TH
VER
SOLUTION

Kieran O'Hagan

THE VERDI SOLUTION

First published in Britain 2009 by Hilbre Publishing
Copyright © 2009 by Kieran O'Hagan

The moral right of Kieran O'Hagan to be identified as the author
of this work has been asserted in accordance with the
Copyright, Design and Patents Act, 1988.

Hilbre Publishing
PO Box 210
Wirral
CH29 9DF

enquiries@hilbrepublishing.com
www.hilbrepublishing.com

ISBN: 978–0–9562469–0–5

This book is a work of fiction. Names, characters, organisations, government
departments, official reports, locations and events, are either the product of
the author's imagination, or they are used entirely fictitiously.

Typeset by Hope Services (Abingdon) Ltd
www.hopeservices.co.uk

Printed and bound in Great Britain by
www.direct-pod.com
Brixworth Northampton

This story is dedicated to the memory of
Morwenna Toleman, an enduring beacon of
light and hope in a profoundly vulnerable
professional world

Acknowledgements

My thanks to South Development Trust and Anthony Gormley for being able to quote from the comments about *Another Man*, on Crosby beach.

The story has had a long gestation. I am grateful to the many editors and publishers, particularly Shona Mullan and Jessica Kingsley, who, during my academic career, responded so positively to my compulsive need to write fiction in order to dramatize painful fact. The book has been subject to many re-writes, and I am grateful to Geraldine Jentz, Andy Gledhill, John Barry and Dinah Weiner for their valued contribution towards that process. Carina Traberg designed the cover and Gavin Rymill of Zarbi Ltd prepared it for the printers. My daughter Christine somehow tolerated my pressure and demands that she read God-only-knows how many drafts. She remained a most dependable and most persistent critic from the outset. Finally, my dear wife Maura, as always, had to live through it all: the obsession, the sacrifices, the near despair and the celebration of completion. With endless love.

'that he who knowing what is right doth it not, should lose the knowledge of what is right, and he who would not do well when he could, should lose the power when he would'
The Confessions of St. Augustine, A.D. 397

PART I

Chapter 1

There was no light to guide O'Neill along the unpaved garden paths and the wet and heavy soil cushioned every step. He didn't mind the darkness; the knock on the door would make them more anxious.

He was at the rear of a rundown Liverpool tenement block of twenty dwellings. Nobody in sight, no street name, little light, no numbers on the filthy battered doors. The only sound was the monotonous cooing of pigeons in a rickety loft.

He smelt the rot and decay all around him, more potent than the night air and the hogweed and nettles that had somehow broken through the concrete rubble of every garden. These sloping back gardens had once been paved but never cultivated and thick green moss had accumulated and colonised both the soil and the paths.

When he arrived he had wandered slowly round the block failing to find a front entrance. Inch-thick steel railings ran continuously from one end to the other, separating the homes from a primary school and a college. At the rear a high brick wall completed the enclosure. The residents entered and left the rear through black metal grid gates, one for every two houses. These gates were conspicuously new and unmarked. They had been recently installed to protect the residents from vandals and from the city's not-too-bright burglars living nearby who invariably found nothing of worth for their trouble and always got caught.

There was a large children's play area at the rear bereft of a single item of play activity; presumably all stolen, replaced, stolen and replaced, until the council had had enough. But it did serve as a dumping ground for passers by, full of litter and graffiti on the crumbling gable end of the block. Outside the back wall perimeter dozens of empty gaudy-purple wheelie bins were lined up, many of them unopened, unused, yet each partially submerged in stinking half eaten junk food and beer cans.

A persistent drizzle and mist blanketed the city, but he could still see an outline of the nearby Metropolitan Cathedral of Christ the King. *Paddy's Wigwam* they once called it, built at the same time as the tenement block. For years tourists had clambered up its fifty-five steps to contemplate its revolutionary design and munificence of light, only to find themselves squelching through the rain that flooded its aisles daily. In thirty years its leaking roof had channelled countless gallons of rain onto the heads of incredulous tourists below. It was once mockingly referred to as the biggest repository of rain water outside of the Mersey, compelling the church hierarchy to contemplate demolishing it. Now fully dried out, some seriously regard it as Liverpool's architectural gem.

Familiar sounds came from inside the cathedral. A choir was rehearsing. He turned towards the main doors, straining to listen. He recognised the music but could not remember what it was called. The voices ebbed and flowed, soaring to heights of power and passion, then descending, slowing, fading to a pianissimo finale he could regrettably no longer hear. He thought it had ended. Then five thunderous beats on a bass drum, doubled and repeated a few seconds later, reminded him what the music was: *Dies Irae* from Verdi's *Requiem*. It all suddenly stopped and a few minutes later began again. It stopped and started again and again. The choir still hadn't got their *Day of Anger* right.

O'Neill paused for a moment, looked around and contemplated the oddity of the place. He was looking for a couple, Madge and her partner McGraw, accused of child abuse. But this was not the place where he usually investigated. Abusers did not normally live within the shadows of a cathedral at the heart of the city's two universities and medical centres and just across the road from its famous *Everyman* theatre and *Philharmonic Hall*. He once knew the area well; he was only a few hundred yards from the Sydney Jones and Harold Cohen libraries where he had laboured through endless garbage about child development and child abuse.

He glanced over the twenty residences of the block. The anonymous referrer had said she didn't know the number they lived at except that it was an 'end house.' It was nearly always an end house, he thought: housing officials contribute to these atrocities by allocating them *end houses*, or even worse, housing them in isolated dwellings, severing them from the community, ensuring that nobody knows what is happening to a child. 'They never mix, never speak to anybody… an them kids never see the light o day!' she'd added indignantly.

But that was no different to the lives of many other kids on his files: curtains permanently drawn, TVs and DVDs spewing out libraries of old films and porn in smoke-filled, window-sealed rooms; babies in their prams deliberately placed as far away as possible, toddlers bribed or warned to shut up. This was the nature of their sensory world; seeing nothing other than incandescent fluorescent screens; hearing voices that meant nothing to them, or music so loud that it deafened them, and always inhaling an all-pervasive stench. Many a time mothers and their partners would open their doors and recoil in anger and resentment from the brightness of the day; natural light was too much for them.

O'Neill approached the end house. This was the one the pigeon loft belonged to. He was sure the birds sensed his presence yet there wasn't a flutter; their cooing never varied. Maybe they really did feel safe and secure in their rickety loft, he thought; maybe they were wonderfully well cared for; he had known child batterers obsessed with the welfare of their dogs and their birds. Then another thought crossed his mind: perhaps it was the pigeon shit all over the gardens rather than bruises on the child that had made a neighbour squeal.

Some kind of material served as a curtain on the living room window but it didn't cover it completely. He could see a faint light inside through its ragged edge and its drooping top. He quietly descended three steps at the edge of the garden onto a concrete path that ran past each back door. He checked McGraw's swollen door for wayward slimy slugs; there were none but the mere knocking on it made him feel contaminated. He wiped his knuckles with a white hankie.

Heavy shuffling footsteps could be heard. The door screeched as it trailed open along a chipped concrete step on the inside.

Frank McGraw stood facing him. O'Neill could not yet see his face clearly because the hallway's bare electric bulb shone in his own eyes, but he could see that McGraw was fat and small with a bushy black beard.

O'Neill felt no need to speak. He just stood there allowing McGraw to scrutinize him.

'Whaddy ye want?' said McGraw, in a voice betraying the nervousness clearly visible in his eyes.

'Shouldn't you be asking who I am?'

'Well... who the hell are ya?'

'O'Neill. Social worker.'

He held an identity card close to McGraw's face. McGraw looked at it, then at O'Neill. The dark tweed jacket that O'Neill wore was old and crinkled; his jeans were well worn at the knees. He never wore a tie except in court where it meant a great deal to impressionable magistrates. Mc Graw didn't seem to notice anything O'Neill wore; he looked anxious.

'Yer not our social worker... it's misses Winters.'

O'Neill smiled. Mrs Winters was the reason he was here. It wasn't his area. Mrs Winters was unwell. Their boss Morgan took advantage of that. He wasn't happy with her supervision of this family. Anonymous telephone calls, school reports, health visitors... they were all concerned. Morgan was burdened like every other inner city team leader with the fall-out from the Victoria Climbié case: memos, new regulations, warnings, and more and more inspections. He had heard enough too, about Jackson the newly-appointed child abuse supremo, to make him more edgy and vigilant. Still, he couldn't get Mrs Winters, nice Mrs Winters, to make sure that she saw the children each time she visited. All she wanted to talk about when she got back to the office was the language of McGraw's partner Madge, *shocking language* that disgusted her and intimidated her. Morgan had given in with Mrs Winters. He could trust O'Neill, not the most congenial of his staff, but reliable. Morgan took all the credit recently, when O'Neill had been congratulated in Crown Court for his realism, a social worker 'who didn't let child abusers pull the wool over his eyes.' A rare event, making O'Neill famous for twenty-four hours and Morgan rather pleased with himself as he was, nominally, O'Neill's boss. Morgan didn't know and had never asked why O'Neill found no difficulty in confronting abusive, threatening clients, or how he was able to walk with ease into a home and demand to see what he was paid to see. But Morgan appreciated it, and O'Neill was always willing to oblige.

'She's sick,' said O'Neill indifferently.

McGraw mumbled something, revealing the reluctance and fear he felt in letting O'Neill in. He led O'Neill through a hall smelling of damp and cold, past a tiny kitchen with an ancient gas cooker, draining boards piled with unwashed dishes and pans laden with hard dripping that looked like wax, bluish and grey. The window above the kitchen sink had never been opened and pools of condensation and dirt lay in the corners of the sill.

McGraw reached the end of the hall and looked round; O'Neill was still staring in at the kitchen.

He followed McGraw into the living room. The stench of shitty nappies, stale urine and vomit came wafting over him. Madge sat near a gas-flamed fire with an infant in her arms. She was twenty-nine years old, but she might have been forty. She had a sallow complexion and more visible bone than flesh. Her grey hair was thinning and lifeless. Her weary eyes were sunk deep in their sockets and her legs bore the deep red tracks that betrayed the countless hours she spent in the same location, in that same position, either in idleness or apathy, or both. She was visibly frightened by O'Neill.

'Social worker,' said McGraw; 'the other one's sick.'

The other one was a pain to be ignored; O'Neill was an intrusion that threatened.

'This the new baby?' he asked, as he walked over uninvited and loosened the clothing about its neck. 'What's her name?'

'Abigail.'

She couldn't be much more than a month old. He carefully placed his hand at the back of Abigail's head and gently brought it forward. For a horrible moment Madge thought he might lift her baby. He felt the exquisitely warm velvety softness of her crown and inhaled its fresh talcumy smells, not yet suffused by the odour rising from the discarded nappies at her mother's feet. His touch reverberated through child to mother and Madge trembled. 'Where's the other two?' he asked. He could hear some movement in the bedroom above.

Not the frolicking about of that older child on a night more than thirty years ago; but an awful subdued sound and movement. Perhaps he had arrived too late, or... perhaps the timing was perfect.

'Bed.' snapped McGraw.

O'Neill glanced at him and saw the struggle between fear and hatred. 'Bring them down,' he said.

'Whadda ya mean?' McGraw stepped forward and clenched his fist.

O'Neill ignored him. 'I came to see the kids,' he said, turning conspicuously to Madge; 'your kids.'

'Ther'n bed,' she just barely managed to say; 'ther asleep.'

'They don't sound asleep Madge.'

'Ye cin see em tamorraw.'

'I need to see them now.'

'Right! that's it!' yelled McGraw. 'You fuck off!'

He had stepped backwards instead of going nearer to O'Neill. He thumbed in the direction of the door leading to the hallway. O'Neill went the other way to a door leading to the staircase. He was halfway up the stairs before the anger of McGraw conquered his fear and he went after O'Neill with a roar.

O'Neill turned on the stairs and watched him, panting already, yet driven by fury. Just like O'Neill's mother's partner all those years ago: oily, fat and bearded, rushing up the stairs of their tiny Falls Road terrace, humiliated because he could not keep O'Neill and his older sister quiet.

O'Neill swung his boot at the rising chin. McGraw somersaulted backwards. Madge screamed as her man lay sprawled in agony at the foot of the stairs.

Within seconds O'Neill stood at the bedroom door. He felt the cold dank air. He switched the lights on. He heard a child whimper and another cry. He walked quickly to the double bed, raised and lowered a grey sheet. 'There Richard, it's going to be all right.' He spoke softly and embraced gently, wondering could the child feel his own pounding heart. He looked over him for a moment and then placed him back on the bed. 'Christopher,' he said, stretching over to the older child who had whimpered. But Christopher didn't move. His face was turned away from O'Neill. 'Christopher,' he said again, lowering the sheets further and gently placing his hand beneath the child's head, levering it round slowly. The skin did not feel right. It was moist but not the moisture of sweat. Christopher resisted him slightly, but he continued to turn the bruised and bloodied face of the child into the light. One of his eyes was swollen and blackened and remained almost closed.

O'Neill closed his own eyes involuntarily. His fist clenched so tightly it shook. He heard the screams of his sister as the punches rained down on her.

A tiny movement of Christopher's head jolted him. He opened his eyes and felt disgust, realising that his own facial contortions had brought a worse fear to the children he was rescuing. He removed the bed-sheet completely. Christopher wore only a tattered unwashed vest. O'Neill removed it and turned him over. He saw the marks of the straps from the neck downwards. The skin beneath the buttocks folded. He turned him round again and searched for burns or scalding. There were none. He held Christopher's two skinny ankles with one hand and lifted them upwards and over. He used his thumb and forefinger to stretch the child's anus. He stared at it for a few moments and thought: McGraw was just a child batterer, not a sexual abuser.

'Christopher,' he said, knowing any utterance was futile. The child had surrendered, not caring whether O'Neill would do him good or ill. O'Neill lifted the scattered clothes and helped put them on. He told Richard who had stopped crying to do the same. He put his arms around the two of them and said: 'I'll be back soon; I'm bringing a nice lady to see you. I want you to stay here until I come back. McGraw will *not* come up to see you, I promise you. Will you stay here until I come back?'

Richard nodded. Christopher never moved.

O'Neill walked slowly across the uncovered creaking floor-boards. He turned, forced a smile and repeated: 'Be back soon.'

On the way down the stairs he took a deep breath, gripping the banister tightly. He entered the living room and ignored McGraw writhing in agony on the heavily soiled couch. Madge stood over him weeping. Baby Abigail lay silent in a pram.

He gazed at their squalor and then leaned over the couch, his head almost touching Madge. He could smell their cheap tobacco, their unwashed bodies and their visible nervous sweat. He grabbed McGraw by the collar and yanked him up. McGraw instantly crossed his arms and begged him not to strike.

'It's not *me* you need to worry about,' O'Neill said in a menacing whisper; 'it's your neighbours and your cellmates.'

He stared into McGraw's eyes and saw the fear. 'Don't go near those stairs, either of you,' he said. He took a mobile phone from his pocket and rang a number. He walked towards the kitchen and turned to them: 'I'll be waiting outside… for a doctor.'

Chapter 2

'You really are asking me to stretch the rules,' said McPherson, Governor of Whixley prison, category C. Despite his exaggerated frowning he didn't really object. He was rather enjoying the encounter.

'But I'm not asking you to stretch them too far though,' Maggie Lynch said with the slightest hint of impudence. She sat on the strategically lower leather chair at the other side of his desk. She wore a two piece dark suit that was neither too formal nor dull. She liked tailored clothes, but they had to look more feminine than corporate.

'For the *death* of a close relative it isn't a problem,' he said.

'His son's *dying*,' she said calmly.

The pitch of the word 'dying' rose dramatically; it betrayed her Liverpool origins as well as an incredulity that she dared not express openly.

He was tempted to say: *he's been dying a long time*, but realised it was a cheap and nasty thought, with an implication that she was being taken for a ride by the family. He had already formed the impression that this petite, smartly dressed, confident woman would be fooled by no one. He didn't usually grant interviews to probation officers, but she had cleverly engineered it during this monthly visit to her client. Her strategy was obviously to personalise, knowing the enormous discretion he as governor exercised on these matters.

'And the six year old daughter who Mr Hargreaves sexually abused is still at home?' he asked, rhetorically.

She knew he would say something like that. A fever of guilt and paranoia had taken hold. Tabloid journalists ruthlessly competed to expose any man who had committed a single child abuse offence during the past fifty years. No matter the nature of the offence, the age of the child, or how long ago, abusers had to quit home and job and flee for their lives. The Government legalised the witch-hunt with legislation certain to be rescinded when everyone realised how unworkable it was.

She once felt like that towards child sex abusers. She was disgusted when she learnt what Hargreaves had done to his daughter. When she had interviewed him to write her probation report – her first such case – she fought hard to resist her loathing of him. She made little effort to find mitigating circumstances for the abuse. She was relieved when he was jailed.

Experience had enlightened and humbled her. Child sexual abuse was more complex than that. She was bewildered and angry when she read the straggling lines that six year old Maria Hargreaves had written entirely of her own volition, asking her father to forgive her (for getting him locked up); Maria begged to see him. It had made Maggie ill. She had inwardly screamed 'NO!' to Maria's plea, but a child psychiatrist warned her that the child *must* see her father. Maggie had to arrange the first meeting between father and daughter in the prison. It was the beginning of the child's slow recovery from the guilt and chaos that well-meaning people, including Maggie herself, unwittingly generated within her.

'I don't think he's going to sexually abuse his daughter when he's visiting his dying son,' she said.

Hardly, thought the Governor, but he couldn't resist asking her: 'How can you be so sure?'

'He'll not be allowed to see his daughter alone.'

Why didn't she say that in the first instance, he thought. 'All right, I'm going to issue a twenty four hour compassionate leave.'

'Could you not make it a weekend?'

He raised his head abruptly; the grip on his fountain pen loosened. 'A weekend?'

'His son's dying, Mr McPherson; they've got three other children including Maria. The parents need a little longer together. They are going to be together at some point in the future. Mr Hargreaves will sleep in one of our hostels; he'll not be with any of the children unsupervised. You'll get a written assurance from my Senior.'

Not worth a fart, McPherson thought; though he remained impressed with Maggie. She conveyed an integrity and courage that reassured him. He signed his approval for a 'compassionate' weekend leave.

Seventeen locked doors Maggie counted on her way out of the prison.

The probation office in central Liverpool was only a half a mile from where she was born and eight miles from where she and her husband Keith and their children Rebecca and Alice lived, in West Kirby, a sleepy little town that few had heard of situated on the Northern strands of the Dee estuary. Maggie went into probation work thinking it was more disciplined and focussed than social work. Now probation officers were increasingly getting it wrong, with consequences as catastrophic as anything that had occurred under the watch of social workers. But she loved the job and was convinced of her own worth. She resented the aspersions cast as a result of the failings of others.

She was thirty three, the fourth child in a Catholic family of six children, descendants of the O'Conors of County Roscommon. She'd never been to Ireland. Unlike her husband Keith she seldom travelled. She enjoyed the occasional short trips to the birth places of her favourite German and Italian composers. But that was about it.

Neither she nor her husband had ever held a driving licence or owned a car. She had a fight on her hands when her employers insisted that she must have a car; but they couldn't prove that not having one would make her a less effective worker. She turned out more effective than most. She wasn't an obsessive environmentalist by any means but she was conscious of the changing perceptions of their life style: once considered *eccentric* and *weird*, arriving at their workplaces on their bicycles or buses, they were now regarded with some envy as fashionable saviours of the planet. In any case, she had never been entirely convinced that travel, whatever the mode, necessarily broadened the mind, made you a better person. At Bristol university ten years previously (where she took theology and music) she never had any inclination to do the back-packing thing, to 'experience' the Sahara, to sail up the Amazon, to hack her way through the Malaysian jungle, or to skip round Aussie land which all her soul mates seemed to be doing. And she lacked a certain empathy for the emerging competitive craze (which more or less proved her point): you hadn't really back packed some believed, unless you'd been struck down with dengue fever, or tick typhus, or schistosomiasis, or until some horrible entamoebic parasite in African fresh water lakes had taken hold in your digestive tract and was ulcerating your gut wall. Seeking this badge of honour was now a national sport amongst back packers, and Liverpool's own School of Tropical Medicine was increasingly being overrun by them.

Maggie was not averse to gambling and risk taking. She made assessments laden with risk every day; but as far as her own personal self was concerned, bodily self abuse extended no further than having her ears pierced. Many of her probation clients on the other hand had transformed their bodies into scrap metal repositories, the most tender and intimate parts masochistically assaulted. 'What kind of scales you got for weighing?' she quizzically bantered them; 'how much do you subtract for the metal?' Other times she exaggerated her expressions of horror at the latest assault and then laughed with them without mockery or contempt.

'How did it go?' asked Mike her supervisor, recognising her footsteps passing the open door of his office.

She continued walking keeping her head low, looking as glumly as she could. She slowed a little but she did not reply nor did she turn her head.

Mike frowned sorrowfully. He was convinced she'd been refused. He had warned her she probably *would be* refused given the current climate. McPherson had to watch his back too; prison governors were despised as much as probation officers and social workers. He imagined she'd got a rollicking as well as a refusal. He sat wondering should he go and comfort her. But he didn't have to because around the frame of the door her dark wavy hair slowly appeared, then a mischievous right eye.

'He's coming home on Friday,' she said, walking briskly into his office with a pleasure devoid of vanity.

'Ah... well done.'

She was at his desk now, leaning over. 'He doesn't have to be back until Monday.'

'What! How did you manage that?'

'By telling McPherson that *you* were a ferocious protector of children, that *you* would personally guarantee their safety for the duration of their father's stay; that *you* had insisted there was no chance of him staying with his children and that *you* would tell him so by letter.'

She smiled broadly then, sensing his pleasure in being manipulated. Of course she said nothing of the kind to the governor. Mike was a *ferocious* protector of no one. He was typical of an old styled social work leadership in the new Probation service. He wasn't a leader. He didn't inspire. He lacked passion and belief. He couldn't withstand conflict of any kind. He just wanted to be liked by everyone, and particularly by people he admired. He admired Maggie a great deal and she, fully aware of his weaknesses strove to focus only on his strengths.

'Oh yes...' he said, trying to look and sound sarcastic. 'Why didn't you try for a permanent release then and compensation; he only sexually abused his six year old daughter; didn't he?'

She was on her way out of his office. She swung round rather dramatically. 'I'll let you know when that's what I'm after Mike and you'll have to write the most convincing letter.'

They both laughed. He kept his eyes on her until the door was closed. He started writing again. Then he remembered something. He looked at his note paper. There was a heading 'McDonald case.' He lifted the internal phone and dialled three numbers.

'Maggie, sorry love; I had a message for you about that McDonald case you wanted to talk about. Do you want to talk about it now? I've...'

'Not now!' she interrupted; 'I wanted to talk about it during supervision; it'll take a while.'

Uncharacteristically brusque, he thought; she was not one who changed mood as quickly as that.

'I didn't want to talk about it now,' he assured her; 'but did you know he'd been charged again?'

'Yes. I heard... he'd stolen a jigsaw.'

'That's right. All I wanted to tell you was that it's been taken out of our hands. Some nit of a magistrate insisted on a Residence Order. Martin's in Hollybank. It's Social Service's buck now. Good luck to them. The social worker rang an hour ago. He wants to talk to you about the case. I wasn't sure whether you knew him or not, Sean O'Neill, an Irishman wouldn't you say? Bit of an oddball if you asked me. Anyhow, that's the message.'

He rang off. Her eyes closed for a few seconds. Her lips tightened. She then opened her eyes and stared long and hard at the opposite wall. She had completely forgotten about her success at the prison.

Chapter 3

At eleven o clock O'Neill drove into the car park of a drab green and grey portacabin office, headquarters of the city's Social Services North East division serving the districts of Kensington, Anfield and Everton. He listened for a few more seconds to Verdi's *Requiem* – the opening bars of the *Dies Irae* in the rehearsal last night would not go away, compelling him when he got home to seek out the CD copy he'd had for more than a decade. He enjoyed listening to it again on his journey across central Liverpool. He switched it off, gathered his papers and briefcase, and mounted the lock on the steering wheel.

The portacabin was located at the foot of Harland Road which rose steeply and stretched into the bowels of Kirby Hill. He paused as always when he got out of the car, gazed round the area and took a rough count of the number of terrace homes for sale. Dozens of large brash estate agent bill boards hung gloomily from the front walls of back to back terrace dwellings. Developers were not yet interested in this area: it was too deprived, too culturally diverse and densely populated.

He walked towards the portacabin offices, once the site of a thriving Methodist church and community; today it was the destination of addicts, delinquents, mentally ill, asylum seekers, battered women, mothers whose kids were taken off them and fathers denied access. Most of these people came to beg or demand, and if they were refused, to insult, attack, or cry. The tramp Patrick Murphy was there every day, half-pissed. Murphy hated O'Neill, a fellow-countryman who contemptuously ignored him.

The graffiti-splattered, knife-slashed notice board pronounced that this was North East Liverpool's 'friendly Social Services office serving all those who may enter.' Police had long ago stopped responding to burglaries and vandalism and the offices had gradually turned into a fortress. Every window was secured by a metal grill riveted to the outside frames. From the inside the windows could only be opened an inch or two. Cleaning them necessitated the removal of the grids so they were never cleaned. It was convenient and cheap not to clean them, as the gathering layers of dirt and grime reassured the predominantly female staff inside that they were invisible to embittered or predatory crackpot clients who might want to leer at them from outside. Blocking out the sun and light all day was a small price to pay.

O'Neill spent little time in the office. He was here because he had to be; it was team meeting time, when new cases were allocated.

Morgan had a pile of files in his arms. The top file had a document attached to it. All the team recognised the heading: CRIMIMAL PROCEEDINGS: 1991 CRIMINAL JUSTICE ACT. Morgan read further hoping his exaggerated mockery would elicit some sympathy: *'for that he Martin James McDonald on the 22nd day of September, 2007, did unlawfully take one jigsaw puzzle of the total value of three pounds and ninety nine pence from the premises of J.R Woolwich and Sons.'*

There were howls of protest. Emma, the oldest member of the team had no sympathy for Morgan. She berated him for expecting anyone to spend time on this drivel when every one of them was inundated with child abuse cases and the media were on another 'useless-social-workers' roll.

'Fifteenth offence,' countered Morgan.

'I don't care if he's offended a hundred and fifty times.'

'He's been cautioned, fined, bound over; he's done community service; he's had two supervision orders, he's done IT orders; he's on a Probation Order…'

'Why's it coming to us if he's on Probation'?

'The magistrates included a residence order; he's in *our* assessment centre at Hollybank; he isn't allowed home until *we* investigate and report back to court.'

The protests evaporated as they did every week. Somebody would take it on.

'I'll have it,' said O'Neill, thinking about the travel allowance and lunch expenses and the opportunity of spending half a day visiting Martin for five minutes. Hollybank was twelve miles from the office.

'Thanks Sean,' said Morgan relieved. He signed his name with a flourish and handed the bulging file to O'Neill. 'That'll please Probation,' he said; 'doesn't look as if they've been able to do much for the kid.'

Norma his deputy glanced at Silvia the team clerk. O'Neill noticed their smirks. He knew what they were thinking: he would do even less for the kid. None of the team were close to him; just the way he liked it.

An hour later O'Neill left for Hollybank. It was a rather incongruous title for the late Lord and Lady McKay's classical-styled mansion with its Venetian windows and central balcony, secluded near the centre of six hundred acres of woodland. In the sixties McKay, a descendant of one of Liverpool's prolific eighteenth-century slave traders, bequeathed all their properties and land to the city's rapidly expanding Social Services. Some thought it was a tax dodge, others thought it was family guilt because of its slave origins; but most believed it was merely a final act on the part of a couple whose lives had been immersed for decades in charitable enterprises throughout the city.

O'Neill entered the spacious reception area and gazed around him. Not a single original item of furniture or painting remained. He chose to stand rather than sit on a soiled threadbare couch most likely donated he thought, by the Salvation Army. It was a cold, dark and lifeless place now, the fumes of disinfectant and polish commingling with the stale human odours of residents who frequently deprived themselves of a daily shower.

A group of lads passed through reception. One of them, red-headed and freckled, came over to him 'Who ye lookin fir Sir?'

'Martin… McDonald.'

'That's Dopey Sir.'

'Dopey?'

Some of the lads sniggered. The red headed one smirked. 'Ees called Dopey. A'll tell Mr Castle'

He scampered away.

A young male Care Officer came through to reception followed by a tall, timid and gawky youth. The youth slowed and then stopped as the Care Officer approached O'Neill. It seemed the youth lacked the confidence to come as close. He was well built with large deep set blue eyes but no sparkle. His complexion was dark, his hair absurdly short and curled, almost rigid. He wore a pair of baggy jeans, a white shirt and an unzipped bluish cardigan. His expensive black leather shoes looked as if they had been polished only minutes before. The Care Officer introduced him and left.

Martin didn't seem to have heard the introduction or maybe wasn't listening.

'Do you know my name Martin?' O'Neill asked.

Martin shook his head.

'Sean O'Neill... I'm a social worker.'

There was no response. His eyes had a pained look of exposure.

'Did anyone tell you a social worker would be calling?'

He shook his head again. O'Neill said nothing for a while. 'How's things?'

'All right.'

It required some effort for him to say that.

'How long you been here?'

'Ah...'

It seemed as though he couldn't answer. O'Neill knew it was two weeks. 'Are they treating you okay?'

He nodded; his top teeth appeared and bit into the lower lip.

'What do you think's going to happen to you?'

He didn't answer.

'What would you like to happen?'

'Go home... mum and dad.'

O'Neill hesitated. He had expected Martin to be the typical fifteen year old delinquent telling him to piss off, then turning his back and ignoring him. He wondered was Martin brain damaged or retarded. But he sensed emotional pain underlying this apparent paralysis; as though Martin knew and understood what O'Neill was asking but just couldn't respond, emotionally or otherwise. He still couldn't look into O'Neill's eyes; he just stared over his shoulder.

'You get on well with mum and dad?'

'Yea.'

'What's wrong with Hollybank?'

'Rough,' he said, and then looked at O'Neill nervously, as if anticipating repercussions for giving an answer like that.

'Rough? What's that mean?'

'Get bullied…'

O'Neill waited, giving him the opportunity to say more, but he couldn't.

'You're a big lad, who bullies you?'

He struggled; either unable to speak or afraid to say.

'What about home… in the street? Do you get bullied there or at school?'

'School… sometimes.'

'What do you do about it?'

'Nothin.'

'How does this bullying start?'

'Ah… em… the jus bully.'

'Do they hit you?'

He nodded once then looked away.

'Don't you try hitting them back?'

'Don't like fightin.'

'Have you never had a go Martin? Have you never felt that you just couldn't take any more and lashed out at them?'

Martin thought for a moment then shook his head in frustration. His whole body was in motion now, his shoulders swaying, his fingers twisting around each other, his feet repositioning, trying to hold himself together as the questioning threatened to tear him apart.

O'Neill's train of thought was interrupted by commotion outside. He got up and walked towards one of the huge reception windows. He looked out and saw some lads clowning with barrows and spades. He looked back at Martin.

'Do you work out here too?'

Martin shook his head again, chaotically, indecisively. It was beginning to get to O'Neill. 'Sorry… what was that you said Martin?' he asked pointedly.

Martin made a huge effort. He only just managed to say 'no.'

O'Neill could hear him sigh with relief as his tongue moistened his dried lips.

'Don't they make you work?'

'Not if ye don't want to.'

Martin sighed again. That was a whole sentence he'd spoken. It was rushed and he had feared not reaching the end. The swaying and fidgeting continued but his head was raised.

O'Neill imagined how much the other kids must torment him. 'I see they've got a soccer pitch out there; do you play soccer?'

'No.'

'Do you play any sports?'

Martin hesitated. He frowned and seemed to be in real difficulty again. O'Neill was tempted to ask him *what was the difficulty*, but then thought there was no point in stressing him further. He told him to wait there. He went down a dank corridor into one of the offices and spoke to Len Castle, officer-in-charge.

'Nice lad Martin,' said Castle. 'He's a big softee though; gets picked on a lot. He's also a poor mixer, which doesn't help. I don't think he'll be here too long.'

'Have you met his parents?'

'I've met his mother... very anxious woman; she can't stand him being here; thinks it's some kind of Borstal.'

'And his dad?'

'Stepdad... no; haven't seen him around; we don't usually see the menfolk in Hollybank. They're all stepdads, or casual cohabittees... glad to get rid of teenagers who aren't their own; though I can't see Martin being too big a problem.'

O'Neill returned to reception annoyed with himself for missing that detail in the file. He seldom read files but he was curious to read Martin's file now. 'Hi,' he said casually to Martin with a smile.

Martin couldn't manage to smile. He stood up and looked at O'Neill through dull defenceless eyes. His 'big softee' 'dopey' look undermined much that was admirable in his physique.

'Right... where were we, Martin... we were talking about sport... You don't play any sport; what about your dad... sorry, your stepdad... does he play sport?'

He struggled again and shook his head.

'How long's he been your stepdad?'

He didn't answer.

O'Neill stared at him anticipating some giveaway tension at the prospect of him having to speak about his step dad.

'What's his first name?'

'Michael.'

'You call him dad?'

'Mum said to call im that.'

'Do you mind calling him dad?'

'No.'

'How do you get on with him?'

He didn't answer. O'Neill waited.

'Do you like him?'

He nodded sheepishly.

'Does he ever hit you... threaten you?'

He shook his head.

'Has he ever abused you Martin?'

'Dunno... what ye mean?'

'Hurt you... or done something he shouldn't have done?'

'Dunno.'

It was a lie, thought O'Neill. 'How long is it since you saw your real dad?'

'Don't remember.'

'Do you miss him?'

'Sometimes.'

'Was he very different from Michael?'

'Ye.'

'In what way?'

He struggled for a moment. 'Dunno.'

'How different is Michael with you? I mean... does he treat you differently from the way your dad treated you?'

He shook his head and looked flustered and confused.

O'Neill said nothing for a while. He knew that these silences and his own inquisitive stare threatened Martin even more. But he found it difficult not to look at him, not to see his suffering.

'I want you to do something for me Martin,' he said.

He took a sheet of paper and divided into three columns. At the head of each column he wrote MARTIN, MUM and MICHAEL.

'Look, it's easy; I just want you to write under each of these headings some of the things that you know about yourself, your mum and Michael. For example, let's take a really simple one, chocolate. Do you like chocolate? Yes. Okay then. Does Michael like chocolate? He doesn't? Right, so one of the differences between you and Michael is that you like chocolate and he doesn't. Now… how about mum? Does your mum like getting up early in the morning? She does? And do you? No, neither do I! So, one of the differences between your mum and yourself is that she likes to get up in the morning and you don't. How about it Martin, do you think you could manage to write a few things in each of these columns?'

Martin stared at the pencil and paper. The muscles of his face tightened, the wrinkles in his brow deepened. A minute later his awkward posture had not altered but the redness in his face had darkened. His eyes betrayed an excruciating embarrassment.

'Any luck?' said O'Neill.

He shook his head.

Images of parents he had yet to meet flashed across O'Neill's mind. He suddenly felt hostile to them.

'Let's forget about this Martin,' he said; 'you can try it again sometime when you feel like it.'

Martin nodded with relief.

O'Neill stared at the tiled floor as if trying to decide his next move.

Martin spontaneously coughed and O'Neill looked into his eyes. 'I often wondered about *my* dad, Martin. You must have felt different from the way I felt.'

Confusion spread over Martin's face. It wasn't a question but he felt it was loaded nonetheless. Even O'Neill's voice had changed; softer, slower.

'My dad walked out, you know.'

Martin remained silent. He didn't know whether or not he was expected to say something in return.

'Yes… and I lived with my mother for a long time.' O'Neill walked across the room and sat on a table top. He crossed his legs, put one hand over his mouth and seemed to be searching for words difficult to find. He didn't look at Martin when he said: 'But it felt different from you Martin. I don't know why my dad walked out, why the marriage broke down. Maybe it was a good job that it did. Anyhow, I was pretty close to my mum... well, there was no dad, so I must have been close to her. And that Martin, is the big problem for me. You see...oh I don't know, maybe it doesn't make sense all this talk...'

'It does! It does!' Martin was visibly animated.

O'Neill then looked up feigning surprise that someone understood him.

'Well, what I'm trying to say Martin is that I didn't like my mum meeting up with other men. You know what I mean? Well... you know you have a dad...'

O'Neill paused when he wasn't expecting to. His act was being sabotaged by the reality. His throat was drying up and his eyes were stinging and his heart was heaving. Deep within he could feel and he despised his own self pity.

''Maybe it's only me,' he said; 'but I was confused I can tell you Martin; I was confused with the whole bloody setup.'

'So was I.'

O'Neill looked at him, startled. 'You were?'

'Yea. A didin know wheer me head was comin or goin!'

O'Neill smiled. He shook his head in feigned disgust and said jokingly: 'Christ... they sure did mess us about!'

They looked at each other and laughed. They laughed quite a while.

Chapter 4

O'Neill was conscious of a sense of trespassing as he drove up the narrow winding lane that led to Lawrence Grove. It was a cul de sac secluded in a private estate in the North West of Liverpool, well away from the city's main boundary roads and yet high enough to afford the visitor intermittent views of the Mersey, the Dee estuary and Welsh mountains beyond. All the city's landmarks dominated by its two cathedrals and the *Radio City* tower were clearly visible.

He calculated that Martin's home, number fifty five, must be near the end. It was indeed the very end house on the right hand side. Beyond it was woodland separated by sturdy high fencing with no visible entrances. Curiously, he could see less of number fifty five as he got nearer to it. Two enormous Western red cedars each three to four metres wide, vibrant green on the outside, waterless brown and rotting on the inside were situated at either corner of the front garden. They joined and were impenetrably thick, blocking sight of the front of the dwelling. He opened a heavily ornamented metal gate and walked slowly along the driveway. The windows were dazzlingly clean but leaded, severely restricting his view inside. He could at least see that the curtains were crimson with unwavering parallel pleats. The front door was oak, with triple-glazed, feature-leaded glass in an oval centre.

He rang the bell and there was no response. He rang a second time. He usually had some sense of when he was being deliberately avoided. He would persist in ringing then. But this was not the type of area he thought, where residents would be scared to open their doors. Clearly there was no one at home. It was his own fault: he seldom offered clients the courtesy of an appointment, preferring to visit randomly, seeing aspects of their lives which they may not want him to see.

He stood staring at the neatly trimmed lawn, the perfectly spruced rose bushes, crocuses, and numerous circles of sprouting daffodils which bordered the lawn. It all looked so symmetrical and boring. Even the parched grass and the absence of any plants beneath the pungent smelling cedars seemed more contrived than consequential. There was a smell of fresh paint in the air, but the area was exposed and high enough to ensure a constant cleansing by a south westerly breeze.

O'Neill stood pondering these extremities of order and harmony, and tried to imagine Martin in the midst of it. A car drew up. He walked slowly down the long narrow drive towards it. The woman driver was trying to do two things at once: look at him and struggle out of her green Fiat Uno with shopping bag in one hand and keys in the other. She looked him up and down apprehensively, he thought. But she walked towards him determinedly.

As she got near to him O'Neill felt a sudden inexplicable chill; it was the face of Martin. And yet, when she was nearer still, he perceived someone very different from Martin. Their eyes may have been identical but they were symptomatic of two different worlds: the dead-like emotionless glaze in Martin's eyes, and in the woman looming towards him, eyes full of vitality and certainty.

'Yes,' she said, now within a few feet.

'Mrs McDonald?'

'No, Greer.' She never flinched, nor did her pace slacken. 'I used to be McDonald. Is it Martin you want to see me about?' she asked, matter of fact like.

'Yes it is,' he replied, fuming at his lack of preparedness; he couldn't recall seeing the name Greer anywhere in the file.

Mrs Greer walked towards him without changing her direction or her pace. She was looking straight ahead, seemingly at the keyhole of her door. She compelled O'Neill to step aside, nearly losing his balance on the edge of the driveway. His arm shot out in case of a fall and he winced in pain as a thorn of one of her rose bushes pricked his index finger, drawing blood. He sucked it, took a handkerchief from his pocket and applied pressure; then he swore to himself.

'I've only been remarried six months,' she said. 'Come on in. You'll have to excuse me. The place is in a mess. I can't get anything done in the morning. I leave the house at half seven.'

O'Neill glanced over the garden again. He licked the tiny drops of blood repeatedly rising on his finger. He was directly behind her now, watching her purposeful approach to opening the front door. Her uncultivated accent was foreign to him; he was no expert on dialects, but he knew she was not from this area. Her simple and direct manner and her speech seemed remarkably self-assured; few of his clients would have been so revealing on the doorstep.

'What do you work at?' he asked.

'I'm a supervisor in Marshall's. They make electrical goods.'

'Like it?'

'I love it,' she replied convincingly. 'I've always loved my work. I wouldn't take an hour off for anything.'

O'Neill stood well behind her as she turned keys in the two different locks on the front door. She deactivated the alarm and led him through the hall. All the doors were closed tight. She went to the far end of the hall and unlocked the kitchen door. The kitchen was pristine. She removed her coat and returned to the hall, opened a cupboard door, placed the coat neatly on a hanger, and put it away. Then she invited him into a spacious living room. The furniture, wall to wall carpet and crimson curtains all seemed virtually new. A large flat screen television with digital box sat in one corner; a computer and printer in another. The room was cold.

She directed him to an armchair and she sat opposite him. He tried to guess her age, perhaps a few years older than himself. Whatever her age, he thought, she made no attempt to look younger. She was dark and of medium height, her large breasts conspicuous in their lack of support and a generally unkempt appearance. Her ancient clothes seemed to have nothing to do with an assembly line. She was an attractive woman, but seemingly lacked the desire to make it obvious. She sat attentively having no inclination to continue with small talk.

O'Neill introduced himself. He said he had to interview her and her husband 'whenever it was convenient.'

'You can call anytime in the evening,' she said. 'I'd like to get a chance to clean up.'

He glanced round. There was nothing to clean up. 'Have you seen him yet, Martin... at the assessment centre I mean?'

'Seen him?' She looked shocked. 'I go to see him twice a week. I'd go more often if they would let me.'

'That's good,' he said half-heartedly. 'Some parents don't bother too much when their kids go into residential care.'

Her expression changed dramatically. Tears swelled in her eyes; her cheeks reddened.

'I just don't know why he does it,' she said. 'He's not that kind of boy. He's big I know... a big softee! He wouldn't hurt a fly. I can't understand it.'

'How does your husband feel about it?'

'Terrible,' she replied, twitching ever so slightly. 'They get on the very best you know.'

O'Neill didn't believe her.

'It nearly broke his heart when the police came that last time,' she said.

'What did your husband do?'

'What would you expect him to do? He had a long chat with him. He was very hurt just as I was.'

'You know about the case conference?' he asked.

She looked at him vaguely. 'Case conference?'

'Yes... only a meeting. We'll be meeting in a couple of weeks' time, probation officer, teacher; anyone involved in Martin's case. We've got to decide where we're going to place him and what we're going to tell the magistrates when we go back to court.'

'Will he be allowed home?' she asked, wide-eyed and apprehensive.

'If it's decided that home is the best place for him... yes.'

'But it is... I know it is!'

'Does your husband think so too?'

'Yes, yes!'

'Good; all we need to be sure of then is that he won't nick anything again.'

He knew that she could not be sure, and that he had silenced her in her efforts to impress him.

'Does Martin have his own bedroom?' he asked.

She nodded. 'He has everything he wants.'

'Can I see it?'

'Oh you can. I have it ready for him.'

'Do you always have it ready for him?' he asked, following her on the stairs.

'I like to keep it in good order. I can't stand things lying around; here it is.'

The handle of Martin's bedroom door was bright and slanted. There was no lock on the outside. She pushed the door and walked in. There was no lock on the inside. The room was just as orderly as the kitchen and the living room below. It was dominated by a centrally positioned double divan bed with matching headboard. At one side stood a small cubic bedside cabinet. On it was an old Phillips' cassette recorder. A single wardrobe had been positioned with barely inches to spare between the chimney breast and the side wall. The wallpaper was bright and flowery; the door, windows and skirting board were painted brilliant glossy white. The wall to wall carpet was the same as that in the living room, though the precision with which it was laid and the absence of any patching indicated intent rather than economy. It all seemed so new, unmarked and undisturbed.

O'Neill was uncertain how to respond. There was a look of expectancy on her face; she expected compliments and eagerly awaited them.

'I did this all myself,' she said impatiently.

'Why? Doesn't your husband help?'

'Not this room. He did the rest of the house.'

'What about Martin, did he help?'

'He doesn't like decorating.'

'Who chose the colours?'

Her brow wrinkled: 'Me. He's not interested in colours.'

O'Neill looked around again, staring at the blank walls and the pristine clean carpet. 'Does he have a desk?'

'Doesn't want one.'

'Where does he do his schoolwork?'

'On the bed.'

'Does he have a computer?'

'Doesn't need one. There's one downstairs.'

'I thought all fifteen year olds had their own computers these days?'

'Not in this house.'

'Does he have a mobile phone?'

'No.'

He looked at her, awaiting an excuse or an explanation. 'Doesn't he want a mobile?'

'Oh no!'

'Does he have an I-pod?'

'A what?'

'I-pod… MP3…' He pointed to the ancient tape recorder. 'It's a bit more modern than that… stores music that you can download from the internet.'

She shook her head uninterestingly.

He moved to the window and looked out on the countless parallel rows of vegetables in the rear garden. Beyond was the surrounding woodland and green fields stretching for miles towards the M67. He could see the motorway in the far distance.

'It's a nice view, isn't it?' she said, having moved silently towards him.

'How long have you been here?'

'Two years.'

He had a strong urge to ask her where she had been before and where had she come from; but he sensed that might have annoyed her and he wasn't certain that she would tell him the truth.

'I'll have to call again to see your husband; is that okay?'

'Whenever you like; call anytime, just let me know.'

'Have you seen the Order your son's under?'

She shook her head, her relaxed confident manner quickly dissolving.

'You should have had a copy.' He handed her a photostat copy. 'Read it carefully. Make sure your husband reads it too.'

She took it with reluctance. She glanced over it uncertain-like. He couldn't be sure whether she regarded it as a humiliation or couldn't read it. He turned to the doorway. He was just about to walk out when he noticed at the foot of Martin's bed only inches from where she stood, a flat round object. It was about eight inches in diameter. At first sight it seemed flat, but then he realised it had a slight circular hump in the middle. It was unusual looking, shaped like a spinning top, or... yes, a flying saucer. He moved towards it. Quite suddenly Mrs Greer moved too and shoved it with her foot further under the bed out of sight. It made a scratching sound on the carpet, telling him it was metal and heavy.

'When do you think you'll be back?' she asked with the merest degree of colour in her cheeks.

'As soon as I can,' he replied, still wondering what it was and irritated with her apparent obsession with tidiness.

'I'll tell my husband; he should be in soon.'

She led him out of the room.

Chapter 5

Maggie was unlikely to forget O'Neill. They had met a decade ago during a criminology course for social workers and probation officers. It was his intensity she remembered most and his tension, the tautness in his lips that gave one little expectation he might easily smile; the fixed piercing stare in the tiny pupils of his green eyes, the lower eye lashes that appeared frazzled to the very roots, the imperfect teeth.

'I'm Maggie,' she said; she was sitting next to him in a seminar.

He nodded and said nothing.

'And you are?' she asked; curious that *she* had to make the effort to ask.

'O'Neill, Sean O'Neill.'

She realised that instead of breaking the ice her effort had inhibited him more. When she eventually did hear him speak in a seminar his voice trembled. He often didn't make it to the end of a sentence, but stopped, struggling for breath, mortified. At times it seemed to Maggie something more than a mere lack of confidence. She had wondered was it his accent, a crude Belfast accent which, when he talked quickly, became more like an incomprehensible babble, emotional splutterings devoid of sense and form, conveying nothing more than the intensity of misery within him.

It was painful that day when he said 'ere' for 'ear.'

'Did you mean "hear"?' asked Tony, a younger student, with tongue in cheek.

Quite a number of the class looked at O'Neill; then they looked at each other, puzzled or amused; there was an air of expectancy in the room.

O'Neill went very red. He didn't know what to say. Maggie remembered the taut muscles of his jaws preventing him from saying anything. She thought Tony had taken him too far.

'Ere!' O'Neill said in a raised voice.

'You mean "here"?' Tony repeated.

O'Neill glanced round him and saw a few more smirks. He pulled at his ear and shouted louder: 'ERE! ERE!' Then he yelled at them in his broad Belfast accent betrayed by his anger: 'What tha hell's wrong wi ya? Do ya think a can't speak?'

He thundered out of the room nearly taking the door off its hinges. Maggie felt sorry for him; it was pathetic, immature. How did he get on the course? she wondered. She speculated on how long he would last. She saw him in the Sydney Jones library a few weeks after; he spent a lot of time there. She pretended not to see him but every time she got the chance she stared at him. He rummaged through his briefcase at one point, emptying it of items which were obviously in the way. One of these items was a tiny pocket recorder which he carefully placed on the desk.

It wasn't until some time later that Maggie realised his voice had slowed; it was becoming more distinct, more confident. He'd obviously been practicing. It must have been really painful then, she thought. And it was still painful, that deep breath he needed before he said anything. But he did stay the course, and his status and his influence altered drastically though not positively for those around him.

As usual nobody volunteered when Spencer their tutor, invited them to do a videoed role play one Thursday afternoon. Maggie would never forget the day. She'd been to the hairdresser during lunch break; she was singing publicly that evening in her local choral society; she had a life-long passion for choral singing.

The students' body language, tense grins and tightly folded arms, told Spencer that he was going to have to beg for volunteers. Then O'Neill surprised everyone by volunteering to play the client. Spencer was grateful. But this had the effect of strengthening everyone's resolve not to play the social worker interviewing him. Nobody felt comfortable with him at the best of times; they certainly weren't going to volunteer being locked in with him in a recording studio with the cameras rolling. The silence that followed became embarrassing and then unbearable. Maggie volunteered and the sighs of relief were palpable.

Spencer gave them an outline of the interview. Maggie asked some questions to clarify; O'Neill asked none.

Maggie remembered his piercing stare as she sat down to face him. She was conscious of the twenty pairs of eyes behind her gazing through the glass panelling of the studio.

The interview began innocuously enough: explain the purpose, set the parameters, establish the aims and objectives; Maggie did all that commendably. Then O'Neill turned on her:

'You don't really give a fuck about people like me,' he said casually; 'You only came out of your office to get your hair done.'

A ripple of humiliation seared through Maggie. The observers, Spencer included, burst out laughing like children.

The laughter, incredulously, compelled Maggie to join in, forcing herself to try to smile and to laugh at her own humiliation!

Then they must have realised that it wasn't funny and that Maggie was the only one amongst them willing to face him. Their laughter ceased as quickly as it had erupted and there was a hushed expectancy.

Maggie tried to recover; she took a deep breath: 'Mr O'Neill, I'm here to…'

'You're here to what?' he said with a scowl.

'Look I know you're angry Mr O'Neill…'

'Do you?'

He played with her, taunting and abusing her. He pretended that he had said enough and that he would listen to her. But he gave her just enough time to regain her poise and then he attacked again. She could see him relishing the effect of his own ugly violence and she trembled helplessly as he finally stretched himself towards her and yelled: 'You're incapable of knowing what I feel!'

From the safety of the screens that separated them, the class was enthralled. The witless Spencer congratulated O'Neill for a brilliantly realistic performance; no one attempted to comfort Maggie; she was a reminder of their own lack of courage.

They huddled together and talked amongst themselves about the likelihood of encountering such a 'real' client after they qualified, and how they might cope with him. Neither Spencer nor any other trainer knew how; they would have disintegrated or run a mile from such gratuitous humiliating. When Maggie had recovered and recalled the experience, she had this awful feeling that the class's self questioning and doubt was precisely what O'Neill had intended. She was convinced that another student Elaine actually left the course because of her role play experience with him.

How could he be so obnoxious and aggressive on occasions like this, Maggie often asked herself, yet vulnerable and inadequate in mere camaraderie? Their fear and distaste of him increased and they avoided him and Maggie knew that they only succeeded in gratifying him. He intrigued her because of the sense of unpredictability he usually generated and because she didn't really know him. She didn't really want to know him all that well. Since Mike her boss phoned to tell her that O'Neill was taking on the case of Martin McDonald, she was lamenting the fact that she had ever led eyes on him.

She remembered the occasion he arrived uninvited, at the door of her first floor flat a few miles from campus. He took her breath away and then she realised that this was the consequence of attempting to reach him. She felt like saying: don't you think you should have phoned? But she couldn't.

'Who plays?' he asked, a distinct note of enthusiasm and familiarity in his voice as he walked into the room and made straight for her piano.

'You do, obviously.'

'And you?'

'I sing.'

He played a Chopin waltz while she made coffee; he played carelessly, unevenly, with a rampant *rubato*, but also, an expressiveness that compelled her to cease her movements in the kitchen, fold her arms and listen. He didn't finish it and she was disappointed.

She handed him a mug of Nescafe. 'Sorry I haven't anything fancier... do you want a biscuit... a sandwich?'

He shook his head and smiled; he held the mug up to her: 'I didn't think I'd get this; I wasn't even sure you'd let me in.'

'Well you're in now for better or for worse.' The resentment he'd caused was fast disappearing. She removed her slippers and sat opposite him, curled up in her usual position. 'Why *did* you come?'

'I felt it would be okay.'

'Okay for what?'

'Just to talk.'

'About what?'

'Em… whatever.'

He didn't really have a clue. Maggie felt she could have trounced him then, about respect, privacy, personal space. Images of his hapless role play victims crossed her mind. But this was no role play and the longer she stared at him, at his hardened face, his unloved, unloving eyes, the more she realised he was telling the truth. She certainly didn't feel under threat. He was merely responding in his own crude way to her kindly impulses in trying to reach out to him. She was uncomfortable with nearly everyone else detesting him because of inadequacies that he didn't seem to recognise or acknowledge.

'You play well; I wanted you to continue.'

'Out of practice.'

'Where did you learn?'

'Belfast.'

'Up the Falls?' she asked, mimicking a Belfast accent.

He smiled.

'It obviously wasn't all that bad,' she said; 'somebody's been good to you!'

He thought about that for a while and then said:

I had an uncle who lived with us; he was in the music trade. He bought this piano from the shop he worked in…' He smiled as if he'd remembered something and needed to digress. 'You know this thing about the working classes in their wee tiny houses always getting the biggest dogs; where I came from they were also wanting to buy the biggest pianos. The living room was 10 x 10, with a three piece suite, and a table, and a television, and yes, a big dog. So when the piano came…'

'Didn't stop you practicing.'

'I suppose not. Then he got married and took the piano with him. His wife was at least twenty years older than him and he was forty. Neither of them played. My mother called him a miserable, spiteful, hen-pecked bastard. She loathed him and swore to me: "Niver worry son… I'll get ya a better one!" So she did, a brand new one, a Zender, Japanese; they were all the rage then, seven hundred quid, five years to pay.'

'So, there were two kind people at least in your life?'

'Kind?'

'Yes, kind! I don't know any kid who had an uncle and a mum each buying him a piano! I don't know of any middle class kid spoilt enough to get two pianos!'

She made him smile and then they laughed, both aware of the drift of the conversation; two rivers of thought and attitude that had always sharply diverged, now converging a little, and him appearing to surrender willingly.

'You're right. I'm an ungrateful bastard!'

'You are!'

They laughed again.

'Where was your dad in all this?' she asked.

'Don't know; never saw him. He walked out before I was born. Went to Kilburn… you know Kilburn? That's where thousands of *good* Irish Catholic fathers went and fathered other kids. They moved around. He ended up with this hag and they drunk themselves silly in a cat-ridden hovel. That was an escape for him.'

'How did you know that? You must have met him sometime?'

'I did. I'll never forget the cats. I never wanted to meet him but I had to track him down one time because I needed his signature for a passport. I had some ideas in my mind of what he might look like; but nothing like what I saw: I met him at a bus stop in Kilburn. He was gross, could hardly move, could hardly breathe, and he was stony broke. I was seventeen. Once I'd got his signature, I couldn't get away from him quick enough. I handed him a fiver when I was leaving… as if he was a beggar. He took it. He mustn't have had any pride or self respect at all. I felt terrible giving it to him. I still have flashbacks about that; I didn't really want to give him money, and it wasn't just the pride thing… I couldn't afford it. But it gave me the chance to get away from him. It was the only way I could get away.'

All the time he had been speaking she noticed his occasional glancing at the huge family photograph above her head; her mum, her dad, her two brothers and three sisters, and herself. Just a family photo as spontaneous and honest as it looked. Her silence gave him the opportunity to get up and have a closer look.

'This is far more interesting,' he said.

'More boring you mean?'

'There's nothing boring about this... it's probably the most precious possession you have and you can't admit it.'

'Okay... I'm sorry. You're right; it's not boring. I love it! I'm grateful.' She got up and joined him. He stared at it for a long time. She wondered what was going through his mind. It was a typical over-the-top family photo, her parents and six lovely teenage children about to break into unstoppable laughter; family togetherness in an unbreakable loving union; it was embarrassing almost; she had intended hanging it elsewhere.

'What does your dad work at?'

'Motor mechanic, self taught.'

'And your brothers and sisters?'

She started from the left: 'Paul there, is a teacher; Sheila, still at college doing agriculture; Emily works in Ford at Speke – she hates it; Caroline's a health visitor. That's me. This is Mark, in finance; he's getting too fat! And mum, she's a nurse.'

She wasn't certain he had heard all that; the fixed stare in his eyes had gone as though his mind had drifted. 'Beautiful family,' he said.

'How many children were in your family?'

She remembered him still staring at the photo when she asked him that. He took a long time to answer.

'I was an only child.'

It didn't sound right. But she was reluctant to probe. 'Well... maybe it was for the best.'

'Why?'

'For your mother.'

'My mother was a whore and a coward.'

'Sean...' she slowly shook her head; 'I'm not sure I wanted to know that.'

He smiled as if to reassure her he wasn't after sympathy and held no grudge against his mother. 'She had it worse than me,' he said; 'came from a mad family, brutal father. Didn't know any better. When things were going well she danced and sang her way around me and couldn't do enough for me, but when things were going bad I was a kind of scapegoat. If my dad missed paying her maintenance, she'd find some excuse to beat the hell out of me and tell me I was a burden and that she should have had me put away. Amazing! But why not? Who else could she kick out at? Isn't it the same old crap that you and me are writing essays about?'

She didn't reply. What was there to say? It made sense of his cynicism, and beneath the surface of his aggression and distrust, his fragility.

'Don't know why I'm telling you this,' he said.

'I didn't ask. You must have wanted to tell me.'

She stood in her bare feet looking up at him. For the first time she felt vulnerable before him. He held out his hands. She had an urge and fear to do likewise, to physically touch him, to help heal him. That's partly why he came, she thought. But when she took his hands, he gently drew her closer to him. He kissed her lightly and embraced her and their arms encircled. She trembled. Their eyes remained open. But suddenly she could see in his eyes a loveless black soul; his embrace then felt like a vice. She wrenched herself free.

Chapter 6

'A man was here… bout Martin.'

Mr Greer looked at his wife. He had not spoken to her since he had sat down in his kitchen chair at the usual time of 6.45pm. He had washed and shaved and changed as he had always done and now he was halfway through the meal she had cooked and served. He resented this interruption; he thoroughly enjoyed her home cooking and the opportunity it provided him to ignore her by fixing his gaze on its ingredients and never looking at her. But her presence was inescapable. If only she would disappear as soon as she had laid the plate before him.

'Another one?' he asked before filling his mouth once again.

'He wants to come back and talk to both of us.'

Mr Greer's vigorous chewing slackened. He looked at his wife for the second time. She never moved. She continued staring at the screen of their kitchen television as she did this time every week night. The casual manner in which she had conveyed this information suggested it was insignificant to her. It was highly significant for Mr Greer. He stopped chewing altogether.

'Who was it? Probation?'

'A social worker,' she replied.

That meant nothing to Mr Greer. Nothing except that combined with his wife's lack of awareness it spoilt a good meal. There was a time when he would have resented her speaking to him during mealtime, for reminding him of her existence. He was no more tolerant now; but he was resigned; he accepted his lot; he just wanted to be left alone, undisturbed, unthreatened.

'Why does he want to see me?' he asked.

'I don't know. The others didn't want to.'

'Did you ask him?'

'He said something about a report; he had to make out a report or something.'

Mr Greer was not frightened by reports. Reports had been made before by probation officers, by police and by teachers. He was contemptuous of all these professionals spending countless hours writing worthless reports. Yet there were reasons why they were worthless, reasons which threatened and burdened him.

Michael Greer suffered the fate of many a man: an unshakeable conviction that he was much more intelligent than his wife, but countered by the realisation that he was infinitely less powerful. He was not a man who sought power; on the contrary, all he wanted was a quiet life, a comfortable home, good food, and regular companionship. Before he first met his wife three years previously the prospect of achieving these modest goals seemed unlikely. He was an uneducated, cripplingly shy, socially unsophisticated man, frugal and hard working. He was a bachelor, a forty year old profoundly unhappy virgin bachelor who never could understand why people always joked about frustrated virgin spinsters. On the building sites where he worked the merest inkling of him being virgin and frustrated would have made his life rather hellish.

After meeting his wife he spent little time on the pros and cons of an offer which had been made very explicit; a comfortable home and family were preferable to his soulless apartment; an attractive, energetic thirty-eight year old – a little peculiar in some respects, though seemingly matured by the bitter experiences of a broken marriage, was much more appealing than permanent loneliness. He proposed and her acceptance convinced him that fate had at last dealt him a kindly blow.

Mr Greer's changing perception of his wife had little to do with her domestic dictatorship. He could easily tolerate, even appreciate the high standards she enforced. Her real power however, was more all-embracing, more profound; it was pervasively manifest in the private, family and social lives of its three occupants. No doubt the fact that such power remained unchallenged was a sorry reflection on Mr Greer. No one was more aware of that than Mr Greer himself. The prospect of a teenage stepchild had worried him slightly; but when he met Martin he worried a great deal more. He wasn't sure why. He had no experience of teenage kids, no experience of any kids, but there was a problem with Martin so obvious that no experience was necessary to discern it. Mr Greer might have difficulty in articulating the problem but by God, he could sense it.

This is what he was thinking sitting in his favourite chair rapidly losing hope that he might be allowed to finish his meal in peace, thinking of that first moment he had laid eyes on Martin, that very second that he smiled and no smile was returned, when he spoke and no reply could be heard. Pangs of guilt surged through him each time he remembered agreeing with her when she explained that he was a shy boy but that he was a good boy. Mr Greer found him a very strange boy. He never did succeed in communicating with Martin. He tried, oh yes, he tried! And he couldn't fail to notice his wife's gratification in his failure

As the union between himself and Martin's mother became inevitable so too did his preoccupation with her son intensify. The difficulty stemmed not merely from the realisation of something unusual and disturbing in Martin, but more so from his conscious surrender to his wife's reassurances that there was nothing unusual or disturbing in Martin. That was bad, bad for Martin, worse for himself.

'He wasn't like that probation officer... what was her name?'

'Eh?' Even when she interrupted his depressing guilt-laden thoughts it was a cause of resentment to Mr Greer. He sometimes deceived himself that it was his wife and her alone that was the problem. But he knew better. He looked up at her. She had turned the television off and was circulating the kitchen with a dishcloth in her hand. He realised how preoccupied he must have been not to have noticed her movements.

'The probation officer... what did you call her?'

He didn't reply. He loathed the naivety and innocence of her voice. Of course he remembered Maggie Lynch. At one time she had seriously worried him. She had got perilously close to the three of them. He became convinced she knew. But nothing happened, and although relieved, he became as contemptuous of Maggie as he had been of all the other professionals.

He continued to ignore his wife. She went out of the kitchen and he could hear the duster flapping as she moved methodically around the living room; it was the same old daily ritual to be repeated again before they retired for the night. He just hoped she would say no more about this new social worker.

'I don't see why the probation officer couldn't come,' she persisted.

'Where'd you say this one came from?' he asked, rising from the table and leaving his unfinished meal on the sink.

'I don't remember. He said he was a social worker.'

Mr Greer lifted his copy of the *Liverpool Echo* and moved to his armchair in the living room. He collapsed into it conspicuously and noisily. He opened up the paper, raised it, and removed her from view. He could forget about the social worker now and his pathetic stepson and his wife. Then he read in the lower half of the front page: *Liverpool Child Sexual Abuse Cases Soaring*. He opened the paper quickly without realising that the article was continued inside. On page three, he stared at another heading: *Expert Suggests All Fathers are Capable of Sexually Abusing Their Children*. He closed the paper in disgust and turned it to look at the back page.

Five minutes later he heard sobbing. He knew precisely the place where she stood in the kitchen. He knew that his defiance would evaporate, that he would rise reluctantly and go to her, and go through the act of trying to console her, reach out to her, knowing his overwhelming desire was to have the courage to do neither.

'It's going to be all right,' he said, stretching his arms on her shoulders, and making no attempt to get any closer: 'He'll be home... wait... in no time at all.'

'The social worker didn't say he'd be home,' she protested. 'He said there's going to be a meeting.'

'Yes, they'll have to have a meeting; that's all right.'

She turned and looked up. He was certain she couldn't see, hear or feel him.

'I want him home now,' she cried.

He had nothing new to say to her: 'It won't be long.'

'They can't keep him away from me,' she said, with determination and fear. She dried her tears with her apron; she appeared a little more composed.

'No they can't,' he replied, conscious of his desire that they would, painfully conscious of the probability that they would not.

'They shouldn't have been allowed to take him. It's a good home he has... even the social worker said so. He looked all around; he even looked in Martin's bedroom.'

'Bedroom!'

'Yes... his bedroom. He asked to see it. I don't know why. But he was very impressed. He said that he could see how well Martin's looked after.'

Mr Greer said no more. You could tell by the ashen colour of his skin that he was having problems digesting that well-prepared, unfinished meal.

Chapter 7

The new child abuse supremo Andrew Jackson was being introduced to childcare staff from around the city. Strikingly handsome with jet black hair and a neat moustache, he had circulated effortlessly amongst Social Services Committee members and front line staff alike. Whenever he listened to or spoke to someone he instinctively moved closer to them; not so much a breach of personal space, but more an intimacy that countered the predominant sense of boring ritual usually associated with such occasions. He would stare unwaveringly at them and smile, convincing the more gullible of his interest and sincerity; but whenever someone else wanted his attention, or whenever he realised he was talking to a bore, he would extricate himself with a subtlety so effective that he didn't even need to apologise.

He wore a dark grey Jasper Littman bespoke suit and a pair of black Oxford lace-up-shoes. Social Services had never seen anything like it before. The suit was made of fine wool and cashmere which combined to produce lustre all the more conspicuous alongside a *Next* ready-made worn by one of his hosts, the beer bellied Director of Social Services, Humphrey Worthing.

Jackson was forty four, unhappily married with two children, and had just moved up from the London Borough of Tower Hamlets, where he overhauled child protection following the scathing attacks on its Social Services department for the horrific death of a four year old. He had begun his career in residential child care and had made rapid progress. His accent and his peculiar dress sense were regarded by some of the kids he cared for as freakish.

Many in his audience were cynical. They believed Jackson was nothing more than a public relations guru hired by Tower Hamlets in the aftermath of frenzied tabloid attacks. They believed he had merely served the customary two years in the child abuse hell-hole of inner city London boroughs, then moved north for an easier life. Liverpool may have one of the highest levels of social deprivation and poverty but it was much less pressurised than London, much less understaffed and a lot cheaper. They regarded Jackson as they did all newcomers introduced with this kind of media-present razzamatazz; he was an irrelevancy, a typical high flying Oxford-educated, overly ambitious bureaucrat who they were convinced gazed at himself each morning and plotted the day's contribution towards his long term goal of a Directorship, then Chief Executive, and then whatever else his limitless ambition may have decreed. Of one thing they were certain: he would have no positive impact on their lives; they had seen it all before many times.

The Chairman of the Social Services Committee, seventy five year old Lord Holtby, introduced Jackson, emphasising how fortunate the Authority was in employing the services of one so distinguished in the field of child protection. He declared that his Committee would continue in its endeavours to ensure that Liverpool had the best child protection services in the country. He then invited Jackson to speak.

Jackson rose and smiled, sensing their anticipation. He appeared consummately at ease within himself.

Unlike a young social worker Eric Houston who sat in the second row from the rear and who stared at Jackson hardly able to believe his eyes. Was this the man Eric thought he was? Eric hadn't long qualified from the University of West London, and apparently, like Jackson, had moved North for an easier life. He was Hackney born and bred, not exactly Bow Bells, but a cockney nonetheless, yet lacking the cockney's spontaneity and humour. There was uncertainty and distrust in his blue eyes. He was of average height, handsome and well built, but inhibited and shy. He could not take his eyes off Jackson, yet he dreaded catching his eye; it might have led to mutual recognition, a *reunion* and conversation that he simply couldn't have coped with. Even anticipating such an encounter compelled him to move his head directly behind the person in front so that he was entirely hidden from Jackson's vision. But occasionally he moved his head back and stole another glance.

Jackson spoke: 'Mr Chairman, Director, ladies and gentlemen, let me begin by thanking you for your kind words of introduction...'

Eric then knew that neither his eyes nor his memory had deceived him. Jackson's voice sent a shudder through him.

Jackson dwelt for a while on the impact of his accent in a city obsessed (or depressed) with its speech.

'Before I say anything more Mr Chairman,' he went on, 'I want to share with you...' (he glanced at the Chairman, and his voice gravely dropped almost an octave) 'this may be breaking a confidence I know, but anyway I'm going to share with you... I want to tell you... my interview... was not easy!'

He paused, looked around, made his tongue in cheek obvious to them all and knew he had the majority of them in a grip of unknowingness and expectancy. Some changed their posture and some fidgeted in preparation for their courtesy laugh.

'There I was,' he continued, 'near the end of the interview, thinking I had done reasonably well, thinking I had a good chance, and the Chairman... this very one, looked me straight in the eye and asked: did I support Everton or Liverpool?'

Many in his audience convulsed in laughter. But some grimaced. 'Oh fuck,' one of them uttered, holding his hand over his mouth, 'not that fucking stereotypical crap! What does he take us for?'

'I gazed around the interview panel, all seven of them. Could I really afford to treat this question as the joke I thought it was?'

Laughter and more laughter.

'You may laugh ladies and gentlemen, and you may well know the answer to that question, but try to imagine my dilemma. I DID NOT KNOW!'

The Chairman and the Director looked at each other, bowed and shook their heads in mock shame. They were enjoying the glow of success they personally felt in the impact Jackson was making.

'And here I have to confess, I have for many years been a keen supporter of...' he paused again, cocked an ear towards them, 'wait for it... yes, Liverpool...'

Cheers and boos simultaneously rose up.

'No no no, that's not my confession... that I have supported Liverpool. I don't need to confess that!'

'Yes you do!' shouted one.

No! No! My confession is that I *did not* admit to supporting Liverpool. The stakes were too high and I was too frightened. I told them... I enjoyed watching both teams but my team was Arsenal!'

It took them a while to settle. He lowered his head, exaggeratedly arranging his papers, and said. 'Of course now I know what you all know: it wouldn't have made the slightest difference how I'd answered that question.' Then he looked quizzically at the Chairman: 'At least I don't think it would!'

Lord Holtby shook his head and they all laughed again. Jackson's smile slowly petered out and his expression became grave, his voice less animated. He raised his eyes, fixed his stare on someone straight ahead of him and said:

'I'm going to be brief. I know all you people are busy.' He paused and glanced round, then he said pointedly: 'So am I.'

I want to put a question to *you*? Why is it, every six to nine months, a child abuse scandal hits the headlines, an inquiry is held, social workers and their managers are held to account, exposed in exactly the same way as the hundreds of other social workers and managers have been exposed in previous enquiries, making the same blunders, the same incompetence, the same unethical and unprofessional conduct in the way they've dealt with the case, the same incredulous blindness to a child being starved, or mutilated, or tortured, or persistently raped, or murdered? Can anyone answer that question for me... why do these tragedies happen again and again?'

No one dared to answer the question and some resented him asking it.

'I've spent nearly twenty years in child protection work...'

'Ten minutes at the frontline,' whispered Peter Ryan, a bearded social worker safely ensconced amongst a group of friends at the back of the hall.

'And two factors never cease to amaze me: we all want to forget the horrors of each report as quickly as possible – and who can blame us for that? And when the next tragedy occurs, it requires someone else, somebody who has nothing to do to with child protection: a lawyer... a High Court judge... a Lord of the realm... paid hundreds of thousands of tax payers' money to point out that we've made exactly the same mistakes all over again.'

'How many of you remember the case of four-year-old Cindy Watson in Tower Hamlets? She was starved, burnt, gagged, locked in an outside coalshed and battered to death. That produced another report. How many of you read it?'

Arms twitched. Heads turned. It could be a risky admission if a question followed.

'Did you know that nearly all the social workers and team leaders caught up in Cindy's case hadn't read the Victoria Climbié report? And all those caught up in the Victoria Climbié case knew nothing about the Kimberley Carlile report? And those caught up in the Kimberley Carlile case hadn't read the Jasmine Beckford report... and the same correlation right down the line: the Maria Colwell report, the Wayne Brewer report, Richard Clark...'

A palpable discomfort spread throughout the hall.

'So what conclusions do you draw apart from the obvious one that social workers on the whole don't like reading child abuse inquiry reports and even less, reading about the professional incompetence responsible?'

Jackson lowered his head and seemed preoccupied with putting his notes in order. Knowing that even the cynics were riveted to him now, his pause extended inordinately. Then he looked up and stared around them. He spoke slowly, softly, yet haltingly, with little of the variation in pitch they had got used to.

'In my office you will not see too many books on child abuse... I make no apology for that. But you will see every published child abuse inquiry report - all seventy of them. When you borrow one of them as I hope you will, you'll see that others have borrowed them before you. I put this to you: If you read an inquiry report thoroughly and concentrate not just on the suffering of the child but on the incompetence of the workers, the team leaders... and yes... managers like myself... people who never in their worst nightmares could see themselves as such… then I guarantee you that you will never replicate that same incompetence; you will never experience the same tabloid ridicule, the same public condemnation.'

He paused a long time again, sensing their expectancy and their need for the crucial crunch line:

'More important, the children that you serve, the children that each and everyone of us here today try to serve, will never experience that same betrayal.'

He lowered his head again and somehow moved his papers without a sound. 'Are there any questions?' he asked.

He knew none of them dared speak.

When would any of them ever have had time to read a seven or eight hundred page report? All they could manage in the typically grinding, futile, emotionally and mentally draining work in the sprawling wasteland of council estates in Liverpool was absorb a few shock headlines shooting out at them from bill boards, tabloids and television news. And then as he was now reminding them, they were more likely to turn their head. How could it be otherwise?

What Jackson said to them was commonsensical and menacing. That it was commonsensical was indisputable; that it was menacing was obvious in the shifting agitated demeanours of his audience. Child abuse literature was notably objective, always aspiring to the cold, detached jargon bereft of the suffering it described, but here was someone communicating to them in a language personal, direct, and, yes, menacing. He was warning them, deliberately and imaginatively transporting them into the vortex that would surely engulf them if they were unfortunate enough to repeat a Climbié or a Jasmine Beckford in Liverpool.

Even without looking up, he sensed the desired tumult in their collective mind. He could *hear* their unspoken admissions and promises made: *I've never read one of those reports… tried to… tried to read several… couldn't stomach them… always said I must read one… must read Climbié… must read it now…!*

He generated a different kind of tumult in the mind of Eric Houston, the young cockney social worker at the back of the hall still alternating between hiding himself behind the person in front for fear Jackson may see him, and yet compelled to steal glances when Jackson was at his most compelling. Memories of a nightmarish childhood swept over him, of his parents killed in a car crash when he was three. He and his two brothers and one sister lived with their aunt and uncle for a while. The couple couldn't cope. They blew it one day and attacked the oldest child. All four children were removed and separately fostered out. Eric was fostered, abused, fostered again and abused, then placed in residential care at the age of six. That's where he had met a much younger Jackson, in 1987, in the London borough of Barnet, in a so-called *family group home* called 'Mareville.'

Jackson resorted to humour to haul his audience out of the depressing and menacing scenarios into which he had purposely lowered them. He gave them a brief biography and told them a few anecdotes from his work experiences. He knew he would make them laugh. He never mentioned his experiences in residential homes. He finished with the usual banalities about his aspirations, about Liverpool being a place in which he had always wanted to work, about its wonderful people and dedicated public servants, its excellent universities and health services, and how much he looked forward to 'getting round' every office, meeting every member of staff. His deepest conviction, he concluded, was in the importance of his 'open door', open at all times to anyone who felt they needed to talk to him.

In another part of the hall, O'Neill and Morgan sat together. O'Neill lay slouched and Morgan sat upright taking in every word. O'Neill had sensed Morgan's rising discomfort. It amused him.

'What do you think?' Morgan whispered to him after Jackson had sat down. He nervously straightened his cuffs and tightened the knot of his tie.

'Hit-man,' O'Neill said casually, still looking straight ahead of him at Jackson.

'Hit-man… what's that supposed to mean?'

'Somebody up there doesn't like the way you're doing things. Brings in a hit-man to do the dirty work.'

'The way *I'm* doing things?'

'You're a team leader.'

'There're twenty team leaders in the department; there're at least fifteen of them here today.'

O'Neill didn't reply. His poker face never turned.

The pregnant silence filled Morgan with dread, the awful possibility that his bosses were gunning for him alone.

O'Neill delivered the *coup de grâce*: 'They'd all better watch out then.'

Chapter 8

In a shabbily elegant Victorian terrace off one of the town's main arteries, Maggie turned the key in the front door as her husband Keith was cooking, her three year daughter Rebecca was drawing and their golden retriever Frankie was sleeping. Dog, child and man (in that order) heard and knew it was her. Maggie let briefcase and handbag slip from her hands, a pleasantly symbolic action at the end of each of her three full working days. She lifted Rebecca and smothered her in hugs and kisses.

A voice from above could be heard: 'Hi mum.' Seven year old Alice was in her bedroom, not so entirely engrossed in her laptop and her MP3 that she could ignore her mum's home-coming. Experience had taught her that that single utterance 'hi mum' was enough to save her from any charge of discourtesy, enabling her to refocus on the things that really mattered in her life.

Rebecca didn't want this little ritual to end; she wanted her mother to continue holding her high, focussing exclusively on her eyes, 'devouring' her with her lips and mouth, talking ceaselessly about 'my darling... missed you so much...' etc. How does one end this, inoffensively, subtly? Maggie's other 'darling' was still in the kitchen, still preoccupied with getting his daughters a meal.

'Oh!' said Maggie, her laughter ceasing and her smile suddenly contracting, 'where's daddy?' Her face was furrowed now with a pleading curiosity. Rebecca's smile contracted too, an instant discomfort, but then a realisation it was a question only she could answer. She smiled proudly, pointed along the hall, and said: 'kitchen.'

'Oh, is he?' Shall we go and see him?'

'There he is,' said Maggie, strategically putting Rebecca on the floor as they reached the kitchen door; Keith was as much entitled to a full-blooded, hands-free embrace as their daughter was. She approached him, drawn more quickly towards him as much by the first eye to eye contact, as by her own needs at the end of the day.

He was much taller than she was, handsome in a sense, not rugged, indeed, incredibly smooth skinned, with large blue eyes that radiated a quiet confidence and conviction. His receding hairline was a matter of indifference to him. He was soft spoken, had never raised his speaking voice in the ten years she had known him. This quietness was not merely an expression of control which he had in abundance, but more so a conviction in the power of reason and persuasion. His humour and calmness when they argued often flummoxed her, made her feel helpless, but never resentful. He was utterly without vanity or triumph.

'Hi there,' she said casually, collapsing into his arms. Rebecca gazed up at them with a three-year-old's intense pride, convinced she was the instrument of her parent's reunion.

They kissed passionately, Maggie prolonging the kiss just a little longer than usual, which Keith interpreted as one of her more stressful kind of days.

As the four of them later sat through mealtime, with Frankie happily stretched out at their feet, Rebecca's litany of achievements was solemnly recalled by her dad, including the compulsory imaginative play: enlisting the help of monsters, doctors, sisters, brothers, and then, not least, her sudden, unrelated and extraordinary phone calls to all and sundry. Keith feigned an expression of exasperation; 'for at least two hours' he whispered; Rebecca rattled on regardless.

'Done ma homework mum!' Alice interjected, as she munched her way through a second helping of pasta and ham. Her strategic pre-empting of the most boring question in the world (*how did you get on at school today?*) relieved her of the tension of anticipating it.

'Well done,' said Maggie; she had stopped asking that question months ago.

She always had an impulse to smile during these rituals. Communication amongst the four of them seemed simple, honest and straight forward, and yet she was conscious of the fact that it was complex and multi layered, and that neither she nor Keith had made any special effort to achieve it. It had come about without anyone noticing or trying too hard. She still kept a diary of sorts, and she had amassed countless hours of video footage of the kids in particular. She had combined, or rather, contrasted this with her working observations of families fragmented, violent, and sexually abusive; she had succeeded in getting a few articles published. She hoped she might write a book on child development some day.

Keith had written several books and recorded numerous compositions. But he had never made a penny out of them. He was a sonic arts composer, a revolutionary, who had discarded conventional music and music-making in his teens, and who relied entirely on subsidies from the Arts Council and various universities, including Cambridge, where he obtained his music degree. He lectured throughout Europe, the U.S., Asia and Australia, chiefly in universities or in institutes of contemporary music. He was especially popular in the Scandinavian capitals, which meant that audiences there could reach double digit numbers! His reputation flourished, and obscure awards were presented to him at obscure venues: the Ars Electronica in Linz; the Euphonie d'Or in Bourges.

Maggie bathed Rebecca, frolicked with her naked little body on the bed, tucked her snugly in, and told her a riveting new story. When Alice went to bed, Maggie joined Keith and cleared up. Later, they both lay half slouched, arm in arm on the living room mustardy settee; it was so shapeless, wrinkled and faded it seemed a thousand years old. She sipped sherry, he drank beer.

When they first met, their mutual attraction didn't make it any easier to admit how unappealing they regarded each other's musical tastes. Maggie pretended for a long time that she was on the verge of comprehending his work, while Keith tried to detour, by humour and mockery, around the afflictions imposed on him by typical choral repertoires. Now they were as frank with each other as they were relaxed.

'What's the next concert?' he asked.

She smiled in anticipation; she knew her reply would amuse him. '*Two Contrasting Requiems: Duruflé and Rutter,*' she said. It was precisely how the program had worded it.

'Don't you sing anything other than requiems?'

She laughed, but her momentary delay in answering suggested they didn't do too much more than requiems! 'Of course,' she replied unconvincingly.

'That's what most choristers sing… requiems! Odd, isn't it?'

'What's odd about it?'

Well… they don't look as if they're suffering. Requiems are about suffering, aren't they? Choral societies are mostly middle class, most of them drawing a pension.' His voice then lowered deferentially: 'with a few exceptions of course. They're usually all Tory and white… you don't see too many black people in a British choral society, do you?'

'How do you know?' she asked; 'there's over a thousand choral societies in the UK.' She felt like saying that she didn't *know* every choral society, and just because there was no diversity at all in West Kirby's, didn't mean that every choir in the country was similarly lacking. But maybe they were. She remembered only the year before when her choir had joined fifty others in the Albert Hall to make up a chorus of three thousand to sing the Messiah. There wasn't a non-white person to be seen. There wasn't even one non-white person in the audience. What was it about British choral societies that made them so exclusively white, she had asked herself. She had felt then she was in a time warp, in the midst of a bizarre British Empire revivalist jamboree; and what better venue for that than the Albert Hall?

They said nothing for a while. Then she couldn't help herself saying: 'I'm envious of you.'

'Why? Don't I let you share my poverty?'

'But I can't share in your success. I can't even enjoy your music. It maddens me that all I want is to hear you play Beethoven on a Steinway, and all I get is you creating a racket in a junk shop.'

He laughed. 'It's mutual. I don't like requiems, and I don't understand the work you do.'

He wasn't patronising her; he genuinely didn't understand human frailty. Her clients and their actions mystified him.

'No, I suppose you don't. But you don't want to. And you're not envious of me, are you?'

No, he wasn't envious of anyone. She honestly didn't know of a single vice he possessed. She remembered him once saying that it was impossible for him to lie. She had retorted that their children were accomplished liars by the age of three, just as he himself must have been at that age. He denied it. He couldn't imagine himself lying at any age.

Soon he would be gone again, and she would depend upon her children (including their lies and manipulations) more than ever.

'Remind me again, how long will you be away?' she asked.

'Twelve days.'

Yes, it was usually around that, she thought. Then she asked him, with no clear reason in mind: 'What will you be doing?'

'Lectures mostly; two performances, and hopefully, a composition. Why do you ask?'

'Because I haven't asked before.'

'Are you sure?'

That could mean: was she sure she hadn't asked the question before, or was she being honest with him, was there another reason why she had asked? There was, but she couldn't share that with him yet.

He was going to Denmark which had a professional appeal for both of them. It was where Keith had his most enthusiastic followers, and for Maggie it was the country with the most radical response to crime, having the least prisoners in Europe per capita of the population. But Denmark was now making waves for a different reason. It was under attack since one of its daily newspapers *Jyllands-Posten* had published cartoons depicting Islam's Muhammed in a less than glorious light. The Islamic community was on the march, particularly in Copenhagen and Aarhus where he would be working. This was bizarre, Maggie thought, inoffensive little Denmark, incapable of hurting anyone. She never shared her anxiety with Keith.

'Yes, I'm sure.'

'But why are you asking now,' he persisted.

'Because I want to know. Shouldn't I know what you're doing, and how long you'll be gone? People do ask me, you know.'

'That's a good reason for not telling them.'

They were quiet for a moment. She was annoyed with herself for nearly causing a stir.

'Who's this social worker O'Neill?' he asked.

His arms stretched just below her breasts. She wondered could he feel the increased palpitations of her heart.

'O'Neill?' she said, trying to sound disinterested. Maybe, hopefully, it was another O'Neill.

'It was on the front page of our local rag. He found this battered kid and had a fight with the mother's cohabittee who did it. The cohabittee ended up in hospital with a broken jaw and was sent down for six months.'

Maggie said nothing. Then Keith laughed and she felt sick.

'Don't you think it's funny?' he asked.

'Funny?'

'Yes. A social worker breaks a guy's jaw and the poor sod gets six months as well.'

She remained silent.

'He deserved more though. He nearly killed the kid.'

'Did he?'

An ironic reproach, not a question. He was again 'simplifying things that he knew nothing about.' That's what she usually said to him.

'I didn't know social workers could be violent,' he said; 'I thought they were all vegetarian and pacifist.'

Now she really did feel like kicking him. She refrained: 'I don't want to talk about that. It's too close…' She was about to say 'to work' and realised the depressing truth of it. He said it for her.

'To work? You've always said probation was different from social work?'

'I could end up supervising that guy when he's released. So will you shut up talking about it?'

She turned away from him and leaned her head on his shoulder.

'I thought you had something on your mind,' he said.

'Yes I have; I'm thinking how easy it is to spoil a pleasant evening.'

Keith said nothing. He held her more tightly and kissed her velvety hair. Perhaps that 'funny' comment had been tactless, he thought. He wouldn't mention anything remotely connected with her work again.

PART II

Chapter 9

September 2000

Dr Abdul Azeer az-Zahrany gazed over the new intake of students in the assembly hall of the Al Jamiah Islamic Academy in Knowsley, the newest Islamic Faith school in Britain. At this time each year he surveyed a sea of new faces, young, nervous, excitable and noisy, and indulged himself in the certainty that somewhere amongst this new intake there was one, at least one whom he could influence far beyond the confines of the school curriculum. He had been doing so for many years now with varying success. He always relished the task of discovering where vulnerabilities lay, of sifting through backgrounds, appearances, intellects, physiques and personalities, before settling on his target. The bloody messes in Bosnia, Kosova and Palestine had aided him considerably over the years, because these relatively better-off Muslim youths of Al Jamiah whom he taught, were no less full of indignation and no less prone to thoughts of revenge, than their Muslim brothers and sisters in the comprehensive schools of Burnley and Blackburn. This year's intake however was different. Amongst them was a ready made target that he would quickly assess. His usually reliable, continuously regurgitated images of the 'slaughter' of Palestinians by Zionists and infidels may not even be necessary. His target was sitting amongst friends in the fourth row of the assembly hall; he was a sixteen year old Somali youth named Sa'eed Jama.

Sa'eed was tall, his face well proportioned, his eyes more grey than green. He had the darkest skin and the shortest hair, features that his former class mates had mockingly reminded him of in the comprehensive school he had previously attended. He had been an oddity to them, a refugee from a country that few of them knew much about. They had perceived his shyness and quietness as a consequence of his blackness and they had located him on the margin of things. His parents hoped

Al Jamiah would be different. Their son was no angel. He prayed five times daily but only because the school and his parents demanded it. He had girlfriends, had sampled booze and detested it, and like many Somali kids, had spaced himself chewing khat and paan even before he was an adolescent. There used to be a hint of mischief in Sa'eed's gentle face, the distant possibility that he was suppressing a smile, plotting some intrigue. He didn't smile often of late.

Sa'eed knew nothing about Abdul Azeer but Azeer and many other staff knew a great deal about him. However *normal* Sa'eed appeared, Azeer was convinced that he must be hurting inside, that he was an angry and damaged youth.

A few months previous to this first day of the new term, Sa'eed's sister Samira and her husband Sharif Mahdi had been attacked by a mob of more than twenty youths in Liverpool's Sefton Park. The mob had encircled them. One of them ripped Samira's hijab off with such speed and force that the beautiful little Swarovski Heart Stick Pin which held it snapped in two. She was seven months pregnant at the time. Then they turned on the husband who hopelessly tried to protect her. They kicked him to death. A few hours later his distraught wife and his parents could not recognise the beaten pulp that lay on the morgue's marble slab. 'RACIST SCUM' ran the headline in the Liverpool *Echo*; 'LIVERPOOL'S RACIST SHAME' ran another. Both families suspected that this had little to do with racism; it was sectarianism, an attack against their faith, their religion, Islam and all that it stands for.

This incident had compelled the Principal of Al Jamiah to convene a staff meeting to predict the likely consequences and to discuss how best they might help Sa'eed recover from his ordeal. Dr Azeer, head of Koranic studies at the Academy, was delegated the task of counselling and supporting him.

Azeer was, according to everyone who knew him, a taciturn and unassuming man. He was actually, a highly successful Al Qaeda operative, an agent and handler. He was one of a breed of operatives who had been coming and going in Britain long before the authorities woke up. His route from torture in the chambers of Cairo's Citadel prison to the manicured lawns of a prestigious faith school in Britain had been a hazardous one. He was born and reared in the well-to-do Maadi district of Cairo, the son of two academics who taught at the Ein Hamms university in Abbasia on the outskirts of the capital. These parents were both the descendants of a long line of illustrious Arab Islamic activists, either continuously under surveillance or harassed by successive Egyptian authorities. It was Nasser's regime in 1966 that executed one of Azeer's distant relatives, Sayyid Qutb, now a revered and iconic figurehead whose writings and martyrdom had contributed to the emergence of a whole new generation of Islamists, including Azeer himself, and a friend, Ayman al-Zawahiri. Zawahiri was destined to become the second in command of Al Qaeda.

During that first term Azeer made contact with his student Sa'eed Jama in exactly the way he had planned. In teaching, he took every opportunity to tell the class how important it was for them to respect Britain and the British way of life; how tolerant and free a society it was; how enlightened and civilized. Each time he made statements like that, he noted Sa'eed's response.

Sa'eed had initially stared at him with incredulity, then anger. Later he pointedly looked elsewhere; then he began lowering his head and biting his lips. Eventually he could take no more and did something that no pupil had ever done in a Muslim faith school: he got up and walked out whilst Azeer spoke.

'Why did you walk out like that, Sa'eed?' Azeer asked him in his office the following day.

Sa'eed had nothing to say. He knew he would be summoned like this and many possible replies to that question had fleeted through his mind; all gone, forgotten. He was at the mercy of Azeer now and probably facing expulsion, but he didn't care.

Azeer sensed the mood; Sa'eed's lips were unusually tight; his eyes defiantly indifferent rather than anxious. 'Don't you care what your parents think? Don't you realise how your sister feels?'

Sa'eed tensed; he hadn't known that Azeer was aware of his sister's defilement and his brother-in-law's murder. 'I hate this country,' he suddenly blurted out; 'I hate this school! I hate you trying to make me respect everything.'

He deliberately and provocatively stretched forward for the last few words and stared Azeer in the eye. He had nothing to lose and he wanted Azeer to know that that's how he felt.

Azeer stared back at him, seemingly hurt and angry. 'You want to carry this bad feeling around with you all day... that is not the way.'

'I don't want anything,' Sa'eed said resignedly, as he sunk back into his chair and lowered his head indifferently. Yet he thought he had detected a tiny ambiguity in Azeer's words and tone. He looked up at him again, questioningly. He wished he could say more to Azeer. No, he didn't want to feel hateful and vengeful all day even though he felt like that often. He wanted to be able to forget. He thought school was the place he could forget. But Azeer provoked him constantly, telling him that Britain was great, a nation of generosity and goodness, as the memories of Sharif's unrecognisable corpse and his defiled sister engulfed him. He emerged daily from the classes and returned to his home where his devastated parents walked around like zombies and his sister swallowed pills all day long. She had lost her baby, perhaps not surprisingly, stillborn. She had been denied the opportunity of normal grieving and closure because the body had not yet been returned to her. In her traumatized state immediately after the stillbirth, she had granted the hospital's request for a post mortem, thinking that the remains would be returned to her in a matter of days. Four months later, they had still not been returned, and her increasingly desperate pleas always provoked the same excuse: the body was still subject to necessary forensic tests.

The family had stopped talking to each other; even Sa'eed's father, a doctor, who had enabled the family to flee from the ravages of Somalia, from the countless corpses and shattered limbs he saw daily in Mogadishu's Hayat hospital, still could not cope with the enormity of his son-in-law's murder and the attempted rape of his daughter. Sa'eed's unheard of early return from school yesterday hadn't even been noticed by his family.

'What are you going to do then?' Azeer asked.

It somehow didn't sound like a question; more a breathing space. Azeer was sensing, scrutinising and probing, just as he had done throughout his adult life. He had lured hundreds of unsuspecting youths, *returning them to Allah* as he believed. Nobody was more cautious and sensitive, ultra sensitive to the danger of the task. But he felt confident with Sa'eed, increasingly aware of the chaos of his mind and the pain in his heart.

Sa'eed nodded helplessly and lowered his head.

Azeer got up from his desk and walked over to him: 'There *is* another way,' he said, his voice much quieter; 'but first you must pretend to ignore these attacks upon Islam.'

'Why?' asked Sa'eed.

'Because they are rampant. They occur every day; in every city, every town.' Azeer spoke slowly, deliberately. 'You must pretend because there is nothing *you* can do; but there may come a time, when you do not have to pretend; when… if you want, you and your many brothers in Islam, can let the world know what *Allah* feels.'

Azeer returned to his desk and opened a drawer. As he walked with his back turned to his pupil, he was quietly confident and conscious of the ambiguity and turmoil he had created in Sa'eed's mind. That was the first objective, ensuring time did *not* heal his wounds, did *not* enable him to adapt in resignation to the atrocity which occurred.

He lifted from the drawer a huge file of newspaper cuttings. He handed them to Sa'eed. Sa'eed leafed through them. He remembered some of them, the ones that had made headline news. None had generated more news and condemnation, and more photographs, than the one at the top of the file: his beloved brother-in-law Sharif, lying in his coffin, and his distraught sister, his anguished parents, aunts, uncles and himself.

Sa'eed stared at the photographs – there must have been at least a dozen photographs and newspapers clippings about the murder of his brother-in-law. He was visibly horrified, yet too exposed and vulnerable to express any anger.

Azeer knew he had not only penetrated his thoughts and his despair, but his very soul. He was unsurprised, unmoved, as the tears swelled in Sa'eed's eyes and began to flow. Sa'eed sobbed helplessly.

Azeer moved closer and put his arms around his shoulders.

'Look beyond them Sa'eed.'

Sa'eed wasn't interested in looking elsewhere; he continued staring at the photographs of his family, blurred by his tears. Azeer waited.

Eventually Sa'eed flicked through some other clippings. He glanced at some of the headlines. He read some of the stories: Muslim taxi drivers, Muslim shop owners, Muslim factory workers, Muslim nobodies and Muslim VIPs... all murdered, kicked to death by British mobs, or knifed or shot or burnt to death by lone racist psychopaths. There were hundreds of clippings.

Then he heard Azeer's voice, grave, sonorous, and laden with an anger that Azeer made no attempt to suppress: 'Muslim blood has become the cheapest in the world.'

A tremor went through Sa'eed. He had thought about leaving home and school many times since the murder; just walking away from the helplessness of it all; from his parent's surrender to an all pervasive grief, from his sister's barren drift into insanity, and from his own hatred that was being rekindled this very moment. For a split second, he had an urge to close the file and throw it to the ground and scream.

'We can choose to ignore this,' Azeer said, 'or we can do what *Allah* commands.'

The mention of Allah again jolted Sa'eed. He silently repeated the words: *We can do what Allah commands.* He looked up at Azeer.

Azeer stood over him imperiously, observing the many changes in Sa'eed's countenance. There were no more tears; his focus was a little more secure, his skin less taut. He appeared to be warming to the direction in which he was being led. He had obviously no hostile sense, maybe no sense at all, of the manipulation that was being applied. He was beginning to be attracted to a possible course of action more logical and hopeful than remaining in a black hole of despair.

Azeer looked down on him, knowing he could now successfully complete his task. He no longer looked like a genial, gentle Egyptian master of Islamic studies. There was a sternness and steeliness about him that few would have recognised. There was a pride, a uniquely Egyptian pride, in his dark eyes and his granite-like cheek bones. There was strength and resolution in his voice and in his movements, in stark contrast to the crumbling heaps of humanity in Sa'eed's own home.

Sa'eed looked at Azeer and Azeer knew the question that was on his lips: 'What does Allah command?'

Chapter 10

Maggie was bussing her way through central Liverpool, a mile long building site increasingly driving motorists and pedestrians frantic. Many parts of the city centre had been flattened; the roads gridlocked, makeshift traffic lights randomly placed here and there, and dozens of super cranes scaffolding most of the city. From the other side of the Mersey, where she often walked with the kids and dog on New Brighton front, she had watched the cranes rise inexorably beyond the skylines of the city's best known landmarks, the Liver Birds, the Custom's House, the Radio tower, and even the city's two famous cathedrals. Everywhere, huge bill posters reminded citizens of what was happening: Liverpool had been designated European City of Culture 2008, and eight billion pounds were being spent, courtesy of the government and the European union, to ensure that it at least looked the part.

Half an hour later, the bus drove into the sprawling Abington Road estate in the north west of the city. The rain had fallen monotonously for hours and the sky was a low blankety grey, silhouetting moss-laden roofs and sparkling new satellite receivers. All entrances led to the centre, thirty acres of unkempt, uneven grass. It used to be a flat green playing field, now it was muck and water, endless pools of brown water, varying in shape, size and depth. The bus circled the field and stopped at the entrance of a cul de sac named Throstle Row. It didn't have a name plate; most name plates in Abington had been removed, vandalised, buckled or burnt.

Throstle Way was the characteristic dumping ground that the council had conveniently created in an estate universally regarded as a dump. All councils do this, and they conveniently choose cul de sacs in the furthest corners of the worst estates. Once they have dumped more than one – there has to be more than one acknowledged hopeless case in a cul de sac, the rot takes hold; the 'good folk' move out, and even more useless hopeless cases move in. Every family in Throstle Way was a broken family, every one of them living on welfare benefits, dependant upon doctors, psychiatrists, counsellors, social workers, priests, citizen advice bureaux, volunteers, and many of them regularly visited by police, or probation officers, or debt collectors or social security fraudster inspectors.

There were no gates in Throstle Way, no numbers on the doors, no lovingly cultivated lawns, no freshly painted wood-work. A few aged cats crouched on narrow slanting window sills and doorways, one of them miaulling for the shelter denied it. Number six was typical, a red bricked semi with rusting window frames and eight-inch door panels that once held glass, now covered with plywood. Lifeless speckled grass, four feet long, completely covered the path to the doorway. Filthy curtains were drawn, upstairs and downstairs. There was no sign of life other than the lingering, embalming smells of last night's carry outs.

Maggie walked up the garden path angry and resolute. This was the least welcoming scenario she had envisaged. As she got near the door she heard the television. She looked at her watch. It had to be the Jeremy Kyle show. She could also hear children's voices. She could not hear their mother. She knocked the door. The voices went silent. She knocked again; Kyle's voice and the screaming abuses of his fodder suddenly ceased. Now she could hear the children's giggles (and she imagined their mother silently begging and threatening them simultaneously not to make a noise). She knocked again, much louder; but silence now reigned. She put her mouth close to the gaping rectangular hole that was once a letter box, and shouted:

'Brenda! It's Maggie. Open the door!'

Still there wasn't a sound. She waited a few seconds, stretched towards the letter box again and began speaking more slowly, more restrainedly.

'Brenda, if I don't get an answer from you, I'll take it you're not there. If you're not there, that means your kids are on their own. I can hear the kids. If I don't get in within the next thirty seconds, I'm ringing the police and Social Services to report two small kids left alone and locked up in their own home. They'll break the door down; now open the bloody door!'

About ten seconds passed. The inside door opened and Maggie, still peering through the letter box, could see the gaunt and bespectacled figure of Brenda slowly shuffling towards her. She was in her thirties and looked fifty. Her cheeks were puffed up red. Her long sandy thinning hair was scattered over the shoulders of her stained and crumpled nightdress. She held a mangled home made cigarette in her right fingers; it was still smoking. She leaned on the porch walls for support. She would never have made it to the front door otherwise. As she reached out for the door knob she could barely open her eyes; she obviously couldn't see the knob. When she eventually got her eyes opened sufficiently, they gazed through old glasses full of dust and grime and smudges. She missed the door knob a couple of times. Her drunken focus was totally skewed and her eyes were unable to bear the pain of daylight. She burst out crying as she pulled the door open. She cried without tears, a self pitying, wailing cry: 'A'm sorry... Maggie.'

Maggie tensed a little. Fifty hours of work and support down the tube; another client on probation for being drunk and disorderly now sloshed. She said nothing. She didn't need to. She moved forward. Brenda stood in her way, not intentionally, just paralysed with fear and still wailing. She managed to get out of the way. Maggie passed her and was momentarily enveloped in powerful gut wrenching smells from Brenda's open mouth and rotten teeth.

Four year old Archie and three year old Grace stared up at Maggie. They stood near the couch their mother had lain on. Around their bare feet on the filthy heavily stained carpet were empty tins of *Carlsberg Special*. Both children were naked from the waist down. Grace's nostrils, upper lip and chin were covered in hardened mucus. Each child's dirty matted hair hung in clumps and their mouths and pyjama tops bore all the signs of a chocolate breakfast.

Maggie breathed in the various stenches and glanced around for causes: the permanently closed windows and drawn curtains, the stale cigarette smoke with no where to go; spilt beer, unwashed flesh and clothes, and the remnants of quick food still lying in cartons scattered about in various parts of the room. She knew that the kitchen would be a lot worse than the living room.

Snappy dresser Kyle looked out of the massive screen into the eyes of his fodder. Although he could not be heard, his gravitas indicated that pearls of wisdom were falling from his lips. Maggie snapped him off, drew the curtains, and turned to the children.

Archie's left knee repeatedly contracted nervously. Both children's eyes were full of apprehension. They both sensed their mother was in trouble and her wailing apologies increasingly distressed them.

Maggie turned on Brenda behind her: she spoke softly. 'Brenda, you're hurting them. Sit down.'

She helped her to an armchair.

Even in her present state, Brenda was conscious of the fact that Maggie had never criticised her in the presence of the children, had never said anything that would have caused her to be angry or distressed in their presence. She knew that Maggie wouldn't even mention *drink* and *children* at this moment; she would though, as sure as hell, *speak* to her on another occasion.

'Who took Angela to school,' Maggie asked.

'Me dad,' replied Brenda sheepishly. More trouble, she thought. The written contract between her and Social Services stated that no matter the weather, or how disinclined she felt, she had to get off her ass at least twice a day and take her oldest daughter Angela to school and Archie and Grace to the playgroup. But it was too convenient not to; Brenda's dad lived round the corner, and, apart from three or four hours in the bookies each day, he had nothing better to do. He couldn't manage the two younger ones, but he was happy enough to get Angela to school and back again.

Maggie turned to the kids. 'NOW THEN… Archie Mulholland and Grace… what have you two got to say for yourselves?'

The children instantly recognised Maggie's barely concealed smile and her grossly exaggerated disproval. Grace looked up at Archie, as if she needed to be reassured that she had read Maggie's face accurately; her brother's face convinced her she had. Archie bit into his lower lip to prevent his own smile; Grace did likewise. They both knew that it was okay.

'SO YOU TWO were not going to let me into the house… am I right?' Maggie towered over them as if threateningly, her arms folded; she was the least threatening adult they had ever known in their short lives. They loved her.

'And I thought you were my friends… umh!'

From behind her, Maggie heard the muffled cry of Brenda: 'It was me Maggie… it was my fault…'

'So what are we going to do now?' she asked them.

'Get dressed,' said Archie, smiling.

'She turned to Grace: 'what do you do before you get dressed?'

'Wash,' said Grace. She swayed from one side to another, overcome with her own sense of cleverness.

'Well done, Grace; so let's get washed and dressed and maybe while we're doing that mum can get dressed as well and clear up the mess and make me a nice cup of tea; can you do that mum?'

Brenda nodded, and forced a smile. Maggie turned to her and almost whispered: 'go and drink plenty of water… a bucket load!'

Maggie returned in the afternoon. A sober, sore headed and contrite Brenda faced her alone in the same living room. She had done what Maggie told her to do: brought the children round to her father's house. Now, she anticipated, the riot act would be read in Maggie's firm and quiet way, and the 'last warnings' about her kids being taken into care would sear through her.

'You've stopped coming to the office, just once a fortnight we asked you to come… you've stopped attending AA… you've stopped taking your oldest daughter to school and your youngest kids to playgroup… you've stopped cleaning the house, feeding the kids properly… regularly… you've stopped being in a fit state to look after them… How's it all going to end, Brenda?'

'A'll niver do it again… Maggie… ah promise ya!'

'Brenda…' Maggie paused; 'It's not *me* you have to prove yourself to. It's Social Services.'

'Yes I know… but…'

'You haven't done anything wrong as far as I'm concerned; you haven't breached the probation Order. You've done well

Brenda, staying out of pubs and not punching barmen who won't sell you another drink.'

Brenda began to cry.

Maggie handed her some tissues; she always carried supplies of tissues; clients like Brenda never purchased them.

'Social Services know that too, but that's not their concern; you know what they're concerned about.'

Brenda nodded as she sank her head in the tissues.

'I'm going to be speaking to Social Services later.'

'Are you gonna tell em?'

'Tell them what?'

'Bout today?'

'Yes Brenda; I have to tell them you were drunk and incapable of looking after the kids. I'm legally bound to tell them that. If an accident had happened, you wouldn't have been capable of doing anything about it. If you'd fallen asleep and dropped your fag, the three of you might have been burnt to death.'

'Yer not going to say that to em, are ya?'

'Nobody needs to say *that*! Unless they're bloody morons it'll be the first thing that'll come into their head.'

'Oh God…!'

'But it *didn't* happen, Brenda; it could have happened, but it *didn't*.'

'Ah know… but it could av.'

'How many mornings have you missed playgroup this last week?'

Brenda shook her head. She dared not say.

'Social Services got your kids placements earlier than most. There's a waiting list of hundreds for these placements. What are you going to do? Give them up?'

'No.'

'And what's this about your dad taking Angela to school every day? Do you think that's right?'

Brenda couldn't see anything wrong with it, but she sensed that Maggie must think it wrong, and she said nothing.

Maggie insisted: 'Well…?'

'Me dad's alright.' There was for the first time a slight resentment in Brenda's voice, a resistance, as though she interpreted Maggie's question as some kind of aspersion on her father.

'I know he's all right Brenda, but it's only an excuse for you not to have to do it yourself. Most mothers do, and lots of them like you have other kids, babies in prams, toddlers they leave off or collect at the playgroup. It's not just taking kids to school; it's about learning more about your kids, who their friends are, getting to know their teachers, meeting other parents… and all that.'

'A don't wanna meet oer parents.'

'No of course you don't, it's much easier not to meet people; much easier to stay at home and get pissed. It's a bloody lot more selfish too.'

'I'm not selfish…' Brenda cried.

Maggie was angry with herself. Brenda wasn't selfish; she'd have given her last penny to anyone who asked for it. Maggie discovered years ago this inverse ratio that was conspicuous amongst her clients: the more destitute, pathetic and broken, the more generous they seemed to be.

The meeting ended not for the first time with the usual promises and commitments. Maggie had no doubt that Brenda would stick to these, for about a week! She would cave in then, as she often did, unless there was someone there to ensure she didn't. Where was bloody Social Services, she asked herself; the kids were registered 'at risk.'

As she was driving out of Abington Maggie was burdened by a sense of foreboding that Grace and Archie would be harmed in some way. It wasn't only that some accident might happen, but more so, that they were readily available for abuse by any of the serial cohabittees for which the estate was renowned. She hadn't attempted to pry – Brenda simply could not have taken it at this moment in time – but she had seen the razor, the shaving cream, the after shave, and a filthy male vest when she took the children to the bathroom for a wash. She wondered was there more than one male with her last night; that was always the worst scenario; and had the drinking continued right through until the morning? All three children were on the child protection register because of similar events in the past, and there had to be a limit on the number of recurrences that Social Services would tolerate.

'Hi Maggie; haven't heard from you for a while,' said Silvia, Morgan's team clerk. It was 4.30 in the afternoon. Maggie was back in her office. Silvia's cheerful voice did not disguise the unease she felt, that Maggie may be bringing her trouble fifteen minutes before the office closed. Silvia had been with the team for years; she knew every case, the most hopeless, the most vile and the most crisis-prone.

'Hi Silvia, who's the social worker for Brenda Mulholland of Throstle Way?'

'She hasn't got one. Used to be Betty Summerfield. She left two months ago.'

'But Brenda's three kids are on the child protection register?'

'Means nothing! We've over twenty on the register without a social worker.'

Maggie closed her eyes and bit her lips. It really *was* a shambles. She was glad she had phoned; a letter or an e-mail would have most likely been put aside.

'Haven't you got a replacement for Betty yet?'

'Yes, Sarah Prescott; she started two weeks ago. But Morgan's taking his time in giving her cases. She's just qualified. Brenda Mulholland isn't the easiest case for a novice.'

'Is Stan in now?'

'I'll try for you.'

She didn't want to speak to Stan Morgan, a reluctance vindicated when he lifted the phone and shouted 'Maggieeeeeeeeee!' based on some peculiar assumption that she enjoyed hearing him address her like that. But he was the team leader responsible for the district of Abington and the only one who could help. So she tolerated the preliminaries that followed about developments in each other's agency since they'd last met. Then she told him about her two visits to Throstle Way and described in detail what she'd found.

'Em...' was the only sound she could hear. She imagined him sitting there at his big desk, the Parker pen sliding in and out of his mouth, enduring the awful dilemma of not understanding what precisely she was worried about and what she was asking for.

'Yea...' he said; 'poor kids... but em... have they been abused?'

'Abused?' She could hardly believe he was asking that.

'Yea... Has she hit them? Did you see any marks?'

Maggie's grip on the phone tightened. 'No, I didn't see any marks. I saw a lot worse.'

He said nothing. She could sense his perplexity, his need for her to explain rather than leaving him exposed like this. But she wouldn't help him.

'What was that?' he eventually asked. 'You mean they're being neglected...?'

'No I don't mean *neglect*. That means bugger all. I mean they're being emotionally abused and psychologically abused; they're kids crying out for basic little responses from their mother, you know... love, pride, joy, curiosity... that kind of thing... and all they get is drunken stupors and all the incapacity that goes with it. If you want to call that *neglect*, okay; I call it abuse.'

She was conscious of the rising levels of sarcasm in her tone and of her own potential for letting rip. She took a deep breath: 'You got them places in a nursery; that could have helped them but you obviously didn't check on their attendance.'

'Well em... yea... it sounds bad Maggie, but it's not much worse than many other kids in Abington.'

Maggie closed her eyes. It was as though he hadn't heard a word. 'You've taken Care Orders on Grace and Archie before. You put the names of all three kids on the 'at risk' register?'

'True, but that was because they were left on their own.'

'They might have been safer on their own this morning; Brenda was paralytic and incapable of looking after them.'

'But she was there. We can't take child protection orders out on kids just because their mother gets drunk.'

'I don't want you to take orders out on the kids. I want you to get a social worker allocated to the family and get Brenda whatever additional help and support she needs.'

He was silenced again. She could sense him wanting to defend himself, or maybe even defy her.

'The kids are not my responsibility Stan,' she said, 'I'm just referring the case, telling you what I found. But if it *was* my responsibility, I'd be worried... about Brenda in her paralytic state dropping her cigarette and falling asleep, and Grace and Archie being burnt to death; or about Grace falling out of the bedroom window and not being found in that jungle of a garden for another six hours; or about either child being sexually abused by the boyfriend she has there at the moment... yes; I'd be worried about any of those possibilities.'

She deliberately kept that possibility to the last, knowing the impact it would have. Just two words, *sexual abuse*, which had many differing connotations. It could mean a man exposing himself to a twelve year old in a public place, or the violent rape of a two year old within the child's own home, or... any one of a hundred other different acts. She knew that Morgan would not be considering such differences; that he would merely be attempting to deal with the alarm bells which the two words had triggered in his head.

'Who is he?' he said, urgently.

'I don't know, but there are plenty of signs that he's there, cohabiting.'

Abington, overrun by cohabittees, whoring their way round all the Brendas at their disposal, and all of them potential sexual abusers. Morgan's team spent ninety per cent of their time with mothers; they barely ever saw the male partners, the cause of all their worries.

She could hear Morgan swallowing, then he gave a little cough and asked her: 'Where's the oldest child in all this... what's her name?'

'Angela.'

'Is she em... safe?'

'No safer than the other two. Fortunately she's at school all day, but I'd be happier if it wasn't her grandad who took her; that's the easy option for Brenda.'

'You're sure he doesn't pose a risk to Angela when Brenda's drunk?'

'I can't be absolutely sure. He's not the most stimulating person to be taking a seven year-old to school every day. On the few occasions I've met him, I've never seen him really engage with any of the kids, but if you're asking do I think he would deliberately harm her, sexually abuse her, no I don't.'

'Okay Maggie,' he said determinedly; 'I'll allocate this one to our new girl, Sarah Prescott; I'll make sure she visits, then we'll call a case conference.'

'Hold on Stan...' She pinched her brow and sighed; it seemed that no matter how she went about this, it made no difference. 'The kids need something more than the statutory supervision of their mother,' she said, irritably. 'Brenda also needs help; she needs a reliable volunteer, something like *Sure Start*; a mother figure there every day for a few months. I could push for it myself, but you people have got far more influence. And if the three kids are on the 'at risk' register, it shouldn't be all that difficult?'

Another silent response. Maybe, just maybe, she thought, she was getting through to him.

'I'll see what we can do,' he said. 'We've first of all got to find out who this cohabitee is and what the risks are.' He paused for a few seconds, then said: 'You know we've got a new child abuse boss, Andrew Jackson?'

'Yes, I heard about him.'

'All charm and dashing good looks-kind-of-thing, but he's ruthless. He's going through as many files as he can manage and calling people in when things don't seem right to him. Jim Hutchinson was flayed by him... gave in his notice.'

Maggie despaired: was he not capable of realising that it was two small kids she was worried about, not his anxieties about Jackson? Now *she* chose to be silent.

'I'll have a chat with Sarah,' he said, 'and maybe do a joint visit with her.'

'Thanks Stan. And will you let me know the outcome?'

'I will.'

Minutes later Morgan was standing in front of Silvia's desk. He could see her hackles rise and the angry frown descend on her face in anticipation of him asking her to do something when she was just about to go home. 'No no, not now...' he said defensively; 'tomorrow first thing, leave me out the Mulholland file; don't forget luv.'

'Mr Jackson's got it.'

He was leaving her desk when he heard that. He swung round, his pallor and shock clearly visible to her.

'Why's he got it,' he said, struggling to control the tremor in his voice.

'I don't know. He's been looking through the data base and picking files at random. He's had three of our files for weeks now.'

'Weeks!'

Ghastly thoughts raced through Morgan's mind. The first was that maybe Maggie's warning was prophetic: something awful really would happen to Brenda Mulholland's two youngest kids. Then he suddenly saw a letter on his desk summoning him to Jackson's office. He would be confronted with Maggie's written testimony that he had listened to only minutes ago – he knew that Maggie would record every word of their conversation. Then he saw himself in the dock of a public enquiry, being mercilessly torn apart by smart arse lawyers who knew nothing other than how to tear people apart. He saw the angelic faces of Grace and Archie alongside his own grotesquely distorted photo in the front page of the *Sun*, his head encased in a pumpkin, mocked, despised, and humiliated in a front page editorial. He read the words of condemnation in the public inquiry's conclusion. He then saw himself facing his own department's disciplinary panel chaired by Jackson, and he heard the cold and cruel verdict: he would be sacked!

He was about to ask Silvia to ring and ask for the file to be returned. He decided to do so himself.

He jotted down a few notes, took a deep breath, and phoned headquarters. Jackson's secretary Priscilla said he had left earlier to visit one of the district offices. 'He spends more time,' she remarked, 'out of his office than in.'

Another warning, Morgan thought. He was relieved not to have to speak to Jackson who would surely have detected the anxiety in his voice. He asked Priscilla for the return of the Mulholland file. He tried to sound calm, matter of fact-like, as if he was just keeping an eye on problematic cases. He stressed that it was a case he could not afford to let slip; that he was allocating it to the young woman who had joined his team only a few weeks ago, Sarah Prescott, and that he would be accompanying Sarah on her first visit.

He knew that Priscilla would convey all this to her boss in the morning: Mr Morgan keen to get the file back, *expressing his concern and commitment about a family and his good intent.* It could not fail to impress Jackson. And he reckoned he didn't have to do anything now until he got the file back. That would take a couple of days at least. He felt much better.

Now he could return to a more interesting matter: another new member of staff was joining his team in the morning. He had been anticipating his arrival for some weeks.

Chapter 11

'Sa'eed... how are you...' Morgan cheerfully shouted out, loud enough for all his team to hear.

Sa'eed was quite taken aback by this unwarranted familiarity. He had met Morgan on only one occasion previously, four months ago, during his interview for the post. He had been informed a few days later of success, but told that extensive checks had then to be made on his suitability for working with children. He had waited for what seemed an eternity for clearance, sometimes expecting a knock on the door by Special Branch, rather than a 'We are pleased to inform you' letter through the post. But the letter eventually arrived, and here he was, on his first morning, rather formally dressed in his navy suit and white shirt, dark red tie and polished black shoes, commencing work as a trainee social worker in the drab headquarters of the city's Social Services North East division, serving the districts of Kensington, Anfield and Everton.

'Good to see you,' Morgan said, smiling nervously as he approached Sa'eed in his usual unhurried pace, with his hand stretched out.

Nearby, Silvia the team clerk was struck by the disparity in height between the two men. Sa'eed was at least six feet tall, Morgan a mere five foot two inches.

Sa'eed tried to smile in return as he shook Morgan's hand, conscious of a momentary intimacy that would have to be tolerated. But he could feel the tensions and apprehensions he had felt over many weeks dissipating.

There was something naïve and reassuring about Morgan, in his smallish green eyes, his double chin and large belly; not a beer belly – he very seldom drank beer and never drank spirits. But he was known to consume large quantities of traditional foods, beef and Yorkshire pudding amongst his favourites, and he was notoriously inactive as well as indecisive. His face overall was a rubbery expressive face – his staff had seen him do excellent impersonations of Les Dawson (a fate yet to be endured by Sa'eed) but it was a face full of uncertainty, and it confirmed Sa'eed's initial impression that he was trying too hard to be friendly.

Sa'eed quickly realised that Morgan was pleasantly preoccupied by his blackness. He was aware that Morgan (and any other team leader for that matter) would have considered him an asset in a Social Services department that had continuously failed to attract enough black people to its payroll. Three quarters of the city's social work caseloads were rooted in minority communities.

Morgan introduced Sa'eed to Silvia. She had felt herself increasingly drawn towards Sa'eed during the ten minutes she had kept him entertained before Morgan arrived. He was everything Morgan was not, and a good deal more attractive than O'Neill who as usual was not there.

Sa'eed met the rest of the team. Then Morgan took him into his office and served him coffee. Morgan appeared less apprehensive now, sitting back on his chair and actually swivelling, less dependant on the desk that separated them.

There was a booklet on the desk which Sa'eed could not yet see. It was the department's anti racist, anti discriminatory policy. Morgan had been studying it overnight, trying to ensure that he could keep a lid on the racist and sectarian sentiments he often expressed to the disgust of some of his team members. When they ridiculed him or condemned him, he usually backtracked, saying things like: 'that's not what I meant...' or: 'I'm only being devil's advocate.' This would make them madder still. He was hopelessly unaware and repeatedly exposed for being so. He knew his team would make him suffer if he dared to breach, in the presence of Sa'eed in particular, the politically correct parameters his bosses had set for him.

'Somalia isn't it... where you were born?' he said casually.

Sa'eed barely nodded. He sensed that Morgan knew nothing about Somalia.

'Rough there at the moment, isn't it?' Morgan tried to give his words some gravitas by lowering his head and frowning.

He could be excused for not knowing that the mention of Somalia risked stirring memories and thoughts that incensed

Sa'eed: the invasion of his country by neighbouring Ethiopia, the US's proxy; the crushing of an Islamist government that had offered Somalia real hope for the first time in a hideous and forgotten civil war that had lasted more than a quarter of a century. Such thoughts invariably led to the same question: why could he not be there, in his own homeland, shoulder to shoulder with his Islamic brotherhood, mercilessly sapping the will of the enemy, before annihilating them? Just as his predecessors had done with the Russians in Afghanistan, just as his Taliban brothers were doing now with British soldiers in Helmond province. Surely Somalia was a greater, more immediate need; a more noble cause, than 'sleeping' in a British Social Services office, enduring inane chitchat from people like Morgan, whilst waiting... waiting... awaiting the call.

It was a long time since Sa'eed had entered a covenant with Azeer. His family were in no fit state then, either to enquire about or object to Azeer's influence; in fact his mother attributed her son's apparent recovery to that influence. It was reassuring to her that Sa'eed had re-immersed himself in their Muslim faith, a guarantee that he would eventually discard all feelings of bitterness and revenge.

After ensnaring him, Azeer carefully planned his alternating pursuits of terrorism and education. When he completed sixth form, he was encouraged to choose college subjects he liked and was good at, but he was also pointed in the direction of study most efficacious to the cause, like engineering and communication technology, and, surprisingly, subjects that would facilitate his applications to work in education, health or Social Services. These areas of employment had long been judged astutely by many senior Al Qaeda agents to be the safest locations for their sleeper cells. They were the most trusting, the least discerning and the most tolerable institutions. Sa'eed chose psychology, sociology and English. He eventually graduated from Manchester Metropolitan University, another 'choice' sanctioned by his handler, for its anonymity and its size, and its potential to recruit.

Sa'eed spent five periods of differing duration in the madrases of Pakistan and in Al Qaeda military camps in Afghanistan. His

85

ideological indoctrination was dominated with an entirely new study of the Qu'ran and Islamic Sharia law. He studied the manufacture of explosives, grenades and mines, topography and land surveys, and the effect of desert and urban conditions on guerrilla operations. He was taught how to booby trap personal possessions. He was instructed on how to blow up buildings and bridges, trains, luxury liners and planes. His specialised training included assassination and torture techniques, surveillance and counter surveillance.

Tens of thousands of young Muslims underwent training like this, but, like Sa'eed, only a tiny percentage of them, the most driven and the most intelligent, were permitted to join Al Qaeda. He was later recruited by Al Qaeda's notorious 055 Brigade, which was all but wiped out by the American blanket bombings in late 2001. He was amongst the sorry remnants of fighters ordered by Osama bin Laden to retreat to the Afghanistan-Pakistan border. He detested this order. He could not stand the idea of retreat; nor did he want to hole up inside the elaborately constructed and fully equipped caves of Tora Bora. He wanted to stand, fight and die, on mountain slopes and valleys, and on the banks of rivers, and in the dirt tracks of villages and towns like Pachir, Landa Khel and Karna Ado. He often stood and stared into the skies whilst his brothers ran, as F18s fired their *Maverick* heat seeking missiles; and F15s dropped their 5000 pound buster bombs that could penetrate 20 foot-thick rocks. It was not that he felt invincible; it was just that he had the presence of mind to realise that running in blind panic was less safe, and that, ultimately, suffering and death in the cause of Islam, was predictable and glorious: *Be sure we shall test you with something of fear and hunger, some loss in goods or lives or the fruits of your toil… to Allah we belong and to Him we return..*

His courage and fanaticism were noted. Azeer's lifelong friend and compatriot, Al Zawahiri, Al Qaeda's deputy leader, took a personal interest. When the bombing stopped, and the Taliban were overrun, the resurrected Al Qaeda, now safely ensconced in the bordering mountains of Pakistan, chose Sa'eed for training that was more demanding and much less appealing than anything he had previously endured. The final consequence of that training, martyrdom, was what he desired, but the path and destination they chose for him to reach that goal was one he could not espouse; it meant lies, deception, betrayal; it meant a return to his beloved family and that could distract him, to his long suffering sister Samira whose stillborn had at last been returned but had been stripped of every organ before its departure from the morgue. Sa'eed dreaded the prospect of returning to England to settle into the corrupt, secular, materially obsessed Western life style that he had come to loathe. Why could he not return to his native Somalia, he had continued to ask, where no lies or deceit would be required, only sacrifice and hardship. He knew the emotional and psychological adjustments that would be required in order to live the lie, particularly when he was in the company of his sister and his parents. But he also knew that he would do what was required. And so too, did those responsible for choosing and preparing him. They were the same people who chose Mohammed Atta as the ringleader of 9/11.

Sa'eed nodded coldly to Morgan, indicating that he wanted no more said about Somalia.

Morgan's eyes kept darting back and forward from Sa'eed to the papers on his desk; these included Sa'eed's application form, his personal statement, photograph, comments and opinions from those who interviewed him. He suddenly thought he knew why Sa'eed had reacted like this: 'I bet you're bored talking about Somalia, Sa'eed...' He let out a squeak of a laugh. 'I can see you've talked plenty about it at the interview.'

The 'joke' didn't register. Sa'eed said nothing.

Morgan conspicuously composed himself, put the papers down on the desk, folded his arms and leaned forward.

'What I'd like you to do over the next year Sa'eed, is spend a little time with every worker in the team. They're all childcare qualified, with a lot to give... and between you and me, some give more than others!'

His indiscretion was accompanied by a weak smile and raised eyebrows. He continued: 'But you need to be assigned to one key worker for the first couple of months. When you get established you'll meet members of other teams working with the mentally ill, the elderly, alcoholic and drug abuse, mentally handicapped, juvenile offenders… all these specialist teams are here, in various parts of the building, and that's ideal, because nearly all the families we help are multi problem families. That way we can keep a pretty sharp eye on things all round.'

Morgan was rather pleased with his presentation; he didn't notice Sa'eed struggle to minimise its effect.

'What is there for me to do,' he asked.

'Plenty Sa'eed! You might be asked to support mothers, get involved with the children, be an advocate representing them at tribunals or negotiating for them in schools; you might be asked to attend court with them, give them a bit of emotional or moral support.'

'What do their own families do for them?'

'Nothing much. They don't have *families,* as you and I understand the word.'

'Do they appreciate this *help* they get from social workers?'

'Not always.' Morgan's mouth slanted and his brow creased; he smiled in anticipation as he said: 'Just wait and see how long it takes for one of them to tell you to clear off!' He released a little patter of mechanical-like laughter; it had no impact on Sa'eed.

'But it's not as simple as that,' he continued. 'We're legally entitled to be involved, and it's the welfare of the children that keeps us there. Anyhow, this shouldn't apply to you. You're only…' Morgan hesitated.

'A trainee?'

'What I mean is that you're not yet qualified to do statutory work. These people you'll be dealing with often try to divide the social worker from the helper. They regard one as a friend and the other as a threat. *You've* got to keep reminding mothers that you and the social worker are singing from the same hymn sheet.'

Sa'eed's fixed stare and his motionless face told Morgan that the metaphor was not the right one: 'I mean… working for the same local authority, with the same responsibilities, and anything that *you* learn regarding the welfare of the children has got to be passed onto the social worker.'

'No secrets then,' said Sa'eed, 'between me and the parent?'

'That's it, and no attempts by the parent to play one off against the other.'

'Okay.'

Morgan then reached over to a pile of literature on his desk. 'You're going to need all this,' he said seriously. 'Department's *child protection handbook*, relevant childcare legislation, health and safety regulations, travel expense forms, anti discriminatory, anti racist policies... and that's only a fraction of what you'll have to read when you get yourself settled.'

Sa'eed took the documents one by one and glanced through them. He was supposed to look and sound enthusiastic but everything he had heard and seen had perplexed him. When he had finished flicking through the material he looked up and stared through Morgan's nervous, innocent eyes. He realised how boring and unchallenging it might be, to *sleep*.

'Who have you *assigned* me to?' he asked, confident that Morgan would not detect his ironical tone.

'Oh yes sorry I forgot Sa'eed... that's Sean... Sean O'Neill. He's one of our most experienced workers. I'll introduce you... whenever I find him! He spends a lot of time out of the office.'

Morgan's smile was accompanied by a wink. Sa'eed looked bemused.

Chapter 12

Mr Cole gazed around the assembled dignitaries in the Great Hall of the university, with conflicting senses of relief and unease. Professor Cummings, Dean of the University Medical School and Head of the Institute of Child Care, was at last leaving on the day before his much heralded Dutch protégé Professor van Hoofdaaker was due to begin. Van Hoofdaaker would be the very first occupant of the new Chair of Fetal and Infant Pathology, which Professor Cummings had established almost single-handedly. Cummings sat at the centre of the Great Hall's magnificent oak dining table, with the vice-chancellor on one side and his jewel-bedecked wife Esther on the other. High above them from each of the four walls, all twenty-two of the vice- chancellor's illustrious predecessors stared down stonily on the happy occasion. The guests were positioned as near or as far away from Cummings and his wife as rank and influence determined, and each had forked out sixty five quid for the privilege.

Of all the shenanigans Mr Cole could recall in his thirty years as Registrar at the university (he would be retiring himself in a few months) none had been as incredulous as those surrounding Cummings' creation of this Professorial Chair in Pathology, to be based at nearby Aldermann's, one of the largest children's hospitals in Europe. Cummings had been the originator and the driving force. He had ignored fair play and wise counsel from a few of his colleagues about the viability of the plan, and about the candidate who in less than twenty four hours time would occupy it. He had always ignored such obstacles, but never so blatantly, or so hurriedly.

Mr Cole and his wife Lisa sat some two thirds of the length of the hall away from the head table. She usually felt interminably bored by these events, and he had long given up trying to engage her. As the champagne flowed, and filoed langoustines in mango sauce were replaced by Navarin of lamb and orange quark soufflé, Mr Cole became more and more preoccupied with Cummings' failings, on a night in which everyone else would talk of nothing else but his success.

Mr Cole's central bureaucratic role had allowed him to participate in every formal meeting about the project, and gave him access to all papers, minutes and correspondence relating to it. None of these things counted for much, because their conclusions were continuously altered in accordance with less transparent but more important meetings between Cummings and the vice-chancellor. Both men towered over Mr Cole in every conceivable sense, and he had lacked the authority and the confidence to challenge them or to openly express the slightest doubt about their intent. That was until he received a strange phone call from Professor Darby of Oxford University.

Professor Darby was the leader of a group of external advisors appointed to oversee the establishment of the Chair and the selection of candidates. It was a mystery to Mr Cole how such people had been appointed. But he was astonished to say the least, and not a little put out, when Professor Darby phoned him and suggested that *names* should be considered before advertising and that Dr Dick van Hoofdaaker *should* be considered as a strong possibility. It was Mr Cole's job as University Registrar to oversee all advertising for senior posts; he had never spoken to this Professor Darby before, and suspected that Darby and Cummings had colluded before he got the phone call. Darbys' telephone *suggestion* was delivered with an arrogance of tone and a choice of words that Mr Cole could only interpret as a command. That annoyed him, convincing him that Cummings had conveyed to Darby that he, Mr Cole, would be a soft touch, would do exactly what they required to secure the appointment of van Hoofdaaker, and would ask no serious questions.

'Yes Cole, what is it?' said Professor Cummings a few weeks earlier, with a brusqueness which convinced Mr Cole that he was approaching him on the wrong day at the wrong time. It was that long walk from the door to Cummings' huge desk which Mr Cole detested, particularly when Cummings was in a mood like this. When Mr Cole got to the desk, Cummings looked up (looked down as a matter of fact, as when he was sitting, he still towered over the slightly stooping, standing figure of Mr Cole). He then stared at Mr Cole over his golden half moon glasses perched on his large nose and waited impatiently.

This had been an encounter of absurd inequalities, in rank, stature and dress, in confidence and demeanour: the upright, projectile Professor Cummings, renowned internationally, an Oxford don before he descended upon Liverpool determined to acquire power and influence more than title (his boss the vice-chancellor was more or less in his pocket as the advent of van Hoofdaaker had shown). And there was lowly, portly Mr Cole, made cripplingly shy by the mere act of walking into Cummings' office, sensing his mood, hearing his voice. It had always been this way. Mr Cole was a Liverpool lad, born and bred in Liverpool, went to a local comprehensive, and had never worked anywhere else. There were barely a handful of Liverpool folk amongst the two thousand academic staff, he had once observed. He was aware of this because he drew up the advertisements for all academic posts, vetted the applications (though had no say in who was called) and wrote to each of those who were appointed.

The brave impulse that had carried Mr Cole to this point had long dissipated, and he sensed that he was about to be annihilated.

'Thanks Professor Cummings,' he began in his usual ingratiating manner; 'I needed to talk to you about... Professor Darby.'

Cummings said nothing and continued to stare at him.

'Em... well, he rang me. I hadn't spoken to him before, and eh... he suggested that names should be considered before we advertise.'

'Don't you agree?'

'Well... of course there's nothing wrong in thinking of who we might like to get the Chair...'

'So what's the problem?'

'The problem is...' Mr Cole hesitated; it was the usual Cummings tactic of forcing the pace, intensifying the pressure and greatly exacerbating the doubts and the lack of confidence of any subordinate foolish enough to cause him a problem. 'Well,' he continued, 'Professor Darby is an external advisor; but I don't think he should be *advising* us on who should be appointed even before the advertisement appears. He said... Dr Dick van Hoofdaaker should be considered as a very strong candidate.'

'And so he should.'

This putdown was bad enough but Cummings said nothing more, enabling its debilitating effect to linger. Mr Cole did not know what to say, which was precisely what Cummings intended. He derived some pleasure observing this helplessness.

'Well I was just thinking that...'

'Yes?'

Mr Cole's tongue failed to adequately moisten his dried lips. But he struggled on gamely: 'Equal opportunities... the new memorandum that was circulated... it clearly stipulated that particular candidates cannot be em... favoured like this, unless the interviewing process has been completed and the panel has agreed. I got the impression that Professor Darby wants me to word the advertisement in such a way as to make it appealing to Doctor van Hoofdaaker in particular.'

His tremulous voice trailed off but he had made it with a sense of relief. He had managed to say all he wanted to say for the first time ever. He could retire now with a less troublesome conscience.

Cummings had stared at him for a few seconds as though he might explode. Mr Cole didn't mind if he did.

Cummings' face relaxed: 'Then you've got to make sure that the advertisement appeals to the widest possible circle.'

Mr Cole waited expectantly for a tirade but Cummings said no more.

That was it then: not a word about Professor Darby's indiscretion.

'Yes...' said Mr Cole, sensing that he had been shit upon from the heights of indifference.

'Will that be all?' Cummings asked him condescendingly.

'Yes... thank you Professor Cummings.' He felt Cummings' mocking laser stare go through him as he made that hateful journey from the desk to the door.

Mr Cole set about composing the advertisement and Cummings duly savaged it to his own satisfaction. Mr Cole noticed that the list of persons to whom he would normally submit the draft of an advertisement for a senior appointment was shrinking; names were being frequently deleted by Cummings and the vice-chancellor.

Mr Cole made arrangements for prospective applicants to visit. He wasn't unduly embarrassed when he heard the bellied laughter of junior pathology staff as they read about the unique opportunities the post offered: incomparable research facilities, modern fully equipped laboratories and morgues, committed charitable funding, and of the collective support and enthusiasm of everyone. If they thought that was funny he mused, how would they react on learning that the only candidate of interest to Cummings and the VC was the thirty-four year-old van Hoofdaaker.

During the interviews, a couple of lone voices amongst the panel expressed concerns about van Hoofdaaker's apparent 'arrogance' and 'brashness'; his relative inexperience and lack of publications. These impressions and facts were of particular concern to Dr Milder, the most senior representative on the panel. She had had a powerful sense of foreboding about van Hoofdaaker, but she also had an unshakeable faith in Professor Cummings' judgement. So she said nothing.

As Mr Cole reflected on all these events of the past they triggered some apprehensions about the present. Amongst tributes that would be paid to Professor Cummings' legacy, Mr Cole knew someone was certain to talk about 'the great contribution to fetal and infant mortality research' or to the study of 'sudden infant death syndrome.' Only Mr Cole would realise the impact of suchlike terms on his wife Lisa. In the previous year their grandchild Monica, aged three, had died suddenly from congenital heart abnormality. Their daughter Rachel and son-in-law David had spent five days in Aldermann's and had then been subjected to an ordeal of police interrogations and social work inspections. They had consented to a post mortem though they hadn't really much choice as that decision had been taken by a Coroner. The inquest had been adjourned and the body had not been released for over a month, an interminable period for the whole family. The experience had taught Mr Cole a great deal about pathology and infant mortality services in his city. He recalled standing shoulder to shoulder with his sleep-starved daughter outside the morgue of Aldermann's and listening to explanations as devoid of common language as was the doctor devoid of human emotion. The doctor really did not see the suffering etched in his daughter's every expression, did not hear her anguished cry, could not feel the searing confusion she felt on being peppered by his jargon, did not understand how anyone could rate his performance as anything other than exemplary. There were moments when Mr Cole himself had wanted to cry out: 'for Christ's sake…'. But temperamentally, constitutionally, he was incapable of doing that. Just as he was incapable of disrupting Cummings' hell-bent pursuit of van Hoofdaaker to remind him of what fetal and infant mortality was really all about. For Cummings, it had become a vehicle for a brazen, unscrupulous scramble for funding and power through which his legacy could be assured before he resigned. For Mr Cole and his family it was about ordinary people's loss, their initial helplessness and hopelessness, anger and incomprehension.

Perhaps Doctor van Hoofdaaker, now elevated to a Professorship and a Chair, might herald a more humanising service. But having been at the centre of the intrigue generated for the sole purpose of appointing him, Mr Cole wasn't so sure now. Professor van Hoofdaaker of course could not be held to account for that.

Chapter 13

Morgan had just spent thirty minutes going through the voluminous Mulholland file, dispatched to him by Jackson's secretary, Priscilla. An observer might have thought he was familiarising himself with the case before allocating it to one of his staff, but he was in fact looking for evidence that Jackson had read it. He was looking specifically for circles and underlining, and for notes in the margins. There were none and he was mightily relieved. Perhaps Jackson didn't even get opening the file.

He stepped out of his office and looked around. He called out 'Sarah.' A woman's face appeared horizontally from behind a computer screen. 'Could I have a minute?' The woman was quite taken back, spoke a muffled 'yes' and looked around at colleagues to see whether or not they knew something that she didn't. She had after all, only been there a few weeks.

O'Neill and Sa'eed sat close behind another two screens. Sa'eed watched O'Neill eying Sarah as she got up from her desk and walked towards Morgan's office. Morgan closed the door behind her.

'When he closes the door like that,' said O'Neill; 'he's in trouble.'

Sa'eed was curious; he was getting used to O'Neill's cynicism. 'How do you know it's not Sarah who's in trouble?' he asked.

'Not long enough here. She hasn't got any work yet to cause a problem. Morgan's probably giving her a case now; it's got to be one he's worried about when it's all hush hush like that.' He smiled.

Sa'eed stared at him inscrutably. He was becoming increasingly aware of the disparity amongst members of the team. *Team* was a misnomer.

Sarah was 25, of medium height with layered long blonde hair and blue eyes that animated with enthusiasm. She wore black trousers and a light grey top with matching elegantly designed court shoes. Her cheerful roundish face belied an impatience increasingly manifest in recent days. She wanted work. She had just recently graduated with distinction from a four year social work degree course.

'I've another case for you, Sarah,' he said, as they later faced each other across his huge desk.

'Oh… good', she said, but only because she felt she had to respond like that. She was certain she could discern an urgency and shiftiness about him which made her suspicious. Of course she wanted more cases, but the thought uppermost in her mind now was that she was going to be offered a case that no one else wanted or would accept.

He allayed her suspicion. 'I got a call on this case a few days ago,' he said; 'alcoholic mother neglecting her kids… we've known her for years. Don't think it's urgent, but it hasn't been re-allocated since Betty Summerfield left. I thought you and I could do a visit this morning… check up on the call I got. I'll introduce you to Brenda the mum, and then you take over; how does that sound?'

Rushed, she thought. He hadn't even asked her was she free to go with him. She sensed that he would have insisted she go even if she hadn't been free. But she had nothing else on. And what of it, she then thought, even if it is a difficult case. She didn't want a non-challenging case. She'd worked with difficult cases on her practice placement and been commended for it. She'd longed to leave college behind, take on the real thing, without a practice teacher peering over her shoulder or filming every word and action she made with clients. 'Okay,' she said; 'can I read the file?'

'Sure, you can read it on the way.' He got up from his desk and placed the file before her. 'Shall we go?'

This was not the way Sarah had learnt to respond to child neglect cases. She expected to have the opportunity to study the file; seek out the basics, the ages of the kids and the type of neglect that was being alleged; parental profiles, evidence to substantiate the allegation, and previous records of neglect or abuse. She would want to contact other agencies, knowing that cases like this always have lots of agencies involved; get their assessments based on their most recent visits (likely to be more recent than her predecessor; she meant to ask Morgan when was the last time Betty had visited; she'd left three months ago!). And Sarah would always want to think out one or two different approaches or strategies, trying to anticipate and prepare for how the parent might react. Just as well Morgan was taking responsibility for this visit, she thought.

'Hopeless case,' he said, as they drove to Abington.

Hopeless?

She had been trying her best to let him know she wanted to read the file, her head exaggeratedly buried in it and her response to his tittle tattle, a stony silence. But even that uncharacteristic discourtesy on her part had no effect. He just wasn't aware that she didn't want to hear, and he was rattling on about this *terrible* woman, about her *terrible* lifestyle, the *filth* of the home, the *layabouts* and the *scum* who queued up each night for a bit of the *you know what*!

'I always say luv… call a spade a spade; call it what you think it really is…'

She was beginning to dislike him. It was not just his crass sexism making the journey increasingly claustrophobic and oppressive, but also, the smell of his cheap after shave, the drooping double chin, the chubby left hand resting on the gear stick only inches from her thigh. She sensed that whatever the reason for his haste in getting this case allocated, he also saw it as an opportunity to impress her. Incredulous, she thought, that he might believe she was impressed.

'Why are we going if you think Brenda's a hopeless case?' she asked.

'You'll see for yourself,' he replied. 'We're only going because the kids are on the register, and we've got a rottweiler in the department on the loose! It's called Jackson.' He released a self-congratulatory laugh as though he was convinced he was outfoxing the rottweiler.

Sarah wasn't interested. She slowly closed the file on her lap and stared straight ahead. She had just heard every childcare principle she'd learnt turned on its head, and watched social work's ethical code being torn in shreds; she'd just felt every potential spark of enthusiasm in herself and in her clients snuffed out.

Morgan was agitated but steadfast in the way he walked up to the Mulholland's front door. She noticed him licking his lips nervously a few times.

Brenda opened the door. She was sober. He spoke to her without a smile, more of a grunt than a greeting. He didn't await an invitation to enter; he brushed past her, as if he thought there might have been some skulduggery being opportunely swept away while Brenda, if he'd had let her, engaged in the usual formalities at the door. But only Archie and Grace were inside the darkened living room, and they were frightened by him coming in ahead of their mother.

Morgan glanced around in barely concealed disgust, sniffed the stale air, and decided the place was infested. He continued standing.

'This is Miss Prescott,' he said; 'she'll be your new social worker.'

Sarah moved nearer, held out her hand and smiled warmly: 'How do you do Mrs Mulholland? I'm looking forward to working with you.' She turned to the children and said in a higher pitch 'And you!' She lowered herself to their level and asked them their names in a hushed tone; her expression was warm and curious.

The children swayed and put their fingers in their mouths. They looked at each other and giggled; they just about managed to whisper their names.

Brenda appreciated Sarah's efforts, but she was still too tense to return the smile. She sensed Morgan was going to read the riot act. 'Wud ye like ta sit?' she said, making a token gesture of sweeping the settee with one hand.

'Thanks,' said Sarah. Morgan remained standing. He ignored the snot-faced kids.

'Another complaint I've got here Brenda,' he said, loudly, wagging his fat finger into her face, then gesticulating towards the file Sarah was carrying. 'You were drunk on Monday, unable to look after the kids; you know what this means, don't you?'

Brenda shrivelled away from him. 'A'm sorry Mr Morgan…'

'A bit late in the day being sorry now Brenda.'

'A promised Maggie… a won't do it again, Mr Morgan.'

'How many promises is that you've made?'

'Ah…'

'Who's living with you?'

'What…?'

'Who's here… in the house… living here?'

Brenda stared at him, paralysed as much by fear as by hatred. She only just managed to control an urge to spring at him, tear his eyes out with her nails, call him a dirty rotten bastard… or something to that effect.

'If you've got a man here Brenda, we need to know who he is. Do you understand? Your kids are registered *at risk*. We've got to know who's living with them.'

'Ee doesn' have anythin to do with em,' she blurted out.

'Who is he?'

'A'm not telling ya.' She burst into tears, doubly humiliated: that he could so brutally and speedily expose her and make her lose control. Her two children rushed to her, each encircling one of her legs with both their arms. The mouth of Grace the youngest child arched sharply; her lips pouted and huge tears rose up in her eyes.

Sarah got off the settee and stretched over to comfort them, but her kindly gesture only served to expose their fear and their distress even more. Archie began crying too. Sarah realised that she had made their plight worse; that they somehow knew her kindness and sensitivity was in response to the cruelty of that big fat man shouting at their mother; and they also knew that he was the boss man, the one who could separate them from their mum. He had done it before. Their cry was becoming an uncontrollable cry of panic.

'It's your kids you've got to be thinking about Brenda,' said Morgan, wagging his finger again; 'do you hear me?'

Brenda's head was lowered as she stared directly beneath her. He wanted to see her face; he wanted her to look at him, to see her mouth and her eyes mouthing the affirmative which he demanded again, loudly: 'DO YOU HEAR ME?'

She did as he asked and comforted the children as best she could. She was still standing in the middle of the living room trapped by Morgan standing before her and by her children who still clung to her with their arms clasped tight around her legs. Her hands alternated between cuddling their heads and wiping her own tears. 'It's okay darlings...' she kept repeating.

Sarah's initial expression of incredulity had slowly altered to one of anguished helplessness. She could not stand this pummelling cruelty and stupidity much longer. Morgan was worse than anything she had anticipated. Her social work friends and her college tutor would not believe this. Morgan was even worse than those idiotic social work characters that they so much enjoyed playing in role-play; the ones so exaggeratedly stupid and unaware that they were certain to wreak havoc and suffering on their clients without realising it. It was always an hilarious indulgence, but no real social worker could be as incompetent as that, they'd all thought.

'You've got a choice luv,' said Morgan; either you tell us who he is or you get rid of him. Is that understood?'

Every muscle in Brenda's face clenched. She managed to shake her head in what seemed to Sarah to be a clear expression of desperation. Morgan interpreted it as 'no', an act of defiance. He raised his index finger again and spoke gravely:

'Unless we know who he is and we're satisfied, we can't have kids who are registered *at risk* living with him. That's the bottom line Brenda! Understand?'

Sarah unwittingly nodded, willing Brenda to do the same. She did.

'That'll keep her in check for three months at least,' Morgan boasted to a shell-shocked Sarah on their return to the office. 'The job's difficult some times,' he added; 'but it's the welfare of the kids that matters.'

Sarah was speechless and full of guilt because she had tolerated it. She could not share her views or feelings with this man. She couldn't seriously discuss anything with him. Her future suddenly felt bleak.

He rabbited on about the foul conditions in which the kids were living, how beneficial it would be if they could be placed in a nice foster home.

Sarah remembered something; she turned to him: 'Isn't there another child?'

He thought for a moment. 'Angela... oh yes, I forgot about Angela. But she's the lucky one,' he said confidently; 'she's at school and doesn't have to live in that crap all day. Her grandfather Charlie takes her to school. You couldn't depend on her mother taking her. As long as Charlie isn't abusing her I don't mind him taking her. I don't care *who* takes her to school as long as she gets there.'

Chapter 14

Professor Dick van Hoofdaaker and Caroline Simms lay in the bed of her luxury apartment, located in one of the most affluent sectors of Liverpool, once the city's crumbling docklands. It had been another perfect ending to their twice weekly fabrication of statistics, making the department's workload appear as though it was expanding inexorably. They had been doing this for months and their bosses had not yet discovered how.

The only witness to their conspiracy was Astral, Caroline's two year old prized Somali cat. It squatted indifferently on its usual resting place, a soft pink cushion on the baroque-carved maple chair in the far corner. Caroline had purchased the chair at an auction, then didn't know what to do with it. Astral had claimed it. Van Hoofdaaker had always been intrigued by this animal, with its cool silvery fawn colours, its large pointed ears and long bushy tail. He first caressed its lustrous thick fur only after Caroline had assured him that it wasn't really as feral as it looked; then he had caressed it ceaselessly, while asking her so many questions about its breed that she got bored.

'How long can this go on?' she asked, her eyes half closed. Within her own mind this question was a recurring one; strangely not a troubling one, but always worth the unserious responses he gave her.

He turned to her: 'Does it matter?'

'Yes it does... when I'm being pestered for histology and post mortem reports that don't exist... and for organs we should have released.'

'Pestered by who? Junior doctors? GPs? Tell them to fuck off!'

'Goldrick is no junior doctor; she's Chair of the medical advisory committee.'

'What has she got to do with me?'

'Nothing. But she's a friend of the Jama family.'

'Jama...' he interrupted, frowning disbelievingly.

'Jama… they're a Muslim family. Samira Jama had a stillbirth. Her father's a surgeon working in Manchester. He saw the body when we returned it and had a fit.'

Van Hoofdaaker uuuumphed contemptuously. 'If it had been anybody else's body he wouldn't have cared.'

She turned and whispered mockingly to him: 'But you didn't say darling, that you were going to strip the body.'

'A bloody stillbirth! I don't understand these people.'

'Goldrick's made a formal complaint to the VC.'

'The VC!' He grunted. 'He's an idiot; tell *him* to krijk de klere!'

'To what?'

'To go get cholera.'

She laughed, caught unaware again by his foolery; he often used Dutch slang to deflect her train of thought; he knew that she was merely making conversation and wasn't really all that concerned.

Mr Cole had introduced van Hoofdaaker to Caroline when he accompanied the would-be professor on a courtesy visit to the pathology premises before the formal interviews. He was surprised to say the least that van Hoofdaaker's enthusiasm never diminished at any point during the visit. Having been privy to the damning criticisms of the project and the Machiavellian intrigues which overrode them, Mr Cole secretly thought that only an imbecile, or at least someone utterly unsuitable, would not have realised how grossly ill equipped and unprepared Aldermann's was for the new Pathology Chair. He expected van Hoofdaaker to do what nearly every other candidate had done, withdraw his application at the end of the visit.

Caroline Simms was even more surprised that anyone could seriously consider the Chair. She may not have been as familiar with the machinations of Cummings and the vice-chancellor in bringing it about as Mr Cole undoubtedly was, but she knew far more precisely than he did about the awful working conditions more than a mile from the main hospital site, isolating her and her equally demoralized colleagues toiling unnoticed for years. When she first heard about the creation of this new Chair, she was convinced that whoever was unfortunate enough to occupy it would barely last a few months. Both Caroline and Cole were wrong; she would quickly find out that van Hoofdaaker was not just aware of the shortcomings that so many had warned about, but that he seemed inexplicably to relish them; in particular the isolated location of their work.

'So you think the VC is the biggest idiot... *of them all*. Do you include me amongst *them*?' she asked, her eyes wide open and frowning slightly. Thoughts raced through her mind; she was lowly in status compared to him, but she was in effect his partner; she had taken risks in persistently lying for him, ensuring he remained untouchable.

'No, of course not. You know who I mean; you must know them even better than I do. Who appointed them?'

He was pandering to her sense of neglect by these same people. They had ignored her until he arrived. Now she was somebody, constantly in demand, forever answering the questions that they were afraid to ask him, blind to the machinations of them both. Her contempt for them was no less intense than his.

She was twenty eight, attractive clever and ambitious, and appeared to have emerged relatively unscathed from her Guildford upbringing, from the affects of a predominantly invisible father and a self obsessed bohemian mother. When Caroline was seventeen her mother simply disappeared one night, returning nonchalantly six months later, with neither explanation nor apology. Caroline survived this ultimate self obsessed act but her ten year old brother did not, principally because the uselessness of the father was the last thing the child needed in trying to come to terms with the desertion of his mother. Caroline herself had little to offer him, being so preoccupied with escape herself. Her brother ended up in an adolescent psychiatric unit (which was not the reason why his mother returned). Realistically, this family and upbringing was something to which Caroline owed little either for her emotional life or mental health, but it may have influenced her morality, her perceptions of the world, her relationships. It may even have influenced her looks; there was a slight tension in her beautiful hazel eyes, a tautness around her lips; a wariness, a distrust. Except when she lay in her lover's arms.

'I like looking into their eyes,' van Hoofdaaker said, 'and listen to them skirting round the issues afraid of offending me or provoking me, and I keep asking... where did they come from?'

'Three quarters of them at least from Oxbridge,' she mused. She didn't really know that, but she would have bet on it.

Caroline chose Stirling university (as far away as possible from Guildford). She graduated in microbiology then moved to Liverpool where she gained a PhD in forensic paediatric pathology research. She started in Aldermann's. She met and married Steve, stockbroker, property developer, rich and handsome, one of the many young investors cashing in on Liverpool's phenomenal expansion. They both made a covenant: they would not have children until he was very rich and she had a successful career.

Over time Steve wanted to renege but Caroline would not yield. This was not unreasonable as she increasingly realised there was no future for her in Aldermann's. Her stance was also somewhat fortified by daily exposure to children's corpses and deformed, diseased and aborted foetuses. She had never met the bereft and traumatised mothers who supplied this vital work material, but she had cultivated a rather negative perception of them, of mothers generally and of those from the great sprawling council estates of Liverpool in particular. She easily fed into the stereotype that these women must 'breed like rabbits' and she often seriously asked was it any wonder infant mortality in the city was so high.

Her disintegrating relationship with Steve and her increasing disillusionment at Aldermann's left her vulnerable and propelled her towards the emerging science of vitrification, enabling her to put motherhood on hold until she decided the time and circumstances were right. She was well qualified to weigh up the risks of this new technique of extracting and freezing her own eggs; she had made explorative trips to the few expensive clinics offering the service. She was convinced then that she must leave Liverpool and start afresh. She had already made numerous applications elsewhere.

Then she met van Hoofdaaker. She was indifferent that morning when Mr Cole had rung to remind her of the courtesy visit, and she had long ago lost interest in an enterprise that, should she change her mind, was likely to impact on her day by day, professionally and possibly promotionally. As the senior researcher in paediatric pathology, any occupant of the newly created Chair was certain to need her and depend upon her, initially at least.

The prospect of van Hoofdaaker being dependant upon her in any sense soon became irresistibly attractive. She did admittedly, when they met and shook hands, resent the sensation that he had held her hand too firmly, too long, and maybe too longingly. But then she said to herself that that's precisely what she should have expected from any of the applicants: an exaggerated enthusiasm and sincerity. But when she later stared into his steel-cold, calculating blue eyes, she sensed something rather unique about him. She was surprised to learn that he was only thirty-four; he looked not particularly older but more experienced than thirty-four. His face was large and rugged; she reckoned there was nothing smooth in the life of this man. Maybe he intentionally tried to conceal it in his antiquated horn rimmed glasses and his boring suit, or in the school-boyish flicker of hair dangling over his brow, something of a cross between a young Alan Bennett and Bill Gates.

But it was his voice that made the lasting impression on Caroline, full of resonance and power. His English was perfect, his phrasing exquisitely constructed, timed and delivered; 'typical Dutch' she remembered saying to herself; he could even swear like an English man, and when he got the Chair he swore often. He sat with her and her team displaying a far too consummate ease and control, every expression seemingly natural, every utterance relevant or amusing. But she knew that he knew the impact that he was having upon her; surely that was a warning to stay clear of this man. On the contrary, it was the unmistakeable sense of risk and dangerousness that made her fall hopelessly in love with him. She was making love to him within a week of meeting him.

'They're reluctant to challenge me,' he said, 'because of all their publicity in appointing me.'

She remembered that publicity. They had encouraged him to respond to every request for an interview, and his youthful rugged countenance and his over-preening confidence attracted much attention. He didn't let them down. He milked the phrase *research that will ultimately save children's lives* for all it was worth – it was worth much more in maudlin Liverpool than elsewhere, and he convinced most of those who saw him that Liverpool would have the best fetal research facilities in the world.

On his very first day in the department he issued two decrees: Firstly, that all hearts removed during post mortems would no longer be dispatched, after dissection and analysis, to the world-renowned collection at London's Great Ormond Street Hospital. They would instead be stored within his own offices and any access to them for research or any other purpose would necessitate his approval. Secondly, he decreed that he would remove every organ of every child's corpse and that these organs would be stored for the purposes of his own research; they must never be disposed of, he warned. He never mentioned parental consent.

Before she had met him Caroline would have regarded such a decree as impractical – she had no moral qualms about the lack of consent, but her instant response to it now was nothing short of awe; a realisation in her own mind that he must be exceptional; he was certainly supremely confident. Soon she was thinking just like her colleagues, that van Hoofdaaker might take their neglected, resources-starved department of paediatric pathology to dizzying heights of success, which is precisely what he believed he would do from the moment he applied.

He did no such thing. Despite the containers of organs accumulating and overflowing in the basement and laboratories and being perilously piled up in his own office and on corridors and stairs, van Hoofdaaker actually did very little. It was Caroline who helped him create and sustain this sham; it was Caroline who provided all the bogus work statistics that were needed, and whose upright professional exterior belied a certain hilarity she felt in delivering them. She knew this could not go on indefinitely:

'But they will challenge you eventually,' she said.

'On what grounds?'

'You're not doing what they require you to do.'

'I'll blame *them* for that.'

'You've already done that and got away with it; they'll be preparing themselves better for the next time you try it.'

'They're in no position to deny it. They're all complicit in Cummings' stupidity. He was determined to establish a Chair. But he never thought it through. Funding was all he was after; big money funding... a million pounds. I knew that the first time I spoke to him. And everybody fell into line. Whenever any of them seriously challenge me I just need to remind them of that. It soon shuts them up.'

She turned and put an arm around him and snuggled closely to him. She would have scorned this aura of impregnability a few years ago; now she felt herself pleasurably suffused in it. Like an addict or a sinner, Caroline could never recall the exact moment when his influence first made her morally transgress; made her tell a simple lie or two on his behalf. But she did have a vague recollection of how easy it got and how bigger and riskier and enjoyable the transgressions became. She would never forget the occasion when she corrupted herself irredeemably. It was during the first of many audits imposed on van Hoofdaaker. His bosses were beginning to realise the character he was. They wanted him suspended. They had given up challenging him directly; he was too aggressive and he cowed them. So they sent the auditors in.

In the days leading up to the audit van Hoofdaaker had shared with her his fears of exposure, probing the nature and the extent of her loyalty to him. On the night before the auditors arrived she was preparing papers for their inspection. Van Hoofdaaker was standing behind her looking over her shoulder. It was not his lustful presence that made her slowly and methodically falsify the figures, but rather a sexually gratifying realisation of the danger into which she was willingly and rapidly descending. She already knew that he was a professional con, a serial liar, a criminal, a lecher, that he was politically and socially infantile in the way he communicated with people and that he was utterly failing to fulfil his contract. Yet she never wanted to leave his side. The seemingly unfathomable depths of his immorality became a magnet to her. His apparent impregnability to bosses who were futilely trying to expose and get rid of him was a constant source of hilarity for her. She then became very much a part of his immorality, making her conscious of a reversal of roles, of her power and control over him. His sense of relief and triumph that night, standing over her, watching her for the first time falsify the figures, was palpable; it reverberated through her. She felt his deep breathing on the back of her neck and his cool surgical hands massaging her throat; then she heard a hushed 'thank you.' Their love making two hours later was violent.

They had been making love for years now. Van Hoofdaaker's marriage collapsed and he blamed his bosses, accusing them of generating within him suicidal levels of anxiety and stress through a cowardly campaign of vilification in trying to get rid of him. But it was van Hoofdaaker who enlisted the foreigner-besotted local press to wage a far more successful campaign of vilification against his employers, making them apoplectic in suddenly finding themselves the target of all and sundry for allegedly wanting to 'rid the city of paediatric pathology services altogether.' This lie would normally have led to instant suspension; but it had the opposite effect, making him more revered amongst his staff and even more feared by his bosses.

'You're always smirking at them,' she said. It embarrassed her sometimes, the way he smirked, like an overgrown schoolboy licking cream.

'I can't help it,' he replied; 'I know it infuriates them but they should know why. Because they're such fucking cowards who can't say what they want to say. I suppress my laughter and they suppress the truth. So I ignore them when…'

She interrupted: 'You're going to have to do those reports; we're going to have to get rid of the specimens and return organs. The place is awash with them.'

'In my own time,' he said, uninterestingly. 'Their brains would make far more interesting specimens.'

'Why are you so obsessed with people's weaknesses?' she asked, frowning; there was a hint of exasperation in her voice.

'I like to know where weakness originates; perhaps it's more cultural than neurological.'

'You'd be better not finding out.'

'Why not?'

'You might take even greater liberties with them; abuse them more than you're already doing?'

He smirked again. 'That would only be one of the consequences; but the integrity of my motive, the search for truth, would remain.'

'*Integrity*' she said incredulously, her mouth opening, her brow creasing. Their heads turned on the pillow simultaneously and their eyes locked. They burst out laughing. Their laughter sent tremors through the spring mattress and the floor as Astral's feral eyes lit on them.

Chapter 15

On a late October Saturday evening, eight-year O'Neill heard his paralytic uncle O'Sweeney stagger from one end of the pavement to the other. His mother yelled: 'QUICK... THE DOOR!' O'Neill sprang up, pulled it open and reached the heavier outside door. He closed it as swiftly and as silently as his little frame would allow. His mother had the lights and television off by this time and O'Neill tiptoed back into the darkness. They waited anxiously. He wondered what O'Sweeney was thinking, what he might do. He hated him. Like nearly every other child in the terraced street, he had been sitting happily engrossed in *Dr No*; it was the first televised recording of the first James Bond film. He wondered would he see the end of it.

It seemed an eternity before O'Sweeney reached the front door. When he did he stopped and stared at the tiny little terrace conspicuously sandwiched by light and noise on either side. O'Sweeney hammered the door, scaring O'Neill. He continued hammering, cursing and swearing. O'Neill and his mother tensed in the darkness, hearing the doors and windows of neighbours opening and voices raised. O'Neill knew his mother would give way and then she would be in a foul mood because she had given way. There'd probably be a row too which would scare him even more.

When he got in O'Sweeney was far too drunk to notice his sister's taut skin and her angry gleaming eyes. This was an indignity he inflicted on her most Saturday nights, since another brother, who had been living there, had left to get married. The family generally felt O'Neill's mother should suffer for inheriting the rented terrace. O'Sweeney had confidence to make her suffer only when he was exceedingly drunk.

He was a short stocky, rather handsome fifty year old, with well groomed sandy hair and blue eyes, a gentle countenance that deceived. When he was sober he walked with an unprecedented military uprightness and precision, chest out, stomach in, eyes straight ahead. But this peculiar gait only accentuated the more common sight of him zigzagging on his drunken way along the pavements, making onlookers gasp each time they thought he'd slip off the kerb.

He spoke to the floor that Saturday night, as he normally did, the saliva slowly dripping from his purple lips. Occasionally he managed to raise his head whenever he thought he had said something important. Then he tried to point a finger at O'Neill and his mother, his direction and his focus at least a metre off target.

O'Neill resorted to slipping in and out of the kitchen for mouthfuls of stew his mother had prepared for Sunday dinner; he liked it fresh and wet, dripping with the gravy that he could still savour long after, seeking it out with his roving tongue in the innermost recesses of his unwashed teeth and gums. His mother didn't seem to notice the comings and goings that night, O'Neill gorging himself to palliate the tension he felt. She seemed to have something else on her mind.

'Am telling ya,' O'Sweeney stuttered half a dozen times, trying to look serious and deepening his voice; but the only articulate sound he could make was a burp or a fart. O'Neill's mother continued with her knitting, pretending to ignore him.

'Am telling ya,' he started again, swaying from side to side, 'a've reared twelve o'em, an never missed a day's work in ma life…'

'Whaddabout your wife?' O'Neill's mother asked sarcastically without looking at him; 'what was she doing when ya were rearin twelve o them?'

O'Sweeney stopped swaying; it took moments for the sarcasm to register. He tried to look at O'Neill's mother but she was purposely avoiding looking at him. She continued with her knitting. His uncle eventually got the point: his quiet spoken, tee-totalling, God-fearing wife was the principal carer of his children – that's what she meant… his wife was a martyr to his weekend binges; she was the arch typical Catholic Irish mother, rearing twelve children whom he hardly knew, rarely saw, and never played with… that's what she meant!

O'Sweeney realised his sister was not prepared to listen to his slobbering rubbish. Even in sobriety he had no defence against her verbal lashings; she was a lot more intelligent than him. But O'Neill sensed she was not being intelligent that night.

'A've never had to desert ma kids...' he eventually said, throwing his head back as if pleased with his wounding. It was a reference to her husband, O'Neill's father, worded to imply that it was her fault; that she was so insufferable to live with that no man would stay with her. 'A fathered twelve o' em... A brought tha money in that reared em... every Friday night.' He shook his head triumphantly.

'Very good,' his mother said, still seemingly absorbed in her knitting. 'Do you think yid recognise yer kids if ya saw them?'

O'Neill tensed. O'Sweeney raised a hurt-laden face. 'Nigh... whadda ya mean?' He knew exactly what she meant. 'Whadda ya mean, Eileen?' he repeated.

'I mean what I say,' she replied emphatically. Often she would try to speak distinctly during their skirmishes; she knew it drove him crazy, when he was struggling for every word.

O'Sweeney shook his head in exasperation. 'A'd recognise em quicker than yer man wud wi your ins'. He made another pathetic attempt to nod in O'Neill's direction. *Your ins.* O'Neill knew who he meant: him and his sister, his battered sister who was taken into care.

'You're like all the rest of them,' she said, searing with hatred at the mention of the child taken from her; 'you're too bloody comfortable to walk out on yer kids!'

'A worked night and day fir ma kids,' he said defensively; 'an a'm still working fir em.'

'You don't want credit for *that*, do you?' She looked at him with an exaggerated incredulity: 'Don't ya think ya should work night and day for yer kids? Or maybe ya think yiv the right to spend day as well as night propping up the bar in the Tavern an forgetting all about them?'

'Whadda ye talking about? Isn't that what yer man's doing in Kilburn now?'

'He can do whatever hell he likes with all the other drunken scumbags; he won't do it here!'

O'Sweeney paused for a while. He was becoming baffled by the innuendo. It seemed he had neither the physical nor mental energy to continue. But then he leaned forward and said quietly, confidently, as though he was having one last throw of the dice and knew precisely what it would do to her: 'Just as well you threw im out... He wudn't a done half as good a job as yer brother.'

O'Neill watched his mother's countenance change dramatically. She stopped knitting. She looked up at O'Sweeney and stared through him. 'What job?'

'Rearin yer kids fir ya,' he replied, smirking triumphantly.

'JESES CHRIST' she yelled, throwing her knitting to the floor, and getting up. She paced up and down the ten foot wide living room and then screamed at him: 'You stinkin slobbering bastard blarging in here of a Saturday night cause your own family despise you... know what ye are... a filthy good fir nothing... not fit to have children... fit for nothin but to be laughed at... yer kids runnin when they see ya comin up the street... cause they're ashamed of ya... ashamed of being seen anywhere near ya... and you come here to tell me that that other useless bastard of a brother reared my children fir me... when all he did was treat me like his own bloody slave. An him as dumb as yerself... he wasn't fit to rear a dog...!'

O'Sweeney somehow managed to spring from the couch and grab his mother by the throat. She yelled and O'Neill screamed. His uncle pushed her against the corner of the room and tightened his grip; he thrust his head to within inches of her mouth and roared at her: 'Yer brother reared your kids fir ya, and if ee hadda bin round when ya were whoring about, ya mightina lost yir wee daughter!'

O'Neill ran into his massive bulk and yelled hysterically. His uncle could neither see nor hear him. His mother's face turned blue. O'Neill screamed and yelled frantically, watching the life blood drain from her. He flung open the door and ran into the darkness screaming. He ran in the direction of his uncle's house, knowing that his aunt Kathleen, if she could get back in time, would save his mother. He ran for his life, sensing the life draining from him, in an image of his mother, dead.

But he was unable to reach his aunt. The cold autumnal air rushed into his gaping mouth and congealed all the remnants of the savoury gravy-soaked stew he had gorged on. He needed to stop, keep his mouth closed and just wait. He did the opposite. He panicked even more, tried to run faster, and the gravy thickened and hardened so much at the back of his throat that he couldn't breathe at all. He managed to reach a gable wall and then he felt unconsciousness closing in. He remembered going down, his hands chilled by the freezing red bricks, choking and drowning in the floods of images of his mother's face turning blue, and his own terrifying helplessness.

'Sean! Sean! What in the name of God's wrong with you?'

Mary, the office cleaner, stood over him, shaking him; she looked petrified: 'God... Sean... I thought you'd had a heart attack... the look on your face... sure a've been trying to talk to you since a came in... are you all right?'

She stared into his wide open fear-laden eyes where tears seemed to swell. His bony cheeks had an unusually paled hue. 'I'm okay,' he said, annoyed and exposed; 'just day-dreaming. I'm waiting on someone.'

'Are you sure?' she asked, unconvinced. Maybe another abuse case had gone horribly wrong, she thought; she had known lots of social workers cry over cases.

''Yes I'm sure.'

'Can I get you a cuppa tea?'

He shook his head and turned away from her, emphasising a desire to be left alone. She resumed her cleaning and eventually moved out of his sight.

It was 5.30. Everyone had gone half an hour before, rushing out stuffing briefcases that wouldn't be open until the morning, hurrying away before last minute emergency calls. Sa'eed had asked to stay, curious as to why O'Neill would want to interview someone at this time. He had never seen O'Neill in the office when it was closing. O'Neill had told him to go home.

O'Neill lifted a social work journal and flicked through the pages. He read an article on the significance of surrealism in social work: '*Surrealism departs from reason and challenges the outer world of reality; it lays greater stress on fantasy rather than logic, and has a dream like quality similar to Freud's dream analysis.'*

He threw the journal to the end of the desk and gazed over the office floor. Ancient filing cabinets lined the walls, stuffed with crumbling files on clients nobody knew anything about. Current files, contrary to the rules, were stuck in the drawers of the desks, or in social workers' cars or in their homes.

A new batch of computers had just been installed, with programs guaranteeing that they would make social workers more competent and their clients more satisfied. Computers and programs were at least more obedient than clients, and they did have the unerring capacity to convince managers that solutions were always possible. One particular program postulated over fifty different causes of child abuse, with elaborate step by step instructions for tackling all of them. Child abuse cases inexorably rose.

His mind wandered again. He placed the ring on her finger and looked into her eyes and could see nothing of the crudity and immaturity in her or himself. He was eighteen and she was seventeen. They both escaped from their misery in loveless sex and marriage, like most of his adolescent clients did. He was ex-delinquent, a criminal record, unemployed and unemployable, only then awakening to the consequences of his past, and about to be consumed by the hatred it would generate. Their marriage lasted a year, just like the marriages of most of his adolescent clients, and he walked out leaving a child and a pregnant wife just like his father did.

The social work lecturer who interviewed him more than a decade later was ambiguous about his experiences; O'Neill sensed she was impressed that he had survived, but concerned that he might be too damaged. It was common knowledge that a good many social work applicants were motivated by childhood trauma, misery, cruelty or loss. He wasn't entirely honest about its effects.

'What time's your visitor due, Sean?' asked Mary.

'Six.'

He resented her intrusion. Then he thought: Mary was an Irish single mother too, with three kids, doing what his mother did once, cleaning offices. That's what most of the women around them then did, cleaned offices, schools, hospitals and churches, on their knees.

'Do you like this job?' he asked her, in a semi mocking tone.

'Oh I do indeed Sean,' she replied in her lilting Irish brogue. 'Sure it's the hours I'm after, and there's many a foreign lass these days would be glad of it.'

Poland seemed to have invaded the city. There were hundreds of Polish 'lasses' looking for work, any work, any hours; anywhere.

'How much do they pay you?'

'Mind your own business,' she replied, unoffended. She continued working around him.

The *minimum wage*, he thought, not a penny more. Suffering Irish motherhood, thousands of them, with their fatherless kids, now competing with thousands of East European students and illegal African and Chinese immigrants, all glad of the 'hours' and the minimum wage paid to them.

He watched Mary move about the office business-like, lifting discarded chocolate wrappings, emptying rubbish bins, placing chairs neatly at their desks. He suddenly thought: she was not *that* unhappy. Their eyes met and he resented her warmth and her kindly caring features. She moved further away from him. She stood before the bookshelves, lifting with care the few at each end, straightening them, placing the end one on each shelf at the appropriate angle of support.

'That sounds like your visitor Sean,' she said, as she heard the car drive into the grounds. She looked out the window. 'Is it a Fiat she drives?'

O'Neill didn't answer her. He got up decisively and walked to the window. He saw Mrs Greer carefully checking the doors of her car. He looked at his watch. She was dead on time. Then she came towards him wearing the same old gabardine coat and holding the tattered straw shopping bag drooping emptily over one arm. Her long black hair remained bundled out of sight by a plain grey scarf. She was unable to see him watching her through the thick dust and grime of unwashed windows.

He went to the reception and greeted her. He anticipated that this encounter would be different, knowing that all his clients behaved differently at home and in a Social Services office. The office could cow clients, could provoke them into a fury, could make some disintegrate. He took her to one of the cubicle interview rooms, asking her about the heavy tea-time traffic and thanking her for making the effort to come. They sat opposite at a very small table, ensuring for him a sustained proximity. He offered her tea, coffee, water with ice, but she refused.

He had asked her to come on the pretext of filling in some forms. But her anxiety was so obvious in her dry taut lips and in her stammering and monosyllabic replies that he wondered did she suspect he may have had other motives.

She certainly had no intention of concealing how she felt: 'Look,' she said, holding out a trembling hand; 'that's how I am the whole day; I'm worried sick about him; I don't know what's happening to him.'

'I saw him Monday; he's fine.'

'I want him home.'

Her pleading tone surprised and annoyed him. She was apparently willing to go on her knees and beg of him.

'What do you think will happen if he does come home?'

She looked puzzled. 'He's going to be good… he's not going to get into any more trouble… is that what you mean… I'm not sure what you mean.'

'No, I wasn't meaning that. I mean what do you think our job will be if he does come home again? You and your husband haven't been able to stop him getting into trouble, so… how do you think *we'll* stop him?'

'Well… you'll check up… you'll come and visit… like the Probation woman used to do.'

He smiled. 'Yes, we'll check up. Is that all you think we might do?'

She shook her head, perplexed and resentful of the fact that she didn't know where these questions were leading. 'I don't know; you're the people that know best.'

'Are we?' She wouldn't have said that in her own home, he thought. 'How long did you say you've been living in Lawrence Grove, Mrs Greer?'

'Two years.'

'It's not like a lot of homes we visit. You must be really proud of it?'

'Yes I am. I've put every penny into it. That's why I work. I wouldn't miss a day's work for anything.'

'Did you always feel that way about having a nice home?'

The expression on her face altered significantly. The pained, pleading expression had gone. She smiled, a smile of childish smug self satisfaction. 'Even before I was married I always longed for a nice home of my own.'

He stared at her for a moment, and suddenly stared at Martin. She seemed to have forgotten about Martin. 'You know, I've never said it before, but it's always struck me how alike you and Martin are?'

She looked annoyed. She shook her head vigorously.

'No?' he asked. 'Well... I think you are; hasn't anyone else said it?' He tried to sound jovial.

She stared coldly at him. Then she stretched towards him, discomforting him, and said in a hushed voice as if in secrecy: 'He's like his father.'

'I've never seen his father.'

She lifted her handbag and opened it. 'I can show you.' She began rummaging, with her head almost immersed in the bag. 'But you mustn't say anything to my husband. He doesn't know I've got these.'

There was an impish glee all over her face. She took a number of photographs from the bag, held them tightly, and looked at each one before handing them to him. 'But you mustn't say,' she repeated excitably. 'Didn't I tell you?' She had barely given him time to look. 'He's the image of his father, isn't he?'

The photographs showed a small hunched figure with rounded shoulders leaning unsteadily against a gable wall; his eyes appeared bloodshot. His lips bore no smile. His whole posture and demeanour conveyed uncertainty and insecurity. He looked ugly and destitute.

O'Neill never spoke. For a second he thought this was some weird kind of humour, but when he looked up from the photographs and looked into her eyes he could see that she meant it. He wondered was she mad. 'He isn't like your former husband, Mrs Greer,' he said emphatically.

'He is! He is! He's his father. I should know.'

She gathered the photographs together and replaced them in her bag. She was visibly exasperated by his refusal to agree.

O'Neill felt relieved that he was not going to have to persist in disagreeing with her, but he also had a sudden inexplicable and conscious desire to expose and punish her.

'What's Martin interested in most?' he asked.

She thought about this for a few moments. 'Bikes,' she said, unconvincingly; 'he's got two. He likes music. He's got a... what's it called... a music thing...?'

O'Neill remembered the cassette recorder he saw on his first visit. She surely didn't mean that!

'It plays tapes and has a radio,' she said.

'A cassette recorder?'

'That's it... he loves it; he's always playing it.'

More to be pitied than punished, he thought. 'Are you proud of Martin, Mrs Greer?'

'Yes yes! Of course I'm proud of him.'

'Why?'

'Because I love him. Why isn't any mother proud of her son?'

'Good question. Maybe because a son might be good-looking, strong, clever and witty.'

'I know he's not clever.'

'Nor confident.'

'He's shy.'

'He's more than shy, Mrs Greer. He doesn't know who he is.'

He waited for some response, but she said nothing. He wondered did she understand.

'What do your neighbours think of him?'

'I don't care what they think of him.'

'What about your husband, what does he think of Martin?'

'I told you... they get on great.'

'But what does he think of him?'

'I don't know what he thinks of him.'

'Does he ever say anything complimentary about him?'

'Yes... I'm sure he does.'

'Such as?'

'I can't remember.'

'Has he ever abused Martin?'

'He wouldn't lay a finger on my son.'

'Are you sure you'd know if he was being abused?'

'I'd see it, wouldn't I?'

Not necessarily, O'Neill thought to himself. But he was disinclined to share with her his suspicion that her husband *was* sexually abusing her son. How could she cope?

'Have you ever heard anyone praise Martin, Mrs Greer?'

She stared helplessly at him, sensing his determination to find questions that he knew she could not answer; she had never been asked such questions before. 'I don't know... please?'

'I've heard lots of people talk about Martin,' he said; 'but I haven't heard anyone say anything nice about him. You called him a big softee...?'

'I didn't mean anything by it.'

'Sure... that's what lots of people call him... and you said he wasn't clever?'

'It's what the teachers told me.'

'Okay. But if these are the only kind of opinions Martin hears about himself, maybe they're the only opinions that he believes about himself; maybe Martin thinks he's incapable of being anything else?'

She lowered her head, and sobbed: 'I love him... he knows I love him.'

Then she began trembling all over, and choking with emotion. She looked up at him, submissively. He stared through her, unmoved.

She said: 'You don't believe anything I say, do you?'

He never spoke.

'I'm not going to lose him. I don't care what you do. I'll stand by him. I've always stood by him. I've always done my best for him. People tell me I've done too much for him. I don't care. He's my son. He's a big boy but he's only a baby at heart. I'll never leave him. He's going to stay with me, because he needs me. He's never been away from me. Not once. That's why it's killing him up there. He can't stand being away from me. But you don't understand because you don't know him. Even in the house he needs me. If I get up and go to the kitchen, he has to get up and follow me. It's funny, isn't it? But that's what he does. I've told him that he doesn't have to follow me into the kitchen, but he still does it. You see? He really needs me. And I want him back. He's my son! He's mine! Oh my God... send him back!'

Her remaining words were muffled as her head fell helplessly towards him. He felt her madness come nearer him too. He stared down on her, and grappled with the images she had unwittingly conveyed. He had listened in fascination and disbelief but when she said that Martin 'follows her around the house' he could not prevent an ice-cold tremor spreading from his neck downwards. He took a deep breath and pressed his feet against the floor. He said to her, conscious of the absurdity and inappropriateness of it: 'The case conference on Martin is a week on Tuesday.'

She was still sobbing into her arms on the table, and he thought she may not have heard. But a few seconds later, she managed to slowly lever her face upwards into view, and he thought and felt that her tear-laden eyes were piercing through him, crying out: *why-are-you-doing-this-to-me?*

Eventually she stammered: 'I... want him home... please!'

O'Neill said nothing. He just stared at her, thinking of Martin, with more anger than pity.

Chapter 16

In the name of Allah, Most Gracious, Most Merciful.

To my beloved and revered Sheikh Omar Abdel Rahmān, As-salamu Alaikum!

Alhumdulallah!

I have been in Britain three months now and I have been given permission to make contact with you again. My father in Islam, Dr. Azeer, has told me many times that I must always believe they are watching me and listening to me. I do believe that. I believe they have eyes and ears in the skies, lens peering through my windows, and microphones in my mobile and in my walls. They probably haven't, but I must believe they have and then I must find a safe way to communicate with you and all my brothers and sisters whom I miss dearly.

So, they may spend millions of dollars tracking me with their state of the art technology twenty four hours a day. But all I have to do is write a letter and carry it into my work and give it to the clerk who posts hundreds of letters each afternoon. She looks at your address and remarks that I am a lovely writer! She is not young, but she is a simple girl who believes she is falling in love with me. Dr Azeer derives much gratification from such indulgences, which confirm that our enemies, despite the sophistication of their surveillance, are essentially corrupt, lazy and stupid.

I want to tell you about what I've seen and learnt in Britain since returning from the place that I regard as my home. I know now that Allah the Compassionate, the Merciful, the Majestic, sent me to you, and I am eternally grateful to you for enabling me, through Allah, to see into my soul and the meaning of my life. I will try to make contact regularly with you, Insha'allah! so that you may judge whether or not I am fulfilling the obligations I have committed myself to.

*My mother and father are overjoyed with my return, though saddened by my 'apparent' lapse from the faith (**Allah, most gracious, most merciful, oft-forgiving, strengthen me in this resolve**). Since the murder of our beloved Sharif, they have achieved a little fame in the local press and radio, commenting on current news* and events relating to Muslims. For their moderation and their efforts in trying to reach out to the infidel, they often receive anonymous mail that makes a mockery of Allah (**Thus will Allah show these people the fruits of their deeds... Nor will there be a way for them out of the fire**). This mail threatens my parents and insults them; it sometimes contains racism and pornography that sickens them, and it even celebrates the slaughter of my dear brother and the defilement of my beloved sister.

Samira has much more to contend with. The body of her stillborn child was stripped of its organs. They have never been returned. Apparently this has happened to thousands of parents. Even with our father's influence, the pathologist concerned has failed every request and every complaint to have the organs returned. Samira still grieves and will continue to do so until the organs are returned to the corpse of the child and buried. I grieve with her, but I must not raise my voice in protest. I must not draw attention to myself.

Islam is being attacked from all sides. After being permitted to establish our own Islamic schools, the same politicians who gave us that right now criticize them for being sectarian and divisive. A cabinet minister has accused them of exploiting their popularity by unlawfully extracting funds from poor parents. His colleagues even advocate them being taken over and integrated into their abysmal state system.

The clothes our sisters wear are criticized daily. When a Muslim woman wearing a chador or a khimar comes into the office, the plight that has brought her there is of little interest to anyone; it is her expression of faith in Allah, and her willingness to exhibit that faith by what she wears, that provokes interest; not the interest of concern and good will, but of contempt and hostility.

Government ministers say they will not speak to Muslim women covered with a veil. They don't know and don't respect that most Muslim women will not remove their veil in the presence of men. These statements I'm sure have some political motive, like courting anti Muslim sentiment in their own constituencies where they feel under threat, but they manage to unleash a whole nation's prejudice against Muslims in general, and our veiled women in particular.

It is now obvious to all of us that the infidels have been harbouring deeply offensive feelings about the clothes our sisters, of their own volition, choose to wear. Every comedian must now make insulting jokes about the veil; every comedy program must include equally offensive sketches about the veil. Thus our sisters are been covertly regarded as lepers or slaves, and now they are banished from the workplace, from the classroom, and from courtrooms and banks. Where do they expect our sisters to go? They have always accused and condemned Muslim men for entrapping their wives at home (ignorant of Allah's advice that they should stay at home). The government now issues warnings to universities and colleges about the increasing number of young Islamic women being radicalised by jihadi extremists! Excellent!

That great arch-Satan Pope Benedict is at it again (**enough for him is Hell – an evil bed indeed for him to lie on**). Dr Azeer has encouraged me to pay particular attention to this Pope. Remember, he lectured in his native Germany (thinking no one outside was listening). He told his audience that Islam was rooted in violence, and he implied that Allah was 'evil' and 'inhuman'. When he was found out, he spent all his time making grovelling apologies to Muslims (the only reason being that he was about to visit Turkey and our brothers in Istanbul were threatening to ban him). Now one of his Vatican henchmen has this week spoken of Islam as a religion of extremes. He says the Pope's speech was justified to counter naïve views of Islam. He warns about the Islamisation of Europe. There's hypocracy for you. They say our faith is rooted in violence, but Catholicism is a faith rooted in nothing more than the shifting sands. ThePope pronounces on great issues but only according to the expediency of the day.

I am sure it is no coincidence that my return coincided with this government awarding a knighthood to Salman Rushdie. His ugly Capitalist-bloated face fails to conceal from me his sniggering contempt for Islam and Muslims; it blazes out from the front page of every paper, every news broadcast. Those of us who wept when Iran lifted the Fatwa are vindicated. The British government laughs at us. They used all the lies and cunning their diplomacy is infamous for, to persuade the Iranians that Rushdie meant us no harm, that he was in fact a friend of Islam, which he proved of course (if you are even a bigger fool) by renewing his faith in Islam. Now the Iranians are made to look ridiculous. They are seething, but they dare not re-issue the Fatwa, which would expose their gullibility in the first instance.

The media here regard us as religious zealots because we protest about the abominable Danish cartoons. Their camera crews roam amongst our brothers and sisters and their reporters infiltrate our mosques in the hope that they hear words and capture images that will demonstrate how 'brutal' and 'barbarian' we are. They say that we have no respect for freedom of expression, or for the British way of life!

The prejudice of their media knows no bounds. It delights in telling us that when Princess Diana fell in love with Dodi Fayed, a Muslim, her aristocratic mother called her a whore. So what? Muslims know how the British establishment regards them. But the screaming headlines YOU ARE A WHORE DIANA revealed not just the aristocratic hatred of Muslims, but also, the attitude of Britain as a whole. Their newspapers merely reflect the views of their readers, who proudly say they agree with Diana's mother: any Christian woman who marries a Muslim must be a whore!

When the head of the Christians in Britain dared to suggest that some aspects of our Sharia would inevitably be incorporated into British law, he was ridiculed and attacked by the press with such ferocity that he hid himself away for three days.

The media repeatedly broadcast programs to demonstrate the risks Muslims pose. Then they pretend to be shocked and horrified when their researchers discover that a quarter of all Muslims supported what our brother martyrs achieved on July 7. Only a quarter! We have still much work to do.

The media learns nothing. They believe they have the right to mock what is sacred to us because they are incapable of realising that anything can be sacred to anyone. They not only trample on the rights of Muslims and mock our faith, but they usurp Muslims' rights to feel. They say: 'how can you feel like that… there is no need for you to feel that way…' What they mean is that 'we non-Muslims cannot feel like that, so there's no reason why Muslims should feel like that.'

The only feelings they understand are pain and gratification. They do not understand feelings generated by faith. They laugh when Muslims try to point out that there are aspects of our faith, and practices and rituals in our devotion, which we cannot tolerate being mimicked or mocked. These touch the very core of our being, consume and purify our soul, and are essentially good and selfless.

127

This is strange babble to our enemies. Nothing touches them if it doesn't gratify them. They no longer believe in souls. They no longer believe in sin. Their only devotion is to themselves. **Those who purchase unbelief at the price of faith – not the least harm will they do to Allah, but they will have a grievous punishment.**

The middle classes boast that they are a civilized and enlightened people, sensitive to the cultures and religions of the world. What hypocrites! They are up in arms, protesting in council buildings, marching with banners on the street. And what is the cause of their wrath: our Imans request permission to pray as they are supposed to pray; to broadcast the Muslim call to prayer in the minaret of the central mosques! The civilised civilizing British are having none of it. Even in their ancient university cities where one might expect tolerance and fair play, they degenerate into howling sectarian mobs determined to silence us. Why does the visible and audible expression of belief so anger them?

The government reassures the people that Muslims are an integral part of British society, and that they have made an inestimable contribution to the British way of life. Meanwhile it churns out new legislation that has only one objective in mind, to keep Muslims under greater surveillance and control. When they capture and imprison our brothers, other prisoners subject them to horrific attacks. They are then denied treatment, and locked in solitary confinement, and if they protest by the only means at their disposal, by refusing to eat, they are then force fed.

The most difficult task I have dear Sheikh Omar, is to conceal my faith and my daily prayer. They have to believe that I am not a true believer, that I am not a good Muslim or a committed Muslim. Some do not even know that I am a Muslim. Some believe that I am too black to be a Muslim! They are more likely to see me as the product of their Christian missionaries than as a soldier of Allah in their midst!

I suffer in this concealment. But I know why that has to be so, and that I cannot succeed were it not so. Yet it still hurts and oppresses me much to watch so many of my brothers and sisters proclaim their faith in the teeth of the ridicule and abuses perpetrated against them, and worse, when I hear them invoke the almighty and the merciful Allah in their suffering.

This abuse and hatred is also an expression of their envy. They realise theirs is a spiritual-less, materially-obsessed existence, and they are frightened and envious when confronted with any form of spirituality or any contempt for materialism. They are incapable of understanding the extent of our contempt: we welcome death.

My time is spent now in settling into my job. I work in Social Services, like many of our Muslim brothers and sisters do. I work with social workers who are supposed to help poor families and protect children. I had never heard of Social Services before I left England. Most people have never heard of Social Services, or, they may have heard of it, but they don't know what it is. Yet within days of starting, I realised the wisdom of Dr Azeer pointing me in this direction. I feel safe here.

It is, contrary to my expectations, interesting work. I'm discovering aspects of British life which I wasn't aware of. I'll share these with you in the months ahead, a self test I suppose, to prove to my employers that I am diligent and effective, but more importantly, to prove to you that I am a sound sleeper! Insha'allah!

My work remains dedicated to Allah. Allah the almighty, the merciful, the exalted, has put me here. I need only think of Allah, and then I inhale a purer air, see into the mystery of things, hear heavenly music, become intoxicated with heavenly fragrances, and feel as though I am walking through the clouds. I am blessed through Allah. I do not know why I have been chosen. I dare not even ask. But I do know that Allah as always "made his signs clear to me".

Through the power and Grace of Allah,

Your loving Sa'eed.

PART III

Chapter 17

'Jeses! Maggie Lynch... a right holy mess you've got us into now!'

Bell Chantler, a life-long friend of the same age, was taller than Maggie, a factor that somehow made her feel and look more conspicuously lost. She could hardly contain herself. Even the lenses of her sun glasses which had darkened rapidly to cope with the glaring light of the day could not disguise the conflicting emotions she felt: disappointment, incredulity, gratification, and an uncontrollable impulse to laugh. She laughed herself silly then, and Maggie, embarrassingly, could do nothing other than join her. As Bell's case slipped from her hands, the two women stood in the middle of an empty road in a foreign land helplessly embracing each other. The laughter enabled them to forget that Maggie had made a blunder.

They had journeyed by rail from the lush rolling hills of Tuscany and now on a hot sultry Sunday afternoon in May, they stood near the exit of a run down station called Busseto, twenty-five kilometres north west of Emilia-Romagne's provincial capital Parma. During the four-hour journey up through the monotonous northern central plains of Italy, they had occasionally shared growing doubts with glances and frowns. Ominously now it seemed, they had been the only passengers to disembark from the filthy carriage of a 30mph antique locomotive masquerading as an Italian train. It was their third and final train of the day. They had boarded at Fidenza on the main Bologna-Milan line, stressing to the guard that they wanted off at Busseto. He had looked at them oddly. When they exited the station and gazed along the desolate Viale Pallavicini, it seemed as though they had disembarked at a ghost town.

How could this be? Busseto (or more accurately, the village of Le Roncole, a mile from its centre) was the birthplace of Giuseppe Verdi. Maggie had always wanted to visit it. She had previously been to Mozart's Salzburg, Beethoven's Cologne and

Fauré's Pamiers. She loved standing in the hallowed ground of these choral giants, walking through the same doorway, sitting at the same desk or piano. Then the visit would culminate with a concert. On this occasion, she and Bell would be attending the famous annual open-air performance of Verdi's *Requiem* in Busseto's Piazza Verdi.

But where then, they both wondered, was the welcome for the hundreds of thousands of pilgrims who visited his shrine every year? Were they the only tourists foolish enough to arrive by rail? When they stepped off the train, they had expected to see the national flag and bunting, and at the very least, a Verdi statue or portrait. They thought they might even hear his music! But Busseto station said nothing about the man. There wasn't even a toilet or a ticket clerk to be seen. There was graffiti everywhere and sickly yellow crumbling walls. Its darkened interior was less inviting than the Liverpool underground.

The tree clad Viale Pallavicini made a sharp left-angle turn at the station as though in flight. They stood wondering in which direction the town centre lay. Three middle-aged Italian women, coolly and stylishly attired to confront the heat of the day, sat on a shaded pavement bench fifty yards from where they stood. Maggie approached them and saw looks of disdain in their half-concealed glances at her bare white legs. The shorts she wore barely reached her knees. She asked: 'Parla inglese?' All three women instantly shook their heads as though some kind of alarm had gone off. 'Where can we get a taxi?' she asked, smiling pleadingly at the women.

'No taxis Busseto,' said one of the women, waving her hand wildly.

'Buses… can we get a bus?'

'No buses… Domenica!' The same woman waved her hands again, glanced at her compatriots and said something that Maggie could neither hear nor understand. The three smiled to each other as though gratified by their own unhelpfulness.

Maggie returned to Bell, crestfallen: 'No taxis… no buses on Sunday.'

'What kind of a place is this?' Bell said, glaring back at the women.

Maggie's brow creased in exasperation; her lips pouted and her head shook ever so slightly, gesturing Bell not to say another word.

They trundled noisily past the women, away from the station, the hardened roller wheels of Bell's bulky case making a merciless clatter on the chipped uneven pavement. They glanced up on either side of them, at the imposing residences of Viale Pallavicini, miserably wondering how exposed they were, how suspicious they may have looked and sounded on this deathly quiet Sunday afternoon. But not a single resident was to be seen; not even the windows of their spacious homes could be seen behind protective shutters sealing the panes from the searing sun.

Perhaps, thought Maggie, this was an occasion when she could finally persuade Bell to ditch her case and purchase a rucksack. Maggie's Berghaus sat silently and effortlessly on her shoulders, whilst Bell's rackety case looked and sounded ridiculous; it didn't seem compatible with her three quarter length Capris.

They had known each other since their early teens when they went to St Dominic's grammar school in Liverpool, and both were members of the school's prestigious prize-winning choir. They had parted company when the then seventeen- year-old Bell with only a few O levels to her credit (and in defiance of her parent's wishes) left school to fulfil a long-held ambition of joining the cadets of London's Metropolitan police. Both women returned to Liverpool, Maggie first after university. Bell spent ten relatively happy years with the Met, but was less fortunate in her marriage. She divorced and transferred to Merseyside Constabulary to be nearer her child-doting parents and the assurance of knowing that in them at least she had a reliable child-minding service for her six-year-old son Mark.

Their reunion seemed inauspicious the way it began. Maggie was emerging from one of the side entrances to Lime Street station on a Saturday afternoon and saw Bell standing shoulder to shoulder with a squad of Merseyside Police. They were all scouring the ranks of Manchester United supporters who were also emerging from the station. It took a few seconds for the memories to register. Their eyes met and Bell barely acknowledged her. Maggie knew Bell had recognised her and thought she'd wantonly severed all connections with her past; but then she realised: Bell wasn't able to respond to her, like the rest of the squad she was concentrating on the profiles of supporters they'd been ordered to apprehend. Bell apologised later.

They sought each other out after that. Bell was living in Meols, a few miles round the coast from West Kirby. Maggie persuaded her to take up singing again and join her in the West Kirby choral society. Their reunion was more or less complete.

They were half way along the Viale Pallavicino now, and were relieved to see what appeared to be a main road at the end: more traffic, pedestrians, and a café or pub. This would surely mean a loo and a quick wash.

'So what do you make of it?' Bell asked fifteen minutes later as they sat refreshed, sipping cappuccinos amongst the regulars.

'Too soon to say. But I'm beginning to understand what Verdi made of it.'

'He didn't like it?'

'He hated it. So did his wife Giusppina.'

'At least they didn't have to arrive at that dump of a station. What did they hate about it?'

'The people, the place, their insularity... they shunned Verdi and Giusppina because they never married.'

'It looks as if they're still shunning him!'

'No no... Verdi's big business here. There's a Verdi theatre and museum... somewhere!'

They glanced around, then looked at each other with doubting smiles.

'When he got rich and famous' said Maggie, 'they decided to build a theatre in his honour. He told them to get lost and spend the money on the poor. They begged him to attend the opening night. He refused. He never set foot in it.'

Bell stared at Maggie with a look of consternation. She glanced around the other customers and then gazed back down the Viale Pallavicino. She could still see the station. Her lips tightened. 'You might have prepared me,' she said.

'That's a hundred-and-fifty years ago I'm talking about! Let's wait and see. I can't believe it's going to be like this on the night. The *Requiem's* booked out… has been for nearly a year.'

Bell didn't know what to believe.

The Podere San Vitale was 'a big white house on your right' according to the website. And there it was, the *only* house, a massive eighteenth-century farm cottage on a country lane that stretched towards Fidenza. The blue Appenine mountains were clearly visible on the horizon. The taxi driver pulled up sharply at the entrance. The gates opened, obviously controlled by someone from inside. They drove into a large sprawling farmyard. There was a dilapidated barn on the left with plentiful bales of hay and adjoining stables. Discarded equipment and farm machinery were scattered about. Two black cats stretched indifferently on a crumbling old rocking chair.

A woman in her sixties, tiny, thin, and very nimble on her feet, came towards them smiling. She had masses of grey hair flowing over both shoulders. Despite the heat, she wore a heavy grey woollen skirt that nearly reached her ankles and a long sleeved white blouse with frills at her wrists. Her husband waited behind until she had welcomed them.

The woman said 'hello' and 'welcome' rather hesitantly, but then resorted to a long speech in Italian, punctuated with apologies for 'speak no English.' They couldn't understand a word but the tone of her voice and her blue eyes were friendly.

They paid the taxi driver and the couple led them in through an enormously wide but low oak-panelled door without windows. They both had to stoop to enter.

They stood in a darkened, airless hallway, engulfed in odours of damp rot, fresh polish and ancient oil lamps that no longer functioned. The woman continued walking to the foot of a staircase. In the far corner of the hallway just before they turned to follow her they noticed a strikingly-carved, multi-coloured wooden statue of St Michael Angelo. His face was curiously feminine. His wings were spread out, each two feet long, and his right hand was drawn back with a sword, about to pierce the heart of Lucifer under his feet.

Verdi memorabilia could be seen everywhere. A small bronze bust stood in a glass cabinet. Stencilled sketches and reproduction portraits hung from ledges. In the landing above they saw two early editions of his *Requiem* and the opera *Nabucca* sitting on an original eighteenth century hall stand. A visitors' book conspicuously rested between the two works.

Maggie and Bell were relieved to enter a bedroom that was much brighter and more spacious than the hallway. It had two divan beds bolted together, each with a walnut baroque headboard. An ancient tallboy stretched almost to the ceiling, making it virtually impossible without a ladder, to reach the top section. Pristine white towels lay neatly over a rack behind the door.

Bell opened one of two large double glazed windows, the one that looked to the east across the road. It was only then they saw a finely-meshed metal mosquito screen that partially dimmed the clarity of their view over wheat and barley fields that seemed to stretch for an eternity. The screens were movable but when Bell tried to raise one, their hostess gesticulated 'no!' She pinched both of her arms alternatively.

'Morsa… morsa,' she said.

They looked out the window at the barren road and saw ditches on either side. The water in them looked foul, not unlike raw sewage.

'She's warning us about the mosquitoes,' Maggie said.

'I thought mosquitoes didn't come out until night,' said Bell, visualising herself lying in bed covered in smelly repellent.

'She's advising us from experience; open either of those screens and we'll both forget about them until it's too late.' Maggie turned to the woman: 'Grazie.'

The woman beamed; another communication success. She then gesticulated that she was leaving and that if there was anything they wanted…

'A cuppa tea,' said Bell.

'Ah… cuppa tea Sì, sì.'

As soon as the door closed they both collapsed on the beds. Nothing was said for a full two minutes. They gazed at the darkened oak beams of the ceiling, tastefully restored.

'Go on,' said Maggie in a mood bordering on despair; 'say it.'

'It's not exactly the Sheraton in Salsburg,' said Bell.

'That was a year ago; a special deal... Expedia's deal of the week.'

'How much did you say this was?'

'180 euros for three nights.'

'Shared accommodation?'

'Correct.'

Do you know what, Lynch? There'll be nobody sharing accommodation with us tonight... nobody in their right mind would come to a place like this!'

'I hear you.'

'You couldn't resist that price, could you?'

'Nothing to do with the price; it was the only accommodation I could get.'

'How are we going to survive three days here?'

'Can you think of an alternative?'

'No. That's why I'm asking. We're stuck, aren't we? No contacts, no car, no buses... why did you persuade me not to hire a car?'

'Because I didn't think we'd need one. I know... I know... I made a mistake.'

Bell said nothing for a while. She wasn't going to let Maggie off the hook just yet. She spoke ponderously, with a touch of brogue that mimicked the old Father Byrne they knew from years gone by. 'May the Lord forgive you Maggie Lynch!'

Maggie sang: 'Kyrie eleison!'

Bell retorted: 'And may the same Lord prevent me ever again falling for your cheap, crazy, *on-yer-arse* ideas.'

Maggie burst out laughing. Bell joined in. Just as they had done when they disembarked at Busseto station.

Chapter 18

The stranger sat in his grey Ford Escort, parked near the corner of Beckwith Hill in the Abington estate. He was strategically parked at a safe enough distance from the Mother of Pity Catholic primary school. He had been reconnoitring the school for weeks now, in between his official visits to various parts of the city. It was the kind of bitterly cold, wet and windy day that he had long waited for.

The school and its playground were situated in a valley junction that seemed to trap and fuel the slightest descending breeze. On days like this every parent knew that the playground would become the eye of a storm, a mini hurricane unleashing powerful gusts of wind that could fell a body, and piercing rain that could soak them through in seconds. Consequently, many of them left their homes later than usual, so that they would have to wait in the playground the least possible time. On a day like this they would forgo joining their little ritualistic gossiping circles that assembled in the same spots twenty minutes before the children were discharged. They would huddle instead under the canopies overhanging the classrooms, hoping the wind would die down, the rain would cease, and the teachers would get a move on.

Other less socially inclined parents waited in their cars on the main road outside the school. The stranger was parked amongst them. As the parents and grandparents streamed past him and in through the thick black steel metal gates to collect their kids, he occasionally looked up from the back pages of his *Sun* newspaper and studied their faces, mostly the faces of very young mothers with babies in their prams, the faces of grandmothers, a few grandfathers, and very rarely, dads. Their apparent lack of awareness and alertness reassured him. For many of them, this was their most boring task of the day, a burdensome distraction from real worries like paying the rent, saving their marriages, thwarting the bailiffs, or keeping Social

Services and police at bay from their wayward or neglected kids. Reassuring too, he thought, still gazing sideways at the hurrying parents, that none of them could sense danger. All the cautions, the warnings periodically issued to parents, the obstacle-laden pathway leading into the fortress-like playground, the CCTV surveillance cameras recording every exit and entrance, and the jolly large, luminous-yellow-clad lollipop woman always smiling as she shepherded both children and parents safely to the other side of the road, – all these safeguards meant nothing on a day like this. The stranger knew it.

At exactly ten minutes past three, four of the all female teaching staff unlocked and opened corridor doors. They poked their heads out of the hothouse they'd worked in all day and felt the cold swirling wind and rain play havoc with their hair. One of the teachers wore a dress that was suddenly blown over her head, but the frequency of such incidents and the decorous silence of the parents caused her no embarrassment at all. She calmly pulled the dress down, and held it tight.

Behind the teachers, rows of noisy children queued patiently; they seemed to know how the system worked. The child at the head of the queue stood obediently, restrained by the arm of a teacher. When the teacher saw the parent, her arm would rise, and the child would run, and parent and child would then dash across the wind swept playground towards the metal gates, towards the safety and comfort of home.

The teachers detested days like this. They couldn't see all the parents huddled together under the canopies, mainly because of their multicoloured umbrellas bobbing up and down. And many in the dense packs of parents couldn't see the teachers. So teachers had to search and shout; and parents had to listen and wait and then wave and shout in return, and beaver their way to the front. If the teacher failed to see a parent, or if a parent had not yet arrived, the child was quickly dispatched to the end of the queue, far back into the heat and security of the corridor. There were usually quite a few straggling parents on days like this, making the task of dispersal infuriatingly longer, and wetter.

The stranger knew as much as the teachers about the straggling parents. He knew about the most consistent stragglers, who they were, how many of them, the directions they came from, and about their relationships with the children they collected. After weeks of surveillance, he had picked out one particularly serious straggler, Charlie Mulholland, an unemployed grandfather, who, like many on the estate, was on long-term incapacity benefit (no more incapacitated than the child he was sent to collect).

The stranger had followed Charlie home one day, in order to follow him to the school the next day. He had watched him in the street and in his local pub, saw how he greeted and responded to his mates and neighbours. He took particular note of Charlie's looks, facial expressions, his gait and his posture. He learnt that Charlie did not, contrary to what the teachers thought, leave home late; actually, he left thirty minutes earlier than necessary, but he stopped at a local bookies on the way, and he never left the bookies until he knew the results of the three o'clock races, then he would run to his battered old grey Ford Escort, and head for the school. Charlie was guaranteed to be at least a few minutes late every day, and more than a few minutes if he collected any winnings. He hadn't noticed during the last few days that someone else had acquired a battered old grey Ford Escort, just like his own.

Charlie was aged forty two, a few years younger than the stranger. He wore a peaked oily cap identical to the one the stranger was wearing. His horn rimmed ancient spectacles and his tatty blue jeans and trainers were very similar to what the stranger had acquired. The coat Charlie wore was a permanent winter fixture for him, a filthy old duffle coat that he used to wear in his teens. It was once a bright fawn colour, now it was dirty grey. The stranger had trawled through jumble sales and charity shops and car boot sales before he eventually found the coat he was looking for, a near perfect match with the one Charlie wore, dirt and all.

Charlie was of similar height and build as this stranger, though their looks and movements were markedly different. The stranger had found it difficult to master the slouching walk of Charlie. He had however enjoyed his attempt at a facial makeover, finding the right shade of pallor to spoil his tan, and making the right brushstrokes to create the impression of shadows and gauntness. Their vastly different mouths posed no great difficulty for the stranger: he had already accumulated an impressive supply of fake teeth that were 'plaque-laden' or 'rotten' or just grossly false. The most important accessory was a tube of blackout wax which he needed to replicate a huge gap in Charlie's lower teeth. It worked perfectly provided no one got close to him.

Just as the teachers opened the corridor doors, the stranger, still sitting in his car, inhaled one last time the stinking cheap tobacco he had seen Charlie use in his local pub. He could never roll fags as expertly as Charlie. This final inhalation burnt up nearly half of the grotesquely shaped fag he had rolled, but he couldn't swallow the smoke, and his mouth couldn't hold it, and somewhere at the back of his throat it tickled, causing him to splutter convulsively. But then he spluttered intentionally in all directions, contaminating the cabin air with a similar stench as that which he knew pervaded Charlie's car. He had previously intended to get out of the car with his fag in his hand, as Charlie sometimes did, have a few quick draws before reaching the entrance and then discarding it; but the rehearsals had convinced him that it was an act too far. Suffice to ensure that the cars where identical in every respect.

He checked that the St. Christopher medallion he'd bought was still dangling from precisely the same location and height on the passenger side as the identical one in Charlie's car. He placed the *Sun* on the back seat, ensuring that its title was visible. His heartbeat quickened. His penis swelled. He opened the car door, and glanced round. There was no sign of Charlie.

He went through the entrance to the playground with some other stragglers. They all had their head low, shielding themselves from the howling wind and the horizontal rain. He slowed as he got to the centre of the playground. He had spent a lot of time studying the way some children and parents greeted each other. He had witnessed various extremes in this regard; children who, as they waited their turn in Miss Watts' row, could barely control their eagerness to see their parents who always felt the same way. But there were other children, and other parents.

143

Miss Watts had disposed of about a third of her class; so too had her colleagues. Bedlam reigned, with fifty or more kids released into the arms of their loved ones who bellowed instructions to them to get their coats on. Parents grappled with umbrellas that threatened to take off, reached out for prams that started to roll because they had momentarily taken their hands off them, left conversations suspended, and made brief farewells.

Miss Watts later swore that she saw Charlie Mulholland approach her diagonally across the wind swept playground. It was the same old peaked cap that caught her eye. More convincingly (she would later plead to the police) Charlie's gait and posture were unmistakeable, both hands in the pockets of his trade mark duffle coat, his short crisp steps, his head rigid, his elbows thrusting excessively, though moving rhythmically with each step. His diagonal hurried approach was also typical, as it was the quickest route to where she stood with the children, in the corner of the school building, and Charlie was always late, and always made a last minute rush to the corridor doors. But he didn't need to do that today; he was curiously early, and he slowed as he got to the centre of the playground; then he stopped, as though he was sensitively aware of her difficulties, and didn't want to pressurise her in any way. He was about fifteen metres from Miss Watts and her remaining children. He nodded to her and smiled, not his usual full blooded happy smile. His lips never parted. But Miss Watts clearly thought there was nothing to smile about, as she had a final look to see him standing there in the biting wind and drenching rain, patiently awaiting his granddaughter.

Then Miss Watts did something unusual. She was a disciplined and dedicated teacher and seldom allowed herself to deviate from the time honoured system of dealing with one child at a time, the child at the head of the queue, the child she held with one steady arm until she caught sight of the parent, and the parent acknowledged her release of the child. Maybe it was the unusual sight of a drenched Charlie Mulholland standing in the middle of the playground, early for the first time she could remember, that made her turn to the remaining children in her class and call out: 'Angela, it's your grandad… Go on!'

A lanky, pale-faced and not very bright seven year old, standing next to the last child in the row, barely managed to look up at Miss Watts, so engrossed had she been in a toy that she held in both hands. Now her large blue eyes had a somewhat vacuous stare with deep darkened hollows beneath them, suggesting either sleepless nights or a pervasive tension. Her skin was taut, her lips were abnormally dry and lifeless, and her blond hair was unwashed and dishevelled. She gave the strongest impression that her repertoire of facial expressions was a limited one: not a flicker of emotion registered on hearing that her grandad had arrived.

She held a Tomagochi, a miniature-sized electronic toy with a screen. The principal character was an alien pet whose destiny was controlled by the owner, tapping in instructions and commands. Angela could feed and clothe this alien, play games with it, induce pregnancy and birth, instil discipline, help it to help others, censor or award it. Many six and seven year olds had Tomagochis when they were all the rage a couple of years ago, compelling Miss Watts to ban them during class. Angela still played with hers every day.

She stepped out of the row, her head still bent over, and her eyes still riveted on her alien. She walked nonchalantly towards Miss Watts. When she reached the open doors, she barely glanced up, caught sight of the stranger, walked towards him, and lowered her head again to resume play with her alien.

This utter indifference to the prospect of going home was understandable to those who knew Angela. In twenty minutes or so, she expected to enter the smoke filled living room of her terrace house in Throstle Way. She would often find her mum Brenda there watching television, with a tin of beer in one hand, and a cigarette in the other. Angela would barely be noticed, either by her siblings or her mother, unless she discarded her coat and school bag on the floor, then her mother might shout at her. This kind of home-coming didn't bother her. It was preferable to what she had experienced before, when she was never sure of finding her mum in one piece, or buckled over, writhing in agony, her eyes blackened and her jaw broken by one of her violent boyfriends. Angela dreaded leaving school to return home during those days.

The misery and squalor of Angela's life was well known to Miss Watts, who often despaired of her mother, Brenda. Brenda never attended a parent's evening, never came to sports day, or school fetes, or Nativity plays. Miss Watts regularly told the principal, Mrs York. Mrs York wrote to Brenda, spelling out their concerns: Angela's limited vocabulary, her lack of progress in comprehension and problem solving, her negligible social skills, her pervasive sadness and sustained periods of indifference or apathy, and her increasing marginalisation within the class group as a whole. Mrs York sensitively omitted another of Miss Watts' concerns: Angela's poor standard of hygiene, which was beginning to be noticed by her peers.

Now something new was about to happen in the Mulholland household, and it made Angela apprehensive. That nice woman Maggie Lynch had been trying to get her mum to stop drinking and to start taking Angela to school. The last thing Angela wanted was her mum taking her to school. It wasn't that she *liked* her grandad taking her; indeed she was aware of reasons why he shouldn't: he was late every day for a start, and she was experiencing a child's increasing social realisation that he was not highly regarded either by teachers or other parents. An even more potent reason, if truth were to tell, was that she and her grandad were fundamentally indifferent to each other; they never spoke a word; they barely glanced at each other. Angela knew what her grandad's all-consuming preoccupation was: whether or not he had backed a winner, and she knew when he had lost or won, simply by the expression on his face and the pace of his movements.

And yet, Angela did *not* want her mother to take her to school. She didn't trust her. She was convinced her mother would soon start drinking again, and there was nothing more embarrassing than her friends and her teachers seeing her mum staggering into the school grounds, barely able to see those who would have taken the trouble to speak to her.

Her grandad hit the roof when her mother pronounced only a few days ago that she was going to take Angela to school herself.

Despite Brenda's denial, he assumed it was Social Services who'd made her do this, and he fumed about 'bloody useless interfering bastard social workers denying him the chance to be doing something useful with his grandkids! He said he wasn't having it! He kicked up such a stink that Brenda asked Maggie Lynch to speak to him. Maggie told him *she* was the one telling Brenda she must take Angela to school. She tried to explain to him that it was in Angela's interests that her mum didn't just stop drinking, but got involved in Angela's school life. He forced a laugh at that, as though abstinence and parental responsibility on the part of his daughter was a joke.

This then was supposed to be Charlie's last day for accompanying Angela. He didn't really believe that; he expected his daughter to be back on the bottle in a matter of days; but he was still full of bitterness and resentment that his daily routine was going to be disrupted.

The stranger watched Angela strolling towards him. He could only see the crown of her head. Her eyes remained focussed on her Tomagochi. Then he turned and walked ahead of her. He walked briskly towards the exit. He even felt confident enough to glance back at her. There she was, a beautiful sad seven year old, lashed by wind and rain, trailing after him, but still engrossed in her toy.

He slowed as he approached the final outer gate of the school. He could risk Angela catching up on him (she wouldn't look at him), but he could not risk close proximity in a bottleneck of parents, anyone of whom might speak to him. Much to his annoyance, there was another child who seemed interested in him. Well… she certainly did look up at him. She was seven year old Tracy Cook in the same class as Angela. She too like the other parents and children, was caught up in the bottleneck at the final gate. The approaching stranger stood between Tracy in front of him and Angela behind him. Tracy shouted to Angela and looked up at the stranger. He turned away from her to look back on Angela, rightly predicting that she would still be engaged with her toy. The bottleneck cleared, and when the stranger looked in front of him, Tracy had disappeared.

He made it to the main road, walked towards his car, looked back again at his prize. Then he quickened his step, abnormally so; he reached the car, turned the key, and opened the back door onto the pavement. He quickly went round the back of the car, opened the driver's door, and got in. He started the engine, looked into his wing mirror, made sure his rear view mirror was obstructed, and prepared to move quickly away from the pavement. He watched the left-hand side wing mirror. She was nearly there... Wow! how dopey she looked, he thought, how easy it had all been!

She instinctively reached out to the handle of the rear door without looking. Her mind as always was still buzzing with the challenge of what next to do with her alien. Despite this preoccupation, something ever so slightly registered in her brain the moment she touched the handle of the door. The surface was somehow different. But this perception was too weak to seriously impinge on her care of her alien. She got into the car. She did not immediately close the door, which is what he desperately wanted her to do. She hesitated for a moment, unburdening herself of her satchel and her lunch bag. The car door remained open.

He could not yell at her. He could not turn round to her. He could only wait, his heart thumping, his brow now sweating. He edged the car forward a few inches, as though he was about to take off. 'Hang on!' she yelled, looking up but unable to see his face in the rear view mirror which he had obstructed. She stretched over his *Sun* newspaper, and reached out for the font-like handle on the inside of the door. She slammed the door tight.

The stranger released a long sigh.

Then Angela had that same perception again, the 'feel' of the font-like handle on the inside was different. This time she was not preoccupied with her alien. She actually thought of the difference, and looked over at the handle of the door. It looked the same as it always did, but it *felt* different. Then she realised that the seat on which she sat also felt different. She placed the palm of her hand on its vinyl surface and made a circular motion.

The car had left the kerb now and was moving away from all the school's traffic congestion.

As she stared at the vinyl seat on either side of her, observing stains that she had never seen before, Angela suddenly realised that the engine sounded different, and that her grandad was driving faster than usual. She looked up to see him in the rear mirror, and wondered why it was obstructed. She saw St. Christopher, chaotically swinging as usual. That momentarily reassured her. But then a certain confusion descended upon her, and a niggling anxiety. Her senses were feeding shards of information to her brain, like microscopic pieces of a jigsaw, and her brain was telling her, louder and louder, that this was not her grandad's car. It was the smells that convinced her it was not her grandad's car, smells she hadn't experienced before. The stale smoke was familiar, but it seemed fused with more pleasant substances that she could not recognise, cosmetic smells maybe. A lightening shiver went through her, and she murmured with a trembling voice: 'Grandad.'

He looked round at her and smiled, and she stared into his strange evil eyes and greasy lips. His mouth opened to reveal the same gap in his bottom teeth as her grandfather had. The rest of his teeth were similarly yellow and black. She screamed. She screamed from the depths of her being and she dived at the rear doors, wrenching at the handles, but both doors were kiddy-proofed. He drove into a quiet side street, and looked around him to make sure no one was in sight. Then he stretched over and punched her with his fist repeatedly. Blood spurted from her mouth and nose. He pulled her towards him, and she stared half consciously into his eyes, and then she saw something that petrified her even more than the punches he rained down upon her: the gap in his lower teeth was not a gap; it was black paint or something, covering an ordinary shaped tooth. He threw her onto the floor of the car. He covered her with a blanket and yelled in a strange dark voice: 'Make another sound and I'll kill you.'

Later he would blindfold her, taste her blood, and gently bathe her wounds, before raping her and strangling her.

Chapter 19

Maggie and Bell stood awkwardly at the main entrance to the Verdi Piazza. They'd been here yesterday, visiting Verdi's theatre and museum, and the square had been almost deserted. Now it was crammed tight, with hundreds of diners and scores of tables merging the services of the colonnaded restaurants and cafes on either side. Beyond the Piazza, the municipal offices and the theatre were brilliantly floodlit. Select recordings of Verdi music competed with animated chatter and children's play. This was a popular family occasion as well as an annual musical extravaganza.

They had tickets that permitted them entrance to the Piazza, but they quickly realised that choosing where to sit was more or less a free for all. Table seats were being rapidly taken and they were looking all around for empty spaces, not certain that their choice would be the right one.

'What does it matter,' Bell said; 'we're hardly likely to be talking to anyone.'

There wasn't a Briton in sight or an English word to be heard.

'Look at the smoke,' Maggie said; 'typical Italian night out.'

At least three quarters of the adults were smoking. They searched in vain for notices designating non-smoking areas. What else could they have expected, Maggie thought to herself, in an Italian town's central Piazza? Another un-anticipated irritant in their lack of planning.

Bell eventually saw two empty seats at a table just below the stage. There were two men already sitting there and neither of them was smoking. They wondered did the men have female partners yet to join them. They watched for a few moments. Nobody appeared. It seemed an ideal location if they could get there; it was near both orchestra and soloists. They began the arduous journey of reaching it through the already settled throngs, uttering 'Mi scusi' and 'Grazie' dozens of times. They eventually made it, collapsed onto their seats and sighed.

The two men turned to them. One was in his late fifties or older, with looks and features very different from the audience around him. His skin was darker, his large sunken blue eyes and his granite like cheeks altogether graver. He looked comfortable and cool, though somewhat overdressed in a tailored poplin seersucker suit. A cream folded handkerchief was neatly perched in the breast pocket.

His companion was at least a third of his age, tall and muscular. His skin was black and his eyes were grey. His short hair had a buzz cut style. He wore jeans and a tight fitting dark red Egyptian cotton T shirt through which the muscles of his arms bulged. A square shaped leather and silver amulet dangled from his neck. He looked at Maggie once, just more than a glance, a momentary fixed stare. His face remained expressionless. He turned back to his older companion.

Bell noticed Maggie's unease. She also noticed the two glasses of iced water on the table. The men had purchased nothing else. Every other table in the square was laden with food and bottles of Lambrusco and Sangiovese.

'Look behind you,' Maggie suddenly said, frowningly. 'Look where we are!'

Bell looked behind: 'What... what is it?'

Maggie pointed to the percussion instruments only a few yards from where they sat. In their anxiety to get to the table neither of them had noticed. The Verdi bass drum, taller than the second percussionist necessary to play it, towered over them. Being near the orchestra was okay, but saddled underneath percussion and the extra large drum during the *Requiem's Dies Irae* was not what they had intended.

Bell let out an ironic laugh. 'I'm not moving.'

They didn't have a choice; there were no seats left.

'Neither am I. At least we know when it's going to be struck.'

'Ah... you are British!' a stranger's voice said.

Maggie turned reluctantly to the older man who sat adjacent to her. She resented his intrusion; they had not fully recovered from the ordeal of getting there; their clothes felt hot and sticky and their cheeks were still a little flushed. 'We are,' she replied, conveying neither interest nor encouragement. She looked quizzically at him and was about to ask: 'And where do you…' but he didn't wait.

'I'm from Egypt,' he said smiling; 'My name's Abdul Azeer. This is Sa'eed.'

Maggie looked diagonally across the table. The youth who stared back at her was obviously not one to engage in social niceties. He was distinctly less friendly and relaxed than his much older companion, and indifferent to what anybody else thought about it. His half smile was as much as he could manage, though it was enough to partially reveal his teeth, stunningly white in the blackness of his face. He continued staring at her, through eyes that seemed unfathomable and permanently tense and cold. His single utterance 'hello' had neither warmth nor enthusiasm.

'I'm Maggie,' she said.

'And I'm Bell.'

Bell sat adjacent to Sa'eed. When she had turned to him to introduce herself, she couldn't help partially exposing her bosom, swelling against the rim of her soft white bra, beneath a satin dress with a plunging neckline. Maggie had earlier bantered her about the dress, its 'outrageousness' for the occasion, but to the surprise of them both, it wasn't nearly as revealing as many in the Piazza that night. 'Hello,' she said to Sa'eed and smiled, unable to interpret his unsmiling face and his steadfast focus which remained resolutely on her eyes. She was sure she saw the tiniest contraction in his nostrils, as though he was surreptitiously inhaling the scents of her perfumes. He gave no indication that it was pleasurable or stimulating.

'Maggie and Bell,' Azeer said, his right eyebrow rising fractionally. He cast glances over both women.

'Abdul and Sa'eed,' Bell said, reciprocating what she discerned as a slightly sardonic tone, and irritated by his sweeping glances. His voice convinced her that she had met him before, but she couldn't recall when or where.

'You come from the north of England? I hear Liverpool in your voice,' he said, smiling.

'How do you know Liverpool?' asked Maggie.

I've worked there for many years. I am the Director of Islamic studies at the Al Jamiah Islamic Academy in Knowsley. Sa'eed is one of my students.'

A real bundle of fun, thought Bell, as she looked at the stony faced youth who momentarily stared at them again. Now she remembered who Azeer was.

'Do you work in Liverpool?' Azeer asked.

'Yes,' said Maggie, anticipating he was going to ask them where, and resenting the fact that she might have to remain civil and tell him.

'What do you do?'

'I'm a probation officer.'

'And I'm a police officer,' said Bell. She sat diagonally across from Azeer, whose expression remained inscrutable, but she was convinced she detected a slight movement of Sa'eed's head. 'We've met,' she added

Azeer smiled at her and opened up both of his massive hands in a gesture of welcome. 'Of course we must have met. I've spoken many times to Liverpool's police; I'm spoken to police forces in most cities in Britain.'

'What about?' asked Maggie, feeling more obliged now to make an effort.

'About Islam and Christianity... how Christians and Muslims can live in harmony; how they view each other; treat each other.'

Maggie silently groaned. They were supposed to be on a musical pilgrimage to the birthplace of Verdi. Azeer's homily, if that's what he was about to deliver, would be as welcome as a supporting bill of karaoke.

'The police have a crucial part to play,' he continued. Everybody has a part to play. You are both Christian I presume?'

Maggie and Bell looked at each other. In Liverpool they could be sacked for asking that. 'We don't ask people what their religion is,' said Maggie, apologetically.

'But surely *you're* not prevented from saying what it is if someone asks?'

'*We* don't expect anyone to ask,' said Bell; 'it's a private matter.'

'Umphhhh,' he muttered, shrugging his shoulders.

Bell disliked his posture and his expressions, similar on the day he spoke to her and her colleagues. She interpreted them, then and now, as his assumption that they should feel privileged because he was engaging them. She was also becoming irritated by the silence of his companion.

'What do you like about Verdi then?' Azeer asked effortlessly, ignoring their lack of enthusiasm to continue.

'Probably what you like about him too,' said Maggie.

'Is Verdi popular in Egypt?' asked Bell.

Maggie winced. She thought Bell had given Azeer a cue for taking off now; lecturing them about how significant Egypt became in Verdi's life; about the origins and the premiering of *Aida* in Cairo; the opening of the new Cairo Opera House in 1871, etc. etc. Azeer seemed just the man who would indulge himself like that.

'Very popular my dear,' he said condescendingly. 'Verdi's *Requiem* is popular everywhere. When they sing it in Egypt there are standing ovations.'

Maggie thought for a second he was mocking Bell, but his expression suggested otherwise.

'And they often perform a second and a third night,' he added.

'They must repeat *Aida* for weeks on end then,' said Maggie.

He thought for a moment: 'Just another opera,' he said, with a weak shrug.

'Have you seen it?' Maggie asked, perplexed by that reply.

'Of course,' he said, after a slight pause.

She didn't believe him. 'Why is the *Requiem* so special in Egypt?' she asked. 'It is a Muslim country, isn't it? I can't imagine a performance of the *Requiem* in Riyyad or Teheran.'

He shrugged his shoulders again with a look that implied he was genuinely hurt by the question: 'Who's bothered about those cities? I'm an Egyptian.'

'But I thought Muslims were not supposed to enjoy Christian worship of any kind,'

'This is a musical concert, not a Christian service.'

'But every phrase sung is a Christian prayer.'

He looked out over the Piazza. His expression altered and he seemed to pause for thought. Then he looked into Maggie's eyes, and speaking rather more slowly, in a lower and graver tone of voice said:

'The *Requiem* is a prayer Muslims can embrace as much as Christians. It's about sin and punishment, and the cry for redemption. The second movement of the *Requiem*, the *Dies Irae*, is based on a medieval hymn by Thomas of Celano: "*The day of wrath, that special day, Will dissolve this age into ash…*"'

'Oh my God,' Bell muttered to herself, wondering how long this might go on.

Azeer forced a belly laugh: 'Verdi is for everyone,' he said; 'Look around you.' He made a sweeping gesture towards the audience: 'All ages, all generations.'

They waited, expecting him to add *all races and religions*. But he didn't.

Members of the Busseto-Parma Philharmonic Orchestra came trickling out of the Verdi theatre at the far end of the Piazza. They walked towards the makeshift stage and were dwarfed by the seven metre tall bronze statue of Verdi that dominated the square. The players took their seats at the same time as they made their customary search for relatives and friends in the audience. Then they waved, shouted and gesticulated. This chaotic custom was repeated by the Busseto Verdi choir which soon followed. The tenors and basses in traditional black dinner jackets and bow ties approached from the left; and, from the right, the sopranos and altos, in their famously resplendent green dresses that contrasted with the rustic Renaissance façade of Busseto castle at the rear of the Piazza.

After an address by the President of the Verdi Society, the orchestra's Leader, a lanky cheerful looking man with glossy hair and thick rimmed glasses walked briskly across the stage with violin in hand. He was quickly followed by the conductor and the four soloists.

Within seconds the Piazza was transformed. The gaiety and laughter, the camaraderie and ceaseless chatter, the riotous and formless motion all ceased as the baton was raised. A hushed expectancy and tension filled the air. Eyes and ears strained in silent competition, watching the cellists watching the conductor, listening intently, hoping to hear the first note, that same note always but only just on the threshold of audibility.

By the time the choir, orchestra and soloists had reached the closing bars of the first movement, a captivated Maggie had her eyes closed wishing it would never end. She had forgotten the encounter with Azeer and Sa'eed. She had become absorbed in the novelty of the experience, the evocative location, the open air, the atmosphere, and she was conscious of all these merging into a climax of some kind, at the end of an eventful week. The chorus sang magnificently and without their vocal scores. How liberating, she thought, singing without being distracted by the written music!

As strings and cellos consummated on the final notes, and the sounds slowly melted into the night sky, Maggie reluctantly opened her eyes and sighed. All the performers looked well pleased with themselves. Perhaps they could hear or lip read the superlatives uttered in whispers spreading amongst the crowd. But it didn't last long. Everyone knew what was coming now. Emotional and physical adjustments had to be speedily made. The gravity and solemnity with which the first movement ended was now being replaced by an agitation, visible and palpable, particularly amongst those who sat at the tables closest to the stage. Bell caught Maggie's eye and nodded above her in the direction of the mighty bass drum. The second percussionist had taken up his position. Members of the brass section had instruments raised to their mouths. The agitation throughout the audience increased. Some were smiling expectantly, or feigning looks of terror, or warning others to stick their fingers in their ears. The conductor cued for silence by raising his baton again.

The opening five beats of the *Dies Irae* came crashing down upon Maggie and Bell. They had risked not putting their fingers to their ears (which would have been a rather un-British thing to do) until they heard the first beat. They couldn't withstand another, and hurriedly thrust their index fingers as far into their ears as they dared.

The basses and tenors pronounced the *Day of Anger*. The sopranos and altos joined in, sounding like the whipped up fury of a thousand shrieking witches. The screaming piccolos trilled above them.

Maggie, still holding her fingers in her ears, turned away from the stage and looked around her. Her embarrassment and discomfort left her almost instantly, because dozens of people were doing as she and Bell were doing. But these citizens of Busseto weren't really discomforted. They obviously regarded the terrifying *Dies Irae* as a game, a bit of fun, an annual ritual, not unlike last night of the Proms. Some of them tapped or gesticulated to the beat; some were flinching, frowning, miming, and laughing hysterically with their fingers still stuck in their ears, as though they were on a fairground roller coaster, pretending to be torn asunder, yet enjoying it immensely. The conductor and the orchestra, consumed in the intensity and explosiveness of the sounds they were creating, cared not a whit about the exaggerated expressions of terror on the faces of the audience closest to them. Nobody seemed to mind.

She wondered what Azeer and Sa'eed made of it. As she turned to look at them, the witches ceased their high pitched screams and the strings raced down over three octaves, the metaphorical dive into Hell.

Azeer and Sa'eed sat motionless, seemingly without emotion, staring into each other's eyes. Neither of them looked at her. She raised her head as though to look over them at the bass drum above, but she glanced from one face to the other. Then she realised their expressions were *not* without emotion. There was something of a pleasurable tension in Sa'eed's face, lips pregnant with a peculiar smile that would just not let go, eyes of cold steel oblivious to anything else in this world apart from whatever was on his mind. It looked as if there was more than music on his mind.

Maggie nudged Bell with her toe and directed her focus to Sa'eed's face. Bell stole a glance and looked back at Maggie with a questioning frown.

The strings completed the lightening descent into Hell, and the thunderous five claps of the opening bars were repeated, punctuated this time by the strikes of the second percussionist. The witches shricked louder.

Maggie was certain now that Sa'eed's pregnant smile had a whiff of mockery or contempt. What she wasn't certain about however, was whether or not Azeer and Sa'eed had nodded simultaneously, almost imperceptibly, on the repeated fifth and final beat. She knew Sa'eed *had* nodded precisely then, because she was sitting diagonally to him and staring at him when he did it. But whether or not she could trust the periphery of her vision that appeared to register Azeer nodding also, she could not be sure. She wondered had Bell seen anything. Although their earlier praise of the *Requiem* seemed genuine, this unspoken communication and expression between the two men seemed far from praise. The thought that she and Bell were being laughed at, reoccurred. But she instinctively knew there was something more; it was not just her and Bell, but the whole audience, the performers themselves, the event itself, that were being mocked.

Well... maybe not, she then thought. But that's what it felt like.

Chapter 20

It was a cold and wet evening as O'Neill drove from his bedsit on the edge of a dingy housing estate to Lawrence Grove. When he got out of the car the only noise he could hear was raindrops. The rain bounced off the window panes yet fell silently and soothingly on his bony cheeks. He unlatched the gates; the bolt felt icily cold. As he walked along the driveway he became aware of the drawn curtains all around him. He glanced at some of them thinking he may be being watched. He stopped for a moment, wondering whether or not Mrs Greer had told her husband about the visit to the office and about the humiliation she endured.

He moved to the door and lightly touched the bell. A thin streak of light spread over the hallway, revealing the unmistakeable figure of Mrs Greer. He would have preferred Mr Greer to come to the door; he would have liked to meet Mr Greer on the doorstep rather than in the living room, to look into his eyes and determine whether or not he was in an attacking mood. When inside, he thought, he must take the usual precaution of positioning himself for a speedy exit, if threatened.

'Oh hello Mr O'Neill, come on in.' She smiled broadly and turned to let him pass her. 'We've been expecting you; isn't it a cold night?'

Had she forgotten that evening in his office, he asked himself; or was this friendliness a mere pretence. They walked along the hallway, through to the living room, and her friendly chat continued.

Mr Greer sat on the settee watching television. He appeared to be a rather small plump figure, wearing glasses with unfashionable frames streaked in orange and brown. His thinning hair and his eyebrows were sandy-coloured. His eyes were small and the eyelids unusually close together, giving the impression of a constant straining for vision. He briefly glanced up at O'Neill and then his nervous focus returned to the screen. Somehow,

East Enders was not registering with him; he was staring at it with other things on his mind. His stiffness and avoidance reassured O'Neill: Mr Greer, he now knew, was not the type of client who would attack a social worker, no matter what the social worker had said to his wife.

O'Neill was directed to the armchair furthest from the settee. Mrs Greer then sat so close to her husband that one of his folded arms was in the way. He moved it, glancing towards O'Neill as he did so.

Mrs Greer's upright posture looked contrived. She waited in anticipation to hear what O'Neill had to say.

'Would you mind turning the television off?' he asked.

'No of course not, Mr O'Neill. I never watch it. I never have time.'

She got up promptly and switched it off. She returned to the settee and again joined shoulders and thighs with a seemingly lifeless husband. The silence closed in on Mr Greer; he looked vulnerable and insignificant without his soap prop. Maybe he thought he was going to get away with staring at a live screen all night as his wife answered the questions.

'I take it you know I saw your wife at our office, Mr Greer?'

He nodded. His wife spoke for him.

'Yes he does, Mr O'Neill. I told him all about it and we're very grateful for everything you're doing for my son, aren't we, dear?'

Her husband muttered something and nodded half-heartedly.

'I have to write a social report,' he said pointedly to Mr Greer, determined to get his attention. 'Do you know what that is?'

He shook his head.

'It's a report about Martin's home circumstances, who he's living with, how he gets on with them, and them with him, and if there's any connection between that and the offences that he keeps on committing.'

'But there is no connection Mr O'Neill,' said Mrs Greer. 'I can't understand it. He has everything he wants, Martin. He gets on the very best with his stepdad too, doesn't he dear?'

She made a fleeting glance at Mr Greer, a command for him to agree in one syllable, certainly not an invitation for him to elaborate. He nodded again and made another inaudible sound that was supposed to mean 'that's right.'

'How long have you known Martin?' he asked Mr Greer.

'About two years.' His voice was high pitched, meek and pained.

'Have you been married before?'

'No.'

'What was it like, taking on a teenager?'

'All right. I never gave it much thought.'

'Didn't you? It's a big move, if you haven't had kids yourself.'

No response. His folded arms seemed to clench across his chest. Either he was feeling pressurised or contemptuous. Mrs Greer looked curiously content.

'What kind of social life do you both have?' he asked, knowing that Mrs Greer was certain to answer.

'Oh we don't have much of a social life Mr O'Neill,' she said proudly. 'We never go out. We never spend a penny on ourselves. Do we?'

O'Neill caught the glance of Mr Greer and saw the rising tension in his face.

'Don't you get bored with each other's company?'

'We're too busy to get bored,' she said.

'Doing what?'

'Oh lots of things… the house, the washing, the ironing, the shopping… and we've got full-time jobs to do, Mr O'Neill.'

'And you Mr Greer?'

He shrugged. 'Television.'

'There's nothing wrong with that, Mr O'Neill,' she said, as if to counter any thought that there *could be* something wrong with it.

'Don't you ever go out?' O'Neill asked, addressing the question to her husband.

Mr Greer shook his head, unable to make light of it.

'What would we go out for days like these? asked Mrs Greer; her brow frowning with the absurdity of the question. 'To get mugged? robbed? No, I shouldn't think so.' She shook her head indignantly.

O'Neill felt himself being taken for a ride. Whatever the question he addressed to her husband, whatever difficulty it caused him, she would rescue him. She was not saying anything intelligent or incisive, but he thought she was being wondrously effective in playing stupid and deflecting him. He persisted: 'Okay, so you don't have much of a social life; you don't go out with each other, what about mates, Mr Greer, do you go for a drink, go to a match?'

He nodded, forcing the lie.

O'Neill stared at each of them in turn, pondering how he might get closer to them. 'You've had a rough time in your first marriage,' he said to Mrs Greer in a conciliatory tone.

'I had,' she replied enthusiastically. 'It was like a bad dream Mr O'Neill. I sometimes thought I'd never survive it.'

'Was he violent, your first husband?'

'Not to me.'

'To Martin?'

'Yes. That's why I left him, for Martin's sake.'

'How did Martin feel about you getting married again?'

'He was over the moon; oh yes, we told him; we discussed it with him. He was delighted… wasn't he?'

Mr Greer nodded with the same tense reluctant obedience.

'Does he ever talk about his father?'

'No! He's forgotten all about him. His father never did a thing for him.'

'Did he ever say he'd like to see his father.'

'Never!'

'That surprises me.'

Mrs Greer stared at him with her mouth open. She was not pleased. 'Why?' she asked, struggling to show some composure.

'Well, that suffering that you and your son came through makes me think he must have some strong feelings about his dad.'

'No no!' she said, frowning and shaking her head emphatically like a despairing teacher. She stretched towards him just as she had done in his office: 'He hasn't got feelings about things like that,' she said; 'he doesn't have feelings about anything Martin. I know my own son.'

Mr Greer's face reddened. His arms clenched tighter.

O'Neill recalled Martin struggling to express the powerful feelings within him. He felt antagonism towards Mr Greer, sitting there in his silent guilt, his sleeves rolled up and his arms folded, and wearing ghastly green house slippers that were guaranteed not to make a sound.

'What's your opinion of Martin, Mr Greer?'

He shrugged his shoulders, as if to cast doubt upon the relevance of the question. Then he said: 'He's a bit childish sometimes.'

'Is he a "big softee?"'

'Yes,' he replied, then realised that O'Neill had put the reply in his mouth.

'Did you ever think of adopting him?'

'Wasn't any need to.'

O'Neill turned to Mrs Greer. 'Did you really expect Martin to be 'over the moon' about you getting married again?'

'Oh yes... I knew he'd be delighted.'

'So he *has* got some feelings?'

'Well... those kind of feelings... yes.'

'What did he say that made you think he'd be happy?'

She flustered, unable to recall anything Martin said. 'I just know he was happy for both of us.'

'Would you have been surprised if he'd objected?'

She looked puzzled; it was inconceivable to her.

'Can you think of any reason why Martin should have objected?'

'No!'

'Has he ever objected... protested about something you've done?'

'No... he's a good lad.'

'Have you ever seen him lose his temper?'

'He would never do a thing like that, Mr O'Neill.'

'Has he ever been violent?'

'Violent... my son? Mr O'Neill!'

'I think you're right Mrs Greer,' he said ironically. 'I don't know what would make Martin angry. I think you could kick him from one end of the room to the other, and still he wouldn't be angry... I mean... he wouldn't show any anger. And do you know why?'

'Mr O'Neill! What are you saying? That's a terrible thing to say. No one would lay a finger on my son. If anybody...'

'I'll tell you', he said, interrupting and then ignoring her. His eyes remained riveted on Mr Greer. 'Because for some reason Martin doesn't know who he is. He doesn't even know what he is. Can you understand that, Mr Greer?'

Mr Greer's silence convinced O'Neill of his fear and guilt.

'It means that he's uncertain about everything and confident about nothing. It means he thinks anything he does or says when people are near him is either wrong or dangerous. So he waits on people telling him what to do: sit down, stand up, speak! He's frightened of people Mr Greer, because they expose him and humiliate him. Yes... despite what you say, Mrs Greer, your son *does* feel a lot; he feels it when people mock him and belittle him. He avoids people. He avoids talking to them. The risks are too high. That's why Mr Greer, I believe that Martin has been abused, seriously abused, and very damaged. I'm not certain how or why, or by who, or for how long. I was hoping you or you wife could enlighten me.'

'Watch you... your tongue!' Mr Greer made what seemed to be a mighty physical effort stretching himself forward, pointing his fist at O'Neill and blurting out, red-faced: 'I've heard enough from you. You don't tell me anything about... you know nothing about what I gotta put up with... I don't want to hear anything more from you. You take your social work somewhere else. There's plenty of kids being beaten and starved... that's where you want to be, social worker! So just you take yerself off!'

The words faltered and faded. His lips were parched, and he appeared to be making futile attempts to huddle himself into mere non-existence. O'Neill's silence exacerbated his difficulty, as if Mr Greer had demanded the stage for a threatened outburst which turned out to be pathetic, and now he had nothing more to say to an impatient audience. Mrs Greer broke the silence. She dried her tears:

'I don't understand why you're being so nasty, Mr O'Neill. We've always done our best.'

O'Neill gazed at the two of them, a moving picture of wounded innocence. His suspicion that the weak, isolated and pervasively inferior Mr Greer was abusing Martin, had become a conviction. Mrs Greer, he thought, was simply mad, comfortably living inside (and outwardly expressing) two or three different personalities, and inflicting emotional and psychological misery on her son. In the flotsam of his work, which he seldom took seriously or cared about, it was becoming a hellishly serious and interesting case.

Mr Greer held the door open and stood there until O'Neill had reversed his car and drove off. He breathed in the night air and sighed. As he reached the living room door he forgot about O'Neill. He paused for a few seconds with his fingers resting on the handle. This was always the difficult part. He opened the door and walked in. She sat there, like a statue, immovable, indestructible, triumphant. Another professional idiot neutralised by her performance. He sat silently away from her, but occasionally glanced at her. He was relieved that she ignored him, didn't even attempt to look at him through eyes transformed, darker, colder, beautiful and menacing. She eventually got up and walked towards the door. The sound and breeze of her movements were oppressive to him. Yet he did not feel good when she'd gone. The silence created a terrible tension within him. He raised his head and looked above. Should he go up? No, not just now; leave it; just let things be. Read a newspaper. Turn the television on. He tried both. He couldn't relax. He got up. He paced the room. He could hear nothing now. He went through to the hall. He walked up the stairs and crossed the landing. He stepped into the bedroom, cold dark and empty. He looked across the landing to Martin's bedroom opposite. He stared painfully. Dare he suffer it? Dare he walk into the bedroom and see, and be seen to see? No. He undressed and lay on his back staring at the ceiling above. In the opposite bedroom his wife lay on her side, her eyes fixed on the bedroom door.

Chapter 21

'*Allahu akhbar*' Azeer and Sa'eed both pronounced, after their ritual cleansing. They continued with the opening sura of the Qur'an: *In the name of God the merciful and the compassionate.* They stood, bowed, prostrated and sat, and when their evening prayer was finished, they conducted their check on the latest monitoring sensor Azeer had installed. It confirmed there was no change of frequencies, no audible giveaway, no possibility that they were being bugged. They double checked on the main computer, programmed to register any frequency change by coded e-mail. They felt safe to begin.

'How do your think your mission is progressing?' Azeer asked him, as they sat opposite on two mock regency armchairs near the imitation fire in an open hearth. It was a week since they'd returned from Busseto.

Sa'eed thought he detected a certain rhetorical nuance in the question. 'Satisfactorily,' he replied; 'you've given me no reason to think otherwise.'

'Excellent. Tell me about your sister. Is she becoming a distraction?'

Sa'eed was disconcerted by the abruptness and tone of the question. He had kept Azeer informed about his sister's worsening plight: unable to get Professor van Hoofdaaker to return the organs of her stillborn, years after he had stripped the corpse.

'She's still suffering,' he replied; 'I see her often, but there is nothing I can do.'

'It's painful to watch a loved one suffer.'

'I am not distracted.'

'Good. Your discipline and your self-belief are admirable. They are crucial assets. Do your two female recruits possess the same?'

'They'll complete the mission.'

'Are you any nearer to choosing a fourth person?'

'No.'

'Are you targeting someone?'

'I'm observing; it's too soon to be targeting.'

'You should bear in mind the priorities. An operative trained and cultivated by ourselves, of our own culture and faith, is always the most effective. But one who has little in common with us will be all the more devastating in their impact. You should seek out a fourth member who is home grown, whose hatred of this country and its decadence is faith in itself. That's what the infidel cannot cope with: being hated and despised by their own. It harms them more than the casualties we inflict.'

Sa'eed looked slightly bemused. He never did familiarize himself with Al Qaeda's scale of psychological impacts made by different operatives. Yet now that he thought about it, it had an inescapable logic that appealed. 'I'll bear it in mind,' he said.

'Good,' said Azeer; 'you can be too cautious in your assessment. Tell me more about the two you've selected.'

'What more can I tell you? You've met them. You've made your own assessment. I've told you everything I know about them.'

'Tell me how self-aware they are.'

Sa'eed frowned. 'Self-aware?'

'I don't mean how clever and secretive they are; I don't mean how vigilant either; I'm sure you have chosen them with care. No. What I'm asking Sa'eed, is how well do they integrate and how conscious are they of integrating? How do you think their friends and colleagues perceive them? Do you think that question ever enters their mind?'

Sa'eed could tolerate Azeer's habitual cat and mouse tactics but not when they felt like an aspersion on his intelligence and his competence. 'They are naturally suspicious and sceptical,' he said with uncharacteristic uncertainty, sensing that Azeer was probing about something else.

'As they should be,' said Azeer assuredly. 'But there is often a price to be paid for too much suspicion and scepticism; too much looking over one's shoulder, trusting no one.'

'How else do we operate?' Sa'eed asked, displaying signs of impatience.

'That is not the question you should be asking,' said Azeer. '*What is the price* is a more important question.'

Sa'eed hesitated, wondering whether or not to give Azeer the pleasure. He knew he had to. 'Which is?'

'One's humanity.'

Sa'eed had enough of this. He stared coldly at Azeer.

'Or should I say,' Azeer added, 'the appearance of humanity.'

His protégé looked perplexed and angrier. *Appearance*? There was no greater source of contempt for jihadists than *appearance*. Wasn't Britain's enslavement to *appearance* and its blindness to its own sinful realities manna from Allah for every Islamist, for every trainer and operative? Wasn't it that same *appearance* that Azeer himself had converted into a most effective tool in the conversion of Sa'eed and many others? He not only made Sa'eed despise *appearance*, but enabled him to discern it far more quickly, to laugh at it, to mock those who so assiduously promoted it. What was Azeer getting at?

'I'm not concerned about how I *appear*,' said Sa'eed; 'I am a servant of Allah.'

'But to serve him well Sa'eed, you must integrate well, and to integrate well you must be certain you know how others perceive you.'

Azeer rose from his seat and went over to his desk. 'The tide may be turning,' he said sombrely, as he lifted some photographs.

Sa'eed stared after him, wondering had he heard him right. *Tide Turning?* It was the tone as much as the words themselves that made it sound like an admission he thought he would never hear.

'The Americans have at last awakened,' Azeer continued as he walked back from his desk. 'They are pursuing us to the ends of the earth. They have driven our brothers off the streets of Baghdad. We are on the run throughout the rest of Iraq. Osama Bin Ladin has apologised to the Iraqi people for the sectarian slaughter that our brothers wreaked upon them; it succeeded only in uniting Sunnis and Americans, the very opposite to what we set out to do.'

Sa'eed was becoming increasingly discomforted. Iraq was a setback, so what? Islamists had endured far worse elsewhere. They would withdraw, regroup and re-enter, and conquer, just as they were doing now in Afghanistan with their Taliban brothers. Why should what was happening in Iraq create doubt in the mind of his mentor, a man whose resolution and certainty had never wavered? Or was it that?

Azeer sank back on the armchair again. 'We have two thousand genuine operatives in this country and everyone of them is more vulnerable.'

No it wasn't just Iraq, Sa'eed realised.

Azeer removed an elastic band from the photographs. 'They are being noticed and monitored, reported on and spied on. They are being exposed and arrested, tried and convicted, and they are being put away for life.' He handed over some of the photographs.

Sa'eed instantly recognised the 9/11 martyrs: Mohamed Atta, Abdulaziz Alomari, Satam Al Suqami, Alshehri... all nineteen of them were there. Beneath them were the 7/7 London bombers, Mohammed Sidique Khan, Shehzad Tanweer, Germaine Lindsay, Hasib Hussain.

'Look at these faces,' Azeer said; 'what do they tell you?'

They told him of comradeship, loyalty, devotion, selflessness and sacrifice. And one face in particular, Nawaf Al Hazmi, told him of eternal friendship. He and Nawaf had met during Sa'eed's first visit to Afghanistan. Nawaf had been personally chosen by Bin Laden for the 9/11 operation. He and his brother Salem, and Hans Hanjour, and Khalid Almihdhar, and Majed Moqed, were the five martyrs who had crashed American Airline's Boeing 757 into the Pentagon. Around his neck Sa'eed always wore the *Al Budah* amulet given to him by Nawaf, a few days before Nawaf disappeared from the al Faruz training camp near Kandahar which they both shared. Nawaf never returned.

But what was Azeer getting at? Sa'eed still had no idea.

'Look at Mohamed Atta,' Azeer said, his index finger falling heavily onto the face of the 9/11 commander. 'What do you see ... what do most people see when they look at a face like that?'

Sa'eed could see only good in the face of Atta: the supreme leader; the inspirer, the perfectionist, the most successful operator Al Qaeda had ever produced. Yet Azeer had obviously something else in mind.

'Muslims prepared to be martyrs are being increasingly exposed because this is their model,' said Azeer.

This! thought Sa'eed, fuming. But he had too much respect for Azeer to believe that his only intent was to offend the name of Mohamed Atta.

'Our recruiting and training are too successful,' said Azeer; 'Operatives are transformed overnight. They become unrecognisable to their families. They disown former friends. They advertise their devotion to the Qur'an and their contempt for infidel values. They express their new found religiosity with fanatical certainty. They avoid contact with anyone who does not share that fanaticism. They become immune to the suspicions they arouse and easy targets for the authorities to monitor. That is why the tide may be turning.'

Azeer poured himself a glass of water. Sa'eed gazed at the opposite wall, sensing that he had much more to say, and that it might be more painful and incisive than what had already been said. Azeer lifted the photograph of Mohamed Atta and stared at Sa'eed:

'To you and the thousands who trained with you, he is a hero without equal. But he was also a fool. They were all fools! Had it not been for the protection that Allah afforded them and the dumbness of the heathens who welcomed them, they would have all been caught.'

Sa'eed's fingers clenched. His lips tightened.

Azeer read his thoughts well: 'Yes! It's sacrilegious to talk like this, isn't it Sa'eed? Let me say more then. They all emerged victorious from their training because their teachers were convinced that they would do what was required of them. Which they did. But their teachers were culpable in creating unnecessary risk. They succeeded in draining every drop of humanity out of them. Every American who had contact with our 9/11 martyrs speaks of their coldness, their unfriendliness, their aloofness. Their neighbours in the cities, the checkout staff at their nearest supermarkets, their student colleagues and their trainers in the aviation colleges that they joined, all made the same observations: never saw them smile; never heard them laugh, could never get them to respond to a friendly greeting, never witnessed them being neighbourly or helpful. No! just cold detachment, emotionless and unreachable, the kind of behaviour that in any country in the world other than gullible, perpetually optimistic America, would have had dozens of agents monitoring their every move. By the grace of Allah, they got away with it!'

Azeer held up the photographs of the London bombers. 'And by that same grace, our brothers here, Khan, Tanweer, Lindsay and Hussain, got away with it. The same fanaticism for all to see; their conspicuous conversions and the rejection of their previous lives, their open contempt for people and values they once espoused. How could the authorities not be suspicious? Only through the grace of Allah.

Sa'eed remained tense and fuming. He didn't know which outraged him most: the perception of his iconic martyred brothers as people who had carelessly and stupidly risked all, or the implication that he himself was risking, in as yet some undefined way, the exposure of his own planned martyrdom. Had it been anyone other than Azeer saying these things, he wouldn't have tolerated it. And yet despite his barely suppressed rage, he wanted to hear Azeer out. He realised that there was more than a grain of truth in what he was saying.

'We are living in different times, Sa'eed,' Azeer continued. 'Allah expects us to learn and adapt. We cannot expect Him to protect stupidity and carelessness for ever. Our operatives are not only betraying themselves by their inability to integrate, to appear human, but they are also being exposed by a rag bag of brainless self-appointed Islamic malcontents in pursuit of a cause which we all share, but who are being picked off by security one by one, and their trials and their convictions making Islam and Muslims a laughing-stock to the world.'

Sa'eed knew precisely the kind of people Azeer was referring to. Some of their faces flashed across his mind: Mohammed Atif Siddique the Edinburgh student boasting to his friends that he was going to become a suicide bomber; setting up a Jihadi website *Al Battar* that anyone could access, with instructions on weapons, explosives, terrorism and Jihad... Samina Malik, the

171

self-styled *Lyrical terrorist* whose hate-filled poems written on the back of receipts in the W.H.Smith branch in which she worked were so psychopathically blood-drenched that they made Abu Hamza's sermons sound like interdenominational prayers for peace and reconciliation; even the courts couldn't take her seriously and quashed her conviction... Abdul Haleem, who Sa'eed regarded as the greatest blunderer of them all, falling for the security service's sting of selling him a load of high velocity weaponry at a M25 service station!

Such recall fuelled Sa'eed's burning indignation. 'So these are all fools,' he shouted; 'why do I need to be reminded of *them*?'

'Because there are far too many of them, Sa'eed. There's one or more being arrested every day. Trials are occurring as we speak. During every one of these trials the revelations of their bungling are hyped up by the press and are meant to humiliate us. Now we learn that British television is going to satirize them, make them an even bigger laughing-stock than they already are. The whole country will soon be laughing at them. But that's only a cover for laughing at Muslims and Islam.'

The pace of his voice had quickened; the volume considerably increased; and his eyes were full of hatred.

'What you must realise Sa'eed is that these fools often have valuable contacts. They regularly flit to and from Pakistan and make contact with important operatives. They stay a few nights in Muzaffarabad or some other camp, learn how to fire a Kalishnikov and then return to indulge themselves in one hair brained scheme after another. They are responsible to no one. The authorities are howling with laughter as they watch them and then they pounce on them. But they're not really interested in people like that. They want to know about the Islamic groups they've made contact with, about the leaders of such groups and the more important members within them. They want to know about who is in contact with whom, and above all, about imminent operations; sophisticated operations, long planned for, to be carried out by genuine operatives like yourself, not by a bunch of monkeys.'

Azeer threw the photographs on the glass coffee table separating them. 'That is the danger, Sa'eed; that the recklessness and idiocy of these people shed light on the whereabouts and activities of those who really matter.'

'I have not made contact with any of them,' Sa'eed said defensively.

'*You* didn't need to.'

Sa'eed's countenance changed dramatically. The expression of strained tolerance with which he had gazed at Azeer for the previous ten minutes changed to one of apprehension. *You didn't need to!* Had he unwittingly betrayed himself? No, probably not; Azeer would not have 'played' with him like this as a preliminary to exposing his failings. But he couldn't be sure. 'Have I done something wrong?' he asked.

'You have missed the whole point Sa'eed. Our operatives have been trained as no others have been trained. They are more technically knowledgeable, more disciplined, more committed, more tested. They have endured more sufferings and privations than any other. They have withstood everything that has been thrown at them. Yet somehow when they finally emerge from their training, a huge chunk of their humanity is missing. 'Emotionless robots' I call them. They have lost the capacity to express emotion as any normal human being may express it. This is what makes them... and *you*, so conspicuous and vulnerable. Your idol Mohamed Atta is the perfect example. Can you imagine him being cheerful or humorous, or stopping to talk to another human being he might bump into or pass by? How long do you think Atta would last *today* if he was unleashed for another 9/11?'

Sa'eed just stared at him. His rage had subsided, but his sense of humiliation had intensified.

'We have produced a whole generation of robotic-like Attas,' Azeer continued; 'in addition to these bungling incompetents who idolise him and who want to get in on the act. And there is a third group, equally brainless and dangerous; undisciplined, uncontrolled.'

Azeer glanced through more photographs as he spoke.

'They want to produce their own great big bangs, to kill more than have ever been killed before. They want to blow up a shopping mall or the Houses of Parliament, they want to smash a bomb-laden 4x4 through the entrance of an airport; they want to poison water supplies, or shoot down a dozen planes simultaneously. They have neither the means nor the wit to shoot down a rabbit! All they succeed in doing is emulating Atta's cold unfriendly stare, arousing suspicion, and being put under surveillance... then leading security to those who really matter. They too have had their day in Kandahar, dabbling in explosives and dismantling their Kalishnikovs, and spending fifteen minutes on counter-surveillance.'

Azeer held up a photograph of two of the five failed London bombers, Muktar Said Ibrahim and Ramzi Mohammed. Their copy-cat attempt at carnage two weeks after the July 7th bombings ended in capture. The photograph showed Ibrahim and Mohammed surrendering in ignominy and shame, half naked on a tenement balcony, coughing and spluttering and their eyes streaming from the CS gas that had engulfed them, and all in the full glare of publicity. He held up another, the failed so-called fertilizer bombers, led by Omar Khyam. He held up a third photograph: six would-be terrorist trainees whose leader, Mohammed Hamid boasted that the 52 deaths of July 7th would hardly be considered as *breakfast* for him.

'You have distinguished yourself in training, Sa'eed, and yet you share the same potentially ruinous traits as your hero, Mohamed Atta, and all these others. You are far too cold, too intense, too insular, too unyielding, too fanatical, too unfriendly. You have lost all sense of proportion, all sense of fun. It didn't matter in 9/11, when the infidel fell asleep. It matters now.'

Azeer gesticulated towards the photographs of the convicted again. 'Look closely at the faces of these incompetents, these fools. I can see you suffering the same fate. Arousing suspicion. I watched you in Busseto. I could see the impact you were having on the two women. Your demeanour, your expressions, your eyes... they will never forget. You not only made them suspicious of your thoughts and feelings; you also convinced them that you were unreachable and that that was the way you wanted it to remain. Thank Allah the merciful that you met them in Busseto and not Liverpool.'

Chapter 22

It was the meeting Morgan had dreaded. Jackson had summoned him and Sarah Prescott to headquarters. Morgan was rushing about in his own office, masquerading as the omnipotent but kindly boss ensuring that his staff were all right and could cope with his temporary absence. Anxiety oozed out of every pore, accentuating the tightness of the collar of his brand new shirt.

O'Neill sat at his desk and mimed his throat being sliced with the edge of his hand as Morgan and Sarah walked past. 'He's for the chop,' he said half jokingly to Sa'eed who sat opposite him.

'For what?'

'He's a twit!'

'You mean he's done something wrong?'

'He hasn't done anything right.'

'He's not going to get much sympathy from you, then; is he?'

O'Neill smiled. Sa'eed looked through him, but smiled in return.

'I'll tell you about it some other time,' said O'Neill.

In headquarters, Sarah deliberately avoided walking abreast of Morgan as they headed towards Jackson's office. She could feel the anxiety in his clumsy haste and could hear it in his voice. She had difficulty enough composing herself for this meeting without being engulfed by Morgan's state of mind. She wore black trousers and a plum-red jacket with matching brooch and scarf, a more formal appearance than usual which, given the circumstances of the occasion, surprised no one. All week she had tried to cope with the predictable yet unhelpful responses of colleagues: their sympathies, their intentional *there but for the grace of God* expressions; their reassurances: *It wasn't your fault Sarah…* She lost control when the young cockney Eric Houston spoke to her for the first time and pathetically stuttered and stammered his way through what sounded like an attempt to provide moral support. 'What is it to you?' she'd snapped at him, sensing that he too must have experienced Jackson's wrath in some comparatively minor way, having no relevance to the gravity of what she and Morgan were about to face. She apologised to Eric.

How could this have happened? She was just weeks into the professional career that she had trained years for and here she was, implicated through Morgan, in a series of events culminating in a child's abduction, and most likely, her murder.

The police had quickly arrested Charlie Mulholland, known to them for a string of petty offences decades ago. It was a cut and dried case. He'd been caught on CCTV. He'd been seen by more than a dozen people (including her teacher Miss Watts) collecting Angela and driving off in the old grey Ford. Then he mysteriously turned up twenty five minutes later, on the pretext of collecting her for the first time. Only one unimportant witness supported Charlie's defence, Tracy Cook, another seven year old in the same class as Angela. She was one of the first pupils out that afternoon, and was waiting, with her impatient mother, at the school gates, for another friend. She knew Angela's grandfather because she usually saw him every school day. Like any seven year old, indifferent to the inclement wind and rain that had lowered the vigilance of parents and staff alike, Tracy's perceptions were sharper, more discerning. She saw Angela and *that man* coming towards her at the school gates, Angela walking behind the man, engrossed in her Tomagochi. At a distance, he did indeed look like Angela's grandfather, but the nearer he got, the more Tracy was convinced he was someone else. The way he walked wasn't exactly the same. The way he had his head bent, staring at the ground, never looking at anybody, and not speaking to anybody... that wasn't Angela's grandfather. Tracy was interviewed along with all the other children in the class, and their parents, and every staff member. Too many parents and staff members contradicted her. That was good enough for the police, particularly when they learnt that Charlie had told all and sundry of his anger at being usurped of this little daily ritual which, despite his awful time-keeping, meant so much to him. If he felt as angry as that, they reckoned, then he must have had some ulterior (sexual) motive for wanting to accompany Angela in the first instance. While there were always plenty of grandmothers to be seen in the school grounds, it was noticeable that Charlie was the only grandfather who took his seven year old grandchild to school and back again every day. He'd obviously been sexually abusing her over a long time, they believed. They also reckoned that Charlie saw the new arrangement not just as an end to the convenience of his granddaughter's availability, but more crucially, as a potential witness revealing to her mother (or whoever else replaced him) what he had been doing to her. They believed Charlie picked her up unusually early on that last day, raped her, strangled her, and dumped her body in the nearby woods – it would be only a matter of days before they found her body, and Charlie would confess.

'Mr Jackson is ready to see you now,' Priscilla his secretary said, in a voice so formal and subdued that it increased Morgan's anxiety substantially.

Jackson smiled as they walked in; he directed them to the two low lonely chairs placed conspicuously apart in front of his desk. His swivel chair was raised to its maximum level and he looked down on them.

'How are you getting on, Sarah,' he asked, with a smile that did little to betray his purpose; 'not the kind of case you were expecting I'm sure, in your third… or is it your fourth week?' He looked at her intensely, contrasting her poise and steady focus with a fidgety Morgan.

'Fourth,' she replied, unnerved by being spoken to first, yet sensing that she was merely being used to increase the pressure on Morgan. 'No, it's not the case I was expecting; I wasn't expecting reporters and cameras on my doorsteps either.'

'We can arrange for you to live elsewhere,' Jackson said, 'until things settle.'

'No thanks,' she replied emphatically.

He turned to Morgan.

'Stan, tell me…' He glanced at the Mulholland file on his desk. 'You and Sarah visited on Thursday the day before Angela was abducted. According to this file you didn't see Angela.'

177

Morgan's knees began trembling. He tried to steady them with his hands. He stuttered: 'No-no-no-no… that's right Andrew. Angela was at school when we called. But I did ask Maggie Lynch about her?'

'I know you did. Mrs Lynch recorded that in her report.'

It sounded good, Morgan thought; but he knew what was coming.

'So what time did you call?' Jackson asked.

Morgan's eyes-brows nearly collided in his exaggerated effort to show this was a difficult question. 'Em… m…'

'Nine-thirty,' said Sarah.

Jackson kept his eyes on Morgan. 'Did you expect to find Angela at home at nine-thirty?'

'No… not really… well…' A life line suddenly came to his mind: 'Brenda Mulholland isn't the world's most reliable parent… Andrew.'

'Could you explain that?'

'She hasn't always got the kids up for school… or got herself up.'

'When was the last time she failed to get Angela to school?'

'Well… she didn't get the kids to the playgroup…'

'But when was the last time she failed to get Angela to school?' He couldn't answer.

'Has the school ever said Angela's not attending?'

Sarah tensed. She lowered her head and focussed her eyes on her clasped fingers. She thought she had seen Morgan at his worse in Brenda Mulholland's home. But this attempt to conceal the fact that Angela had nothing to do with his visit was too much for her. She thought it dastardly that he should attempt to divert Jackson's attention away from his own failings, onto an additional, newly invented *neglect* on the part of Brenda. As if the poor woman didn't have enough to contend with! Sarah imagined Brenda sitting at home devastated, trying to cope with her daughter's abduction as well as the condemnations and the lurid innuendos in a tabloid press. She knew Jackson was going to screw him now and she had no sympathy for him.

Morgan shook his head.

'So what you're saying,' asked Jackson; 'is that you were checking on whether or not Angela *was* attending school even though no one suggested she wasn't?'

'No no...'

'What then?'

'We got a referral from Maggie about the two younger kids at risk... and...'

'All *three* children are on the child protection register, are they not?'

'Yes... but the referral was especially about the two younger ones.'

'But all three are on the register?'

'Yes.'

'When was the last time they were seen before your visit on Thursday?'

'About... em... three months before that.'

Jackson stared through him and Morgan felt his whole body trembling now. He knew that Jackson knew the answer to every question he asked. Since Angela's disappearance, he had repeatedly asked the same questions of himself. The answers stared out at him from the pages of the Mulholland file and tortured him.

'How are you going to explain that to a public enquiry?' Jackson asked.

Morgan gulped. He couldn't speak.

Jackson held up two A4 sheets of paper. 'This is the referral from Maggie Lynch the probation officer, and this is *her* recording of the conversation she had with you. Did *you* make a recording of your conversation with her?'

'Ah... well I made some notes.'

'Where are they?'

'Well... just a few details I wrote down...'

'But you haven't got them?'

He shook his head.

'Do you dispute any of the contents of Maggie Lynch's report?'

Morgan was beginning to realise that every question was a trap, and every response he gave ensured he fell headlong into it. He shook his head again.

'You discussed Angela during your conversation with Lynch,' Jackson said.

'Yes! But I mentioned her first,' Morgan replied hurriedly. It was the only opportunity he was likely to get. 'Maggie hadn't any concerns about her, but I wasn't too sure. I thought we *should* be concerned.'

'What were you concerned about?'

'The possibility of her being sexually abused.'

'The possibility? But why were you concerned? You just can't be concerned about a *possibility*. Was there nothing more tangible for you to be concerned about?'

Morgan remembered what Maggie had said. 'Well... it's not ideal for a grandad to be taking the child to and from school every day.'

Sarah grimaced.

'Why not?'

He was stumped.

Jackson waited a few moments, looked again at Maggie's report and then said: 'You *did* ask Maggie Lynch did she think the grandfather was okay?'

'I did, yes.' Morgan perked up a little. He was still in deep trouble, but here was Jackson acknowledging that he had the foresight, the social work intuition, to recognise the danger. The fact that he had actually sought Maggie's assurances that the grandfather was not sexually abusing Angela, and that that same grandfather was now languishing in a prison cell charged with her abduction, could only mitigate against his neglect of the case. He hoped.

'Did you intend seeing the grandfather and making your own assessment?'

'Ah... well, not as such. It might have been difficult talking to him about that.'

'Did you need to *talk* to him about *that*? Could you not just have arranged to visit, say, when he was bringing Angela back home from school? Get to meet him, see how he was with *all* the kids, see how he responded to you or Sarah. Did any of that cross your mind?'

'No not really... I was more concerned about...'

'Concerned? Were you really concerned?'

'Yes I was.'

'But not concerned enough to make sure you saw the child or meet the man you thought might be abusing the child? How did you intend assuaging yourself of your concerns then?'

'Well that was only the first visit... I would have made sure Sarah would have done all those things you're talking about...'

Jackson looked at Sarah and saw her lips tighten with contempt.

'Did you contact the school and ask was Angela exhibiting any peculiar signs recently?'

'No.'

'Do you think if her grandfather had been sexually abusing her, she might have exhibited some signs... in the classroom... in play?'

'She might have.'

'Did you share your fears about what might be happening to Angela, with her mother?'

'No.'

'Why not?'

'Well... it didn't seem right at that time.'

'Because?'

'The two younger children were there and...'

'Of course they were there. What did you expect, when you chose to visit knowing that the older child, the child that you were *concerned* about, would *not* be there? Did you mention Angela at all to her mother?'

The slight increase in the volume of Jackson's voice and the strained incredulity in his expression convinced Morgan that he was closing in. He would normally have lied his way out of these situations, but he was ever conscious of Sarah next to him. He knew now that this was the reason why Jackson had summoned her too; she was a witness to his incompetence, and his face would burn on every lie he told. This was a lie he could not tell.

'No,' he said, sheepishly.

'So you visit because of a hunch that Angela might be subject to abuse from her grandfather; but you chose to visit during school hours when it was almost certain she wasn't going to be there; and you made no attempt to share your hunch and your concerns with her mother; in fact you didn't even mention Angela to her mother?'

Morgan's head leaned to the left; he swallowed, bit his lip, and his parched mouth silently cried out for water. He said nothing.

'The probation officer Lynch made a referral about the two younger children. She gave a detailed recording of what she'd seen. Did you make any assessment of the children's welfare when you were there?'

'Well... not as such.'

Jackson never spoke for a few moments. He appeared to nonchalantly glance through the file. 'How long were you there?' he asked abruptly, without looking up.

Morgan willed himself to tell a lie, despite Sarah's presence. The truth, somewhere in the region of five or six minutes, would surely damn him. 'Em... I'd say about quarter of an hour.'

Jackson looked at Sarah again. She was having difficulty now in constraining herself. The word 'liar' was written all over her face.

'Lynch says she discussed with you the need for help for this woman; did you discuss that when you visited?'

'No.'

'Did you offer her any help?'

'No.'

'Did you think of offering her any help?'

'No... well... I couldn't see how we could help.'

'Lynch suggested the need for a volunteer. She mentioned *Surestart*; she says you committed yourself to looking into it; did you?

'Well I did... but... em...'

'Yes?'

Well I just thought it wasn't right for Mrs Mulholland; I didn't think she was capable of making use of it.'

'Did you offer it to her?'

'No.'

'Did you contact the probation officer and tell her the reason why you'd decided not to offer any help?'

'No.'

Jackson turned to Sarah: 'I think you can leave now Sarah.'

For the second time he had spoken to her when she was least expecting it. She had stopped listening to both men. She had been staring over Jackson's shoulder with a glaze in her eye, contemplating her future and still trying to comprehend how this had all come about. Her future certainly did not lie here. She got up and walked towards the door.

Jackson called after her: 'Don't speak to the press under any circumstances, no matter how much they may tempt you. And thanks.'

She nodded but said nothing. She paused and sighed as she closed the door behind her.

Jackson returned his gaze to Morgan.

Chapter 23

In the regenerated docklands, outside the Tate Gallery in Liverpool, orderly columns of men and women of different ages, nationalities and social class waited patiently. Tate London had been persuaded to move the Turner prize exhibition to Liverpool to coincide with its coming status as European City of Culture. Television cameras were on hand and an impertinent young interviewer provoked shrieks and giggles by asking (off camera) how many in the good natured crowd were hoping to see dirty knickers and camel turds? Actually most of them were there to see the work of Zarina Bhinji, joint favourite to win the prize. Her exhibits were as uncomplicated and powerful as the emotions they expressed. Liverpool's intelligentsia had taken the artist, a former Uganda refugee driven out by Idi Amin, to their hearts. Strategically placed bill boards had for weeks now, shown her sad and beautiful face peering down on the city's inhabitants.

Later that same day, near waste-land in the Abington estate, another crowd gathered. It had begun with mostly young men and boys knocking on doors, apparently to gain recruits. It wasn't orderly in the flow of its movement or in its direction; but there seemed to be some kind of leadership determining its goals. The most prominent individuals in this crowd were two men, one aged about fifty, and the other in his late teens. They carried rucksacks heavily laden down with unseen contents. The older man was called Nick McManus. He was pock-faced, beer bellied, and short of breath; he had huge ears and false teeth. His eyes were tired and bloodshot. He wore trainers with bunion splits in their sides, and filthy jeans too small to encircle his considerable girth. He looked the least fit of anyone in the crowd, but he was decisive and purposeful, and people clearly looked to him for guidance. He had an ugly and an angry face. There was little humour in this crowd.

The younger man who appeared to be McManus' deputy was his nephew, Darren Toby. He was good looking up to a point, but he had ulcerated sores around his lips and his upper teeth were showing clear signs of decay. He was tall and thin, and in contrast to his uncle, he moved speedily though not gracefully. He had a scar that ran down his right cheekbone and disappeared somewhere amongst the multiple tattoos of his neck. Dozens of tiny blackheads were embedded in various parts of his face, mostly in the cavities between his nose and his upper lip. He wore a red tracksuit and conspicuously heavy boots. The hood of the tracksuit was pulled up over his head and tightened.

Both uncle and nephew were Abington born and bred. Both were long term unemployed; both had a criminal record; both frequently assaulted their wives; both often indulged in their passion for organising pit bull terrier fights (usually to the death) and both were child abusers in the sense that nearly all the parents in Abington, through the wretchedness of their own upbringings, could not help but deprive their children of things that the good folk of Liverpool (good folk everywhere) normally took for granted: like decency and cleanliness, an awareness and inquisitiveness about the world, fair play and an open mind. Social workers who worked in Abington could not afford to think of such *privileges*. If children weren't being battered, buggered and raped by cohabitees, they were lucky kids and the workers were relieved. Darren and his uncle however, did not feel deprived living in Abington. For the second time this week, they felt driven and inspired by the *goodness* of their *cause*.

The mob spread out, its members going from door to door. Sometimes more than one person from the same house would join them. As the mob got larger its members became more confident and less furtive. They no longer spoke in whispers. They joked and laughed and swore. In this crescendo, onlookers would have agreed that the most frequent comment – maybe a *command* – was: 'we need ta finish the job.' Others responded with 'shoulda finished when we started.' Such responses were invariably greeted with nods of approval and pleasure, an intensifying camaraderie spurring them on. But their intent was clearly malevolent.

'Finishing the job' meant burning Charlie Mulholland's house down. It was a prospect the mob had been relishing for days.

They had already held marches and banners pronouncing Charlie's guilt, and warning him never to set foot in Abington again. They had appeared on news broadcasts, on front pages, and best of all, on the giant BBC News 24 screen in Parker Street in down-town Liverpool. They had received thousands of congratulatory e-mails and letters from like minded groups, and they even provoked sympathetic editorials in a couple of the tabloids.

Charlie Mulholland never imagined in his wildest dreams how much he would transform the lives of the mob in Abington. Generally these were miserable self-destructive lives. Nick McManus for example was widely perceived by his neighbours as a lazy bastard who never did an honest day's work in his life, and who derived a great deal of sadistic pleasure watching pit bull terriers tear themselves to pieces. Yet he had recently worked solidly for days and walked dozens of miles panting for breath, all in the cause of castrating paedophiles. He could barely string two sentences together, and yet he was now enthralling journalists from around the world, all straining to comprehend the scouse garbage falling from his lips.

McManus was a totally unaware person, blessedly unaware of his physical ugliness and of his selfishness; incapable of understanding let alone accepting his failure as a husband and a father and a grandfather (when his daughters weren't there, he still derived much satisfaction from encouraging his grandchildren to beat the shit out of each other). And he was forgetful too; he conveniently but genuinely forgot the time he sexually assaulted an eleven year old niece, the sister of Darren, when she was staying over one night. It must be said however, that although social workers, had they known, would have slapped their emergency protection orders on the table and speedily removed the child, she herself didn't regard it as it any big deal. Darren himself had sexually assaulted her many times, and at the age of eleven, she'd already had a series of sexual liaisons with the boys of her choice. These were not uncommon experiences in Abington.

A psychoanalyst may have posited the idea that McManus and more than just a few of the mob (who also had sexually abused under age children) were enraged by Charlie Mulholland simply because he subconsciously reminded them of themselves; they were then projecting onto poor Charlie all their own sins and punishing him, banishing him accordingly. This clever trick of the mind was certainly less painful than acknowledging their own guilt or engaging in some kind of self flagellation which they may have felt they deserved. But this theory could not apply to McManus. He marched at the head of the mob conscious of the awesomeness of responsibility given to him by a people who generally regarded him as *not a nice man*. But he had worked hard for this responsibility; it was no more than he deserved.

It happened one night when he was slouched in front of the television with his fifth pint in his hand. He cursed and fumed watching the tragedy of Angela Mulholland unfold. His wife had for more than thirty years been listening to him cursing and fuming on a whole range of news topics and ignored him. He had never met any of the Mulholland family before and yet he had roared out: 'A cudda told ya it was that bastard' as Angela's grandad was once again rushed into a station by a large group of nervous police officers. That was the moment McManus was stricken with something he later interpreted as divine intervention. He let out another roar: 'E'll niver touch anuther weein in this estate...' and then with great difficulty he managed to raise his hopelessly drunken bulk from the armchair, belched and farted a few times, and marched... he actually tried to *march* towards his front door. He got it open and *marched* out. Two hours later, he *marched* back again, grinning like a Cheshire cat: 'A've organised a *march*,' he said to his wife.

News of Nick McManus' renaissance spread wildly. The more he spewed out his hatred of paedophiles in general and Charlie Mulholland in particular, the more popular and influential he became. He was conscious not just of his rocketing authority but of his unifying powers. He *unified* Abington. Just as he was able to forget about the afflictions which assailed his much abused body, he was also somehow able to make the people of Abington forget about their divisions and their wretchedness. People who loathed each other, attacked each other, and who betrayed each other to social security fraud squads now locked arm in arm as

187

they marched and chanted PAEDOPHILES OUT! OUT! OUT! They wanted to finish the job.

McManus and Darren led the mob up Shepherd Lane, along Glendalina Avenue, and down Houghton Road. They had tactfully chosen this longer route to Charlie Mulholland's street because the shorter route would have meant passing Charlie's daughter's house in Throstle Way. McManus had had an ugly confrontation with Brenda the first time he led a march to Charlie's house. She had recklessly dashed in front of the mob, her two kids Archie and Grace screaming and clinging to her knees. She swore at the mob that her father hadn't touched the child, that he wouldn't harm a fly. But McManus and his mob *knew* different. They were not so gullible. They had flung Brenda and her kids to the side of the road and marched on.

They came down Houghton Road as darkness was falling. The whitewashed graffiti on the walls of Charlie's house was clearly visible. Every window had been smashed, the two front door panels kicked through, the contents of the bins strewn all over the garden. They'd used a ladder to paint the longest and biggest message from one end of the house to the other CHARLIE YER A PERVERT AN A PAEDOPHILE AN WE'RE GONNA KILL YOU.

Darren and McManus lowered the rucksacks from their shoulders. They opened them and removed ten empty beer bottles, a litre sized petrol canister, and a pile of dirty rags. They half filled the bottles with petrol, soaked the rags and stuffed them into the necks of the bottles. The mob gathered round them, each of them hoping to be given the honour of throwing the first blazing rag through the open windows. Mc Manus lined the bottles up. He looked at all the expectant hate-filled faces around him. He picked the youngest, thirteen-year-old Jimmy Breen. He handed him a bottle. Jimmy's eyes lit up and his heart pumped furiously. He licked his lips and gaped at the bottle. McManus cautioned him to be careful as he pulled a lighter from his back pocket and lit the rag. 'Quick', he said; 'get up close and aim for the far wall!' Jimmy ran at the open window and threw the bottle. A glorious orange flame engulfed the whole of the living room, lighting up furniture and pictures already scarred by the bricks they'd thrown in on earlier occasions. The mob cheered. Little Jimmy beamed with pride. Mc Manus and Darren put a match to the remaining bottles. The mob grabbed them and ran towards the other windows of the house, front and back. The whole house was in flames. The mob was ecstatic. The fierce crackling somehow made Jimmy's penis erect.

It took less than ten minutes for the house to be gutted. Then some in the mob bemoaned the fact that their white-painted message to Charlie, spread from one end of the house to the other, had melted. The heat was too intense. 'We'll paint it again' someone said; 'it'll look even better ginst the black.'

Chapter 24

Maggie was preparing her kids for bed. There was no escape for her. Every news bulletin, every headline, every sympathetic expression in the faces of her colleagues neighbours and friends would remind her of the half eaten corpse of Angela, the doomed child of an alcoholic mum. The body had been found not as the police expected, near to the school in Abington, but more disturbingly for Maggie, in her own West Kirby, in thick undergrowth surrounding the war memorial on the top of Grange Hill. A cheery cocker spaniel *Prince* had sniffed her body out, and stood barking with tail proudly wagging, until his elderly owner arrived at the grisly scene. Everyone believed that Angela had been raped, and most likely strangled.

The first Maggie knew of the abduction was on her return from Busseto; she picked up a *Guardian* for the rail journey to Liverpool. She saw the photograph of Angela and was physically ill when she read the opening paragraphs below it. In the days that followed, she had a perverse need to calculate precisely where she was and what she had been doing at the moment the abduction occurred. Her holiday diary told her that on that Friday afternoon, she and Bell had been fooling about in one of the more luxuriant boxes of the Verdi theatre. They each had held grotesque looking lorgnettes, through which they had gazed in feigned contempt at the imaginary citizens of Busseto below. They had photographed each other. Tourists who passed by and laughed with them offered to photograph them together. She would never be able to look at those photographs again without seeing Angela.

Her first visit to Brenda after she got back was surreal. She couldn't get into the house. She could hardly get into the front garden, every space laden with flowers, cameras, tripods and cables, and groups of photographers, journalists, neighbours and strangers. These people knew a home without boundaries when they saw one, and they had quickly recognised the powerless guilt-ridden lone mother they were there to report on, unable to put her head outside the door, let alone tell them all to fuck off. Unlike middle class suburbia where such media comings and goings would have been frowned upon, the residents of Abington, particularly the children, welcomed this circus. Their faces and their homes were being seen all over the world, their *grief* creating a cauldron of bottomless pity that oozed out of every visiting politician, clergy and counsellor, few of whom had ever before set foot in Abington.

Maggie was preparing her kids for bed – quality time – with less quality than usual. She tucked Rebecca in and told her an imaginary story with a little more haste than usual. Rebecca calmingly sucked her thumb and listened intently. She stared into her mum's eyes and frowned as if perplexed, as if sensing something was not quite as it normally was. But it was a good story with enough suspense and drama to divert attention from the minuscule changes in mum's face and voice.

Maggie then went into Alice's bedroom. She kissed Alice goodnight and shuddered. Alice was just a year older than Angela. The faces of the two children and two mutilated bodies momentarily fused in her mind. She saw Angela's rotting corpse in the thick undergrowth less than half a mile away. She knew the spot well. The murderer had been only a half a mile away! 'Night mum,' Alice replied without looking at Maggie, her head still buried in *How to survive Summer Camp*.

She hurried downstairs and switched the television on. She had heard earlier in the day that the police *and the mother of the child* would be making one of those ritual pleas to the public at a press conference to be shown on BBC's *Northwest Live*. She convinced herself it was best to avoid it but now she felt she had to watch it.

Brenda Mulholland was flanked by two family liaison officers, one a detective and the other a female constable who permanently supported her with an arm around her. Where were her friends and relatives, Maggie wondered. She could think of at least one friend, Henny McCann who Brenda would have greatly appreciated being there. But maybe the police said no! They needed total control and Henny and Brenda together would not guarantee it. If Maggie had known Brenda was going to be asked to do this alone she would have volunteered to be there herself.

Brenda looked her usual wretched self, just what the police were looking for to yield the maximum public response. Her greyish uncombed hair dangled lifelessly, her face was gaunt and dazed, and her eyes seemed suspended above deep red hollows. She wore a black stained dress that Maggie recognised.

Maggie felt consumed by guilt, not about any perceived inadequacy in her work with Brenda – she had been personally thanked by the city's chief probation officer who'd read the file in a hurry once he'd learnt his department was involved, but simply about the sheer injustice of it all.

The conference was led by Chief Superintendent Tony Marshall, in overall charge of the case and his assistant Detective inspector Vicky Adams. After introductions Brenda got her cue and blurted out a few sentences about her 'dear lost child' 'sweet angel' 'couldn't live without her' etc. She kept glancing at the sheet of paper on the desk. She begged the viewers to help the police find the killer. 'Please, please, please… don't let it happen to any other child…' She broke down and could say no more. Rows of cameras clicked and flashed.

Maggie stared at Brenda and her heart heaved. She felt both anger and pity. She was painfully aware for the first time of a bizarre contrast arising out of these rituals. The parent was utterly helpless and anguished, didn't have a clue what was happening, and was always willing to be led every step of the way, and to be told what to say and do. But the police and journalists knew precisely what was happening; they feigned sorrow and sympathy and remained coldly dependent upon the parent's anguish and helplessness. Later, cynical editors would seek out the most anguished shots and decide without an emotional tremor what might make people cry.

Marshall cautioned his audience that just because an arrest had been made, it did not mean that the crime had been solved. Everyone knew this was a barely coded reference to the torching of Charlie's home. 'The investigation is ongoing,' he stressed; 'We need the public's help.'

The scene switched from the conference to the news room of the *Northwest* studio. A grim faced Austin Goodwin, the show's anchor man, seemingly carrying the conscience and outrage of a whole city, sat opposite three men. He introduced them: 'Professor van Hoofdaaker, our regular contributor on issues to do with the death of children; Andrew Jackson, Inspector of Child Protection Services in Liverpool, and Sean O'Neill, a senior social worker who has worked for many years in the Abington estate; he was recently you may remember, involved in a high profile child abuse case and was commended by a high court judge.'

Maggie froze at the sight of O'Neill. She closed her eyes and took a deep breath. She opened them and stared at the three men and tried to make sense of it. She had heard of van Hoofdaaker but she had never met him. But it was Jackson and O'Neill she was more interested in, the child abuse supremo rubbing shoulders with the foot soldier! She speculated. They would surely have found each other, she reckoned: Jackson, scrutinising social service offices and files throughout the city, creating mayhem and fear; and O'Neill, fearing no one, probably gratified that Jackson was kicking many asses that deserved to be kicked. Of course they would find each other, and Jackson would have recognised immediately the social worker he could depend upon. It was most likely Jackson, she concluded, who had suggested that O'Neill appeared with him.

'Now gentlemen,' Goodwin began; 'I needn't remind you... we're not here to discuss Angela Mulholland's case, which, as the superintendent has stressed, is on-going, but if I could begin with you Professor van Hoofdaaker, just how important is this discovery of a body?'

'Of fundamental importance,' van Hoofdaaker replied. 'The nature and cause of death will be established, as will any injuries external or internal inflicted before death. It's also likely to reveal the time and location of death and if it proves to have been an unnatural death, it's certain to provide information about those responsible.'

He continued, with the same consummate ease that would once again infuriate his far more qualified, but less articulate, less photogenic bosses and colleagues.

Goodwin attempted to signal to him that he had said enough. Then he turned to Jackson less differentially, and asked him in a tone distinctly rhetorical. 'Mr Jackson, we *do* know that the child is dead, and that the child was on Social Services protection register... I know that we can't discuss this particular case, but...'

'But you're doing your very best to discuss it Austin,' Jackson interrupted.

'No no!' he said defensively; 'But the reality is... and the public know... far too often... we seem to have another shocking example of Social Services incompetence in failing to protect children for whom it has a statutory responsibility?'

Jackson looked at Goodwin with a patronising incredulity: 'Protect them from what?' he asked.

'Protect them from harm,' Goodwin replied, failing in his obvious attempt to look equally incredulous.

'We're responsible for protecting *some* children,' Jackson replied; 'but very few in the population as a whole. We protect them from harm or neglect that they might suffer in their own homes. Sean here... who has far more experience than most, will I'm sure, agree with me that that's a big enough responsibility, without also being responsible for whatever might happen them on their way to and from school. Social workers can't be held responsible for abductors or murderers who may be lurking outside the school gates!'

A chastened Goodwin felt himself floundering. He turned to O'Neill, determined to change tact, play safe. 'You've been working in Abington many years Sean; how has this tragedy affected people? What are people saying? What are they doing?' Goodwin tailed off weakly with conspicuous insincerity.

'They're devastated,' O'Neill replied, 'as we all are...'

Maggie frowned. The residents of Abington had never known such excitement; had never had so much to talk about, had never felt so useful and important answering journalists' queries with varying degrees of passion, truth and nonsense.

194

'Their hearts go out to Mrs Mulholland and her family,' O'Neill said, his expression not entirely compatible with the compassion implied in the words.

He was annoying Maggie now as well as puzzling her. She had watched and listened to the heartlessness and vindictiveness other clients in Abington had willingly and enthusiastically expressed to her: 'what did she expect... letting that dirty oul bugger take her kid to school every day... we all saw it comin... the kids should have been removed years ago... the woman just isn't fit to have children...' The speed and brutality with which Abington turned on Brenda and her father had depressed her.

'They're very fearful,' O'Neill said; 'as you would expect.'

Ferocious, not *fearful*, thought Maggie. She'd seen them organising marches, carrying banners, and demanding the return of the death penalty.

'They're worried naturally, about their kids' safety,' O'Neill continued. 'Many of the parents don't let their children out now and those that do insist on knowing where they are.'

'Rubbish,' she said to herself. She'd been there twice in the last week, and had seen the same children in the same streets, still unsupervised for hours. She had seen them assembling around journalists and camera men, gate-crashing interviews, centring themselves between the camera and the reporter when interviews were taking place. Then they would jump and shriek obscenities as they tried to reach the height of the camera's lens. The police often had to disperse them, but like hyenas in the pack they simply bided their time. They were having the time of their lives.

She was beginning to resent the game he had obviously set out to play. Jackson must have known he would play it like this. Perhaps he was the instigator, or at least they had colluded for whatever perverse reason. She watched the discussion for a few minutes more then switched it off in disgust.

Chapter 25

Consultant paediatric cardiac surgeon Hugo White and staff nurse Molloy emerged from the theatre and briskly made their way to the parent's suite. Nurse Molloy carried a clipboard in one arm and a brown envelope in another. The surgeon was still wearing his blue and white theatre garb, complete with mask pulled down below his mouth. He looked the more agitated of the two, less confident in his stride, yet more anxious to get the job done. His companion, a cheerful middle aged woman with tinted blonde hair and designer spectacles, moved steadily and purposefully, her head held high, her esteem considerably enhanced by the surgeon's dependence upon her. She knew exactly what she had to do, and she was visibly bristling with confidence. She did most of the talking, unaware that the surgeon wasn't really listening. He was being drawn inexorably towards an acknowledgement of failure, and she was about to reap the benefit, another child's body which he and his team had laboured most of the afternoon, to keep alive.

The parent's suite wasn't too far from the reception area, discreetly tucked away behind an inconspicuous doorway in the main corridor of the hospital. Hospital staff had tried hard to humanise this facility, ensuring that when parents entered, they were struck by its exceptional cleanliness and the fragrances of fresh flowers, its mini library, radio and television, and (always appreciated) its own toilet and washing facilities. The day and night skies were visible too, unlike in so many of the hospital's hermetically sealed corridors.

None of these privileges had any impact on the woman who lay on a makeshift bed near the centre of the room. She was in her early thirties, and had obviously been denied sleep over many nights. She heard their footsteps approaching, and managed to haul her dishevelled body up before they entered. She knew by the look on the surgeon's face that her son Carl was dead.

'Mrs Sloan,' he said as he approached her, 'I'm sorry… we did everything possible, but the odds were too great. His heart was too weak. We know now that the congenital condition would have killed him in a matter of days.'

As it had done to her first son Shane less than two years ago, both parent and surgeon simultaneously thought. It might have eased the surgeon's burden if he had been able to say that both children died from the same condition, but he was a sensitive man, and realised he couldn't; at least he couldn't at that moment.

During the previous days, he had prepared her well, emphasising that there was only a one in five chance of two week old Carl surviving the surgery, yet willing to respond to her pleas that he do anything, try anything at all to save him; the odds had been slightly higher for Shane.

Valerie Sloan lowered her head and turned from them. She did not cry. There were few tears left in her sleepless sunken eyes, but the remains of dried tears where everywhere, in mangled tissues, on the shoulders of her grey blouse, on the lap of her blue jeans. All she could think of was the moment she handed her son Carl to the nurse for the last time, and he had looked at her, stared through her, she believed, for the last time. 'Thanks Doctor.'

Nurse Molloy stepped forward, slowly, gravely, unlike the brisk confident strides that had brought her here. Her demeanour had changed too, her face full of sympathy and concern. She was a staff nurse in the ward where Carl had stayed days before his condition had rapidly deteriorated and he had been moved to intensive care.

'Would you like to ring your husband dear?' she gently asked.

'My partner… in a minute.'

'Can I get you something? tea? coffee?'

'No thanks.'

The surgeon nodded to the nurse. He turned to the mother: 'I'll leave you with nurse Molloy now,' he said; 'don't hesitate to come and see me, you and your partner, anytime.' He hurried out into the corridor. He felt relief and unease, conscious of nurse Molloy's assignment. He could never understand why it couldn't wait. He regarded the memo from van Hoofdaaker, that it shouldn't wait, as idiotic and callous.

Nurse Molloy paused for a brief moment trying to conceal the deep breath she took before saying another word: 'Mrs Sloan, we know what this means to you… and maybe this isn't the time to ask you, but your son Carl, even though he's dead, can help other children with similar conditions. If you would give us permission to do a post mortem, permission to look at his heart, it'll help us understand how these congenital heart conditions develop.'

Valerie raised her head and stared at nurse Molloy. To a less experienced, less confident nurse, the mother's expression may have read something like anger and disgust, prefacing an outburst accusing her of cruel insensitivity; but Nurse Molloy knew there was no such threat. Since Professor van Hoofdaaker's arrival, she had as instructed, made the same request of dozens of bereaved mothers, mothers of different intelligence, race, class and religion. Invariably, they all reacted in the same way. They barely heard what was said and knew not what was being asked of them. They were, quite literally capable of signing their lives away at a moment like this. This made it easier for nurse Molloy to open the envelope that she had carried under her arm and remove some papers. There was a post mortem consent form with separate space for instructions from parents on what they might allow or prohibit; and an authorisation form for mortuary attendants already signed by van Hoofdaaker in anticipation of Valerie's consent.

Valerie nodded and shook her head, a rather pitiful gesture revealing her confusion and helplessness. Nurse Molloy placed the forms on the coffee table. She pondered her options of putting a pen in Valerie's hand, or waiting; she chose the latter and placed the pen on top of the forms. There was no hurry now, she thought; the forms would be signed.

Valerie leaned forward with one arm propping her chin and her long auburn hair almost touching her feet. Outside the family suite, small children occasionally ran noisily past, a sound that usually seared through her but which now didn't even register. 'This is my second baby,' she cried 'Why?'

Nurse Molloy resisted the opportunity in such a plea: *that's what we need to find out dear, why?* This was a moment when she must say nothing, sit down beside the mother and place her arms around her knowing that her gentle embrace would unleash a greater profusion of tears, anger and bitterness.

'I dared not hope that this would be different,' Valerie said. 'Before Shane was born I used to imagine what it would be like to cuddle and feed him, to clothe and play with him, to smile at him... but not Carl; I couldn't concentrate on nice thoughts like that; I kept getting flashbacks; seeing Shane taken from me, watching him fight for life in a glass cage, wired up like something out of this world... I was so scared I didn't even want to try again; but my partner did! He didn't pressurise me; he just talked about it every time I was willing to listen, and then slowly but surely my own resistance caved in... all the nice thoughts about having babies taking over me.'

'And why not?' whispered nurse Molloy; 'there'd be something wrong if you didn't have those nice thoughts no matter what's gone on before.'

'But why me? What's wrong with me? Why can't I produce a normal child?'

Nurse Molloy clasped her: 'Don't ever believe that dear, because it isn't true. Your health was perfect during the pregnancies. Both your babies died of congenital heart failure, and that may have nothing at all to with your health, or your partner's.'

Valerie began to cry; nurse Molloy gave her some paper tissues. 'That's why a post mortem would be so helpful dear. Aldermann's has the best pathology service in the country now, run by Professor van Hoofdaaker – he's a world famous Dutch professor who's doing incredible work... haven't you heard of him? He and his team will leave no stone unturned to find out about this congenital heart condition that both your sons died of.'

Nurse Molloy was conscious of the fact that her assurances were groundless. But she felt no qualms about that; experience had taught her that many working class parents were greatly assured by the mention of the word 'professor' particularly if it prefaced an unmistakeably foreign name. She also knew that no matter what she said to bereaved parents, it was likely to be forgotten the day after. And it wasn't any insensitivity on her part to be talking about a child who had died eighteen months ago rather than comforting a mother on the death of her second child only an hour ago; the two were inextricably fused in this mother's mind.

Nurse Molloy removed her arm from Valerie's shoulders and stretched over to the consent form. She took a pen from her pocket and gently nudged it into Valerie's hand. She didn't notice that the expression on the mother's face had altered. No longer bereft or helpless looking, her head was raised and she was staring at the pale blue wall opposite; her reddened eyes were wide open and pained; the furrows of her brow had deepened; her lips tightened. Had nurse Molloy looked at Valerie, she would have instantly recognised perplexity. But she was looking instead at the consent form, which had two very large Xs scrawled in pencil, her own scrawls. She pointed at them: 'There and there,' she said.

'What...?' Valerie felt the pen in her fingers and saw the consent form on her knees.' She looked up at nurse Molloy: 'How will they find out about this heart problem?'

There was a certain incredulity in the voice that made the nurse, who was pointing her finger at the first of the scrawled Xs, look up at Valerie. Voice and expression then combined to convince nurse Molloy that something was wrong. Her mind worked furiously: had she said something inappropriate?

'They'll examine Carl's heart,' she said.

'How?'

'Well... they need to remove it before they examine it.'

'When?'

Nurse Molloy was hesitant. Her hesitancy seemed to vindicate the mother's purposeful query, now being made in a discernible, and for nurse Molloy, discomforting crescendo: 'When will they examine my son's heart?' she repeated.

'As soon as they can, dear... what's wrong?'

'How long will it take?'

'Em… well, a week maybe.'

'Will they let me know what they find?'

'Of course dear… good heavens, of course they will!'

'Do they still have Shane's heart?'

Nurse Molloy stared at her as though she hadn't heard her, or as though she believed that this mother, in her distress, was confusing her two sons. But Valerie's expression gave no indication of confusion. Her eyes remained moist and reddened, but they were animated; her focus was steadier, and her tone resolute. Nurse Molloy then felt her own confidence and poise beginning to desert her. The mother spoke first:

'My son Shane was buried eighteen months ago. Did I bury him without his heart?'

'Good Lord No! Mrs Sloan…' Then she realised she should not have said that; how could she know the heart had not been retained for on-going research, and that this mother had consented, but in her turmoil, couldn't remember; or worse, her consent had never been sought.

'I had forgotten… I'd completely forgotten,' said Valerie; 'but now it's all coming back to me.'

Nurse Molloy looked at her, wondering and worrying where this was leading.

'I gave you consent for a post mortem on my first baby, on a form just like this.' She held up the consent form. 'Don't you have any record of it?'

Nurse Molloy glanced through the file on her clipboard. 'It doesn't look like it dear' she said, apologetically. 'It may have been removed for administrative purposes, I'll have to check… I am sorry dear.'

'You carried out a post-mortem… more than eighteen months ago, and nobody told me anything about the results. I got so fed up waiting for them I forgot all about them. All I got from you was a telephone call six weeks later telling me my son's body was available.'

Nurse Molloy felt riveted to the shiny new floor. She swallowed, and when she was certain that Valerie wasn't looking, her tongue momentarily ran along her dried lips 'I'm terribly sorry, dear… I… I'll look into this and…'

'Oh for CHRIST'S SAKE!... WILL YOU STOP "DEARING" ME!' Valerie burst into tears and cried with anguish. A few moments later she said: 'So you remove the heart?'

Nurse Molloy sensed the rhetoric of the question and the bitterness of tone; she realised that her response would be fraught. Now she reckoned that Valerie had consented to a post-mortem, but wasn't told what it entailed. She took a deep breath and dared to enlighten her.

'Yes we do... we need to remove the heart in order to examine it.' She peered nervously into Valerie's eyes trying to determine the impact of her words. Then she thought: how could something as logical as what she had just said have escaped this poor woman? How can you examine a heart without removing it?

'That's not what I was told,' Valerie replied, each word struggling to emerge from the emotions that were almost choking her. She continued defiantly: 'I was told they would take a tiny piece of tissue from his heart.'

Nurse Molloy had a sinking feeling around her own heart. Whoever had told this lie had unwittingly ensnared her. She was afraid to speak. But she had to stay the course, listen to the anger and the anguish, and then somehow make amends.

'Now you want to remove Carl's heart?'

'No... not if you don't want us to.' But this was another lie. Nurse Molloy knew that van Hoofdaaker would insist on the removal of the heart, and that she was expected somehow to convey to any 'stubborn' parent (thankfully she had only ever met one before) that if they did not consent to a hospital post mortem, they could face the prospect of one by a Coroner. It was a ploy that van Hoofdaaker had personally used often in his past, one that had raised eyebrows in Aldermann's but no moral objections. A Coroner was certain to permit pathologists to do whatever tests 'it deemed necessary' and for as long as it may take, to assist the court in its findings. Nurse Molly had no stomach for such a potentially explosive leverage at this particular moment.

Valerie burst into tears again. She buried her head in her hands and made fiendish and helpless gurgling sounds. Nurse Molloy watched her in fear and pity.

'You must not remove my son's heart,' she eventually cried out.

'No of course not.'

'You can do for Carl what you said you would do for Shane... you can make the incision... you can take the sample... and that's all!'

'Yes... okay... I'm sure that Professor van Hoof...'

'And I want to know why I did not get the results of tests on Shane's heart.' She turned deliberately, determinedly, and stared into nurse Molloy's eyes as she continued, her voice rising: 'Why you kept his body for six weeks; and if you removed his heart, did you put it back, or have you still got it, because you still haven't done your tests... Oh God... and my son Carl...'

She buried her head again.

Nurse Molloy stood over her, helplessly. She realised the pointlessness and the dangerousness of uttering another word.

Chapter 26

Half an hour after nurse Molloy's difficult encounter with Valerie Sloan she made the return journey to her ward. It was approaching 5.0'clock. She had intended going straight to the mortuary but the outcome convinced her that a phone call to the pathology department was more urgent. Once pathology knew what had happened she reasoned, they would inform the mortuary that only tissue sample was required.

'Caroline,' she began on hearing the *leave a message* instruction in an empty pathology office; 'I'm putting Mrs Sloan's... Carl's mother, I'm putting the consent forms in the internal mail; consent limited to incision and removal of tissue; strong objections to anything more. And serious questions about her first child Shane. She says she didn't get the results of tests. She's asking do we still have his organs... his heart... she went on and on about his heart. I'm on duty tomorrow afternoon; ring me and I'll fill you in on the details. Bye.'

The next morning Caroline handed van Hoofdaaker the consent forms and relayed the brief message. He glanced through the forms and then calmly crushed them in his two fists. He threw them at a waste paper basket and missed. Then he winked at her, turned on his swivel chair, and resumed writing.

'Em...' She knew that was exactly what he would do.

'Nobody else in this fucking place has to hang around waiting for authorisation from stupid parents,' he said. 'If you're a surgeon, you operate; they would never stop a surgeon from operating, would they? If you're a nurse, you nurse; if you're a domestic, you clean up. I'm supposed to be running paediatric pathology and I can't make a move because this fucking place gives parents the right to let me do or not do my work.'

She was sympathetic to this perception, but she could not resist the temptation of gently provoking him. 'It's a difference in culture, my dear; when the Brits lose their loved ones, they're actually encouraged to believe that the corpses are precious to them, have some meaning for them. We're expected to put our arms around the bereaved and let it all gush out. Two weeks later, most of them have forgotten and don't care much what we do. We've got to play along with that. You made a tactical blunder in decreeing that we pressurise them for consent within the hour of death.'

'It wasn't a tactic. It's common sense.'

'But it isn't *consent*.'

He shook his head in exasperation. 'Consent…? When did we start needing consent? I spent five minutes on *consent* in twelve years of training. Tutors know that as soon as we qualify and get ourselves submerged in patient ignorance, we quickly forget about consent.'

'We're not supposed to forget about it,' she said, 'There is a law in this country upholding it, the Human Tissues Act.'

He swung round on the chair to look at her. He acknowledged her expertise in legality and was grateful for her lack of conviction in applying it. 'I've never heard of it,' he said.

'You're no different to those who have, and who have conveniently forgotten about it.'

'What does it say about consent?'

'That you should have no reason to believe any surviving relative of the deceased would object to what you intend to do with the body of their loved ones.'

'What?'

It was the first time she'd seen him grapple with language and meaning.

'I know,' she said; 'it's typical legal-speak. The problem is that before you decide on whether or not any relative might consent or object, you've got to tell them candidly and precisely, what you're going to do with the body.'

He frowned disbelievingly: 'It's a joke!'

'No. It's section one, subsection three,' she said rather smugly.

'You expect me to give parents the details of a post-mortem?'

'Not me darling, the law.'

'Before asking for their consent?'

'Correct.'

'It's madness… Who pays attention to this law? I've never heard Barnett or Parker or any of the others give details of a post-mortem to a parent.'

'Of course not, they wouldn't dare; they're just as negligent as you are, but they at least know there's a law to be broken. They're willing to ignore that law when they feel that it's too painful and difficult to apply.'

'So I'm not the maverick you make me out to be; this is the way it's always been in Aldermann's?'

'Well yes, more or less; except for one big difference: I think your subordinates genuinely feel the pain of parents, and really couldn't stomach inflicting any more pain on them by describing what a post-mortem entails and then asking for their consent. They were all relieved when *you* came along and offered to take responsibility for all post mortems, whether there's consent or not.'

'So what *is* this difference then; how am I different from them?'

She appeared to hesitate, but was merely savouring the moment. She spoke slowly and emphatically: 'Because darling, you don't feel anyone's pain.'

He smiled.

'And your reason for not telling parents is different too. It's not because you don't want to distress them further, it's because you know they wouldn't let you do it.'

'If they could see the benefits,' he said almost instantly.

'They're not likely to see the benefits when they've just lost their dearest.'

'So I'm expected to wait around for this… culture change, is that it?'

'That isn't going to happen either. You're going to have to deal with it in your own way.' She walked away from him and lifted the crumpled forms from the floor. She returned to his desk and dropped them. 'But not this way; too risky.'

He laughed:

'How are you going to deal with the matter of Sloan's first child,' she asked.

'I'll write to her.'

'And say what?'

'That the heart was replaced.'

'But it wasn't.'

I'll tell her it was. She won't challenge me; she'll be relieved, she'll probably even apologise to me for believing that I did such a wicked thing, keeping her son's heart!'

They glanced at each other as he pulled his swivel chair over to the screen and began typing. His eyes were animated and he smirked like a schoolboy about to engage in some prank. She stared at him in anticipation: was he going to lie in print, on his own personal, expensive heavily embossed paper that he insisted on having from the day he arrived?

'But you did keep it darling,' she repeated, moving to his shoulder, leaning over him and watching him type. She half whispered in his ear, as though he needed reminding of his errant ways: 'you didn't only remove his heart and keep it; you removed and kept every other organ, as you told us you would do, and as you did with the Jama stillbirth, and hundreds more; so many whole organs you've removed and kept that we have not yet been able to catalogue them all; we don't know where half of them are. We used to be very careful about storing hearts in Aldermann's; but now we have so many hearts we haven't enough containers for them or space to store them. So many hearts darling, that I've had to instruct your incredibly loyal staff to begin storing them four to a container rather than two. Are you aware of all that, my darling?' She kissed his ear, a typical 'full stop' gesture to yet another of her ironic lectures on his behaviour, a source of amusement to them both.

The smile spread across his whole face. 'What's the problem then,' he asked; 'no records, no organs…? I can just say the heart was replaced… No! it was never removed; that's what I'm going to write.'

She watched the screen, wondering would he dare write that. His two stilted index fingers bounced over the keys:

Dear Mrs Sloan,

I was deeply saddened to learn of the death of your son Carl. Any death in Aldermann's is a cause of great sadness amongst our staff, but more particularly so when we devote so much time and effort in attempting to discover the cause of death, so that it can be prevented in the future. I was shocked to hear that a junior member of staff may have accidentally misled you into thinking that your first son Shane's heart had been removed, and that you did not get the results of tests we conducted after gaining your consent for the removal of organ tissue.

Since coming to Aldermann's, I have repeatedly emphasised to my staff the importance of caring for parents as much as we do about their children, and that if a parent is unfortunate enough to suffer the tragedy of loss of a child as you have just done, we make every effort to respect their wishes and their feelings.

You will understand I'm sure Mrs Sloan, that when Shane died, we needed to find out the nature of the coronary disease that was responsible. But this did not necessitate me removing his heart. In accordance with your wishes, I simply made a 3-inch incision sufficient to enable me to place my left hand into the body cavity. I was then able to assess the condition of many of your son's organs merely by gently touching them and feeling them for size and abnormalities. I removed some tiny samples of tissue from the heart and lungs, less than half an inch in size; I made no further invasive exploration, and your son's body was returned to you, undisturbed.

As for not getting any test results, these of course would have been sent to your GP, who should have contacted you. I am very sorry that this did not happen, and I will investigate the matter further.

I want to thank you for your help and cooperation in your hour of pain. I can't even begin to tell you how significant these tests on the hearts of both of your sons are in the study of heart disease. There are children not yet born who will live because of your courage and selflessness in giving us the opportunity to advance paediatric care.

If there is any matter arising from the contents of this letter that you wish to discuss further, do not hesitate to contact me, by letter or phone.

Yours sincerely,

Professor Dick van Hoofdaaker

Caroline put her other arm around him as she read it. Each sentence made her clasp him more tightly. By the time she neared the end, she was trying desperately not to laugh: his audacity; his outrageousness. It was the flourish of his signature that punctured her restraint and she laughed loudly. He merely smiled, gratified. He really had lost all sense of dangerousness, she thought. And he obviously *did* believe that this mother, whoever she was, would apologise to him. Caroline herself believed it. She laughed again.

Later that morning, van Hoofdaaker arrived at the mortuary with two of his male staff. He greeted the mortuary attendant Ted with his usual smiles and banter, and handed him an authorization form. Ted nonchalantly glanced at the top of the form and noted the name Carl Sloan. He read no further and led them to the corpse.

Within an hour, Carl's brain, heart, lung, aorta, thymus, spleen, liver, pancras, kidney, intestine and adrenal glands had been removed. The eyes of van Hoofdaaker's clinical assistants were riveted on him as he worked. Occasionally they glanced at each other, awed by his speed and his efficiency. They could hardly keep up with his running commentary.

PART IV

Chapter 27

'You don't believe in the job, do you?' Sa'eed asked O'Neill.

It was a measure of the rapport developing between them that Sa'eed could challenge him like this without offending him. He had been with him all morning visiting clients in Abington.

'You mean I don't take the job seriously? Would you take any of that lot seriously?'

Sa'eed didn't reply. He just smiled.

'All you do is keep an eye on the kids and have fun,' said O'Neill.

Sa'eed was initially puzzled by the respect many of the Abington residents gave to O'Neill. Once he had examined babies and kids in his usual intrusive manner and was satisfied, the conversation between him and the parents seldom deviated from mutual banter. He had no interest in a family's general welfare; he laughed when Sa'eed asked about whether or not they were receiving the help they were entitled to; he said he didn't know and didn't care.

It was in sharp contrast to the nervousness and the shilly-shallying Sa'eed had witnessed elsewhere. He'd been out with everyone in the team now.

When they left Abington, they headed for Hollybank. 'This is about a fifteen year old called Martin,' O'Neill said; 'being messed up by his mum... and stepdad.'

'Messed up?'

'Yea, messed up, damaged... he's an emotional and mental wreck. I think his stepdad's sexually abusing him and his mum's too crazy to notice.'

'Will they be there?'

'Good question. His mum's entitled to be but I don't think she will be. She knows what I think.'

'So you can't let him home then?'

O'Neill said nothing.

Sa'eed became aware of a lengthening silence. He turned round to look into O'Neill's face, to see why a simple question had seemingly silenced him.

'Yes I *can* let him home,' O'Neill eventually replied. 'That's what I'm going to try to do. I'll have difficulty convincing some of the people here today, but Martin has to be home.'

'Why?'

'Wait and see.'

Sa'eed stared at O'Neill. O'Neill sensed his perplexity and smiled: 'Wait and see,' he repeated.

Sa'eed relaxed. He'd interpreted the silence wrongly. O'Neill had merely been scheming and dwelling on another of his unconventional strategies, the obstacles to be surmounted, and the people he would offend. His methods and motivation remained a constant source of curiosity to Sa'eed.

Maggie had mistimed how long it would take her to walk from the nearest bus stop to the gates of Hollybank, and she hurried along the entrance hall annoyed and flustered. As she approached the conference room she heard the ritual greetings and small talk, telling her the meeting had obviously not yet begun. She opened the door hesitantly, prepared to apologise to the host Len Castle, Officer-in-Charge of Hollybank.

There were eight people in the room, some with their backs to her, and most of whom she had expected. She had not been expecting to see Andrew Jackson; surely he would have regarded this case as piffling, taking him away from weightier matters like the Mulholland murder. But maybe he wanted a break from that. Then a more troubling thought came to her; perhaps Jackson had learnt from O'Neill that Martin's case was no piffling matter; maybe he had read the file and realised this for himself.

Jackson was holding court to most of the group, initially proclaiming that he dare not mention the Mulholland case, but then casually though intentionally revealing insider details, and adding a particular gloss to his responsibilities in the whole affair. He nodded and smiled at Maggie as she passed, as though he had been looking out for her.

214

'Maggie, how are you,' he said, with undue familiarity; 'I've just been told you live in West Kirby and you don't have a car; I could have picked you up this morning; I live in Caldy.'

'Oh do you,' she said, wondering was it a subtle admonishment for being late, or a pretentiousness in letting people know he lived in exclusively rich Caldy, a mile from her own home. 'Thanks. Sorry… I didn't realise the distance I had to walk from the bus stop to here.'

'Not a problem,' he said; 'plenty of warming up to do. By the way… excellent case notes you sent on that Mulholland case. Thank *you*!'

He resumed engagement with the group around him. She passed them by.

Priscilla, Jackson's secretary, was there to take the minutes, looking much more chic than Maggie had ever seen her before, in her red dress and white top, her hair transformed through flicked out layers with a heavy graduated fringe; Maggie bantered her about how well she looked, saying it was obviously linked to her 'rising status' since Jackson arrived.

'Not all he makes out to be,' Priscilla said rather secretively. She glanced back at Jackson, as if to reassure herself he was too distant to hear her.

Maggie looked at her curiously, waiting for an explanation. Priscilla said nothing more, but the look in her eyes bordered on disdain.

As well as Castle, DC Wright from Juvenile Liaison was there, and Bob Williams from Martin's school, and Mrs Spinner from Educational Psychology, and Dr Millwize, a psychiatrist. She had never met the doctor before. Her first sighting of the remaining two people in the room, O'Neill and Sa'eed, stunned her. She really had to stare at them for a few seconds and convince herself that she wasn't imagining things. She was expecting and dreading O'Neill, but Sa'eed Jama… standing alongside *O'Neill* of all people, both of them now looking at her, and sending tremors through her.

They stirred unconnected memories in her: a fleeting discomforting encounter with Sa'eed and Azeer in the Verdi Piazza in Busseto, and her sustained encounters with O'Neill all those years ago. O'Neill nodded and said 'hello.' She reluctantly went towards them, acknowledging others as she passed.

'Hi,' she said, wondering did her looks betray the tremor.

'Hello Maggie. This is Sa'eed, Sa'eed Jama, our newest trainee social worker. Morgan insists he spends some time with me.'

His tone was ironic, suggestive of contempt for Morgan, but he also sounded as though he was deriving some satisfaction from his trainee shadow.

'We've already met,' she said.

'O'Neill looked frowningly at both of them. 'Have you?' He felt put out. 'How come?'

Maggie turned to Sa'eed. His face and his expression were somewhat softer than she remembered, without tension, his eyes no longer inclined to stare coldly or fixedly. His smile seemed genuine and warm.

'How are you?' he asked, 'very nice to see you.'

'I'm okay,' she said, then turned to explain to O'Neill.

'We met in Busseto in North Italy, at an open air performance of Verdi's *Requiem*. Did you enjoy it?' she asked Sa'eed, remembering that she and Bell had deliberately avoided him and Azeer after the concert.

'Excellent… amazing. But too close for my ears.' He touched both ears with his finger tips.

'Yes, we were just a bit too close,' she said.

'So you're still singing Maggie,' said O'Neill, half interestedly.

'Still trying.'

'Where?'

'Same place; West Kirby. We're joining up with twenty other choirs to do the *Requiem* with the Philharmonic at the Metropolitan cathedral.'

'Twenty choirs? That'll put a few bums on seats. Will there be any room for an audience?' He shrugged his shoulders. 'I heard the *Requiem* being rehearsed there a few months ago. Trust Liverpool to choose a requiem to celebrate the *Year of Culture!*'

'Not just one Sean; they're doing half a dozen requiems throughout the year, Verdi, Fauré, Britten… Apparently requiems sell out more quickly than anything else.'

'Morbid!' He turned to Sa'eed. 'What's your interest in Verdi's *Requiem* Sa'eed? I thought Muslims could be shot for listening to music like that.'

Sa'eed shook his head and laughed.

'We've been through all that,' said Maggie; 'it's what I thought too, but apparently it's not so; Verdi's big in Egypt, isn't that right?'

Now *she* was being ironical. Maybe she was taking a risk too, in reminding him of a conversation with Azeer that had perplexed her, and of cryptic communication between Sa'eed and Azeer that had disturbed her. She continued, raising her eyebrows and smiling at Sa'eed, but still speaking to O'Neill: 'The *Requiem's* so popular,' she continued, 'that they have to put on repeat performances.'

'Why don't you join a choir here and sing it Sa'eed?' chirped O'Neill.

'I might,' he said, more seriously than O'Neill had intended. 'I know it well enough now, but I need to find a choir that's not too particular about who joins it.'

'That's us!' Maggie said, jokingly. 'No auditions, no musical training, just hard work and enthusiasm. We could do with lots more tenors. Are you a tenor?'

'I think I am,' he said.

Elsewhere the party was becoming restless; Jackson's hold was loosening; there were momentary lapses in the conversation, sighing and glancing away from each other, a collective agitation. Eventually, Jackson said: 'Okay folks, shall we sit ourselves down and get started.'

They sat around four formica topped, tubular-legged tables pushed together. Occasionally some of them looked up at the high ceiling, at the oblong fluorescent tubes replacing Hollybank's priceless chandeliers; at the ornamented flaking cornices, and the original and vast pulley windows. They wondered how elegant the room must have looked when Lord and Lady McKay graced it with their presence.

Jackson invited them to introduce themselves.

Sa'eed sat next to O'Neill; Maggie sat opposite to them. Len Castle sat on the right of Jackson at the head of the table; Priscilla sat on his left. Further down the tables, the silver haired Mrs Spinner and Dr Millwize sat opposite Williams the teacher and the plain-clothed DC Wright.

Jackson thanked them all for coming and made a special welcome to Sa'eed, wishing him well in his social work career. All eyes gazed at Sa'eed with a mixture of inquisitiveness and approval. Sa'eed thanked them.

'Are we expecting anyone else?' Jackson asked, looking at O'Neill.

'Martin's mum *was* invited,' said O'Neill, 'and said she'd think about it; I don't think she'll be coming.'

'And you and Len invited Martin, but he felt it would be too difficult for him?'

'That's right.'

'Okay. Let's start, folks…'

Maggie cringed; if it wasn't *folks* it was *you guys*. She still hadn't found an effective way to counter *you guys* being frequently drawled out by her daughter Alice.

'This is not a child abuse conference,' Morgan said, 'in the sense in which we normally understand the term, but having looked at the file and discussed it at length with Sean, I have to concede that there may well be a child abuse aspect to this case.'

Maggie wondered how much of the incomplete file he had read.

'This *child* Martin,' said Jackson; 'he's in Hollybank subject of a residency Order; he's been a persistent offender. Can we have your staff's assessment, Len?'

Len Castle opened his file. He was a small and stocky man, mid-forties, bald headed, casually dressed with open necked shirt, quiet spoken, but confident and respected within Hollybank by staff and kids alike. He spoke for five minutes about Martin; the 'most untypical' kid he had ever seen in Hollybank, so withdrawn, soft, lacking in confidence, meticulously clean, very poor academically, always yearning to go home, always looking forward to his mother's visits, – his stepdad never visits. He gets picked on by the other kids; that was the biggest challenge facing Len and his staff, preventing him from getting picked on, him and another kid Damian Atkins, nearly as big a softee as Martin; good friends they are; mutually comforting and supportive. Len concluded by declaring that he and his staff couldn't see any point in Martin staying at Hollybank.

Jackson took a few notes, thanked Len, and looked at Bob Williams. 'Is this the Martin that *you* know, Bob, or is he someone different…? Can we have the last school report?'

'Almost identical,' said Williams. He was a dapper little man, highly attentive and eager to please. He read out his report and added: 'there's one problem you didn't mention Len, because I know you haven't got that problem… if only we could keep some of our lads locked up too!'

They all looked at him quizzically, except Maggie. She'd been to the school during her own enquiries; she knew what Williams was getting at.

'The attendance is abysmal,' he said; 'in fact, if he hadn't ended up here for thieving, we might have been thinking about suspending him.'

'So what's going on?' Jackson asked.

'I don't know,' Williams replied.

Jackson looked round the group. 'Do *you* know, Maggie? You probably know the family better than anyone else here.'

'I've not sure anybody knows this family.'

'I think the mother's on another planet,' said Williams.

Smiles all round. Maggie remained tense.

Jackson looked further down the group. 'Mrs Spinner, you've carried out psychological tests on Martin; would you like to share your findings with us?'

'Certainly,' said the silver haired lady, opening her file and placing the prepared papers before her. She raised her spectacles from around her neck and implanted them firmly on her nose. She could just about see her papers over the open lapels of her thick green jacket. 'At the interview,' she began, 'Martin presented as a very cooperative, pleasant, but extremely inhibited boy. Formal assessment confirms recent findings, and suggests that Martin is operating within the very limited range of ability and for practical purposes may be regarded as ESN.'

She paused for a moment as if the gravity of her words demanded it.

'Martin experiences problems of a perceptual cognitive nature. He is right handed, but experiences problems of right/left discrimination, and manifests specific learning difficulties. Some degree of motor coordination is apparent, and his manipulation of objects is occasionally clumsy and ham-fisted. His handwriting is not distinct or well formed. Formal testing provides data suggestive of cerebral pathology, possibly associated with brain injury at birth. The deleterious behavioural and perceptual cognitive ramifications may, therefore, overwhelm his performance on formal intellectual tests, and thus contribute to an apparent under estimation of his intellectual capacity. The evidence therefore, suggests that Martin's low level of achievement at school stems from attentional and/or perceptual cognitive deficits associated with cerebral pathology and not from intellectual shortcomings per se.'

She never looked up when she finished. She methodically gathered her papers together and placed them in a file. She rested her outstretched hands on the file and waited, confident in the knowledge that no other contribution could match her own. All she had to do now, she believed, was tolerate a load of anecdotal dribble in the contributions that would follow.

With due deference to her age and status, Jackson thanked her for her 'excellent report', combining 'scientific facts' with 'crucial observation'. 'Does anyone want to ask Mrs Spinner any questions or make any comment?' he asked.

'Martin isn't clumsy or hamfisted,' said Maggie quietly but determinedly.

They looked at her with bemusement, Jackson with some irritation, and Mrs Spinner, witheringly. The gold chain of Mrs Spinner's spectacles quivered ever so slightly: 'The Burt-Schlisinger Co-ordination tests were used,' she said, addressing the chairman.

Silence reigned.

Maggie ignored Mrs Spinner's indignation and spoke directly to Williams: 'I'm surprised you didn't mention the discus, Bob? Isn't he good at the discus, at school sports in general?'

'Yes he is,' said Williams, feeling caught out. 'But I don't think throwing a discus is going to help with the problems he's got.' He forced a laugh.

Everyone was curious about this discus revelation.

'But don't you think it's worth mentioning?' Maggie persisted.

'Well... maybe it is. But if you were to ask my honest opinion, I'd say he'd be much better doing something else. An employer isn't going to be interested in a lad who spends a lot of time on his own throwing a discus and who can't read nor write, and has no social skills whatsoever.'

He felt better after that.

Len Castle unexpectedly spoke. 'Maggie's right. It's not just the discus; he's good at a lot of other sports.'

All eyes switched to Len.

'I didn't think anything of it until just now...' he continued; 'but he is very fit and strong. We take a group to the Lancashire show every year; it just finished two weeks ago. The Army has a recruitment stand there and an obstacle course for potential recruits... or bored kids! Martin was the only one of our lot who finished it; scored the highest by a long way. He got a plaque to prove it though that didn't make him popular with the rest of them! I wasn't there myself but Steve... Steve Pender, one of my staff, said he was very impressive.'

'And yet,' said Jackson, 'he gets picked on.'

'All the time.'

'Somebody might do it one last time.'

Heads nodded.

Maggie's intervention was unplanned; a simple gut reaction against the injustice of labelling Martin, of denying an unusual talent in a lad generally credited with none. She had no idea how her challenge had impacted on them; but when she happened to glance at O'Neill, it seemed as though the impact on him had been considerable. His face was motionless, but his expression seemed pregnant with anger; he was flushed, tense, his eyes riveted on her, his mouth tightly shut. Then she realised that he wasn't even seeing her; he was staring at her, but she was sure he was thinking of something else.

'Just how good is he at discus throwing?' Jackson asked Williams.

'Good... very good,' came the reluctant reply.

'Where does he rank in the school as a whole?'

Williams looked exasperated. There was still no escape from the trap that had been unpredictably sprung on him. Why weren't they interested in Martin's pathetic spelling, reading and writing, he thought to himself. He was rummaging through the file notes as Jackson pressed him and he saw something which obviously pleased him. He then spoke emphatically, with more volume than his voice normally carried:

'The best in the school. He would do well in competition... if he would attend. But he seldom attends when the school's competing. As I said earlier his attendance generally is awful, but you can be certain of one thing: most of the days that he doesn't attend are sports day or when we're competing with another school. He truants a lot – we all know that, but for most sports days, he always has a note from his mother. He's 'had a cold' or 'a flu', or he's 'had a fall', or something like that. Can't do much about it when his mother's providing him with a note.'

'Are you saying she *deliberately* prevents Martin from attending when the school's competing?' Jackson asked.

'Well no, I wouldn't go that far. But the coincidences of illnesses or whatever on sports days are hardly credible. And these letters she sends... I have some of them here; the woman's nearly illiterate it seems. Here, see for yourselves.'

He passed one along to Jackson; O'Neill reached out his hand for another. O'Neill stared long at the incomprehensible childish scribbles. He handed the note to Sa'eed and he then looked across to Maggie. They looked at each other for a few seconds, without warmth or ease, as if sensing in each other a depth of involvement and awareness about the case that the others probably could not share.

Jackson detected the uneasy calm of the group. A cloud of perplexity seemed to have descended upon them, with no one willing to risk analysis or speculation.

'Could we hear your views now Dr. Millwize.'

'Yes of course,' the doctor answered. He had remained earnestly passive and detached throughout the meeting. Even the moment of friction between Mrs Spinner and Maggie had failed to stir him. He placed his hand in the inside pocket of his well worn brown tweed suit, and removed a single crumpled piece of paper. He opened it up and read:

Dear Mr Castle,

On behalf of Social Services, I have examined this boy in your establishment, and found him quite normal in every respect. He is a very presentable lad who appears to have remorse for the offences he has committed. I find him quite dull intellectually – this is borne out by your staff I believe. There's no doubt in my mind however, that he is not suffering from mental disorder of any kind.

They watched him and waited expectantly for an exposition. But he replaced his crumpled piece of paper and said no more.

Jackson looked at him and asked with barely disguised incredulity: 'Is there anything else you'd like to add, *doctor*?'

'No. I really can't see that this boy has a psychiatric problem.'

Jackson was in difficulty. He didn't know which was the more offensive: the doctor's apparent indifference or his quiet yet overbearing confidence. He could not let him away with this: 'Would you like to comment on the psychological tests that Mrs Spinner carried out?' he asked.

'No.'

Jackson was fuming. He would have to personally approve a £500 fee for this man, for the four worthless sentences that he read out, and which he, Jackson, had already seen a copy of, before the conference. He did not pay him the usual courtesy of thanking him for his *contribution*. He turned to Maggie with some relief and said: 'What can Probation tell us about this case, Maggie?'

'I think we're probably making fools of ourselves,' she replied.

Jackson stared at her with his mouth open.

'What's the purpose of the meeting?' Maggie asked.

'Purpose…?'

'The purpose isn't clear to me. We're supposed to be dealing with someone who won't stop committing offences. He's been in court eight times. Magistrate and police are laughing at us. Are we or are we not going to make a decision?'

Jackson calmly called upon DC Wright: 'Are you laughing at us?'

Wright smiled and shook his head. Jackson looked questioningly around the group wondering was there some common knowledge about the case that only *he* knew nothing about. He was reassured. Everybody looked as bemused as himself.

'What decision do you think we should take, Maggie?' he asked, with a hint of condescension in his eyes.

'I believe he should remain in residential care, because I don't think any of us are in a position to say that he won't commit another offence if we allow him home. He hasn't committed an offence since coming here.'

'Where do you suggest we put Martin?' O'Neill asked.

'I don't know... wherever Social Services think appropriate.'

He looked at her, disbelievingly. 'Anywhere, so long as we don't let him home?'

'Yes... unless you want to see him in court again.'

'Why are you so convinced he'll appear in court again if he goes home?'

'Because nothing's changed.'

They stared at each other. O'Neill seemingly wanted to push her one more time: 'What needs changing? Is he being abused?'

She paused for a second. The whole group stared at her.

'I don't know,' she said.

'Give us a profile of his mum,' said Jackson; 'I don't feel I know this woman.'

Maggie took a deep breath: 'She's 38 years old, a supervisor on an assembly line in a local factory. She's been married before to a man called McDonald. She married him when she was 19. They had Martin. She says that her husband was alcoholic. She left him, met Mr Greer and got married. She is... too over-protective of Martin... she doesn't let him take normal risks.'

They all stared at her, waiting for more. She knew it was the blandest statement she had ever made in her professional life.

Unexpectedly, Dr Millwize spoke: 'What's her maiden name, may I ask?'

Maggie froze for a moment. She glanced at O'Neill, and felt his piercing stare go through her. 'Phillips,' she said, looking back at the doctor.

He pondered the name for a while; 'hmmm' he said, without explanation.

'Do we know anything about her childhood... her upbringing?' Jackson asked.

There was no response.

'Shouldn't somebody have enquired about that?' He looked at Maggie.

She shook her head in apparent disgust. 'I'm sorry... I can't see the point. I'm leaving!' She lifted her bag from the floor, flung it over her shoulder, got up and hurried out of the room, slamming the door behind her.

Jackson stared after her, his face crimson with anger. 'Sorry about that folks.'

'What's her full name?' Dr Millwize asked.

'Maggie Lynch... she's a probation officer,' Jackson replied, unwittingly.

'No no, not Mrs Lynch... the boy's mother?'

'Oh Mrs Greer? Sorry doctor. Her full name... I should have it here.' He fumbled noisily with the papers, grateful for the diversion.

'Marian Patricia Greer,' said O'Neill, before Jackson could speak.

'Thanks Sean,' said Jackson. 'Yes. I have it here now; Marian Patricia. Why do you ask, Doctor?'

'Marian Patricia...' The doctor scratched his chin and pondered again. 'Mrs Lynch said her maiden name was Phillips? No, I must be thinking of someone else.'

Chapter 28

O'Neill stood still and silent at her office door. His expression gave nothing away, unlike Maggie's sudden agitation on seeing him. She didn't know how long he had been standing there. She should have known because his dark lean figure blocked at least a third of the daylight streaming in from the hallway.

'Aren't you coming in?' she asked casually. She managed to look away from him, and tidy the file in front of her. Then she closed it and joined her hands across it. Her fingers clenched. 'Where's your trainee, Sa'eed?'

'Having a break.'

'I bet!'

'He pretends to be cool but he's overwhelmed. He never stops asking questions about the job.'

'And every answer you give shocks him?'

He smiled at her.

'I thought you might be paying me a visit,' she said; 'Priscilla phoned me, and Len Castle too... and now you! They all think I'm cracking up. Whatever you ask me, don't ask me if I've got a problem. And don't be sympathising with me because of what happened to Angela Mulholland.'

She wondered how that sounded; hopefully disarming him; she at least expected him to be less boringly inquisitive than the others.

'Why do you keep your door open?' he asked, coming nearer.

'Fresh air.'

'You've got windows.'

'Yes, I keep them open too. See?'

'You'd prefer open plan wouldn't you, every one together, seeing each other?'

'Yes, why not?'

'That's not how you felt yesterday.'

He was sitting by a window now, stretching his arms behind and above his head. His comment seemed a mere observation, but his tone sounded as though he meant to mock or ensnare.

'Were you… shocked?'

'No, I wasn't shocked. You raised your voice and walked out, but I don't believe you lost control.'

That could mean anything, she thought. Did he mean it was contrived?

'Why *did* you come?' she asked.

'You were supposed to contact me.'

'Yes I intended to, but there wasn't much to talk about.'

He got up and came forward, and leant upon her desk. He stared into her eyes, yet not in an accusatory way. 'Did you forget?'

'No, but anytime I remembered, I was in the wrong place.'

'Probation doesn't think much about social work, does it?' he asked, half mockingly, as he returned to his seat.

She smiled. 'We keep our distance, and right too. We're civil servants employed by the Home Office; we're no longer *social workers*.'

The *Sun* and the *Mail* aren't impressed by that distinction.'

'Never read them.'

'We're all parasites Maggie, and unemployable.'

'Nice to know Sa'eed's being trained by someone who believes in the job.'

'Sa'eed knows I *don't* believe in it.'

'What are you doing with Martin then?'

'I'll tell you when I get him home.'

'I must be a fool Sean; I ask clients to tell me what my job's about. They keep telling me I'm helping them and they appreciate it. I can't argue with that.'

'You could enlighten them.'

'Oh how? By trying to tell them what *you* think?'

'What you and I know.'

'You're talking in riddles. My clients wouldn't understand you.'

'Wouldn't they? Have you ever told them about social work training? You did some of that, didn't you? Remember? learning to reach out to clients; *empathise*… now there's a word! Give them hope of climbing out of their dung heaps, offering them *compassion* and *commitment*; telling them that there's more to life than competition and failure. One of the big lies, that!'

She laughed. She'd heard it before when she was unable to laugh, because it always sounded like a personal attack, with his own experiences explicitly and embarrassingly thrown in. 'Bit heavy for a lot of my clients,' she said.

Mike her supervisor walked in, his head buried in a basket of files. He was nearly on top of O'Neill before he saw him.

'What about that Simeon case... oh hello... sorry Maggie; I didn't realise you had company.'

'It's okay.'

It wasn't really. She wanted Mike to leave.

'I'll call back,' he said, nodding and trying to convey concern. He left without saying a word to O'Neill.

'I suppose probation's full of people like that,' O'Neill said

'Mike's all right. You know nothing about him.'

'Except that he supervises you.'

'I'm not complaining.'

'But you know he's not fit to supervise you.'

'He's got a lot of strengths that you know nothing about.'

'Yea... I'm sure he's a wonderful guy. As good as Morgan. How long would either of them last in another job?'

'I can't understand why you're still doing this job. You think it's hypocrisy and yet you get your kicks out of it. You believe everybody around you is useless. Seems stupid to me if that's the only satisfaction you get in the job.'

'It's not. There are kids out there needing something more than all that crap you and I had rammed down our throats. I've held onto that *something more*. I don't believe parents; I seldom give them the benefit of the doubt; I never try to understand their *social* and *economic* difficulties; I don't waste time looking into their deprived childhoods; I don't give a damn if they're black or white, Muslim or heathen, middle class or no class... I can't stand that cultural relativism bullshit! If they're abusing their kids and lying about it, I'll see through them quicker than anybody else. And yea... I'll make them suffer... and I'll probably get some satisfaction out of that too!'

She despised and pitied him. She wanted to gently mock him but refrained. It would not have alleviated her from her own guilt.

'Boring… Sean! Do you bore your clients as much as you bore me about your past? It's your past you're on about, isn't it?'

'I didn't bore Martin.'

She stared at him with uncertainty. She couldn't think of any positive reason why he might have done that. 'You told Martin about your childhood?'

'I told him a few things… I *empathised* with him,' he said ironically. 'The context was right. It helped open him up a little bit.'

So he *had* come to talk about the case, she thought. But what was he getting at? Maybe he did know something; maybe he had come to try and bait her. No, she then concluded; he could not have sustained this calm if he'd known anything.

'You probably got through to him without crap like that,' he said. 'I didn't know what you were trying to do at the conference; I expected some resistance to him going home, from Wright or Williams, but I wasn't expecting *you* to resist in the way you did.' He smiled and added: 'it was the best conference entertainment I've seen for a long time. Poor Sa'eed didn't know what was happening. And you succeeded in annoying Jackson; you should be more careful about the enemies you make.'

She wanted to get up and scream at him, but instead quietly asked him: 'Is that what you've come to say to me, Sean?'

'It's not a very subtle apology.'

Apology? What next, she wondered.

'I didn't make it easy for you,' he said.

'You weren't supposed to. You wanted Martin home… I couldn't see why. What are you going to do with him when you get him home?'

She was surprised at the length of time he took to answer, as though he was considering not answering at all. Then he leaned towards her and said:

'I'm going to prove that he's being screwed by that stepdad creep Michael; and I'm going to prove that his mum knows about it and colludes in it. Then I'm going to remove Martin from them both, permanently.'

Maggie suddenly felt weak. She wanted to cave in there and then, quit her pretence of naivety and frustration, shake her head and yell YOU FOOL! Or laugh contemptuously at him. But she did none of that. She had worried thinking he had come maybe to interrogate her, or goad her, or toy with her, and now she knew he had merely wanted to impress her, with his analysis and solution, more ludicrous than any of the conjectures she herself had posited when she first took on the case. Her sense of helplessness deepened.

'How do you know Michael's abusing him... why are you letting him home, then?'

He stared through her again. 'Don't tell me you didn't at least *suspect* that's what was happening to him?'

'No I didn't... I never...' The first blatant lie, she then thought to herself.

He looked at her ambiguously. 'It's bloody obvious.'

'Not to me, Sean.'

She felt sick. It was the truth, but just another word: not to me, *now*, Sean, would have been truer.

'You know they have a loveless, sexless relationship, don't you?' he asked.

'No I don't know. I may have thought that at times, but how different is that to many other relationships? That's no reason to believe he's abusing Martin.'

'Does he have a relationship with anyone else?'

'Not that I know of.'

'Does he have any friends, any social life?'

She shook her head, and then realised he interpreted it as a surrender to his *irrefutable* logic. He was incapable of recognising that it was her expression of self-disgust.

'Have you ever seen a guy so dominated, so weak?' he asked.

She hadn't. She knew what he was driving at: Michael Greer displayed all the characteristics, the classic indicators of a sexually abusing father. Again she felt like surrendering in despair, but then she felt she had to resist. Not to save O'Neill from himself, but more a reaction to the guilt consuming her. What else could she do? She was watching a man galloping blindly towards a cliff edge, and she knew that if she had the courage to stop him and tell him what she knew, he was certain to gallop towards that same cliff much faster.

'I know that's the way he appears Sean; but you can't be certain. Maybe there are reasons in the relationship...'

'Screwing his stepson is one good reason. He's a paedophile. You should have seen that before me: you've plenty of them on your caseload.'

So she had. She said nothing for a while. There was nothing for her to say other than what any other colleague or indeed any normal human being would have said. But she felt like a hypocrite when she eventually did say it: 'Why haven't you done something about it? Why haven't you told Morgan and the police?'

He burst out laughing contemptuously. 'For what? So that they'd go charging in with all guns blazing; so that they could arrest him, and he'd deny it, and she'd deny it, and Martin would deny it, and the creep would walk free from the station and he and his wife would ensure that police and probation and Social Services would never get anywhere near them again?'

'Why are you letting him home then?' she asked, managing a frown of incredulity; 'Are you going to break in some night and catch Michael Greer in the act?'

He laughed again. 'I'm going to unravel them... bust their system. I'm going to do it slowly, methodically. Marian Greer is the key. But I can't do it without Martin being present. You know what she's done to Martin, don't you?'

'I'm not sure what *you're* doing to him; I know she's done him harm.'

'Harm! You call it *harm*? He's unable to look at another individual without feeling a sense of doom because he thinks that they may speak to him, or ask him a question, or seek his opinion, and he'll disintegrate if they do... you call that *harm*? Not to believe that you are anyone else other than the buffoon that your mother and step-dad make you out to be... you call that *harm*? And who's the chief beneficiary? Marian Greer. Half illiterate, half mad, driven by some perverted need to ensure her son doesn't grow up, that he remains like that for ever; enslaved to her while he's being screwed by his stepdad. And the slightest hint of change, of him escaping, of being somebody else, being a real human being... would make his mad mother's life not worth living. So that's just... *harm*, is it?'

It was pretty incisive, and yet in one respect dangerously wrong.

He got up and paced her office. He spoke in a much slower, mellower tone: 'When I made my first visit to the home,' he said, his head lowered and his gaze fixed on the floor, 'I asked to see Martin's bedroom. It was a revelation. I knew there was something wrong with the way she talked about the room and about Martin. I saw the discus lying under the bed, but I didn't know it was a discus. I've never seen a discus close up before. I was going to ask her what it was, and I'm sure she anticipated that, because she pushed it out of my sight. I quickly forgot about it.'

He came closer to her and looked down on her: 'But then you Maggie were not going to let us forget about it. You must have been seething listening to Spinner: *Cerebral pathology… brain injury at birth.* I looked at you when she said that. You knew what was happening to Martin. You knew the significance of the discus. No wonder you never wanted him to return home.'

She was a heroine then! She looked into his eyes and could see the gratitude that he could not express. She looked away. It was too painful.

He moved away from her desk. She prayed that it was to leave. He walked towards the doorway. She was sure that he would turn round and say something else. And although she dreaded that, she had something herself to say to him; a question to ask, and her charity willing him to give a reply different to the one that was in her mind.

'Sean, is there any other reason why you wanted Martin home?'

She sensed that he repeatedly invited her to ask that question, but he didn't answer.

Chapter 29

Nothing would stop Samira now. She had got off a train in Lime Street station during the early morning rush hour and was making her way through the moving masses of passengers, uncharacteristically defiant towards their curious, hostile or even their pitying glances. It was the police she feared most, clutching their Heckler and Coch machine guns and strategically located at each entrance to the station. They couldn't harm her but they could humiliate her. They could stop her and order her to remove the veil. Worse, they could ask their female colleagues to search under her jilbaab.

Her perception of Islamic dress had undergone fundamental change. She had always happily worn it, but she had been guided more by fashion and beauty than by the Qur'an. She had been wearing the most eye-catching turquoise hijab with matching silk trousers and sandals on the night she was nearly gang-raped and her husband was kicked to death. She had never worn anything like that since. She eventually escaped from the resulting depression and despair with the help of a local Iman. She began seriously reading the Qur'an all over again and the commentary and interpretations that came with it, only to be tormented by the realisation that the warnings of what might happen (what did happen) were always there:

And say to the believing woman that they should lower their gaze and guard their modesty; that they should not display their beauty and ornaments... And stay in your houses, and do not display yourselves... Allah wishes only to remove evil deeds and sins from you, to purify you. A woman is likened to a sweet creature. Everything about her is an attraction for spectators. Islam protects her by enjoining her to cover herself, so that she does not attract the swamps of flies and dirty creatures.

Now she was completely covered in a black baggy jilbaab, a black niqab veil and a black hijab. Muslim sisters were being penalised for covering themselves like this; banished from classrooms where they taught, disciplined in hospitals for not rolling up their sleeves, mocked and spat at on the streets, the object of scorn and vitriol in phone-ins and editorials. Even Cabinet ministers courted favour by saying how alien and divisive Islamic dress was. And that's how she felt on her journey, alien and divisive when she noticed other passengers sitting anywhere else in the carriage other than near her. She had four seats to herself.

Such hostility reassured her. It was the *test*, part of the *affliction* that Allah had promised. She always responded by uttering the prayer He'd provided: *To Allah we belong and to Him we return.* She was not only doing what Allah had asked, she was increasingly shutting herself off from a world inexplicably callous and brutal.

After the night in Sefton Park the child in her womb had meant nothing to her. She was too grief-stricken, too traumatized, too defiled. She just wanted to die. But as the long days and nights passed her by and she lay motionless and silent in her darkened room, she increasingly realised that she was not alone. She had initially ignored the rising commotion inside her, then resented it, and at one point detested it. But she could not prevent herself from getting curious about it. Loneliness and despair caved in. This *thing* inside her was the living embodiment of the only man she had ever loved. This *thing* might even look like him. She began speaking to her baby; she began preparing for the birth: attending ante natal classes, converting a spare room into a nursery, standing for hours in her local library flicking through the myriads of books on birth and childcare. Then one morning, less than a week before she was due to deliver, she could feel no movement. She could have enquired of her surgeon father but she chose to ring her elderly GP, Dr Abdi, one of the few Muslim women doctors established in the north. Dr Abdi reassured her that it was quite normal that babies so large and heavy in this advanced stage of pregnancy often relax before the big occasion! 'But come in anyway,' she told her. Before examining her, Dr Abdi checked her charts to reassure Samira (and herself). The scans and all the other tests confirmed there were no high risk factors or abnormalities. Considering what Samira had endured, it looked as perfect a pregnancy as they might have hoped for. But when the doctor placed the sonicaid on Samira's abdomen, neither of them could hear the fetal heartbeat. The display screen registered nothing. Samira stared into Dr Abdi's expressionless face, straining to read what she herself was now feeling. But Dr Abdi was a traditionalist; had never really taken to the sonicaid; had always believed it was likely to let her down when her own ears would not. She opened one of her drawers and lifted out an old Pinard stethoscope. Samira later recalled the daylight sun's rays brilliantly reflecting off its beautifully varnished beechwood. Was this not just a reflection of sunshine but also a ray of hope? Maybe. Dr Abdi lightly massaged and manipulated Samira's abdomen. She positioned the Pinard and bent over so that Samira could not see her face. Samira watched the crown of her doctor's head moving around her abdomen. Then it was over. Dr Abdi's face remained expressionless but her eyes spoke volumes. She regretted reassuring Samira before examining her. Now she had to subject her to the ghastly ritual of hospital tests to prove what both of them already knew. And worse, Samira would have to carry the corpse for a few days longer, meet smiling friends and relatives in the street, unable to tell them that her priceless baby had become nothing more than a burdensome lump.

Neither her surgeon father nor her GP could convince Samira that her unborn child may have died from any one of a number of causes. For her there was only one cause: that summer's evening in Sefton Park, during which she had joyously flaunted her beauty and her happiness. She cared not what anyone said, or what anyone might do. She was so distraught that she didn't even hear the request being made of her for a post-mortem. And even if she had heard, she couldn't have cared. Her father consented on her behalf in the expectation that the much heralded Professor van Hoofdaaker could demonstrate some congenital failure that had nothing to do with her husband's murder. Muslim clergy had assured him that Islam did not demand the usual speedy burial for a stillbirth.

Months later, it was her father who first mentioned that the body had not been returned. He had already enquired and protested and got nowhere. He mentioned it to Samira in an attempt to stimulate her, motivate her, anger her; anything to shake her out of an apparent hopelessness and torpor. It was easier than he had anticipated. She had become obsessed with the fact that she never set eyes on the lifeless face of her stillborn son. She had become laden down with guilt because she had refused to look at him. Now she needed to look at him before burying him.

Neither Samira nor her father could have realised how difficult that would be; it took eighteen months for the hospital to release the body. Samira stared at the sickly grey corpse in horror. Her father had warned it would not be a cuddly infant child that she would want to lift and caress. But even he, who had spent half his professional life piecing together bits of bodies in the hell hole of Mogadishu's Hayat hospital, was stunned. He saw instantly the incisions that had been made. He knew the eyes had been removed and some padding substituted. When he shepherded his distraught daughter to another room, he fetched a pair of latex gloves and returned. He manoeuvred his gloved hands around the body, confirming what he suspected. Virtually every organ had been removed. It was a poorly stuffed skin they were about to bury.

That was six years ago, six futile years of complaint and enquiry, with letters from her father, from her GP and her MP, and herself, begging them, pleading with them, weeping over the phone, threatening them; and all these attempts to have the organs returned to complete the burial, thwarted by indifference, and arrogance, and obfuscation. She had tried many times before to do precisely what she was doing now this day, but her nerve had always given way, and she had slunk back to her home again, to the darkened room, to despise herself even more.

She had seldom ventured out, and she had not seen Liverpool's seething city centre for years. She felt she might collapse or disintegrate if these armed uniformed men, hostile and suspicious, confronted her and demanded she remove her veil. And why shouldn't they so demand? Islamic terrorists in bus and railway stations and airports up and down the country had for years made fools of Britain's police and security personnel by enrobing themselves in burqas or niqab veils and walking on by. But no more. She knew that these cops in Lime street, like their counterparts elsewhere, now perceived female Muslim dress differently. Every burqa or nicab or chador was a potentially escaping suspect or suicidal maniac strapped up with two kilos of nail-bomb. Their eyes had immediately latched onto her as she emerged from the platform. As she got near them they stared into her beautiful fear-laden eyes and she couldn't stare back at them; she just hoped that her poise and her movements would convince them that she was no terrorist.

She sighed with relief as she reached the nearest exit and ran down the station's filthy gum-strewn steps. Strong currents of wind rushed in beneath her baggy jilbaab, swelling and contracting it in different places, making her body and her movements look grotesque. But her niqab remained securely fastened.

She had steeled herself for this walk. Walking precluded the possibility of close claustrophobic proximity to anyone in a taxi or a bus. She could just imagine bus passengers and taxi drivers staring at her through cold hostile Islamaphobic eyes.

She turned left and walked along Lime Street for about fifty metres. She reached the junction at Skelhorne Street. She glanced up for approval to cross but the pedestrian lights with the flashing little green man beckoning one to walk towards him in safety had disappeared. There was a new system now, a slower system, with the green and red lights much smaller, and a button at one's fingertips. She stood nervously in the midst of passing throngs, still feelings their eyes riveting in on her. Many of them ignored the lights. She hurriedly joined them.

She stopped at the forecourt of the Adelphi Hotel and opened her map. She was quite a diversion for some passing pedestrians and drivers: a Muslim woman covered from head to toe, standing outside the city's most famous hotel, map-reading. Some couldn't take their eyes off her, probably thinking she was a very rich woman, married to a rich Arab, and both of them staying in the Adelphi's executive suite.

Nearby, the busy junction at Ranelagh Place was in gridlock. Traffic crawled down the steep hills of Brownlow and Mount Pleasant into the junction only to be met by makeshift detours, temporary traffic lights, and heavy trucks and equipment serving the scores of workers who were drilling the roads and laying new drainage. Explanations and apologies for the inconvenience were posted all around. This was a cause worth suffering for: Liverpool European City of Culture 2008. Just forget about it and walk on past the thickening clouds of dust and debris, the deafening noises, traffic going no where yet spewing out filthy noxious substances as drivers inched their way through the mayhem. Just grin and bear it.

But Samira didn't have to. As other pedestrians raised their ineffective hands and cursed and spluttered and spat, her niqab and hijab serenely and securely covered her head, nose and mouth. She hadn't anticipated how appreciative she would feel at this moment towards her precious Islamic dress. She prayed thanks to Allah again.

Half an hour later, without realising it, Samira was walking adjacent to the high wall surrounding the hospital grounds. If she had stepped back from the wall and moved to the pavement's edge, she would have seen the L-shaped four storied building, quintessentially Victorian in its workhouse-like drabness and darkness, in its permanency and indestructibility. This hospital once had an enviable reputation. It saved lives, many children's lives, and the lives of children who would become famous. It saved the life of the *Beatles'* Ringo Starr when he was six years of age and nearly died of peritonitis. The people of Liverpool had loved this hospital. Even its children were its benefactors, donating their pennies through *Auntie Joan's Children's Corner* appeal in the *Evening Express*, paying for additional cot beds and a regular supply of toys. A long time before the hospital was built, there used to be a cemetery here for the children of paupers. Thousands of them were buried here; cholera victims mostly, buried in their own infested clothes, wrapped in a tarred canvas covering. Some locals were convinced that the ghosts of these children occasionally arose from the dead and walked through the hospital grounds. Fortunately nobody told Samira about this.

The wall stopped where the entrance jutted onto the pavement. There were six wide steps leading up to the swinging doors. This was the hardest part, maintaining her poise and control when she walked up the steps, pushed her way through the doors and headed for the part of the building that Professor van Hoofdaaker had annexed as soon as he had arrived. She held her head high and walked past the busy main reception area. On her left was an arched corridor. A sign with an arrow read: Fetal and Infant Pathology. She trembled as she glanced at it but she didn't hesitate. Within seconds she was hurrying down the long corridor rehearsing for the hundredth time what she would say to him and wondering what he might say or do in return. Then a slow dawning realisation came to her: this didn't look like the corridor of a busy hospital. It was stacked on one side with coloured storage containers of some kind. What were they stacked there for, she wondered, leaving barely enough space for stretchers and trolleys? At the end of the corridor there were breaches in the stacks of containers around two doorways, one marked Reception and the other Professor Dick van Hoofdaaker: Department of Fetal and Infant Pathology.

Samira's heart pounded. She dried her sweaty palms beneath her baggy biljaab and repeatedly moistened her dried lips. But she would not turn back now.

Without knocking, she opened van Hoofdaaker's office door with one hand; her other hand remained sunk deep in her biljaab. She had rehearsed this moment many times, willing herself to move briskly, confidently, determinedly, and then to confront him. As she opened the door, she noticed the same coloured and same shaped containers stacked high to the ceiling inside the office. She opened the door wide and walked further on in. She came to a sudden halt, a look of horror spreading over her hidden face. She did not immediately see van Hoofdaaker. He was there all right, slouched on his huge swivel chair, but he was totally blocked from her view by the body of someone else, a woman with her back to Samira, wearing a white medical coat. She was stretched across the top of van Hoofdaaker's desk, leaning on one elbow at one end of the desk, and both her naked legs dangling casually over the other end. One high heel shoe clung precariously to her foot; another lay on the floor below.

Chapter 30

'Idiots!' said Mike, banging the desk with his fist, but not that loudly nor with much conviction. He didn't do *anger* easily, although his neck was red and warm around his starched collar.

Maggie was standing at the other end of his desk watching him reading a letter from Jackson: '*Conference agreed that Martin's problems are fundamentally home-based. These problems have got to be tackled in the home therefore. It means intensive work with the family. Martin will be strictly supervised by Mr O'Neill. Any help the parents need will be provided. The consensus of opinion was that separating Martin from his parents would not be in his best interests…*'

'How many more offences does he have to commit?' he asked rhetorically.

Maggie reckoned that he had heard about her outburst and her walkout, and that these gestures of indignation stemmed from his guilt at not being there to support her. That's what he was supposed to do: accompany team members to case conferences. That was the last thing she would have wanted.

'Where's the new case you mentioned?' she asked, having heard enough.

'What… Oh… Simeons… yes… but don't you want to talk about this; they're sending him home after fifteen… fifteen convictions!'

'I know what they're doing.'

'Do you want me to…?' He didn't know what she wanted him to do. 'No, I suppose it's pointless phoning Jackson.'

Maggie looked at him blankly realising there was yet more to endure. She could see him struggling to think of something ingratiating to say.

'He'll be back in court in a week I bet,' he said, re-reading the letter. Then he put it down. 'Right… that Simeons case…' He opened the file and flicked through what looked like no more than half a dozen pages. 'Carla Simeons, two years probation for assaulting two police officers trying to arrest her. She's had a string of convictions...' He hesitated, and looked up at her. 'Em sorry Maggie... we never did have a chat about the McDonald case, did we? You remember... that day you said you wanted to discuss it with me... we never did discuss it, did we?'

The frustration swelled within her; she bit her lip and her fingers clenched, but she could not hold back: 'Oh for God's sake forget about it Mike! That was months ago. It isn't important anymore'

He pressed further back in his swivel chair. He was hurt and perplexed.

'Sorry,' she said, holding up her hands.

'It's okay.'

She took the file from his desk.

She returned to her own desk and tried to read through the Simeons case. She couldn't concentrate. She thought of the irony of asking Mike her supervisor to forget about the McDonald case, and her lie: *it isn't important any more*. She closed the Simeons case file and stared at the opposite wall, just as she had done that day when Mike phoned her to tell her that O'Neill, the 'Irish oddball' was taking over.

She knew much more about the McDonald case than anyone else. She wasn't absolutely certain about the role of Mr Greer, but she knew exactly the nature of the crimes being committed against Martin.

Her first contact with Mrs Greer had followed her usual formal letter: 'As you know, your son Martin... etc. etc. I should like to call on Monday next, 7.30. Please phone or write if that isn't convenient.'

Mrs Greer had made her feel welcome. 'I'm so glad you called Mrs Lynch.'

Martin and Mr Greer were there. Martin said nothing. He sat on a wooden chair in isolation from Mr and Mrs Greer. Mrs Greer launched into a tirade against him. Martin still said nothing. It was obvious to Maggie that he was incapable of saying anything. Maggie herself did not have much success in being heard. She tried interrupting on a number of occasions but to no avail. Then she noticed a change of tone. Mrs Greer's anger was replaced by scorn. Mr Greer joined in. Maggie watched in revulsion yet unable to comprehend. Their ridicule of Martin was not spontaneous. It seemed and felt contrived, systematic, and devastating in its effect.

She went back to the home again, hoping that what she had witnessed was an aberration. But she saw it all again. She spoke to Martin alone against the *advice* of Mrs Greer. Then she spoke to them together. Mrs Greer remained so nice to her, so friendly, so grateful for all she was doing for her son, and Maggie knew she was doing nothing for her son, because Mrs Greer was mad, yet with that peculiar impregnable lucidity of madness. She was systematically and intentionally tormenting her son, ostensibly welcoming every bit of advice Maggie could offer, yet sabotaging every effort Maggie made on Martin's behalf.

'Has he never had any interest in girls?' she once asked Mrs Greer. A similar question to Martin himself produced that crippling tension she was getting so used to.

'No Mrs Lynch; it's strange. Isn't it? I wouldn't stop him if he wanted to go out with girls.'

'Have you ever seen him talking to girls… at school… or in the street?'

'No I haven't, come to think of it.'

There was something wrong in the way she was looking at Maggie; a rigidity in the pupils of her eyes and a strain in her lips.

'Unusual, isn't it?' asked Maggie, watching, wondering, full of uncertainty.

'I suppose it is. Why do you think he has no interest in girls, Mrs Lynch,' she unexpectedly asked. Her stare was less intense; her lips a little more relaxed.

'I don't know. I was hoping you might know.' Her gentle probing was getting nowhere. She sensed she was being played with. 'Some kids become sexually aware more quickly than others… for different reasons.'

Mrs Greer looked at her for a few seconds before responding: 'The teacher says his behaviour is very good. They've never made any complaints.'

'Complaint about what?' Maggie asked, frowning with perplexity. 'What's behaviour got to do with him becoming sexually aware?'

'I don't know Mrs Lynch; all I know is that I've tried to bring him up decent-like; it breaks my heart to see him get into trouble like this.'

Maggie despaired. She attempted to explore the matter with Martin himself in her own office. He remained silent. She thought at first he knew nothing about sex. She later thought, just like O'Neill, that he knew a great deal about sex, that he was being buggered and bribed and blackmailed by Mr Greer. She tried to gain his trust and confidence; to reassure him that it would be safe to disclose what was being done to him. Then she realised the futility of trying to assure him about anything. Like all the other professionals she couldn't even communicate with him.

She tried talking to Mrs Greer about this *development* thing. She even dared to explore with her the possibility that Martin was being sexually abused by Michael Greer. It was a moment that Maggie would never forget, the look in Mrs Greer's eyes, making Maggie feel that she was going to be laughed off the face of the earth! It was that same sickening moment that the truth dawned.

She traced the origins of Mrs Greer with much difficulty. Marian Greer had previously been married to Dez McDonald. She discovered his whereabouts through the courts. She visited him more than a hundred miles away, in her own time at her own expense. For some reason, the sight of an alcoholic in a doss house was not unexpected; her initial reaction was that here was someone who may have at least put up a fight. He was suspicious of her, thinking she was a local fraud inspector. She eventually convinced him that she was only there to try to help his son. He cried.

She asked him about the marriage.

'She was a nutter!'

'Maybe she thought that of you.'

'Oh no… I didin need to be a nutter; just weak, too weak… not able to cope wi' er. A was scared of er. It wiz them eyes of ers. They gimmee the creeps! They looked as like they're sneerin at ye. Maybe a imagine it now, but the first time I met er, I had this feelin, you know… that she was all over me and through me like… an there was nothing a could do about it.'

Maggie asked him what he knew about her background.

'Don't know anythink. She told me nothink. A wasn't interested anyway.'

She was going to ask him about Martin when he said casually: 'A know she was in a home once.'

'A children's home?'

He nodded, unaware of the significance of what he'd just said. If it was true she would have no difficulty in finding the *home*.

'How did you know that?' she asked.

'A saw the name of the home engraved on a fork she had. She mustave pinched it. She blew er top when a mentioned it; snapped it outta ma hand... A thought she's gonna ram it through me.'

'How do you know she just didn't work there?'

'Cause a mentioned it again. It was somethink she hated to be reminded about.'

Maggie smiled quizzically: 'And so you mentioned it to her lots of times? Can you remember the name of the home?'

'St Joseph's.'

'The town... the address?'

'A don't think that was on it.'

She asked him about Martin. He fell silent as though a great black shutter had been drawn between them. She saw tears swell in his eyes. He sobbed pathetically.

'A went to social workers. A went to the NSPCC. All they wanted to do was interrogate me an prove a was lying. They said a had drink problem.'

She imagined his predicament: needing the drink to tell them something that cast all kinds of aspersions on him. She had to ask him: 'what was it you told them?'

Unexpectedly he held his head high: 'A told em she was screwing Martin.'

'Why didn't you prevent it yourself?'

'Cause she denied it. An Martin denied it. An I niver had proof. A niver realised till it was too late... she could do whatever she want with Martin; the only thing Martin dared say about er was ee loved er... fucking wench!'

'Did you ever see her abusing Martin?'

'No... but this is the thing... ye won't believe me... but's it true... she wanted me to see er screwing im.'

Maggie was not as shocked as he had anticipated.

'She'd start as if she was gonna screw im... snugglin up to im, putting an arm around im. An she'd be watchin me like a hawk to see how a was gonna react. A went beserk, an she'd laugh at me, sayin a must be crazy thinkin she'd ever do somethink like that. An the weirdest thing of all, she'd get Martin to deny it and laugh at me too. A thought a must be goin crazy... a niver believed that kind o thing could happen; a thought a was getting obsessed or somethink. But a know now... she was just testin me. She would've bin cockahoop if a'd let er screw Martin and watched er doin it. She would've had me as well then, known a daren't mention it to anyone. She would've had me both ways: a niver saw anythink an a cud say nothink; an if a saw anythink, a was as guilty as er. Who was goin to believe me anyway, sayin ma wife was screwin ma son? Social Services an the NSPCC didin believe me. One of the bastards tried to git me to admit it was me who was screwin im all along! "Mothers don't do that kind o think," he said, "an there's plenty a fathers doin it who'll blame anybody but themselves".'

Maggie believed him, and he knew she believed him. Why didn't he just kill Marian Greer? she asked herself. Or at least, just walk away sooner?

Then she thought of Mr Greer. She could see both men on either side of the woman who trapped and defeated them. And there was something else in her mind, some haphazard words and phrases from a distant past in her own life trying to fall into place. She focused on the words and forgot about the men. Eventually she could see the words and hear them: *That he who knowing what is right doth it not, should lose the knowledge of what is right*, and she realised that the words and the men were one and the same thing. Worse than that, she knew she had an affinity with both men.

She couldn't stand this thought. She must tell Mike now. She got up and walked out of her office, down the corridor past Judy the receptionist. Usually there was a word, a smile, a gesture exchanged. But not on this occasion. She walked past the board on which staff signed themselves in and out. She never looked at it. But a few minutes later, having slowly returned from Mike's locked office, she was staring at the board and reading that he had gone out for the remainder of the day.

Judy stared at her. She knew there was something wrong. Too serious obviously to intrude. Maggie walked back to her office.

Her phone rang. Judy spoke: 'Maggie, it's Dr Millwize… can you take it?'

Maggie tensed. Her momentary pause made Judy think she might not take it. 'Maggie… are you okay?'

'Yes I'm okay; I'll take it.'

'Good morning Mrs Lynch. That case conference on the McDonald boy… there was something awfully familiar about his mother and I couldn't trace what it was. But I've managed too now and I thought I'd better let you know…'

'Oh… I'm not involved now doctor.' Her face turned ashen; her head felt light, her heart leaden. She had rushed to her boss's office to unburden herself of a terrible guilt; now she knew not only that she would need to carry that burden a little longer, but that she must take on another.

'I know, but you've worked with her longer than anyone else. I did phone Mr O'Neill the social worker but he's not there; I thought you should both know that the boy's mother was once a patient of mine.'

'Was she?'

'Yes she was I'm afraid. I was convinced it was the same woman we were talking about, but that maiden name she gave you, Phillips, that confused me. I suspect she uses aliases like that when anybody asks about her past.'

Maggie bowed her head.

'As I was saying Mrs Lynch…'

Chapter 31

O'Neill stopped the car on the busy A580, between Kirby and St Helen's, about a mile from Knowsley Safari Park. It was a misty morning, with the sun certain to break through later in the day. He had just come from Hollybank, with Martin and Sa'eed in the back seat, chatting to each other. Sa'eed had deftly manoeuvred the chat onto sport, and then athletics, and then discus throwing. Martin quickly warmed to the black stranger who seemed to know a lot about field sports. He proudly showed Sa'eed the little plaque he had been awarded for successfully completing the army obstacle course. Sa'eed and O'Neill made a big deal of it.

'Will this do?' O'Neill asked Martin.

Martin nodded and smiled. There was brightness in his eyes, a combination of excitement and apprehension. O'Neill kept looking at him waiting for the reply. He always insisted on Martin replying to any question asked, and he would ask Martin to repeat it if what he said wasn't clear or assertive enough.

They got out of the car and O'Neill opened a large map of the city. He placed it on the bonnet. The strong south westerly winds blowing over the exposed A580 threatened to rip the map apart; all three men had to use both hands to secure it. Martin's huge hands held down the Northwest and Southwest of the city. 'Does this make sense Martin,' O'Neill asked him.

He glanced at the map. 'A think so.'

'Can you point to where we are now?' Sa'eed asked him.

Martin stared hard and long at the map, looked up in the direction of the city, looked back in the direction they had come from. He was confident enough but he hadn't yet learnt how to use a map.

'We're on the A580,' O'Neill said. 'We're driving into Liverpool. Back there is St Helen's. I want you find the A580 on the map.'

He found it quickly and was pleased with himself.

'Well done Martin,' said Sa'eed.

Martin traced the road in both directions with his finger, spending more time in exploring its path into Liverpool city centre. Sa'eed asked him to pause a number of times and to read out significant landmarks. He told Martin to encircle them on the map and write them down on a notebook which he handed him. O'Neill then asked him had he any idea of where his home was on the map.

Martin again ran his finger along the A580. The finger stopped on names he recognised. He didn't speak. O'Neill asked him to say what their names were.

'Kirby… Gilmoss… Aintree… Fazakerley…'

'Fa… what?' O'Neill asked smiling and feigning surprise.

'Fazakerley…' Martin repeated, sharing the joke with O'Neill; 'Big hospital there,' he said. 'Walton… there's a prison there… There's Bootle…' His finger followed the Mersey coast, northwest. 'Crosby… Great Crosby… It's around here… Lawrence Street… There it is, Lawrence Grove.'

'Well done. Do you think you could walk it?'

Martin looked at O'Neill wondering was he serious. Then he looked at Sa'eed, to see if this was a joke they were both sharing at his expense. But Sa'eed looked just as serious as the tone of O'Neill suggested, and he glanced at Martin with raised eyebrows as if to say 'well… could you?'

Martin gazed in the direction of the city. It seemed far far away, maybe a million miles away, a million miles of the unknown. He had never experienced this freedom and respect before. He smiled embarrassingly, his tongue darting over his lips. Then the pleasure of the prospect suddenly left him, and he frowned. 'My mum…'

'It's okay Martin. I told her this morning that you might be walking home.'

'What did she say?'

'She said it was okay, as long as you think you can do it, and you have a mobile phone.'

'I haven't.'

'Yes you have.' O'Neill produced two mobiles from his pocket.

'I can't…' Martin stuttered, unable to say he didn't know how to use one.

'You can't what?'

Martin said nothing, as if he had suddenly changed his mind, either that he *could* use a mobile, or at least wanted to learn.

O'Neill handed him one and showed him how. Then he and Sa'eed tested him. Within five minutes, the three of them were standing a few yards away from each other on a busy trunk road talking nonsense into their phones. Occasionally Martin could not contain himself and burst out laughing.

'So keep it on,' said O'Neill. 'Ring us if you need to. Keep it in the *locked* position when you're walking just in case you make a call accidentally. Okay?'

'Okay,' he said, still unable to stop grinning.

O'Neill said: 'I think it'll take you three hours to walk that distance.'

'I think he could do it in less,' Sa'eed said.

'Let's have a bet,' said O'Neill; 'I bet you £10 you can't do it in three hours.'

'And I bet £10 you can,' said Sa'eed.

Martin felt overwhelmed. He burst out laughing again, no longer able to withstand the pleasurable tension gripping him; the realisation that these men were 'playing' with him; but a different kind of play; unlike the degrading and cruel baiting he endured so often at the hands of his parents.

'It's easy,' he said. Then he smiled embarrassingly and licked his lips. Three hours on his own. A mobile in his pocket. Nobody to bother, bully or humiliate him.

O'Neill gave him the map. He and Sa'eed got into the car and moved off. They both raised a hand and made a gesture to Martin, something between a wave and a salute. They watched him for as long as they could in the car's rear and wing mirrors. They could see him still grinning. They both felt assured watching the huge strides that they knew would probably get him home in much less than three hours.

O'Neill had lied to Martin and to his mother. He had told Mrs Greer that Martin would be making his own way home… by bus! She wanted to collect him, but O'Neill insisted: Martin was going to have to become more independent, more savvy about the world, move about more freely, stand on his own two feet.

Mrs Greer had begged O'Neill not to allow her son to make such a dangerous journey; she said he had never done anything like that before. All the more reason, O'Neill told her, that he should be trying it now. O'Neill had left her in a state which he knew could deteriorate into panic as the hours went by.

As they drove further away from Martin, Sa'eed turned to O'Neill: 'Why the risk-taking?'

O'Neill thought for a moment, genuinely puzzled. 'You call that risk-taking?'

'For *you*,' he stressed.

'I can live with it. That's what social work used to be about, risk-taking. Now it's taboo. Nobody takes risks anymore. Shit scared. Morgan will probably find out about it in six months time and it'll be too late for him to complain.'

'But Martin's mother will find out tonight; how does that make it easy for you to work with her later?'

'Good point Sa'eed. I'll tell her more lies to explain why Martin didn't after all get a bus. But she's got to understand that she ain't alone anymore; she hasn't got Martin all to herself; big Brother's watching… that's me. That's the bottom line. She's got to face that. This'll be painful for her today but it'll help in the days ahead. There's going to be a lot of pain in this case.'

Sa'eed pondered for a while. He thought it was the most pompous and immoral utterance he had heard from O'Neill. And he had heard plenty of them.

O'Neill drove to the first roundabout and straight on towards the city centre. He turned left into a cul de sac, drove to the end of it, reversed and then parked his Volkswagen behind a BMW. They could clearly see through the windscreens of both cars, looking out onto the A580. They calculated that Martin was about three quarters of a mile from where they had left him.

Martin soon came by. He glanced along the cul de sac without slowing. When he had passed, O'Neill and Sa'eed got out of the car and hurried to the main road. They gazed at the massive upright striding figure of Martin distancing himself from them second by second.

O'Neill's memory drifted back to that moment in Martin's bedroom when his mother tried to prevent him seeing the discus. He gazed after Martin, imagining him throwing a discus. He had never watched a discus thrower before, and now he wanted to watch Martin. He imagined what he would be like. He imagined it would be worth seeing. Sa'eed and he returned to the car and sat for another ten minutes.

Martin soon approached a main junction. To the right, was Kirby; to the left, Knowsley. He looked left and right a number of times, and was tempted to try them. Why not, he felt he could go anywhere now; nobody to stop him. He walked on and then slowed at the next junction, where the A580 met with the A5208. He stared at a hotel situated at the junction, at the big fancy cars in the car park, at the landscaped front, at the guests coming and going. He looked up at the bedrooms and wondered how rich the guests were.

He walked under the M57. The roar of motorway traffic above and its echoing below frightened him and made him run. When he emerged at the other side he slowed and looked back. He acknowledged to himself that his fear had been groundless; the M57 was not about to collapse onto the A5208.

The sun shone gloriously now. There was a forecast of rain for late evening, but the blue and grey clouds nestling around the distant Welsh hills seemed as static as the coastline itself. O'Neill and Sa'eed had moved forward to the hotel that had attracted Martin's attention. They had watched with binoculars from a quarter of a mile back. Every passing vehicle had fleetingly blocked Martin from their view and then he would reappear again, striding on. O'Neill lowered the binoculars and just stared after him. 'That's enough,' he said… we'll leave him now.' They turned round and walked back to the car. Sa'eed could sense O'Neill's underlying anxiety.

They drove out of a side entrance to the hotel. They went to see some of O'Neill's other clients. Sa'eed realised O'Neill wasn't concentrating; that he was still anxious. 'You could always phone him,' he said.

Half an hour later O'Neill did phone Martin and felt bad about doing so.

'I'm sorry, but the person you called is not available.'

'Fuck! He's turned off!' O'Neill frowned then smiled. He looked at Sa'eed. They were both thinking the same: did Martin really deliberately turn the phone off? There was something impressive about that: sheer bloody defiance, cutting himself off from the world, controlling his own world. But it made O'Neill even more anxious.

They drove back to the route. They calculated that Martin should be approaching Walton Hall Park or thereabouts. O'Neill parked the car in Barnsbury Road opposite the park. They walked back onto the A580 and kept looking in both directions. There was no sign of him. An ambulance came racing past, lights flashing, siren screeching, cars on either side of the road doing their good citizens' best to get out of its way. A thought came to O'Neill's mind: how Morgan and his team would gloat if anything happened to Martin. What an asshole! *Making a fifteen year old 'retarded' child on a court residency Order walk the dangerous walk from one end of Liverpool to the other.*

They returned to the car and drove back onto the main road. They drove as far back as the M57. They circled the roundabout and returned towards the city. Perhaps they had missed him, they both conjectured, going into a shop. But there were no shops around. Perhaps a passing lorry had blocked their view. But it was hardly likely that it be blocked again and again by lorry after lorry just as they were passing Martin! They turned off the main road and stopped. O'Neill couldn't think clearly. He knew that if anything untoward had happened to Martin, he was in big trouble. Of all the blunders he had made, the one that would ensure he was sacked was lying to Marian Greer that her son would be returning safely by bus!

It was nearly six o'clock and they had spent more than two hours searching. A thick blanket of cloud had descended. It was darkening fast. They drove to Lawrence Grove. Sa'eed glanced all around him, surprised by the relative prosperity of the area.

O'Neill tried to psyche himself up to face Mrs Greer. He stopped the car outside number fifty-five and looked at the house. He felt strangely curious as well as apprehensive. They walked up the garden path. O'Neill reached for the bell and pressed firmly. Dull muffled footsteps could be heard hurrying towards him.

Mrs Greer opened the hall door and saw the vague outline of their two figures through the heavily leaded glass of the front door. The one behind O'Neill looked like Martin, taller and broader than O'Neill. She sighed with relief. But when she grabbed the knob and flung open the door, she stared horrified into the eyes of Sa'eed.

She stood before them, unrecognisable. She wore black. Her black hair had been brought to life again, shining, flowing, almost reaching her large white breasts, exposed outrageously in a black satin shift. She wore a necklace that sparkled, and ruby ear-rings that danced discordantly with the movement of her hair. Double bracelets jangled on her wrists. The street lamp some yards away cast light upon the red moist lipstick she wore, making her lips sensual and ugly. Her beautiful eyes were full of fear and hatred because her beloved son was not there, and the social worker responsible, was.

O'Neill's countenance changed dramatically. His face had a deathly pallor, and his lips appeared to quiver. 'Hello... isn't he... back yet?' he stuttered. It was all he could manage.

She didn't reply. She stared at him, her eyes going through him. He felt as if she knew him, knew what he was and what he was doing.

'Don't worry,' he said, unconvincingly; 'He'll be here soon.'

'He better,' she said, slamming the door in his face.

They retreated down the garden path. O'Neill was still shell-shocked. Sa'eed noticed neighbours opposite staring at them and then slowly releasing the curtains from their finger tips. It was as if neighbours didn't care whether or not the two men saw them staring; as if... like Maggie, they could have told O'Neill, months ago.

Chapter 32

Martin was relieved to be out of Hollybank. He was desperately in need of his mother. He knew what would happen when he got home, but he still helplessly needed to be with her. Hollybank had been a claustrophobic, humiliating hole.

There were some who had really enjoyed making life hell for him: Niggy, Bowlsie and Hutchinson. They didn't know they were making life hell for him. He'd thought about it often, and decided they were too thick to know. There was one time when they went too far though; it was in the gardens of Hollybank; they just laughed and laughed at him. He couldn't escape. He didn't know what to say. That was always his problem, not knowing what to say; too choked with embarrassment to be able to say anything. It was in that garden that he felt this urge to lift the spade and smash the skull of Bowlsie. When he thought about it afterwards, he had trembled, knowing that if Mr Pender had not called them in, he wouldn't have been able to stop himself and he would have been charged with murder and locked away.

But he wasn't thinking unpleasant things like that now. His pace slackened and he raised a hand to his inside pocket. A sense of pride swept over him as he fingered his trophy. He'd spent hours polishing it, and he smiled to himself when he thought of the impact it had made on O'Neill and Sa'eed. He wondered how his mother would react. He wasn't sure.

Walton Hall Park was the first indication for Martin that Sa'eed would win ten pounds and that O'Neill would lose: he was away ahead of schedule. That's why he went into the park, walked around, and found the boating lake at the far end of it. He sat on a small jetty watching noiseless tiny ripples of water stirred by a gentle breeze. He took the mobile from his pocket and scrutinised it. It looked ancient in comparison to the models his schoolmates used. Maybe this one had been used for many years. But he was grateful nonetheless. He unlocked it and began exploring. He was intrigued by the contents of the menu. He dipped in and out, *Messages, Contacts, Call register, Settings.* Some of it made sense, some of it didn't. He phoned his home, and beamed all over as he waited for his mother to lift the phone. But a bolt of terror suddenly went through him. He dabbed his index finger violently, in panic, seeking out the *off* key. He hit every key. He got it! It was off! He sighed. It was a near escape, a lightening realisation that his mother would have gone berserk on hearing his voice on a mobile phone as he walked a distance of fifteen miles from far beyond the boundary of the city. And when she got him home she would have exacted a terrible revenge, as she did often.

He left the park feeling despondent. The city centre still seemed far away but who cared? It was increasingly within his sight and his ability. He was on the main road again, passing tiny Ivernia Road, Saxonia Road and Lusitania Road. What did those names mean, he wondered, and why were they called Roads, when they were so narrow and short, less than a hundred meters long?

He made his way down Walton Lane, and came onto another park with lakes, Stanley Park. But he'd seen one park already and this one didn't look much different, and he didn't fancy wasting precious time… the clock was ticking.

He reached Anfield Road. Anfield…? Was this the famous Anfield? He'd never been to a match in Anfield. He just had to go down here, drab decaying Anfield Road, bordering Stanley Park on the left, and a host of tiny streets and terraces on the right. So where is it? he asked. There! The mighty Anfield. The Cop! He literally stumbled onto it; he'd expected a huge drive leading up to it. What a disappointment! Old rusting wrought iron gates with the legendary *You'll Never Walk Alone* barely decipherable on the semi-circle top of them. A lone statue of the great Bill Shankly stood outside the empty Anfield shop. He walked right round the stadium. A few flags were fluttering from the sunken roofs of a main building so ugly and dark. It never looked as awful as this when news cameras filmed thousands of supporters queuing to get into it or streaming out of it. To think that inside this place, Gerrard and Carragher and

Torres and Kuit mesmerised their fans… they too were athletes like him, making poetry out of motion on grass. He idolised them but his mother detested him watching them. And he never watched them in the company of others; the rituals and the exuberance of fans terrified him.

He left Anfield and backtracked because he was uncertain of where Anfield Road would lead him. He went down St Domingo's Road right through the heart of Everton. Its grounds and shops looked just that little bit more up-market than Anfield. But he never did support the Blues and so he didn't hang around. He got to the end of Everton Road and his instincts told him to turn right into Brunswick Road. He sensed that he couldn't get lost now, that every road was descending into the city centre with the tips of many of its tallest landmarks clearly visible. He was aware that he was deviating from the route wildly now, but he didn't care.

A motor cycle dealers caught his attention. He crossed the road. There were more bikes on the pavement than in the showroom. They were all new and gleaming. He hesitated, wondering was there any risk in walking up and down the many rows to browse over these magnificent machines. He gazed at the names, some of which he was familiar with, Suzuki, Yamaha, Triumph, Norton, and names he had never heard of, Veli King, KTM, Adley. Some of them looked monstrous, others grotesque. Three youths arrived and made a bee line to a bike raised on a platform inside the showroom. It was a dazzling violet-blue, imperious-like, well spaced from lesser models around it. Martin moved closer to the entrance, as inquisitive about the youths as he was about the focus of their attention. They couldn't be any more than two or three years older than himself. *The New Kawazaki Concours 14e*, a notice read. He knew nothing about bikes but he could see this was something special. He could see the myriads of reflections of the youths in its gleaming chrome and metallic paint as they walked around it, their eyes riveted, their mouths opened. They recited to each other various specifications below the title: 1352CC, 4-Stroke, Injection DFI, Inverted telescopic fork, Tetra Lever… They 'phewed' and 'ahhhhed' and 'emmd' endlessly. He didn't know what they were talking about, except that they coveted it. So did he. He felt this desire creeping over him to mount it, to switch ignition, to throttle and to roar back up the road he'd come down, on out past the spot where O'Neill and Sa'eed had left him to walk, and further on past that hole Hollybank where he would keep the horn blaring and the speedometer needle would be touching 200mph. Those thoughts excited him.

He walked further on into the city centre, down Islington, Lime Street, St George's Place, St John's Lane. He gazed in all directions. He'd been in this area before. He didn't remember when but he was certain of it. And he knew the bus route home. But he had no intention of getting the bus.

He read on a small marble monument:

HERE FELL POLICE CONSTABLE MORTIMER,
15th July 2007

He slowed then stopped. It looked rather incongruous here standing outside a shop front. It was almost new with a shiny mauve surface. At the top it had the crest of Merseyside Police. It said nothing else. He stared at it and pondered. Then he remembered. It was that night when Sergeant Mortimer signalled a car to stop and enquired of a driver for some identification. The driver put his hand in his pocket, pulled a revolver and shot the sergeant in the head and face. It was only about a year ago. It wasn't pleasant; yet he dwelt on it for a long time, imagining the incident second by second, and the sergeant collapsing in a pool of blood.

He passed an Adult shop and strained to keep his eyes on voluptuous half naked women as he pretended not to be looking at them at all. He felt differently about these women to the way he felt about his mother. He wanted to stop here, but he was driven on by embarrassment and fear; the fear of someone noticing him and his mother finding out.

He walked on and soon found himself in a downtown market. It seemed bedlam here, a vitality, colour, language and laughter that normally would have frightened him. But he wandered on in through the stalls. He tried to avoid stall keepers catching his eye, or, worse than that, saying something to him. But so many stall keepers caught his eye and spoke to him and tried to sell him this and that, that he got used to it. He even laughed at it. By the time he was leaving the market, he was confidently shaking his head and repeatedly saying 'no thanks.'

He was wandering aimlessly now. He turned into a narrow darkened alley. It widened considerably at the end where there seemed to be much space and light. He looked back, apprehensive about straying too far and getting home late. He knew he was never going to get back home in three hours now. O'Neill would win the bet.

He hurried on down the alleyway, which opened onto a redeveloped part of the city. In the centre, there was a huge glass-domed building, still reflecting the fading light of the day. He stopped and stared at it. Then he smiled as he recognised it: Liverpool's newest sport's centre. He ran to the entrance. It was one pound to get in; three pounds to swim; four pounds to weight train. He didn't know what to do. His heart was pounding. He paid only to get in. He clutched his purple ticket, and pushed his way through the turnstile, relieved that the receptionist did not speak to him.

He followed the directions leading to the visitor's balcony, and gazed down on an international-sized swimming pool. It was the largest swimming pool he'd ever seen. It wasn't full by any means, but there were enough people there, mostly young people, swimming, jumping, running, diving and yelling to create a noisy and pleasant chaos. He envied them. He wished he could swim like that. He wished he could float like that. He wished he could dive; dive off that board and come up again. He wondered why his mother never wanted him to learn to swim. She always made a fuss and made excuses about how dangerous the water was, and how easy it was to get a chill and pneumonia and to die. He watched necking couples his own age joyously clasping each other, above the water, below the water, watching others watch them, watching others like him envy them. They didn't seem to be in any danger. He breathed heavily. His lips were parched. He became agitated. He thought of his mother again. She'd be angry if she knew what he was doing now; she would say that it was evil and wicked. He couldn't understand.

He moved on. He looked down on brightly lit squash courts. He quickly passed them by. He watched table tennis and badminton in the two halves of the gymnasium. Then he came to the weight training. Mr Barnes, his PT instructor repeatedly told him that he had to do weight training to improve his discus throwing. He knew that but his mother wouldn't let him. He had a near irresistible urge to drop from the balcony and get stuck in. There were three very muscular types already there, sweating, consumed by their weights, their jerks, their sit-ups; they never once looked up at him. He looked at them and felt he could do just as well.

He spent a long time watching them. Too long. It was getting dark and wet outside. He thought about his mother and he thought about O'Neill and Sa'eed. He turned and made his way back to the entrance. He would come back here some day.

Chapter 33

The woman who had been stretched across van Hoofdaaker's desk swung round just as Samira blurted 'sorry', convinced that she had made a terrible mistake. Van Hoofdaaker rose angrily from the desk.

They stared at Samira, both stricken by the intrusion, by her anonymity, her veil, by her beautiful eyes staring back at them. Nobody ever walked into this office without permission; the requisite knock always afforded them time to cease whatever dalliances they may have been indulging in.

'What do you want... who are you?' van Hoofdaaker snapped. Caroline Simms had manoeuvred herself off the desk, and was staring incredulously at the stranger.

Samira glanced at their large coloured identity cards pinned to their opened white coats.

Simms hastily patted and pulled on one side of her misshapen dress underneath. It had lowered significantly on that side as a consequence of the way she had lain across his desk. She seemed also to want to raise her hands to her hair, to restore the cut and smooth out the waves mangled by the hand she had leant on.

Samira barely managed to say: 'I am Samira Jama...'

She realised now that she had *not* made a mistake. This was the right office. This was Professor Dick van Hoofdaaker, the man she needed to confront. She had anticipated gate crashing her way into some kind of grand order, formality and space; and then her audacity to be met by understandable and righteous indignation. But she had never considered stumbling upon a squalid little affair in a hopelessly cluttered office, in which the same ghastly blue and red containers touched the ceiling on every wall. Who was this slut, she asked herself.

She had planned this confrontation on the basis of tumultuously shifting perceptions as to why she had been denied the organs of her still born child. The least critical perception was that it was merely cold heartless bureaucratic delay, and that the people at the centre of it were probably good and hard working doctors simply too busy to know how much she was suffering. But as days turned to weeks and months and years, she no longer viewed them so charitably. Now, as she stared at them through the prism of her veil, she regarded them as sick, sordid and corrupted people. Now she believed that even if they had known what she had endured, they wouldn't have given a damn. They were no better than the thugs who violated her and widowed her. They were worse, they were educated professionals, and they had, through their indifference and their negligence, subjected her to many years of hell.

She was certain that Allah had guided her here today, had given her the strength to do what she was going to do. It wasn't nearly so difficult now as she had predicted. She realised that the crippling fears that had prevented her from doing it before had been rooted in her own ignorance, in her own generosity of spirit, her inability to think so badly of them. Neither of them could see the hand that was still buried in her jilbaab, tightening around her father's cherished Somali dagger.

She charged at van Hoofdaaker and yelled in a voice that she didn't even recognise: 'Where are the organs you removed from my child?'

Van Hoofdaaker's hope that this was merely a hospital cleaner who had lost her way, another of those token weird ethnics who seemed to be popping up in the hospital and university precincts more often than necessary, evaporated. Her charge to within inches of his face disgusted him more than it discomforted him.

'What organs... what are you talking about?'

'His heart... his brain... his lungs... his eyes... where are they?'

She continued staring into his eyes; she could not see that it was Caroline Simms who was visibly shaken by her question.

Van Hoofdaaker barely heard the question. He could only see a half crazed woman in a ridiculous disguise outrageously invading his premises.

'Get out!' he said.

She didn't move. 'Where are my child's organs?' she repeated, knowing he could feel nothing of her pain, vindicating her determination to stay her ground.

'If you don't get out, I'll have you taken out,' he said.

It was her invisibility that disturbed him most. His iron will and his contempt depended so much in looking at faces; looking for cowardice in the eyes, uncertainty around the mouth, the feebleness of bodily gestures. He could see none of that in Samira. But he could sense an unshakeable conviction, and he could see a terrible anger in her eyes.

'I want my child's organs,' she said; 'I gave you his body that you were to return in a few months. You held onto it for eighteen months. You stripped it before you returned it. My father is a surgeon and knows that you removed every organ from it. You've ignored every request I've made, every letter, every phone call, every complaint. I'm not leaving here today without the organs of my child!'

It seemed for a moment that she had penetrated his cool exterior; there was a flicker in his eyes, and he swallowed hard. His lover's grip on the edge of his desk, tightened.

'You cannot barge your way in here demanding organs.'

''My child's organs!'

'Anyone's organs. There is a process.'

'A what?' she yelled at him.

'You must leave… at once,' he said, aware of the rising crescendo of anger, and of his inability to avoid fuelling it.

His lover was more capable, more flexible. She tried to sound sorrowful and meaningful. 'Whatever has happened Mrs… Jama, this is not the way to rectify it… .we can talk about this…'

'No we cannot *talk* about it,' Samira shouted. She hated Simms for trying that; she preferred the honest coldness and the arrogance and the insensitivity of van Hoofdaaker. 'I've talked about it for six years. I've begged you… I've written to you… My GP has written to you… My MP has written to you… I've made complaints about you… and the only thing I've got in return is to hear that people are looking into it! Now do you understand? I'm not interested in talk. I want my child's organs! I want them now! Where are they? What have you done with them?'

A deadly pause followed. Simm's eyes were full of fear. She knew that nothing was going to pacify this woman. For a few seconds it seemed that van Hoofdaaker was feverishly weighing up possible strategies, but then he turned sharply, rushed back to his desk and lifted the phone. He started dialling; he was seething, yet composed enough to maintain his focus on the digits. But as he dialled he could see in the periphery of his vision the looming black shadow descending on him. He could hear it, the uneven rustling sounds of her billowing biljaab. He could somehow feel it, a burden, a threat. It descended fast and menacingly, and when his lover screamed he ceased dialling and glanced up, and a look of terror spread over his face as he saw a magnificently curved dagger raised above his head, its buffalo-horned handle gripped by Samira's two small hands. She lunged the dagger, not swiftly enough to strike him, but terrifyingly enough to make him drop the phone and leap backwards, losing his balance and collapsing into the containers packed eight feet high against the rear wall. Two columns buckled under his weight and the four highest containers came crashing down round him, bursting open with the sound of breaking glass. Large thick jars inside the containers had shattered, and tiny hearts and lungs and livers and brains floated around van Hoofdaaker in a pool of formaldehyde, dense, vaporous, and so pungent it caught his panicky breath, making him cough and splutter. He thought he was doomed, that she was upon him, that the deadly blow was already in flight. He scrambled towards the other side of his desk unable to avoid kneeling on broken glass and syrupy formaldehyde.

But Samira was no where near him. She hadn't moved since her attempt to deliver the initial blow. Simms hadn't moved either, her eyes riveted in terror to the floor, unable to cry out, unable to run. Van Hoofdaaker looked up as he scrambled, relieved and astonished that she had not finished the job. Then he realised why; and realised why he had little to feel relieved about.

Samira stood deadly still, transfixed by the sight of the floating organs. A weird moaning sound came from her trembling lips, unbroken, rising in volume and pitch. She raised her head and looked at the other containers. Then she looked down at van Hoofdaaker, half-hidden and scared, crouching at the other side of his desk. She raised her head again and peered at the containers all round the room. She ran at them, randomly. She pulled two top containers far enough for them to collapse unto the floor, bursting open as the others had done, revealing similar contents. She still held the dagger. She moved to another row, and another, the whole office floor soon awash with tiny organs now floating in a sea of formaldahyde.

Van Hoofdaaker and Simms watched and waited. Simms trembled in terror, unable to cry out, unable to run and throw herself into the arms of her lover, lest she draw attention to her quaking self.

When Samira reached the containers furthest away from them they made a dash for the door. But they couldn't avoid the organs. They squashed them, and slipped and slid on them, the precious organs they had so assiduously collected and stored for years. Simms screamed as she fell headlong into an accumulating blubbery mass.

Samira no longer saw them. As they reached the door, her frenzied plunder continued and intensified. So too did the crescendo of her weird moaning; now her mouth was wide open and her eyes were full of madness.

Van Hoofdaaker and Simms were gone and the containers were still collapsing to the floor. By the time they got back with six security guards, every container lay opened, and every glass jar lay shattered. It took all six guards to disarm Samira, but not before each of them had unwillingly, helplessly, and humiliatingly slipped and fallen repeatedly on a gut wrenching, organ-laden floor.

Chapter 34

Sa'eed sat with O'Neill in the car just outside Lawrence Grove and never spoke. He could sense that O'Neill still hadn't recovered. Occasionally, he felt he should excuse himself and leave O'Neill alone. But he was fascinated by what he had seen; he didn't want to leave. He didn't know what it all meant, the sight of a woman, a mother, demonstrating a wanton lasciviousness, the apparent desire of which was hardly believable, too sickening to contemplate. The memory of Mrs Greer had been so powerful, so all-consuming, that it had temporarily made him forget why he was there. But as this morbid fascination waned, he realised that it was not really all that much of a diversion; it was in fact, a vindication, a reassurance.

Martin's plight was different to that of dozens of abused and neglected kids Sa'eed saw each day. His home in Lawrence Grove seemed another world away, and Martin's parents were definitely not *child abusers* in the sense in which Sa'eed had come to understand the term. Yet whatever was happening to Martin, whatever they were doing to him, seemed infinitely worse than anything Sa'eed had witnessed on the streets of Abington. And judging by the cold silence of O'Neill and the repeated tightening of his grip on the steering wheel, it looked as though O'Neill himself had never encountered anything like it either.

Sa'eed continued silently waiting, hoping that O'Neill would say something, curious as to what he might say, yet still picking up the vibes of a crushing anger and humiliation within him.

O'Neill was the social worker Sa'eed was initially least comfortable with, the most cynical and the most suspicious. But he quickly learnt that O'Neill's cynicism and suspicions were narrowly based, and even more narrowly applied. O'Neill was not all that different from his colleagues, they were all engrossed in the misery and the suffering and the dangerousness of their clients; they all faced the consequences of decisions they took on behalf of their clients. But whereas they searched for solutions that minimised risk, O'Neill made decisions laden with risk. His risk-taking was on a grand scale, entirely compatible with the extent of his cynicism and contempt. He was so self-obsessed in his risk-taking and vanity that Sa'eed's own sense of risk working alongside him diminished daily.

Sa'eed had for some while now realised why his mentors had guided him to this type of job and why it made for perfect cover. Despite plots being frequently exposed and foiled, and arrests of terrorist suspects being made virtually every day, he felt safe working in a Social Services office. He was convinced that even though the eyes and ears of the security services were becoming more prevalent and effective – enough to worry Azeer – they were non-existent in this kind of working environment. There was something about welfare and health and education departments that made the employees within incapable of ever imagining a terrorist sleeper in their midst. Sa'eed's brothers in terror: Mohammed Sidique Khan, the *community worker* in Leeds helping special needs kids before causing carnage in the London underground; Dr. Bilal Abdullah, saving lives in Paisley's Queen Alexandra Hospital before trying to incinerate a thousand innocents in Glasgow airport; dentist Sohail Qureshi in Barking, teaching assistant Zahoor Iqbal in Birmingham… there were many of them, the common factor linking them not so much their disparate terrorist deeds or intent, as their place of work and the shock and disbelief of their welfare, health and teaching colleagues. Sa'eed knew that every single person in the office, the cynical O'Neill included, would express an identical shock and disbelief when his mission had been accomplished. They simply would not believe he was capable of such a mission. The dual role of helper and mass murderer was inconceivable to them. Whatever its origin or cause, this was an attitude of mind preciously conducive to enabling Sa'eed to settle and integrate, as Azeer had commanded.

'I'm going to leave you back,' O'Neill said, his voice hushed and tense. He was still gripping the steering wheel, staring through the windscreen, seeing nothing through a blanket drizzle rapidly descending. 'I don't want you to say anything to anybody… is that understood?'

'Okay, but shouldn't we be looking for him again?'

O'Neill slowly turned his head. Both men stared at each other, only half of their faces visible in the yellowy light, each uncertain of precisely what was in the other's mind.

'Why?' said O'Neill, his voice full of contempt; 'so that we can get him back to *that* more quickly?'

'Does that mean when he turns up you're not going to let him home?' Sa'eed asked him innocently, certain the answer had to be *yes*.

O'Neill never replied.

Sa'eed waited, but still O'Neill never replied.

'Are you sure of... what I'm thinking... *that*?'

'Say it, Sa'eed!' he snapped at him. '*Am I sure* Martin's being fucked by his mother?'

Sa'eed winced. The language pained and disgusted him almost as much as the deed.

O'Neill stared through the windscreen again, shook his head slowly and released an exaggerated ironical sigh. 'Oh yes... she's fucking him all right!'

'Why was she flaunting it, if that's what's she's doing?'

'She didn't know what she was doing tonight. She was driven crazy by him not getting home. She was out of her mind coming down that hall. Then she opens the door and sees me and you and no Martin! She couldn't cope. She didn't give a damn what we thought or what we knew.'

'I thought she was very controlled.'

'Doesn't mean to say she isn't mad.'

'Madder than you thought, then?'

'Mad up to a point. It's been convenient for her to play mad... and *stupid* and *naïve* and *innocent*... anyone of those will do if the question you're asking her is difficult, or exposes her. I once asked her did she think Martin was being *abused* by her husband. She said *he wouldn't lay a finger on her son*. I asked her was she sure she'd know if he did. She said *she'd see it, wouldn't she*... Christ! She must have laughed her head off when I left. She's made a bloody fool of me.'

'She must have made a fool of everybody then?'

'No... not everybody!'

267

Sa'eed waited. He was sure O'Neill was thinking of Maggie, but couldn't admit that.

'What are you going to do when you drop me off?'

'Come back here.'

'What for?'

He didn't answer for a while. Then he said ambiguously: 'I need to be here when he arrives.'

'Are you sure he *is* going to arrive?'

'Yes'

'It's... awkward, isn't it?'

'Neither of them will know.'

Sa'eed thought for a moment. 'What's that mean?'

O'Neill turned away from him and switched on the ignition.

They drove slowly down the main road from Lawrence Grove towards the city centre, both men scrutinising pavements left and right, searching for Martin.

When Sa'eed got out of the car in Smithdown Lane he bent low, looked at O'Neill, thanked him and wished him 'good luck...' He wanted to add *whatever you do*. He had some inkling of what O'Neill intended, but felt he dare not mention it.

The two men half smiled at each other.

Chapter 35

It was convenient and necessary for Mr Greer to be in Anthony Gormley's *Another Place* on Crosby beach on the day that his step-son was returning. The beach wasn't far from his work or his home.

Seven teenagers were gaily painting another of Gormley's penises with coloured chalks nicked from school. Mr Greer often pretended to ignore such antics, when the reality was that it triggered pangs of envy and guilt; it was so ordinary, just kids having a harmless bit of fun.

A few of the teenagers noticed Mr Greer and cautioned the rest to ease up; they all watched him and waited until he had passed them by. They continued then, combining their artistry with running commentary and sexual innuendos. When the work was completed, they took turns with mobiles to film each other grasping the penis, simulating wanks, blow jobs and buggery, and feigning expressions of ecstasy. They shared their films and laughed ceaselessly.

Mr Greer often wandered down to the beach just to get away from it all. He would walk for miles on the rain-swept sands. He could relax here and gaze across the Mersey at New Brighton, or at the oldest observatory in Britain on Bidston Hill, or at the Welsh mountains beyond. It was the Mersey itself that gave Mr Greer most pleasure: a quasi industrial landscape dominated by yellow and red dockyard cranes bordering the dry docks, and ferries criss-crossing between Liverpool and Birkenhead, and the giant container ships chugging their way from port to sea. He could just about tolerate the wind turbines recently installed at the mouth of the Mersey, reasoning that however much a blot on the landscape, they were a helluva lot better than sending men three thousand feet beneath the earth to dig out coal; his father had died young, one of the thousands of miners in the Northwest afflicted with pneumoconiosis.

Few came to share these sights. But tens of thousands now came to pore over Gormley's one hundred strange cast iron sculptures carefully spaced and positioned over two kilometres of the beach, half of them being totally submerged during the high tides. They had been made from the moulds of Gormley's own body, and were mounted on three meter high foundation piles, sturdy enough to withstand small kids climbing all over them, and the corrosive effects of sea, wind and rain.

Mr Greer had been intrigued when he first saw the sculptures. He didn't know exactly what it was about them, other than something compelling, some naked force emanating from them, particularly when one looked at them from behind and saw them half submerged in the water, mere dots beneath a boundless perpetually moving sky. Then he took the trouble one day to look at the Crosby Council's notice board:

'Another Place harnesses the ebb and flow of the tide to explain man's relationship with nature... This sculpture exposes to light the nakedness of a particular and a peculiar body, no hero, no ideal, just the industrially reproduced body of a middle aged man trying to remain standing and trying to breathe'

He didn't know what that meant but felt that it meant something to *him*. Usually he walked amongst the sculptures in a state of melancholy, deriving some perverse empathy from their permanently sad unsmiling faces. But increasingly, he would find visitors amongst them too, walking around them staring quizzically at the large drooping genitalia, joking and laughing and photographing themselves in various poses. Toddlers were usually hoisted onto their hulking six foot high shoulders.

He had been certain the sculptures wouldn't last a year; convinced that the penises in particular wouldn't last a week, that they would be a coveted possession in the streets of nearby Malborough estate. He had imagined mobs of drinking teenagers with hacksaws descending onto the beach on a Friday night and engaging in a competitive mass castration. Yet here he was four years after they had been laid, walking amongst them again, every single one of them beautifully discoloured and scarred by the elements but nevertheless intact.

He left the beach and made his way to the Admiral's Inn. A few words passed between him and Jamie the barman, but his expression made it clear that he wanted to be left alone. Jamie served him his pint of bitter and obliged.

'I'll be working in tonight,' he had told his wife when he heard Martin would be discharged. It was humiliating but not intolerable. He had behaved like that many times. He had long ago realised that there was a part, an unwholesomely large part of his wife's existence from which he was excluded. It had been a slow dawning realisation, denying him the chance of a gut reaction. He actually had to *think* about it then and deny it: 'I must be imagining it; it's too bizarre, too vile, impossible!' But combined with the reality of his own sexless loveless life the truth would not go away.

He had once plucked up the courage to mention *it*. He never got far. 'What do you mean… what is *it* you're trying to say?' she railed at him. The relationship between her and her son was 'a loving relationship… a very special loving relationship compared to what you read about these days…'

Mr Greer had adapted well by becoming an actor of sorts. To those who knew him he was the salt of the earth, a dependable worker, a loving husband, frugal and thrifty, forever sober, maintaining home and a child not even his own. But conscience didn't fall for that. It pounded him, encircled him with a mirror and made him want to scream or run away, not just from what was being done to Martin but from his tolerance of it.

How could he tolerate it? He was initially scared and now he was petrified by the consequences of not tolerating it. The shame, the stigma, the continual fear of being identified wherever he went, with whoever he might be. To be stared at, analysed, judged, condemned, or worse than that: to be ridiculed, mocked or pitied. He was a *Daily Mirror* reader. Oh how they would love a story like that! How merciless and ruthless it would be. Mr Greer accepted a long time ago that it was not his destiny to rescue Martin or to enlighten the world.

On reflection, the initial shock in finding out was no more shocking than the ease with which he settled in. His wife was a marvellous cook, ever so clean and methodically carrying out the domestic routines that provided him with a comfort he had never known before. But there was more than that. There was real substance in the *appearance* of marriage, family and home; it gave him a status he had craved after. The life of a virgin bachelor had been a miserable one. He would never choose to go back to that. So he chose *appearance* and settled in; and when he became convinced of the invulnerability of her madness he felt more secure. He chose to play his wife's game, consciously devised by her, the rules dictated by her, the table set by her, the dice thrown by her, and the results always the same. Mr Greer knew why he behaved towards Martin the way he did: it was precisely what his wife desired, and incredibly now, it was what both of them needed to survive.

His train of thought seldom deviated on these occasions when he would sit with head bowed staring at the remnants of foam in his pint. He always ended up asking: how had it come to this? But he invariably answered the opposite question: why it shouldn't have ended up like this: he was a decent working class bloke, never harmed anyone, couldn't stand the suffering of innocent children. Which is why in a city store one Saturday morning, with all the authority and determination of an NSPCC inspector, he had grabbed the arm of a wretched mother who was trying to control her uncontrollable child by punching the living day lights out of her. Other shoppers who had tried to ignore the child's screams or had guiltily fled in other directions, had then stopped, gathered, looked on, admired and even envied the brave Mr Greer. Whatever happened to those kindly and courageous impulses?

He had vague memories for answers, of the time for instance when he suddenly realised he was laughing at Martin against his will and couldn't stop laughing at him because of a powerful sense that it was what his wife wanted. He recalled feeling guilty about this, and highly perplexed about the mind and motivation of his wife. Eventually it became clear: his wife had a pathological hatred of her son, and he, Mr Greer, was a vital component in the manifestation of that hatred. His own presence seemingly intensified her hatred of her son, varied its expression, and improved its *effect*. He tried to hide from this hideous truth behind a preoccupation which was somewhat ironical: how could a mother hate her son so much, he repeatedly asked. But it didn't seem to matter any more.

Mr Greer's marriage had become a sick joke. He soon found himself laughing longer and louder at Martin. Often he wanted to curse God, or something, for allowing him to be ensnared in this abomination. Why me, he had asked, from a good home, a loving home, a happy home. His three younger brothers and sisters were married. They had seven children between them and another two on the way. Christmas was the worst time: to look into their tiny faces, to reluctantly play with them, hand over their presents and be kissed and hugged by them. They asked him: why don't you have children, uncle Mike?' and if their parents were within earshot, he would be so embarrassed he could not even give a joking reply. It was his sister Janet he feared most of all: the questions she'd asked when she first met Mrs Greer and Martin. She had been suspicious yet discreet in what she said, but when she had been in their company long enough her eyes betrayed a terrible concern. She never shared this, not with him anyway. But he brooded on the possibility that she had shared it with others. Her own husband? Or his two younger sisters? Or God forbid, with his elderly mother! This prospect of their knowing and acting out their own charade of not knowing drove him to despair.

The gods remained indifferent to his curses and anguish and his guilt, and as time passed, the once kindly and good Mr Greer stumbled upon more unpalatable facts about himself: that he was actually capable of scapegoating the helpless buffoon of a son for his own misery and sin, and amazingly, that if he could not be released from the role of accomplice in the emotional and sexual abuse of Martin, then there was some satisfaction to be gained from becoming an even more effective abuser and accomplice.

It had lasted years now. Conscience was dead. But he still felt vulnerable when various officials poked their noses through the door expressing their concern for Martin. Maggie Lynch had worried him. For one horrifying moment he was convinced that she knew. She caused him sleepless nights because she said nothing and he had convinced himself that she had said everything to somebody else. But nothing happened. Now there was the Irishman O'Neill, a bothersome fool.

He was astonished and relieved that Martin had been allowed home. It could only mean that O'Neill had no real idea of precisely what was happening to Martin. It was obvious O'Neill suspected something was happening but he was no nearer to the family *secret*, the nature and the extent of the abuse of Martin and the vital part it played in the sustenance of their sham existence. The persecution of Martin and its consequences was the most effective diversion from Mr Greer's complicity in it.

It was nearly eight; the bar was filling up; filling out too with an assembly of smoking *lepers* outside the front entrance. Two couples sat near him about the same age as himself. Probably locals from nearby Brighton-le-Sands, he thought. Their separation was instant: the men talked football, and ignored the women. The women complimented each other's style, place of purchase and price, and ignored the men. This could not go on.

'Tell im bout the 185 luv,' one of the men eventually said, nudging his wife.

His wife ignored him until she'd finished her sentence. Then she turned to her husband and said 'What?'

'The 185... tellin Joe here bout that trip to London.'

Now the four of them were united. Three looked at the appointed narrator. 'Oh the new train!' she said, after a momentary delay and an expression that suggested she may have appreciated her husband reminding her of it.

She began at the beginning: the alarm going off, the light breakfast because they wanted the real thing on the 185, served with the 'most expensive champagne, would you believe?' Then the taxi to Lime Street; Raymond gave the driver a £5 tip; it was that kind of day. They didn't have to walk far. First Class was on the first and second carriage. 'Oh the luxury... and the speed: two hours an ten minutes, and there we were in Euston! Ye gotta try it Linda.'

Mr Greer occasionally glanced over at them. They never noticed him. They made him acutely self-conscious. Just like he felt in passing the teenagers earlier, he envied these couples' ordinariness and their simple boring chat and one upmanship and companionship. They just seemed… well… yes, so ordinary.

It was a silent night. The sky was clearing. He meandered his way homeward, strangely content, unusually conscious of stars above him and the occasional shuffling of his feet below. Alcohol did not make the usually sober Mr Greer a brave man. He felt no malice or resentment. Increasingly, alcohol relaxed him against all the odds.

Chapter 36

As O'Neill drove quickly away from Sa'eed's flat many differing thoughts raced through his mind, punctuated by Mrs Greer's two lonely threatening words 'he better.' He was convinced that Maggie knew; that she had lied, contrived, and made as much of a fool of him as Martin's mother had. This was obviously why, he thought, Maggie didn't want Martin to return home, and why she behaved so bizarrely in an attempt to keep him from home. It was galling to think that he had confided his own thoughts to her, uneasily and guiltily so, and that he had always believed in her courage and her moral certainty. He wondered how long she had known and why she hadn't revealed it whenever she may have suspected it. Was it because she didn't know how to handle it, a mother fucking her fifteen year old son? How different it would have been, he thought, if it had been some bald headed old pervert buggering his five year old stepchild.

She must have been relieved, he reckoned, when Social Services took over the case. But then she must have been depressed on hearing that the case had been allocated to him! To think that he had been inspired by her behaviour at the case conference and actually went to her office to tell her so! And that parting question she asked: *is there any other reason why you wanted Martin home…?* Surely that had stemmed more from her own guilt in doing nothing than any suspicion about what he intended doing himself.

Who else knew, he wondered. Michael Greer obviously knew. It was all beginning to fit now. His hatred of Michael Greer swelled. The stepfather's guilt and fear were no less manifest than Maggie's. His complicity in his wife's fucking her son was worse than the fucking itself.

He parked the car near the entrance to Lawrence Grove and sought out the path that served the back entrance to the homes. Before going down the path he had one more look along the main road in both directions. He intended being only a few seconds at the back. It was imperative than Martin did not return whilst he was away.

He reached the rear of Martin's home and quietly unhinged the latch of the gate. He walked on the soft wet soil. He reached the back door leading into the kitchen and gently turned the handle. It was unlocked. He stood listening, pondering, trembling. He was sure that Mrs Greer was at the front of the house, peering through the curtains, anxiously awaiting her son. He didn't know for certain, but he had a powerful sense that Mr Greer was not there. He reckoned that Mrs Greer would have ensured her husband's absence for the home-coming of her son. He closed the kitchen door and retreated down the back garden. He returned to his car and waited. The wet darkness would serve him well.

It was nearly eight when Martin turned off the main road into Lawrence Grove. His feelings of pride and exhilaration had slowly given way to apprehension. He didn't notice the car parked amongst other cars; he didn't see O'Neill who sat motionless in the darkness.

O'Neill stared after Martin and felt relief and vindication. Then his pulse quickened rapidly as he gently opened and closed the car door. He calculated that it would take Martin about a minute and a half to reach the front door of his home, and that it would take *him* less to sprint round to the back of it. He got there breathless and tried the back door. It was still unlocked. He opened it and listened.

Martin did not reach his own front door alone. His mother at the window had seen him appear from afar, a huge erect figure looming in the distance, reaching towards her, striding towards her, larger and larger, out of the wet darkness, out of the void of those past few agonising hours. To life she came, dashing through the open doorway, down the driveway, and onto the street, throwing herself into his arms.

'Oh my son, my son!' she cried, burying herself in his massive self and clutching him with grim gratifying determination.

O'Neill heard her run out. He pushed the back door, stepped into the kitchen, closed the door, and hurriedly dried his wet shoes on a thick mat. He dashed through the kitchen, into the hall, and reached the stairs. He took them four at a time. He was on the landing now and didn't know where to hide. He could hear Martin and his mother walking back on the driveway. He looked at the bedroom door opposite Martin's. He opened it and the room felt cold, empty and unused. But he could see vaguely the outline of two single beds about a meter apart. He moved to beyond the far one and lay on his back on the carpet floor. His heart pounded so much he thought it might explode; his panting breath sounded as though it might deafen him; it would surely betray him. He tried hopelessly to control his breathing. He pulled his white handkerchief from his pocket and covered his mouth, hoping to muffle the sound.

Now he could hear their voices… and he could hear other voices and see other faces. He opened his eyes suddenly, fearfully, but there was only darkness all around. Still he could see and hear, that night more than thirty years ago, the memory of his mother and her boyfriend down below, warning him and that older child to be quiet. He did not want to be quiet; he tried not to be; noise was defiance, noise was protest; noise was power over the black bearded man they both loathed. But that same man came thundering up the stairs, and the older child, having thrown O'Neill back onto the bed, could not get herself back into it on time. She screamed and tried to run, just the kind of provocation the man needed. He didn't touch O'Neill, but the sister who had rescued him was carried away in a stretcher that night. He never saw her again.

Martin smiled embarrassingly as she led him by the hand. He had expected her to rush out like that and throw her arms around him, but it was confusing and embarrassing nonetheless. He had longed to see her; he so desperately needed her; yet as he had got nearer to her throughout the day, the turmoil of his mind intensified.

She closed the front gate behind her tightly. She released him only when they were inside. She smiled at him and gazed all over him as she retreated from him in the hallway. She put her tiny hands, palms outstretched, behind her back and pressed the main hall door until it too closed tightly. Her eyes never left him.

She made a great sigh and walked towards him slowly, almost methodically. His timidity assured her. Nothing had changed. She placed her two tiny hands on his burning cheeks. Now she could *feel* his submission. But he interrupted her and what he had to say annoyed her considerably:

'A've somethin to show ya mum.'

"Oh... what is it?' she said impatiently. He had never interrupted her preparation before.

"A trophy.' His hand darted into his inside pocket. He held the heart-shaped trophy out to her. Beneath the hall light, the dazzling reflection caught her eye a number of times, and she blocked out the reflection with her hand. Then she took it from him. She read the inscription.

Martin stood silent and looked at the trophy in his mother's hand. Then he looked into her eyes hopeful of approval at least. He had wanted so much to show it to her and yet some niggling doubts about how she may respond had troubled him. Now her joyless, praise-less looks convinced him. She placed the trophy on a hall stand and said:

'Your coat's wet; take it off.'

He obeyed.

'It's heavy; what have you got in it?' She was searching each pocket before he had time to reply. She felt the mobile and took it out. Her face darkened. She held it up to him.

'Mr O'Neill lent it to me in case a got lost,' he said sheepishly.

'Did you use it?' she asked threateningly.

'No.'

She threw the mobile on the carpeted stairs, deliberately without care.

'Your shirt's wet too,' she said; 'let me help you.' Her voice betrayed the irritation she felt.

He stood there, immovable, sensing her mood, her determination, her power over him. But he was more concerned about what she might do with his trophy. He hadn't the confidence to ask her for it, or to stretch out and retrieve it from the hall stand. He feared he would never see it again.

'You're wet through,' she said, her voice lacking the concern implied.

'I'm all right mum,' he protested nervously. He wanted to say: *give me back my trophy and I will feel wonderful.*

'No No! darling, you're wet through. You need a bath. You'll get pneumonia if you don't have a hot bath. Come along…'

'But mum…'

'I know darling, come along now. I'll get the bath ready for you.'

'But I can do it myself mum.'

'Of course darling; I know you can.'

She took him by the hand again. He didn't notice that she had reached out with her other hand and lifted his trophy. She led him up to the bathroom. He stood awkwardly as she leaned over to turn the taps on. He just stood there, one end of his open shirt hanging over his trousers. He stared at her bent over. She was barely two feet away from him and the bathroom walls seemed as if they were closing in on him. A terrible urge to oppose her intensified within him. But he never could and he knew he wouldn't, even though he suddenly saw the dazzling shine of his trophy in the bottom of the waste bin where she had thrown it.

'Now you get ready,' she said, turning towards him; 'I'll have some warm fresh clothes for you when we're finished. Come along now; let me help you; it's sticking to you, that shirt; turn around; that's it.'

She stood behind him, her face enveloped by a mass of muscular white flesh. He did not see her closing her eyes and the running water drowned her sighs.

An hour later, Mr Greer reached the garden gate and stared at the drawn curtains on all the windows. He closed the gate gently. He had no wish to disturb. His pace slackened along the driveway. He tensed in his attempt to lessen the impact of opening and closing the front and hall doors. He switched on the table lamp and slowly and quietly lowered himself onto his usual armchair. He heard movement somewhere, the creaking of a bed, feet on the floor. It seemed to come from the bedroom above, the cold, loveless marital bedroom. That could not be, he thought; how could she be there? Why isn't she asleep in her son's arms, in Martin's own room? He had given her all the time she needed as he always did. He had not expected to see her until morning. He switched the lamp off.

He closed his eyes and tried listening attentively again. There seemed to be ever such slight noise and movement. It almost seemed as though it were on the landing and moving down the stairs. Maybe he was imagining it; maybe he was so drunk and so fearful of her descending to humiliate him in his drunkenness, that he was hallucinating. Yes, that must be it; he could hear nothing now. But a few minutes later he felt a heavy presence all around him. Not her. Who then? Was he going mad? He knew he should have opened his eyes and sprung up to confront whoever it might be. But his eyes remained closed and he prayed that it was only his imagination. Again he could hear nothing.

A minute later he heard a tiny clicking sound, just like the noise of the key turning in the back kitchen door. He sighed in relief, the relief of not knowing, of being left alone. His head fell to the side. Strange that he should sleep, still hearing and thinking about that train, the 185, hurtling towards Euston.

Chapter 37

Eight year old Alice Lynch danced her way around the lake in West Kirby's Ashton Park, and paused at the bowling green, covetously eyeing the thick carpet of spongy wet grass. There was no one about on this cold autumnal morning, except her sister Rebecca and her mother and Frankie all trailing behind her. She longed to run onto the grass and do her latest somersault, and to hear Maggie say 'well done.' It didn't matter that she was wearing a heavy fleece, hat, gloves and scarf; she was utterly confident. But she wouldn't dare somersault on a bowling green. So she just continued dancing, gyrating, gesticulating and singing as she waited on them: *'We're all in this together… we're all in this together…'*

Maggie unexpectedly had to return home early from work today. For the second time in a year, her children's school had been flooded. But she had intended coming home early in any case after her outburst with Mike. It had never happened before and she felt terrible. She wrote a note of apology to him and left it on his desk. She knew it would probably overwhelm him.

She'd left the office today saying: 'That was it! No more!' And she'd made a momentous decision: she would confront O'Neill. She would tell him herself. She would admit she had lied to him. Surely even O'Neill, despite his cynicism, would understand; would accept that she lied to protect him?

She did not easily tell lies, not even as a tactic to divert the children alongside her. Lying was alien to her in her own upbringing and in her own private world of thought and feeling. She had lied not only to O'Neill but to Mike and Dr Millwise; indeed, to everyone who had attended the conference, one lie begetting the other. This was incredible to Maggie: that just like her clients she had fallen into the commonest pit hole, *that he who knowing what is right doth it not, should lose the knowledge of what is right, and he who would not do well when he could, should lose the power when he would.* She was as intrigued as she was disturbed that these throbbing poetic rhythms were beating louder; these Augustinian gems, long forgotten, and which she had laboured to remember and write about all those years ago in Bristol university. They were increasingly being heard when she was least expecting them, or needing them: *tomorrow, perhaps tomorrow, maybe tomorrow, or presently; leave it but a little, and presently, presently, had no present, and her 'little while' went on for a long while...* She had learnt them off by heart, dissected and criticised them, argued over them, dismissed them, but always ended up treasuring them. Then like everything else she learnt on her theology course, she forgot them. Until recently, that is. Like distant drums in a wilderness, they had returned and would not die away.

Nothing remains the same. The first opportunity to *do the difficult but right thing* is always the golden opportunity. The second is always less of an opportunity than the first. The third contains the risk of exposure and criticism for ignoring the first and second, and so on. But she had never thought of it like that. She'd never felt the slippery slope beneath her.

It was that phone call from Mike that changed everything: *'that MacDonald case, Maggie; do you want to talk about it now?'* That was the golden opportunity lost. If only she had talked about it before Mike shocked her then with the news that O'Neill was taking over the case. Had she instantly told Mike what she knew, she would have been entirely in the clear. Martin would have been removed and her only burden would have been wondering how O'Neill would cope, and restraining herself listening to the many willing him not to cope. He may never have found out, because Mike could also have shared the information with O'Neill's bosses, who would surely have insisted that the case went to anybody but O'Neill.

They continued along Rectory Road and onto Village Lane, heading for Caldy Hill high above Stapleton Wood. It was only four or five hundred yards from their home, an ideal place to take Frankie for a walk before his one and only meal of the day. When they reached the first entrance to the wood Frankie was unleashed and went bounding up the hill. He was soon out of sight on the winding path, carpeted by a thick fertilizing boggy mass of putrifying leaves. The path made its way through gorse, bell and cross-leaved heather and flattened brownish bracken.

'Smell,' said Maggie, and her children's little nostrils inflated and contracted, Rebecca's mind feverishly wondering what was there to smell. Occasionally the last remaining leaves, wrinkled and brittle, were still being parted from the branches of trees, and were aimlessly gliding around the visitors. The oak and sweet chestnut, the beech and birch, the ash and sycamore all seemed dead, their barks a sickly white or grey, overburdened with statuesque branches that stretched themselves through all kinds of contortions. Further in from the path, only the dark green holly and the red berries were vibrant in the cutting wind.

Alice and Rebecca ran after Frankie, until they got to the first turn. Then they stopped and waited for Maggie. True to form, Frankie returned and ran off again.

Suddenly Alice crouched, put her fingers to her lips, and demanded silence: 'shhh…' Her mum and sister obediently complied. A loud chirping whistle could be heard. Rebecca strained to see; it had to be a big bird to make a sound like that. 'There,' whispered Alice; she pointed; 'it's a robin.' Rebecca stared but was puzzled. It was so tiny and clearly visible with its orange breast and its repetitive curtsying as it pranced about on leafless twigs and branches. The children seemed transfixed by its sounds and its movements. It stopped prancing though its tail continued flicking. It stared back at them. Its staccato like chirping graduated into soulful song with rippling crystal-clear cascades of sound that lasted four or five seconds. Rebecca must have been overwhelmed by the sound because she suddenly let out a 'whoopee!' and began to dance. Maggie smiled and the robin continued to sing.

A bearded man passed them by and didn't speak to any of them. He was kitted out just as well as they were, with walking boots and gortex, a woolly hat and green rucksack. Maggie caught only his side profile, and thought she knew him.

Frankie behaved rather oddly. Normally he would sniff at any passing stranger's legs and then resume his interest in whatever the kids were doing. But on this occasion he raised his nose high in the air, sniffing repetitively and followed the stranger.

Another dog owner perhaps, thought Maggie. Frankie followed the man for some thirty yards, round one sharp bend after another. He appeared to get excited, darting his head in front of the man to look up at him inquisitively, searchingly. After about fifty yards and numerous winding bends, the man stopped and looked behind. The family was nowhere in sight. He removed a makeshift kitchen foil bag from his pocket. He opened it and allowed Frankie to put his nose into it. But he was holding it in such a way that the dog could only sniff and not retrieve the freshly cooked meat that was in it. Frankie whimpered and repeatedly stretched out a single paw to the man pleadingly. Then he heard Alice call out his name. The stranger quickly closed the bag, put it back in his pocket and walked on. Frankie turned and looked in the direction of the call. Neither of the children could yet be seen. He looked after the quickly disappearing stranger. He was panting furiously, salivating and still holding a paw of indecision in the air. He whimpered again, turned away from the stranger, and ran back to be with Alice and Rebecca.

They were nearing the end of their walk through the woods. They emerged into the main body of heather, and crossed it diagonally managing to avoid tripping on countless stools of birch cut down. It would need cutting again in a few years if the beautiful heath-land was to be maintained.

Away from the dense undergrowth and the winding paths, Maggie's thoughts drifted back to O'Neill. She would no longer *not do well when she could*; she *would* confront him no matter what obstacle might be placed in her way, no matter how he might react. She would prepare him for the scandal that would ensue. She would reach out to him all over again, even though his skin would be reptilian cold and his eyes would be full of hatred and betrayal and those all around him would gossip and laugh. She wondered why she cared, but then asked herself: did she really care? Maybe it was just pity – there was always something pitiful about O'Neill, his isolation, his brash cynicism and contempt, his conviction that most people around him were stupid and didn't know, didn't know what they were doing. Maybe it was fear. Maybe she was still attempting to achieve an intimacy spurned all those years ago. Or could it be, bizarrely, that she herself was wanting to hold onto the knowledge? She was the only person who knew about Marian Greer and she couldn't deny that it wasn't just simply the *disbelief* and *horror* she felt at what she had found out; it was also riveting; revolting, tragic, and if she was honest, when O'Neill blathered on and on in his ignorance about the ignorance of others, it was sometimes gratifying.

The straight path they were on was one of many that led through the heather to the perimeter of Stapleton Wood. All these narrow paths led to a tiny junction, and from there the dense woodlands dropped sharply to one of the exits in Fleck Lane. To exit onto the lane required another of those winding trails that snaked its way downwards, firstly through trees, and then six feet high gorse.

They were about a hundred yards from the junction. Two men were also approaching it on different paths. They were going to reach the junction much sooner than Maggie and the kids. Frankie as usual was well in front, and moved closer to one of the men. He was the bearded stranger who had passed them earlier. He was a lot older and taller than the other. Neither men gave any indication that they were together or that they knew each other. The older man reached the junction first and it seemed that he wasn't even aware of the other man some thirty yards behind him on another path. As the older man descended out of sight, the younger man quickened his pace, and suddenly left the path. He walked straight through the heather and descended the steep slope where there was no path.

Maggie, still deep in thought about O'Neill, saw both men. But their disappearance over different locations on the perimeter of the heath ensured no lasting interest in them.

Frankie reached the junction only seconds after the stranger had disappeared and then quickly went after him. There was nothing unusual about Frankie dashing to the exit below, nor, while he waited for the kids who always got there before Maggie, indulging himself with unhurried prolonged sniffing around tree trunks and exit posts, and making his own mark.

But he had run after the stranger because of another potent scent: freshly cooked meat in kitchen foil which the stranger was now holding out to him for a second time. He rewarded Frankie this time with a small piece of meat. It was swallowed whole. He held the bag out and allowed Frankie to bury his nose in it. But again he had his thumb and index finger sufficiently tight around it to ensure Frankie could not reach the remaining meat. Then he quickly moved on and Frankie followed. The descending zigzagging path through the tough prickly gorse was too narrow for the dog to get ahead of him. Ravenous and tempted beyond endurance, Frankie fell in behind, moving in a crouching, slave-like way, so close that he repeatedly had to avoid being caught by the stranger's back heel on every step.

Rebecca struggled to keep up with her sister. They had both reached the junction. Alice began descending. She broke into a trot then she started running. Rebecca cried out in frustration and stamped her feet, knowing once again she would not be able to keep up with Alice. She returned to the junction to wait for her mum.

Maggie caught up with her. This was normally the only time and place when her vigilance relaxed, when she knew that Alice and the dog were running down a single winding path about seventy yards long that led nowhere except to the exit on Fleck Lane, a salubrious residential cul de sac. Alice often spurted ahead like that despite Maggie's cautions or admonishments; she was always breaking out of the shackles of patience and tolerance that her much younger and slower sister demanded.

Maggie had no idea why she was suddenly gripped by the memory of the two men disappearing over the ridge and of one of them descending on the path that Alice herself had gone down. Her brooding preoccupation with O'Neill ceased. She had the urge to run, but the ridiculousness of the panic it implied, in broad daylight, in crimeless, leafy, sleepy West Kirby, restrained her. Only for about two seconds though. Then a real panic took hold and she lunged forward. She reached out a hand to Rebecca, clasped it tightly and called out 'Alice!' There was no reply.

Maggie was no different to any other responsible parent. She was no more or no less cautious, cleverer or vigilant in protecting her children. She hadn't let Alice get that far ahead of her. She herself could easily sprint down the winding slope in less than ten seconds, and the myriad of thoughts now racing through her mind included the calculation that Alice, even running down the hill at her maximum speed, could be no more than three quarters of the way down. But she was out of sight, and there were at least a dozen U-turns to navigate through the dense gorse before reaching the bottom.

Maggie had never anticipated obstacles or emergencies which might play havoc with such calculations. Even the most obvious one, that when danger threatened her oldest child what would she do with her youngest child? She ran down the hill for a few yards, called out 'Alice' again, and realised how hopeless it was. Rebecca could not stay on her feet and was being literally dragged along. It was hurting and distressing her. Maggie knew she dare not succumb to the temptation of leaving Rebecca in order to find Alice. She swung round and lifted Rebecca and ran as fast as the burden would allow her. She was acutely conscious of how her precious burden might cause her to trip. She was in the depths of panic now but she was determined not to trip.

Alice hadn't heard her mother call out because she was standing at the rear of the stranger's black Baby Transit Ford and she was laughing hysterically. The stranger stood beside her laughing too. They were laughing at Frankie who was in the back of the van gobbling down the fresh meat. Frankie had jumped into the open rear when the stranger, just before Alice emerged from the exit, had held the meat out to him one last time before scattering it. The pieces lay at the bottom of a metal grill secured against the two seats.

'What are we going to do now?' the stranger said, still smiling broadly; 'If I try to pull him out he'll bite my hand off.'

Alice laughed again. 'No he won't,' she said. 'I'll get him.' She raised a foot and grabbed the inside of the van to lever herself in.

'Can you manage?' He made no move to go near or help her

'Yes,' she said, keeping her head low as she moved further into the van. 'Come here you bad boy!' She pulled Frankie away from the meat and retreated. She laughed, pleased at her initiative and her success. The stranger stretched his hand in to take over and said 'thank you.' He grabbed the dog by the collar and yanked him out of the van with such brutal strength and speed that he let out a yelp. When he landed on the ground he was six feet away from the van. Alice's laughter ceased. Still crouched over in the back of the van, she strained to look into the stranger's eyes. His violence shocked and angered her. She was just about to shout at him 'why did you do that?' but the stranger already had his hand on the ends of both doors which he slammed shut in her face. She screamed. She was locked in, trapped on the floor of a van between the door and a metal grill. The stranger dashed to the driver's door.

Maggie reached the exit. She saw the stranger dashing to the front of the vehicle and her terrified daughter screaming at her through the miniature windows at the rear. She saw Alice helplessly beating the windows with her tiny clenched fists. She screamed. She almost dropped Rebecca as she charged at the stranger.

Then from a thicket a few yards from the exit, another man hurled himself across her path and ran towards the car. He was the smaller much younger man who had left the track above. He held a short very thick branch in his hand. Maggie felt doomed: 'his accomplice... two of them... paedophiles... murderers... my daughter lost...' But she continued her charge, knowing that the older, taller broad-shouldered man would fell her in one blow... that the younger man would surely smash her skull with the thick branch in his hand. But she didn't care. And then suddenly she stopped. She stared. He was not an accomplice, this younger man. He was attacking the stranger with a ferocity and hatred that momentarily paralysed her.

She dashed to the back of the van. She wrenched the handle that released both doors and flung them wide open. Alice threw herself into her mother's arms and buried her head around her neck and sobbed. Maggie quickly ran to Rebecca, who was too petrified at the spectacle to cry out or to make a move. Maggie reached down and lifted Rebecca and both children sobbed uncontrollably. Frankie, still cowed after the stranger's brutal wrench, remained at Maggie's feet and barked ceaselessly.

The stranger had succeeded in reaching the van door but not in opening it. The first blow from behind caused an instant blackness and then a terrible pain. His hat and glasses fell off revealing a bald head that just did not look real. The second blow felled him and he collapsed onto the cold ground, but still held onto the handle of the door with one hand. Another blow smashed into the knuckles of that same hand. He yelled and released the handle and his bloodied numbed fingers left a trail of parallel lines through the dirt and grime on the door as they slid lifelessly to the ground. He turned to look up at his assailant. He pleaded 'don't... please don't...' but another blow struck him across the temple and another across the ear and cheek. He cried out in pain and his open mouth felt the full force of another blow. Within seconds he was coughing and spluttering, convinced he would choke in his own blood.

Eric Houston, the young cockney social worker, stood over him with weapon raised. It was a poise of both triumph and mercy. He did not strike another blow. He reached down and pulled off the stranger's false beard and bald cap. The bleeding bruised face made the stranger almost unrecognisable, but not to his attacker, nor to the mother of his victim. His familiar thick black oily hair unwound and fell backwards limply. Maggie came towards him with both children still clinging around the back of her neck, their eyes shut tight, and neither of them able or wanting to see anything. She looked down on the stranger and gasped. It was Jackson.

Chapter 38

When Jackson gave his inaugural address all those months ago, word quickly spread about his aura of confidence and menace. It wasn't too long before many others besides Morgan felt threatened. They were right to feel threatened. But amazingly, the young cockney social worker Eric Houston who had sat hidden from Jackson at the back of the hall on that same day had also felt threatened.

In his early teens Eric had sworn to track Jackson down and castrate him; in his late teens (when the news was frequently dominated by the topic of sexual abuse and the exposure of officers-in-charge of residential homes) he merely wanted to join the growing numbers of adults claiming that they too had been sexually abused while in care. He had watched these victims appearing almost nightly, many of them being interviewed in secret locations, their faces covered, their voices disguised as they recalled the abuses perpetrated against them. It could have been his experiences they were describing. But Eric never did join them, could never bring himself to seek help or support. When he was training to be a social worker he avoided child sex abuse seminars and role plays. He confided in no one.

Jackson had sexually and violently abused Eric for more than two years in *Mareville*, the Barnet family group home where he was officer in charge. Eric's increasing realisation that he was not alone, that there were literally thousands of kids in care being similarly abused and that many of them were prepared to talk about it publicly, only added to his sense of failure, his lack of courage. The abuse itself had imbued him with lasting and far more damaging feelings: self-disgust and loathing, guilt, shame and a crippling inferiority. He had eventually decided to leave London, go North, and – how cruelly ironic it then seemed on hearing and seeing Jackson addressing the packed hall – make a fresh start!

But how could he have felt so threatened? He was in the uniquely privileged and powerful position of being able to bring Jackson to his knees, of sensationally writing to the Director of Social Services and telling him what Jackson had done to him (and he had no doubt in retrospect, had also done to others). He could easily have ripped off Jackson's veneer of respectability and probity, and expose not just a child abuser, but a psychopath too (Eric could never forget the gruesome smiles accompanying the pain Jackson inflicted).

He could alternatively have chosen to expose Jackson in a more common and mercenary way, making himself rich at the same time: he could have phoned the *Sun* or the *Mirror* or, more profitably, some public relations firm, Max Clifford for example; everybody knew about Max Clifford. The most attractive proposition in Eric's mind, however, was to confront Jackson himself; to walk into his office without knocking, to close in on him, to stare at him, and to quietly say: 'Do you remember me? You buggered me when I was a kid... you buggered me nearly every night!'

But from the moment he had watched Jackson mesmerising people more intelligent, experienced and cynical than himself, Eric knew that he would do none of these things. He knew that if he had accidentally bumped into Jackson (let alone go gate-crashing his office to confront him) that he would most probably have shrivelled up, and that the toweringly confident Jackson would have stared down on him and babbled on as though they had never met. He knew that even if Jackson had recognised him and recalled the group home in which their lives had crossed, he, Jackson, would have been able to behave as though it were a joyful reunion between them both. It would have been Eric who would have been stricken all over again with guilt and shame and fear, the lasting legacy of abuse. *I was horribly abused by that man* was a reality converted in Eric's distraught mind to something like: *I must have been a sub-human, brainless, despicable and cowardly child to have been chosen and groomed by him... why me?*

Worse than that distorted perception of what he had been as a child, was the self-perception that rapidly developed with his new-found proximity to Jackson: Eric felt himself a coward, with no self respect, without dignity, every bit as much a hypocrite as Jackson himself. That is what Jackson had made him.

Jackson's confidence and standing was such that he had nothing to fear from Eric, and Eric's weakness and helplessness was such that it drove him to near despair; it was Jackson his former abuser, who had threatened *him*, threatened his sanity and his well-being, his work performance and his prospects.

Eric drifted into a solution of sorts: he began following Jackson around, clandestinely. He convinced himself at the outset that this served some useful purpose; it certainly had its appeal, a whiff of subterfuge and intrigue, and the sense of just a modicum of freedom and power over the man who had imbued him all his life with a sense of powerlessness.

The delusion took hold. It felt to Eric as though he was merely biding his time, building his confidence, and that he would pounce when the man under his surveillance least suspected it. That was a gratifying thought. But it was only when he wasn't following Jackson that such thoughts had any potency. They melted away as he trailed behind and watched the man whose every stride and posture, whose whole countenance and appearance oozed the confidence that Eric himself had lacked.

If he had been honest with himself Eric would have admitted that those clandestine activities had no beneficial impact at all; they were merely an expression of his continuing helplessness and frustration. He became aware of other consequences. His hatred of Jackson intensified, watching him yet still unable to confront him. So too did his own self-loathing intensify not merely because he eventually realised he was getting nowhere but more because of his fear, his cowardly fear of being seen and being challenged. That was the most painful thought: that if Jackson discovered what he was doing and challenged him he would not have been able to tell him; he would not have been able to say: 'You bastard… you destroyed my life and I'm going to get my own revenge on you, some day… when you're least expecting it; that's why I'm following you!' No, he would have been much more likely to have gone red in the face and deny that he *was* following him, and thereafter be consumed by his own self-loathing and his uselessness.

That was Eric's legacy, the long term consequences of Jackson's bestiality, his Jekyll and Hyde existence all those years ago. The grooming process had lasted months and was all sweetness and light. For the six year old Eric, it was also richly rewarding: he received many privileges and gifts. He was so enamoured of Jackson's *kindness* that he didn't even realise the abuse had begun: the casual availability of pornography that he was certain to stumble on in Jackson's office which was always locked when Eric and he were there; the photographing of a half naked Eric on Jackson's bed; the *innocent* wrestling after they had both shared a bath. By the time Jackson had sexually assaulted him, Eric hadn't even realised what had happened. And by the time it had graduated to painful penetration, it was far too late for Eric to cry out. The nature of the threat was frightening enough to ensure that he would continue to do whatever Jackson demanded of him.

As Jackson later advanced through the echelons of the child protection industry, Eric in many ways remained a terrified, dysfunctional, undeveloped child. In his work he had insights and empathy that he could share with no one, least of all with the children whose experiences of abuse were not dissimilar to his own. He recognised the full extent of their pain and their fear; and he strongly advocated the counselling and support that he could never face up to himself. He dwelt on their suffering for morbidly long periods and he hated their abusers every bit as much as he hated Jackson. He often asked himself who were Jackson's victims today, and how did he find them? In residential care he didn't even have to look. He wondered too, what sexually gratified Jackson now? What perversion? What kind of violence? When Angela Mulholland was abducted, raped and strangled, he actually thought… no… more than thought; he dared to hope! He certainly believed in the possibility that it was Jackson. Yet his paralysis intensified. If he could not confront Jackson about the *reality* of his crimes twenty years ago, he was hardly likely to do anything about a *suspicion* and a *hope* that Jackson had done something infinitely worse in the present day.

He was equally helpless when he plucked up the courage to speak to Sarah Prescott before she and Morgan were confronted by Jackson. He knew he could not mention his suspicion that Jackson was the abductor and the murderer, but he honestly believed that he could at least manage to tell her that Jackson was a paedophile and a hypocrite! He told her nothing and Sarah humiliatingly silenced him for his efforts.

Like every other childcare worker however, Eric had known that paedophiles stop abusing only if caught, convicted, imprisoned and treated. He conceded that that was maybe what had happened in the intervening twenty years since he'd last seen Jackson. But he also knew that even if *that* had happened, Jackson must thereafter have lied his way to the top; he would never have been employed otherwise. Eric hoped that Jackson had remained the liar and paedophile he had always known, and his suspicion that Jackson was also the murderer of Angela became a conviction; a convenient conviction, because it convinced him that Jackson would compulsively attempt something similar again. The task of following him then, seemed less futile than he had originally thought; in fact it became an obsession.

Neither Maggie nor her daughter Alice would ever know that, but they were unlikely to forget the consequences.

Chapter 39

In the name of Allah, Most Gracious, Most Merciful.

To my beloved and revered Sheikh Omar Abdel Rahmān, Assalam Alaikum!

Alhumdulallah!

My dear Sheikh Omar,

I see that BenezirBhutto has at last been dispatched to hell. I stand in awe of the brothers who martyred themselves for this Holy cause. I hope to meet them soon. I will recall them in my prayers.

I also need to pray for my beloved sister. She could take no more from the people who stripped her son's corpse of every organ and refused to return them. She has attacked the one in charge and awaits trial and punishment. She should instead be awarded because she has exposed him as a liar, a fraudster, a lecher, and a so-called doctor who has brought misery to the lives of thousands. He has been sacked. She has however, put our family in the spotlight and created risk for my mission. Allah protect us.

Here is news for you: Tony Blair, the God-father of anti-Islamic crusades in Afghanistan and Iraq, has become a Catholic. His Pope congratulates him. His people laugh at him, reminding him of the misery and suffering he has inflicted upon the world, and his refusal to acknowledge it, or to apologise for it.

The despicable Danes, still believing they are a civilized people, have dared once again to publish their blasphemous cartoons. But do they think that that's the end of the matter?

Our Lord is the Lord of the heavens and the earth.

*I have been working for many weeks now, Dear Sheikh Omar, and, as promised, I will tell you something of what I have learnt. My dear father in Allah Dr Azeer, chastises me for betraying my purpose through the way I look and act in everyday things. He advises me that I know not the time I may be called, and until that time, I must integrate more convincingly in the surroundings in which I find myself. **He who forsakes his home in the cause of Allah, finds in the earth many a refuge.** I must appear as an ordinary and* enthusiastic team member, honest, sincere and dedicated in the job that I am supposed to be doing. I must learn to write about what I do, as I am frequently tested on this each time I learn something new. You will quickly realise that the nature of the work, and the character of the people entrusted with the task of instructing me, provides impenetrable cover.

Something strange is happening to me (Do not be alarmed dear Sheikh Omar). My ultimate mission has always been driven by the majestic, all-seeing, mightily powerful, Allah, who has shown me the way, who has exposed the enemies' faithlessness and their sins, as well as their hatred and fear of Islam – all reason enough to make war against them. But the longer I 'sleep' in their midst, the more aware I become of other reasons to pursue that mission.

You have often stressed the need to 'Know thy enemy' and I have concluded that there is no better way to learn about this particular enemy, than by knowing how they treat their weakest and most vulnerable members. **And why should ye not fight in the cause of Allah and of those who, being weak, are ill-treated and oppressed… whose cry is 'Our Lord!'**

This is, dear Sheikh Omar, a sick and corrupt society, a country in which children are frequently murdered, a people that abuses and neglects its children on an unimaginable scale. Everyone here lives under the illusion that this is a civilized country, a highly sophisticated and developed country. But in the care of its own children, it is a failed state, a broken state, no less so than my own homeland, where war lords rule and foreign armies roam. The children of Somalia may be killed or maimed, may go hungry, may be orphaned, may be dispersed; but in some ways, their well-being and their prospects are brighter than many of the children I am presently working with every day.

I work in a team that's responsible for protecting children and helping the families of children. This is such a peculiar team that I find it difficult to believe they are capable of helping anyone. They are so different, in age, background, values, education, attitude, and conviction. They all do however, have one thing in common: they are unbelievers. They have no religious Faith. They pride themselves in that. They flaunt their heathenism as though it were a badge of honour. They think that's an advantage in their work, despite the fact that most of their work is with immigrant families and cultural minorities who cannot live without Faith. They know nothing of how mighty Allah, Allah the compassionate, instructs 'us' in the work that 'they' are supposed to do. They pontificate on 'religion as a cause of people's woes.' 'Faith' and 'enslavement' are synonymous to them. **As to those who reject Faith – if they had everything on earth, and twice repeated, to give as ransom for the penalty of the Day of Judgement, it would never be accepted of them, theirs would be a grievous penalty.**

I work in a district of Liverpool called Abington. It is a poor part of the city, supposedly owned and run by the local council. It has high unemployment, more broken families, more drug abuse and child abuse, more drunkenness and more criminals gangs than anywhere else in the city. Most of the residents are dependent on state benefits. I used to think this kind of place was unique to Liverpool, but I know now that it is typical of all big cities of the UK. They all have their Abingtons.

Everyone knows about these places; they are large, ugly sprawling featureless scars on the landscape, and are so riddled with crime, violence, cruelty, suffering, self-hate and aggression, that no stranger dare visit them, except of course the police and the professional classes (with whom I temporarily belong) who have built careers on the misery of the inhabitants, and who make fleeting visits to their homes maintaining the charade that they are doing something useful for them.

Britain is apparently now designated the worst place in the world for children. I can see why in places like Abington. Britain has the highest divorce rate, and the worst relationships between children and their parents than anywhere else in Europe (in truth, there are very few genuine 'parents' in Abington; there are far more 'invisible' parents, 'substitute' parents, parents who are nothing more than lovers and boyfriends of the mothers, with no real bond or commitment with the children).

I have asked every day since working here how has this situation come about (and I have to confess to ignorance and disinterest when I lived here previously). According to the literature I read, it has its origins in stupid politicians wanting to make things easier for people. They made it easier for parents to divorce and desert their kids (over 50% of children are now born out of wedlock); they made it much easier for kids to commit crime and get away with it; they made it easier for pregnant teenagers to get abortions, and they relaxed their laws on

298

decency and morality, causing a rampant pornography and sexual depravity (It has also caused the highest rate of sexual diseases amongst teenagers). The politicians were unable to see that by making things easier they made society and families more fragile.

Our Holy Qur'an asks: **Why were there not, among the generations before you, persons possessed of balanced good sense, prohibiting men from mischief in this earth... the wrongdoer pursued the enjoyment of the good things in life?**

Tens of thousands of children couldn't cope with their parents separating. Many remained with their disintegrating families and endured emotional and psychological abuse as a consequence; and many thousands reacted to the marital disintegration so badly that that they had to be removed and placed in large residential complexes. The staff who worked in such places were invariably unqualified and incompetent. The managers in charge were often brutal and deviant.

I have just found out dear Sheikh Omar, that one of those managers has been working amongst us. He is at present in a prison cell, charged with the abduction of one child and being investigated about the abduction and murder of another.

When I first heard this news I was astonished. I had met this man. But even more astonishing was the fact that my colleagues expressed little surprise. When I asked about this they directed me to books and reports in our library documenting hundreds of cases of high profile managers of children's homes, who have been convicted of the most heinous crimes perpetrated against the children under their care. The manager I speak about once managed such a home in London, and he has now been exposed (and nearly killed I should also say) by one of his victims.

Much heart searching has gone on in response to these revelations dear Sheikh Omar, but not surprisingly, in this heathen country, very little soul searching. It is the soul that requires scrutiny. The government is not likely to be guided by our Holy Qur'an which could have told them the real source of the problem: **Have you seen him who denies the religion? He is the one who harshly rebuffs the orphan and does not urge the feeding of the poor... Serve Allah... and do good to parents, kinsfolk, orphans, those in need, neighbours who are near, neighbours who are strangers.** But these faithless carers know not of Allah; care not for any God.

As I see it, all the misery and destructiveness in places like Abington is caused by fragmented, disintegrating family life. There is no longer any shame or guilt involved in a family break-up. A government minister recently said that 'marriage is irrelevant to government policy.' Child care experts repeatedly tell the politicians what family disintegration is doing to children; and the anguished voices of the children themselves cry out with their own testimonies. But all this counts for little and the politicians ignore it.

In Abington, I see children cared for by strangers. I see dozens of single, separated, divorced, predatory men, exploiting the poverty and loneliness of single mothers. I see men who are alcoholics, drug addicts, psychologically scarred by their own upbringings, aggressive in temperament, already criminalised, devoid of education or training, inarticulate, unconfident... all having occasional or full time responsibility for caring for children. How can such men offer anything more to children than the violence and brutality to which so many of them have become accustomed? I see many such men, young men, yet ugly and haggard, slouched into themselves, with beer tins and cannabis joints, enveloped in smoke filled corners, and oblivious to the needs of the children they will ultimately abuse. I look into the faces of children misfortunate enough to have these pathetic creatures as carers and I see terrible silent suffering.

In this country dear Sheikh Omar, you cannot take in a stray dog without animal authorities interrogating you and your family to ensure that you are fit to provide for the animal; yet there are countless utterly inadequate men, switching partnerships and children with ease, with no oversight by anyone, no questions asked.

Three children, usually babies, are murdered in Britain every week by so-called parents. Often they are abused and starved and tortured by their 'carers' before they are murdered. Tens of thousands of other children are officially registered 'at risk.' That means they too could be murdered, or, they are at risk of being seriously harmed.

*My colleagues tell me that ten years ago the worst cases of child abuse deaths were always headline news. Public enquiries were set up to investigate the circumstances of the deaths. Damning reports were produced. Day after day the cases would be discussed and judgements and condemnations made. Everyone would agree that 'this **must** never happen again.' Politicians always declared that it would **never** happen* again. But it always did happen again. It happened hundreds of times again. Many years ago, it happened to a child called Victoria Climbié. The murderers of Victoria plunged new depths of cruelty and sadism. They beat her and starved her and tied her up in the bath to fester in her own faeces. They accused her of being possessed by the Devil. Once again the politicians said NEVER AGAIN! But again, the politicians were wrong. There have been many similar cases since the death of Victoria. Here are some of them (You can be certain that by the time I write to you again, there will be just as many more).

5-year-old Danielle; her squalid, miserable suffering life inflicted by her drug-crazed mother's boyfriend ended only when they both stuffed her into a sack and threw it into a canal.

Leticia, a 4-years-old disabled child, battered, burned, bitten and tortured to death by her mother and her mother's boyfriend (often it is the brutal boyfriends who perpetrate these crimes and mothers too cowed and too weak to stop them).

Samantha, aged 3. Her mother and boyfriend trained their dog to attack her. They starved her and beat her to death.

Two-year-old Casey, murdered through asphyxiation whilst her 21 year old uncle who was supposed to be minding her, was raping her.

Three-month-old Aaron, beaten and burned to death, his face held over a gas fire by his mother's boyfriend.

One-year-old Edmund, his face so swollen from the daily beatings that local children referred to him as the elephant baby. He was eventually beaten to death.

Jessica, murdered when she was just 54 **days** old, after suffering 54 days of physical torture and sexual abuse, at the hands of her father.

These are just a tiny fraction dear Sheikh Omar of the total number. Is there any other country in the world that does this to its infants and its small children, so often and so predictably?

This is the country that believes Islam is a barbarous religion and that Muslims are a cruel people. This is a country so fragmented it can no longer understand Muslim communities that hold together.

There are no Muslim Abingtons. There are no hundreds of thousands of Muslim fatherless children. There are no sadists and torturers amongst Muslim mothers and fathers who have Faith and who believe.

The British condemn us for daring to openly pray. They mock us for our expression of faith. They are outraged and legislate against us when *we arrange marriages to ensure that our children do not end up in similar scrap heaps and sewers as the children of Abington. They have no impact on us and that is why they fear and hate us. But maybe we should be reassured that the country that fears Islam most protects its children the least.*

My mission is safe. Through the power and Grace of Allah,

Your loving Sa'eed.

PART V

Chapter 40

Maggie stepped into a steaming hot foam-laden bath and lay motionless for fifteen minutes. Her head rested on a thick sponge. She sighed and breathed deeply with her eyes closed, concentrating on nothing more than releasing the tension in her body. She did this methodically; firstly limb by limb, then her shoulders, neck, brow, eyes and mouth, alternatively straining and relaxing each of them over a ten minute period, then sighing and sinking into her own dead weight.

It was a Monday evening, four days after the events in Stapleton Woods. She was on compassionate leave. Her children were safely tucked up in bed. Jackson was in a police cell facing certain conviction and a life sentence for the abduction of her child, and still being interrogated about the rape and murder of Angela Mulholland. His wife and children were in hiding somewhere back in London, and his two homes were being taken apart by forensic scientists.

The tabloids were in ecstasy: *Child Protection Tsar Arrested on Charges of Abduction and Attempted Murder.* The fact that Jackson worked in Liverpool made their attacks on social workers and Social Services more vitriolic. The broadsheets took a more dispassionate view, listing the names of previous paedophiles who had similarly ensconced themselves in child protection agencies.

Maggie had spent a long time with the police since Thursday. It hadn't been an entirely recuperative experience. She was forbidden access to Alice's saviour, Eric Houston, incredulously arrested and on bail, suspended from work, and facing the prospect of being charged with inflicting grievous bodily harm. She was the principal and only witness. What else could she say other than (thankfully) she had watched a man dementedly violent, and she had been convinced that he intended killing Jackson. It would matter not to the prosecution that his violence served a noble cause. They would strive for his conviction. This was all due process she knew, but it was crazy nonetheless, monstrously unjust. She desperately wanted to see Eric to thank him.

Her parents had stayed with her for long periods. She also had to contend with countless expressions of gratitude and relief, phone calls, e-mails and texts, from her neighbours, relatives, colleagues, friends old and new, and total strangers. In Keith's absence she relied on her friend Bell more than anyone else. Bell had stayed overnight for the first two nights and had been willing to stay longer. But both women knew that normality was much more of a priority than dependency.

Maggie was grateful for these overtures whatever their motivation, but they exhausted her. She dreaded another good will phone call, another visit. It was Keith she wanted to hear from, wanted to see walking through the door. He was in Denmark, participating in a three week seminar on 'Order, Complexity and Beauty' jointly presented by scientists and sonic art composers (of whom he was the most prominent) in the university of Copenhagen's department of musiocology. She had spoken to him twice since Thursday and wondered on each occasion had her voice betrayed that *something* had happened. Apparently not; it was just as well she wasn't speaking to him face to face. And why should she tell him? The children were safe and would never be alone or out of her sight again, certainly not until he returned; and she herself was being supported (and suffocated) by kindness. What was the purpose in telling him then, when it was certain to make him quit whatever he was doing to return on the first available flight.

This selflessness however, could not withstand certain vulnerabilities felt despite all the support she was offered. The image of her terrified daughter beating at the tiny window… what might have happened…? what would have happened…? haunted her day and night. She was aware like everyone else of the periodic exposure of abusers amongst high ranking Social Services staff, and particularly staff who had, like Jackson, begun their careers in residential care. But she still couldn't come to terms with the circumstances of his exposure, nor the magnitude of what he attempted, nor the bestiality and psychopathy which it implied.

Keith's return would not make all her problems go away, but it would certainly make life more tolerable. Something entirely unforeseen finally broke her selfless resistance to telling him what had happened. The news from Denmark was that all was not 'order' and 'beauty' in down town Copenhagen. There were riots every night. Two weeks before, Danish police had uncovered an assassination plot on the life of Kurt Westergaard, one of the artists who had drawn the Mohammed-mocking cartoons. The Danish public were outraged as the plot unfolded. Islamist extremists had been imported from Tunisia to help in the murder of the elderly, much admired artist. Danish editors retaliated by re-publishing the cartoons. The Islamic community was incensed. Now Muslim mobs were running amok.

She rang Keith earlier in the day on the pretext of ensuring he was all right. She was hoping that he would *not* be all right, that he might say something like 'things were getting a bit scary' or, he was 'feeling anxious...' She would take that as a cue for telling him what had happened. But he laughed at her, explaining that where he was he may as well have been a million miles away from the riots. He had heard and seen nothing. She had nothing to worry about, he tried to reassure her. She burst out crying and apologised. She cried again and apologised. He had never heard Maggie cry like this before. It was so profuse and intense that he feared something calamitous. He waited and then she told him. She began by assuring him that she and the children were safe and well. He listened in stunned silence. Her attempts not to dramatize made the impact of her words greater. The same nightmarish images that had wakened him in the middle of the night flashed across his own mind, of Alice raped, murdered and dumped in a ditch whilst he was being feted within the indulgent cloisters of Copenhagen academia. He never interrupted her. He resisted asking her any questions. When she'd finished he said: 'I'm coming home... I love you...' She put the phone down and wept with relief and joy.

That was six hours ago. He was due home in an hour.

When the doorbell rang, her sudden jolt made quite a splash. It annoyed her. She sat upright in the bath and listened carefully, but the only sound was the muffled crackling of the white honey-combed foam nestling around her. Little quivering bundles of it clung to her smooth skin and were quickly evaporating.

The doorbell rang a second time, the same duration, the same pressure. It was unfamiliar; certainly not Keith. He could of course have got home an hour early, but he would not have forgotten his keys. Maybe it was Bell, or another neighbour, or the police again. She gripped tightly on the sides of the bath, wondering whether or not she should ignore it, and then she worried as to whether or not the children had been wakened by it. She could feel the hot steamy sweat gathering on her brow.

It rang a third time. She couldn't stand it. She got out of the bath and dried herself quickly. She donned a velour dressing gown that was heavy and black. She moved through the landing to the window of the front bedroom and stared down on a solitary male figure. She could not see his face. She instantly thought it was Eric Houston, defying bail conditions and creating problems for both of them. She would have to tell him to leave.

As the visitor reached out to ring the bell a fourth time he raised his head and glanced over the house. Her heart sank as the living room light revealed the one person she did not want to see: Sean O'Neill. But he was obviously determined to keep on ringing until she opened the door, even if it did waken the kids.

She put slippers on and rushed down to the hall. She opened the door: 'Sean…? It's very late… I was…'

He interrupted her: 'Can I come in?'

'Not now Sean; not tonight, it's too late; Keith's due home in an hour.'

'I'll be gone in a quarter of an hour.'

'Sean…'

'We need to talk.'

'We will talk… when I'm *able*.'

That silenced him for a while. Would it be enough, she thought, to remind him of what she'd been through? Would it not shame him? Make him go away? It was his 'friend' Jackson who had done this to her, and here was *he* gate-crashing her home on presumably an entirely different matter. How insensitive could he get? A swelling resentment came over her, more powerful than the guilt and anxiety her first sighting of him had provoked.

'Martin's unable to talk too,' he said, quietly, pointedly. 'I'm sorry about what happened to you and Alice. You escaped. I'm glad you did. There's no escape for Martin.'

They stared into each other's eyes. She sensed danger in letting him in, and danger in refusing to let him in. But her resentment was turning to anger.

'I'm sorry Sean, you'd better go.'

He made no move and continued to stare at her, baiting her it seemed, to do something rash. She felt herself rapidly losing control, exacerbated by the realisation that she'd made another ghastly decision: refusing the offer of a police guard at her door. But that didn't mean she couldn't ask for their help now. 'If you don't leave, I'm going to ring the police.'

His face creased up contemptuously: 'What for? To admit you withheld information about a child being abused?'

She attempted to close the door in his face. But she didn't get it closed tight. He had one foot in the door, and both his hands were pressing it against her. If only her children were not there. She gave up and the door opened. He stepped in from the cold and darkness of the night and closed the door behind him.

She steadied herself, trying to suppress an almost over-whelming urge to lunge at him. She hated him. She had never felt hatred for anyone before. He must have deliberately chosen this moment knowing that her husband was in Denmark, that her traumatised children would be soundly asleep, and that she would quietly endure whatever he might say to her, for their sake. It wasn't just an intrusion; it was a pollution of her home by his destructiveness and his own self-hatred which had for so long been blinding him to the obvious.

'Did you need to do that?' she asked in a trembling voice, conscious of his inability to sense her seething irony.

'I told you, we need to talk.'

It was a semi demand that she allow him into the living room to sit. He was not going to converse with her in the hall.

She was livid, but with no safe options left.

'I have to dress,' she said, hurrying up the stairs. She looked in on the children before returning in sweat shirt and jeans. He was in the living room, sitting on the old settee leaning back relaxed and comfortable. She purposely avoided sitting near him; instead, she pulled out a high stool from under a table and looked down on him.

'Well?' she asked, waiting and wondering what he might say first. He was gazing around the cluttered room.

'You knew she was fucking him,' he suddenly said, staring into her eyes accusingly.

'Don't use that language here!' she barked at him recklessly, her wariness momentarily eclipsed by a raging indignation.

'Raping him! Screwing him! Is that better?' His voice was loud and full of contempt. 'You knew she was screwing him and probably doing it for years?'

Not strictly true, she thought. Of course she *felt* and *believed* it was true and Martin's father Dez McDonald was convinced it *was* true. But that was no proof! That wouldn't stand up in court. A barrister would make mince meat out of Dez McDonald. Despite his chilling testimony to Maggie he had in effect seen nothing. The barrister would dwell on his failings and his bitterness and direct the jury's attention to that *decent, loving hardworking mother.* The barrister would then ask them did they really believe she was capable of such an abomination, particularly when her (programmed) son would strenuously deny it.

A calm descended upon her, not just because she had suddenly conjured a defence to which she would rigidly adhere, but because he so obviously hadn't yet discovered what she truly feared.

'What are you talking about?' she said, psyching herself to plead ignorance and shock.

'Marian Greer screwing her son.'

'I thought you believed that Michael Greer was abusing him?'

'That's what you wanted me to believe. You looked at me as if I was a f... as if I was a moron when I told you that's what's I believed. You knew it wasn't him; you knew it was his mother.'

'I didn't know anything of the sort. There were times when I *thought* I knew.' She heavily stressed the word *thought*, as though she meant to caution him about his own erroneous certainties.

'You didn't look or sound like somebody who didn't know.'

'But I didn't!'

'Oh don't play dumb, Maggie! That was the reason why you wanted Martin away, because you knew she was screwing him. But you never said that. You deliberately went off on this tangent about his offending, as if that was the problem, and you tried hard with a little bit of drama to convince everybody else that that was the only problem.'

'No... you've got it all wrong.'

'You couldn't handle it, could you?'

'Handle what?'

'A mother screwing her fifteen year son.'

Oh God, the pity of it! she thought.

'Much easier,' he continued, 'if it *had* been Michael Greer screwing Martin.' There was a taunt in his voice and a gleam in his eyes.

'I don't understand what you're saying. You start off by saying I *knew* his mother was sexually abusing him. I may have thought she was... I used to think his step-dad was sexually abusing him. But I've never been absolutely certain about either. Now you're saying that I would have done something had I been certain it was one and not the other... that somehow I couldn't cope had it been his mother! Is that what you're saying?'

She stared into his cold green eyes unwaveringly, knowing that he was searching for the merest hint that she was lying.

'How long did you intend letting it go on for?' he asked.

'Letting what go on?'

He never spoke.

'I presume you're talking about Martin,' she said, maintaining the tone and the expression of incredulity; 'and not this... sexual

311

abuse you're so convinced about. We can at least agree that Martin's being abused. Maybe that's the only thing we can agree on. He's been abused horribly, in different ways. He's still being abused. Why? I don't know. And I suspect you don't know either. But I know the consequences for Martin. I *didn't* intend letting *it* go on. I tried to put an end to *it*. You stopped me. The only way to put an end to *it*… whatever abuse we're talking about, is to gradually move him somewhere else, away from both of them. But it's got to be done, as you said, with care; not by Social Services going in *with all guns blazing*. I think if they did that Marian Greer would kill herself. But that's no reason for you or anybody else to send him back home, and forget about him, or for you or your bosses fooling yourselves talking about doing *intensive work with the family*! You did Martin no favours in returning him.'

It wasn't a lie. It wasn't the truth. Yet every sentence contributed to a crescendo of hypocrisy and cowardice steadily beating within her. She was heavily conscious of the fact that she had sabotaged the last remaining opportunity to tell him. She wouldn't have dared tell him in the sanctuary of her own home.

He pondered and looked slightly bemused, uncertain how to respond. He was obviously aware that she had, wittingly or otherwise, put the spotlight back on him. There was an air of resignation about him when he slowly got up and said 'I still don't believe you didn't know what she was doing to him.'

'I can't help that Sean.'

It was the only safe retort and another blatant lie. He was going. It would be all over soon.

He briefly turned his back on her. He glanced over myriads of family photographs on the four walls, on the mantle piece and on the top of the folding coffee tables. There were multiple photographs on huge frames, single photographs on their own stands, and recent photographs unframed, dangling in the corners of paintings and artefacts. Her children dominated the photographs, every pleasurable emotion captured. In the chimney recess another family photograph caught his eye, much older judging by the hair styles, the clothes and the faded colours. He moved closer and scrutinised it. It was the photograph of her own family, her mother and father standing over her and her five brothers and sisters, unable to contain their laughter. He was just as captivated with it as he had been ten years previously when he had stood in her pokey little flat and asked her about each family member.

'Yes,' she said, 'same photograph.'

'Just as beautiful.'

He walked towards the door. He turned to her and said: 'You didn't ask me how could I be certain Marian Greer was abusing him?'

Was that an invitation to ask him? He obviously wanted to tell her. She didn't want to know. She sensed something awful was coming. He was going to tell her whether she wanted to know or not.

'When we chatted in your office' he said, 'you asked was I going to break in. It was a good joke and we both laughed. But that's what I did. I broke in. I didn't see Michael Greer... I saw Marian Greer... screwing Martin.'

She felt great waves of sorrow and revulsion sweeping over her, unsteadying her. She was standing in the middle of the room and there was nothing to reach out to except him. She turned her head away from him unable to look into his eyes, unable to cope with the guilt she felt. His bravado and his extremity in the cause of truth were in some perverse way supposed to impress her. It made her physically ill, disgusted, choked. She suddenly burst into tears; it was the only response her tense fragile mind could tolerate.

He didn't know what to say. Her crying intensified and he reached out to touch her. She shuddered and shook her head and said quietly: 'Please go, Sean.'

He was silenced. He opened the living room door to step into the hall and a terrifying scream rose up from a child at his feet. He looked down into the eyes of Alice who had obviously been huddled with her ear to the door listening to him, another man, another stranger, causing her mummy such pain. Alice's eyes were full of terror as she rushed past him and threw herself into her mother's arms.

'Please go,' Maggie repeated.

Chapter 41

O'Neill heard nothing of the limbering conversational delights of a Monday morning: Emma's hair-do, Silvia's new outfit, Morgan's wedding anniversary and family get- together, and a couple of sensations in the weekend press. The clerical staff had something else to talk about.

'Who watched Strictly Come Dancing?'

'Oh... wasn't it brilliant?'

'I couldn't watch it.'

'Alisha's going to win.'

'Can't stand it... that big long pause, before they tell ye the winner; our Trish puts a pillow over her head!'

'I thought Gethin and Camilla should have went through; I'm not saying they would ave won, but they should ave got through to the finals.'

'Yea, that's what I think. Isn't he gorgeous, Gethin?'

'Emmm...'

'Wasn't he the one attacked by an alligator in Louisiana?'

'You're joking?'

'Choosy alligator. Wouldn't mind attacking Gethin myself.'

'I watched that *Trial by Night* serial thing, the last episode. Anybody see it. There was a social worker in it; he was called out to look after an old man's budgie! He didn't look like Gethin Jones either.'

The clerical staff burst into fits of laughter. Their banter continued. O'Neill never raised his head; he never heard them.

'Did you know McGraw was released last week, Sean?' Morgan stood at his desk wanting to be reassured. 'Reckon you'll be going out to see him?'

O'Neill ignored him. He saw McGraw somersaulting back on the stairs. He heard Alice Lynch screaming as she looked up at him and ran past him. 'Sometime,' he eventually replied.

Morgan was about to leave him. 'By the way Sean, Probation sent some more papers on the McDonald file over; they're very old papers, more to do with Mrs Greer than her son... what's his name?'

'Who sent them?' O'Neill asked, raising his head for the first time.

'Oh Maggie Lynch's secretary Judy, with an apology from Maggie. She's still on sick leave. I'll leave them out for you.'

Morgan left. O'Neill stared at his desk again. Moments later Mary the cleaner spoke to him: 'Are you all right,' she asked, wary that she may have disturbed him and he might snap her head off.

He looked at her kindly caring face, her warm blue eyes: 'yes... yes,' he replied. He wondered: did he really look the way he felt. Then he asked himself: why's she concerned about me? He watched her walk away from him conversing with others. She had a friendly word for them all. He suddenly wished she hadn't walked away from him.

He visited Christopher in the foster home before going to see McGraw. The child had made a full recovery. He asked O'Neill when was he going home.

'Ask your mum when she comes to see you?'

'Mum says to ask you.'

He thought it significant that Christopher never looked at him, as if the child sensed and feared O'Neill's power in determining when he could go home. Yet he was brave enough to put O'Neill on the spot, knowing that he would probably be fobbed off once again. This had been going on for weeks now, the child's inexplicable yearning to return; his hope raised each time O'Neill visited, then shattered before he left.

'That man, Christopher... he's back in your house now,' said O'Neill. He seldom felt the need to defend himself, either directly or deviously, to a six year old.

Christopher looked puzzled. He stared up at O'Neill. 'Who... me dad?'

The question pained O'Neill. He detested kids encouraged by stupid mothers to call every lover and layabout 'dad'. He looked down on the child and noted the changes brought about by his removal from this so-called 'dad': the bright alert eyes, the well nourished face, the spurt in growth. 'McGraw... Eamon McGraw,' he said loudly; 'he's back again.'

'A know that!' 'me mum told me!'

'And what do you think of it?'

'A wanna go home.'

'Why?'

'A jus wanna.' Christopher looked up at him with exasperation. O'Neill was the great obstacle in his way. He figited and got off his seat and walked about the toy strewn room of his foster parents, picking up comics and toys and looking at them with indifference.

'What if he beats you again Christopher?'

Christopher stared at him and O'Neill could see the bitterness in the child's heart. He realised he shouldn't have asked that. When he turned to walk away he could feel the child still staring through him.

O'Neill returned to the tenement block near the cathedral where it had all begun. Christopher's brother Richard, three and a half foot tall, struggled to pull the back door free from the chipped concrete step. He kept shouting in a high pitched piercing voice: 'Hold on... stuck... it's comin...'

The commotion caused a stir among the pigeons in the loft behind O'Neill.

'Have ya got our Chrissie?' Richard asked proudly, with a beaming smile and a stand to attention as he pulled the door free.

'No, I haven't Richard.'

'When's ee comin?'

'Not for a while.'

'Why not?'

'Have you asked your mum?'

'Ask her what?'

'Ask her why Christopher can't come home yet?'

'Can't come home?' Richard looked puzzled.

Why are the innocent and the helpless the most forgetful and forgiving, O'Neill suddenly and inexplicably asked himself.

'Is you mum in?'

'Yes... will a git er?'

'Well... I don't want to be standing here all day.'

He watched Richard scamper through the kitchen. He had seen Madge and McGraw through the front room window. He knew they'd both be reluctant to face him. He hated these follow-ups. His work with McGraw was done.

Inside, Madge sat in her usual place near the gas fire watching a television panel game and peeling potatoes in a dilapidated metal basin. The water was thick, slimy and nearly black. He watched the pieces of skin fall monotonously from her bony hands into the foul looking liquid. She barely raised her head as he came in. Her baby Abigail slept soundly.

McGraw had his back turned to O'Neill entering. He was pretending to tidy up. O'Neill remembered him sprawled at the foot of the stairs, the blood oozing from his mouth. McGraw eventually faced him and sat down on the settee. He looked tense and withdrawn; he'd lost a lot of weight.

'When did you get out?' asked O'Neill, unsure of what else to say. He felt curiously uncomfortable.

McGraw didn't reply for a moment. He looked at O'Neill, his brow furrowing in disbelief. 'You put me in; *you* should know when a got out.'

Richard moved quickly to the side of McGraw and whispered something in his ear. He had an impish smile as he waited expectantly.

Richard's intimacy with the child batterer disturbed O'Neill. McGraw shook his head at Richard and said 'later.'

'Please dad... lemme bring it down now?'

O'Neill was aware of McGraw's predicament: just out of jail and on licence, he must feel that however he responds to Richard would be wrong in O'Neill's eyes.

O'Neill rescued him: 'Have you something to show me Richard?'

The child obviously had a toy or something that he needed to show O'Neill. O'Neill needed to get it out of the way before serious talk with Madge and McGraw.

'Yes!' shouted Richard.

'Well... I'd sure like to see it.'

Richard didn't wait for approval from McGraw. He scampered out of the room. His tiny steps could be heard double fast on the bare wooden stairs. A few seconds later he was descending the stairs, much slower, more carefully. He came into the room with a large cardboard box punched with tiny holes. He sat close to McGraw, occasionally looking up at him and smiling.

There was a heavy silence.

'That looks very secret,' said O'Neill.

Richard was itching to let him see. 'It was nearly dead, wasn't it, dad?'

'It's not dead now, is it?'

'No', said Richard emphatically; 'it's nearly better.'

'I wonder what it is.'

'Wanna see?' He sat waiting to spring off the seat to show O'Neill, but he also sought an expression of approval from McGraw.

McGraw nodded. Richard dropped to the floor on his knees and removed the lid of the box. He was bulging with pride. His eager fingers disappeared, searching, fumbling; a great commotion was taking place at the bottom of the box. Eventually his hands came out empty, and he looked at McGraw pleadingly.

McGraw's fat fingers went into the box. They reappeared, nestling around… O'Neill stared with revulsion. The massive hands of McGraw firmly held some kind of large bird that had endured a terrible mauling. O'Neill could hardly look at it. It should have been dead, he thought; better dead. It was bald from the beak, over the raw pinkish head, to its neck. One eye seemed to have been gouged out of its socket. All over its body were varying sizes of raw flesh, where something or somebody had ripped through the soft, blue grey and white, richly patterned plumage, leaving streaks and dots of coagulated blood, too far embedded to be removed.

O'Neill's stomach churned. It had to be a sick, sickening joke. And yet, there was Richard, rapturously proud, oblivious to the waves of nausea threatening to overwhelm O'Neill.

McGraw held the bird with one hand now and was examining it with the fingers of his other hand.

'What is it?' O'Neill asked; 'a pigeon?'

'Rock dove,' McGraw replied, his eyes remaining on the bird.

It meant nothing to O'Neill. 'What happened to it?' he asked helplessly.

'Our pigeons got it,' said Richard, instantly.

'*Your* pigeons did that?' asked O'Neill.

Richard nodded his head vigorously.

'It's strayed in from the coast,' McGraw added; 'doesn't belong here.'

'Will it recover?'

'Bout a week should do it.'

'I found it,' said Richard, sticking out his chest and smiling. 'They wudda killed it, wuddinda, dad?'

'Yip. We just gotter in time.'

Why didn't they let the pigeons kill it, thought O'Neill. The churning in his stomach had ceased, but he felt hot and his head was light.

'This'ill grow again,' said McGraw, running his hand through the plumage. He spread one of it wings. 'The legs and feet are okay.'

'What about its eye,' asked O'Neill.

'It can see outta thisin,' piped Richard.

'What have you done with it since you got it?'

'Cleaned it down, fed it… it was much worse than that.'

'Nursed it,' said Richard.

'How do you know it won't happen again?

'It might happen again, probably will.'

'Where will you release it?'

Crosby, Formby… somewhere up the coast.'

Nothing more was said for a few moments. O'Neill felt disorientated, uncertain how to proceed. His heart wasn't in it when he turned to Madge and said: 'I need to speak to you, Madge… I need to speak to you both. Can you ask Richard…?'

'Ask him what,' said Madge, contemptuously.

'To leave the room for a while?'

McGraw put the bird back into the box, turned to Richard and said: 'Leave it back and stay upstairs til I call ya.'

Richard did as he was told. 'Okay dad.'

O'Neill wanted to say thanks but couldn't. What am I doing here? he asked himself. 'I'll need to call weekly,' he said.

Madge wouldn't look at him. But he sensed her mounting anger.

'Christopher and Richard's names are both on the child abuse register,' he said, almost as an apology. 'I've got to call regularly.'

'Ee's done is time!' Madge said.

'Not enough,' said McGraw, looking straight into the eyes of O'Neill for the first time and sensing his difficulty. 'You think a'll beat Richard, don't you?'

'No I don't,' he said. He could feel the force of his gratifying kick on McGraw's jaw. 'But *we* can't be certain.'

It was a long time since he sheltered behind the anonymous and the ubiquitous *we*. He turned to Madge only to escape the stony stare of McGraw. But he didn't see Madge. Instead he saw himself taking Martin by the hand and delivering him back into the arms of his mother. He saw himself lying on the bedroom floor, trying with his hanky to stifle the sound of his guilt-laden, pounding heart. He saw himself crossing the landing, and in the heat of their hideous passion, opening the door enough to let him see and stare at her ugly naked contortions over her son. He heard Maggie asking him: 'Is there any other reason why you're letting Martin home?'

Suddenly Madge screamed at him.

'Why ya fucker! Why can't ya leave es alone?' She leapt up and faced him. Her knees were bent, as though she were ready to pounce. Her bony fist was clenched tight around the old knife she'd been using to peel the potatoes. 'We told ya what ee was like when is father walked out. We asked yous ta help es cause wa cudn manage im. Did ya? Did ya fuck all?' Yir fancy Mrs Winters an er crony Robson... I showed them the shit in the drawer an the coat blockin up the toilet... every day for a year ee was doin somthin like that. An all yous people did was talk about im punishin me for what is no-good-fuckin father did. But what help did ya give? Fuck all. Then tha getta fucker like you to do their dirty work for em. An ever since ya blackened that door, a can't walk out fir fear of people starin at me, runnin away from me, an the whole fuckin country starin at me in the papers as if a was a fuckin witch. A'll tell ya somethin else: every time I go an see im, ees askin: when can a come home mammy? when can a come home? An a'm telling im to ask you cause yir the one that knows. But yir a fuckin coward who won't tell im anything! You throw it back to me! Whaddo *ya* think then? A'm a livin with a murderer? Well yir a fuckin tosser if ya believe that!' She lifted her arm and pointed to McGraw. 'If it wasn't for im yid have Richard away too. He beat Christopher cause I took a fuckin overdose! A cudn' stand it any longer. A wanted to be able to manage but a cudn. An yous lot did fuck all ta help when a asked fir it. Christopher's my son an a love im. But it wasn' my fault is fuckin useless father walked out onnim. A still love Christopher, but a don't want im home as long as rats like you are hangin about.'

Chapter 42

Sa'eed and Samira sat opposite each other in the lounge of their parent's home. She didn't need to wear the veil in his presence but he had requested that she do so. He didn't often converse with her and she had no doubts about why he was doing so on this particular occasion. She had been arrested and charged with assault. Although the good family name and her own impeccable reputation would probably save her, there was a distant possibility that she might be imprisoned. Attacking Professor van Hoofdaaker in his own office was a serious criminal offence. She intended wearing the veil in court and in the current climate of police and judicial hostility to veiled Muslims she knew she might just be unlucky.

This possibility of imprisonment and the blemish on the family name was not however Sa'eed's principal concern. He intended her to think it was but he had weightier matters on his mind. His responses to what she had done had fluctuated wildly. Initially he was preoccupied with a perceived danger that her interrogation might pose for him – the police were certain to want to interview other family members. That made him angry and he deliberately had not made immediate contact with her for fear of protesting or saying too much. He had spent a lot of time calming and psyching himself for this encounter, wanting to appear both reasonable and authoritative, caring and concerned. But the more he had dwelt upon the bizarre and utterly non-political nature of her actions (which any half decent lawyer could easily link with the atrocity she suffered and its aftermath all those years ago) the less dangerous it seemed. A bigger concern was that she might do something similar or even more outrageous in the future. This might prompt some enterprising journalist to try to get to the bottom of it, maybe thinking family members could be the key. He imagined himself being confronted by a journalist during the least guarded moment and hearing the words: 'You are the brother of Samira

Jama… could I have a word?' There was real danger in that scenario, he thought. He needed to assess for himself: was her action merely an aberration and could he be sure that she would never do anything like that again?

He had become increasingly aware of both the similarities and divergence in their two lives stemming from the same event. They had both been scarred and tested by a Muslim-hating atrocity all those years ago and both had found refuge and redemption in Islam. But Samira was still suffering, still at the mercy of forces apparently deaf to her needs, bureaucratically insensitive enough not to return the organs of her stillborn. He had always known about her plight, but had never dwelt on it nor sought to explore the details of it. He had never wanted to get involved; there was too much potential within it for distraction or exposure. Now he realised, through her action, what it had done to her and what a monstrous crime it was. He did not however assume it was her veil and her religion that made them treat her like that. He had moved beyond that instinctual sense of Muslim victimisation, interpreting every wrong as a typically Western, Christian, anti Islamic activity. He knew that the people who did this to her, probably had no religion at all and no sensitivities for the faiths of others. He had learnt from his father about the rumours circulating within hospitals and medical schools, that many mothers of all faiths and none had suffered similar experiences as that of Samira. This was not an anti-Muslim thing; it was, he now believed, something rotting at the core of a valueless, irreligious professional life itself. It was exemplified as much by the callousness of van Hoofdaaker as it was by the brutal cynicism and voyeurism of O'Neill. Van Hoofdaaker and his colleagues were worse in one sense. They were faceless people who wreaked suffering and despair on bereaved mothers from the seclusion of their impenetrable fiefdoms hidden away in the obscure corners of university and hospital cloisters. Although he could not say so, he admired Samira's daring and courage in getting through to them and confronting them. He would never have thought her capable of anything like that.

'You must have known what this would do to our parents,' he said, focussing on the safe and selfless issue of family honour, fulfilling his role as elder brother. 'To our father in particular,' he continued, 'his job, his reputation... why did you do it?'

Samira stared at the floor near to his feet, which he wrongly interpreted as embarrassment and shame. She had been asked the same question by her parents, by her sisters in the mosque, and by her family's Iman, Abbūd al-Zomer. The police had also asked her more than a dozen times. She had no difficulty in replying then, unlike now. She sensed that was not really the question her brother wanted to ask.

'I didn't set out to do it,' she said without looking at him. 'It happened. I don't know how.'

'That's not the way it was reported. They said it was premeditated.'

'It wasn't,' she insisted. She looked up at him, imploringly. 'I went seeking justice. I found even greater *injustice*; I couldn't help myself.'

Sa'eed's focus on Samira weakened. He said nothing for a few moments. He looked away.

Was that a gesture of disappointment or disproval, or something worse? Samira's eyes expressed both apprehension and puzzlement.

'But our parents, our home, our standing in the neighbour-hood... did you consider none of that?'

Maybe not. Her *own* standing had been on a downward spiral in any case. Their nearest neighbours, the early retired Camerons had distanced themselves ever since she wore the veil. The usual tendencies of middle England avoidance and reserve were brought into play to ensure they never had to face her, or worse, speak to her. When they heard her in the garden they ceased spontaneous conversation and spoke to each other about their flowers and shrubs. They spoke in whispers, muffled tones, turning their heads away from the fencing that divided the two homes, unaware that they were only fleeing their own prejudices and inadequacies. They had continued acknowled-ging the existence of her parents and occasionally went out of their suffocating ways to speak to her father; but since the news of Samira's arrest broke they seemed to have locked themselves away from the family altogether.

'This neighbourhood is not *my* community,' she said.

'But it is our parent's. Where else is there for them to go?'

She couldn't answer. Their father's job enabled him to go anywhere in the country. But she knew as Sa'eed did that their parents were unlikely to go anywhere. They just wanted to retire quietly.

'They're established here,' he said. 'They are respected. They were in a television studio advising Muslim youth on citizenship the same day that you were attacking a medical professor in his office.'

Again she did not respond. It was not guilt or remorse. Her eyes remained alert and focussed; indeed, there may even have been a hint of scepticism in them, as though she might think their tête-à-tête was a sham, or that his ironical contrasting of her actions with those of her parents lacked conviction.

'You've invited unwelcome attention,' he said calmly. He scrutinised her eyes and her posture.

'You mean the press... or the police?' she asked.

'Both.'

'Which do you...' she hesitated; 'fear... most?'

Sa'eed's expression never changed; yet the question and more so the hesitant delivery hit him like a bolt of lightning.

'I don't *fear* anything,' he said, conscious that it was the first deliberate lie he had ever told her.

'Why would the attention of the police or press be unwelcome to *you*?' she asked. It almost sounded as though she was playing with him.

'Unwelcome to our parents I meant,' he said with emphasis.

'But not to you?'

'Yes, to me as well,' he conceded reluctantly, yet inquisitively. 'I have a job and a reputation too. I work for Social Services. Why shouldn't I be worried when you attack a professor in Health Services. What do you think *my* colleagues would make of it? Social Services... Health Services... they're linked; I meet people from Health Services every day. I met a consultant last week who knows our father well. No I don't want people talking about me or the police interviewing me because of some crazy behaviour by you!'

She lowered her head and was silent.

'I'm sorry,' he said.

'Perhaps if I'd thought about consequences like that it could have prevented me doing what I did.'

'But you didn't and so here we are.'

'I don't want to make your task more difficult.'

'What do you mean… my task?' He struggled to control the vulnerability rapidly spreading through him.

'I *will not* make your task more difficult.' She spoke slowly and emphatically, observing the impact of her words and feeling the need to reassure him.

Samira was not the kind of challenge Sa'eed had contemplated during his eight years abroad. What was she about now, he asked himself. What did she know? How could she know? What had he done wrong? He had left no clues, kept no diary, always burnt relevant literature and correspondence as soon as he'd read it. He dared to feel some kind of relief. He rose from his seat and walked over to her and knelt before her. He unclipped her veil without touching her hair. He gazed searchingly at her eyes, her lips, her cheeks and her brow and he saw only beauty and pain and truth. She hardly moved, but her eyes challenged him again to trust her.

He replaced the veil and returned to his seat. He knew now that his anxieties had been misplaced. She would pose no risk to him.

He stared at her again, overwhelmed by a surge of conflicting emotions and questions. What made this happen? How could she have arrived at such a resolution after what she had been through and was still enduring? Her mental torment and physical decay, dutifully reported in letters from his mother, had been for him the only cause of pain and doubt in a jihadi existence otherwise profoundly satisfying to him. Perhaps that was his mother's intention, to pain him sufficiently that he might return. He had read the letters imagining Samira rotting away in a suburban wilderness whilst he strove daily to attain the heights of spiritual fulfilment and physical rigour. She had no one and he was blessed with the luxury of living within a community, an international Islamic Sharia community with a camaraderie and a purity of purpose and sacrifice that was quite simply indescribable. He had prayed daily for her. He had once asked Sheikh Omar Abdel Rahmān, his mentor and spiritual guide, could he take a short time out and return home. Sheikh Omar said 'no' and encouraged him to pray harder. Allah must have heard. Now he realised she had not only recovered through the grace of Allah, but she had apparently chosen a path similar to his. She was neither a martyr nor on a mission as he was; but that closest proximity to her beautiful face only a few minutes before, staring into eyes that could tell no lies, convinced him that their perceptions of the world were moving closer. She'd obviously known about his task or at least suspected it. If he'd even had thought of that possibility before, he would have predicted (and dreaded) her hysterics and panic and her screaming pleas for him not to do whatever he intended to do. But here she was calmly reassuring him, in effect wishing him well. She would not only support and protect him, she was willing to sacrifice herself for him. He smiled at her and she smiled in return and his sense of pride swelled.

'How did you find out? How long have you known?' he asked.

'I've known nothing,' she replied definitively; 'I only had a sense of you not really belonging here anymore.'

That sounded ambiguous; a complaint that he had not or might not share with her, or a declaration that she need not or did not want to know.

He felt the need to rise and pace the room but knew that that would not release him from the temptation of telling her.

'I have been chosen,' he said quietly.

'For martyrdom?'

His pause seemed an eternity to her. Her eyes again begged and willed him to trust her.

'A mission.'

'Martyrdom?'

'Yes.'

She clasped her hands tightly and raised them to her chin. She closed her eyes momentarily. 'Allah createth what he willith,' she said, in a near whisper.

'You don't know anything,' he said, 'and yet you are now an accomplice.'

'Am I?' Her eyes glistened. Her tone was semi-mocking. She was contemptuous of the danger implied.

He had something to say to her and he knew its effect. She would either rage at him or stare at him in disbelief. It was not, he then thought to himself, necessary to say it, but then he felt he had to say it for *his* own sake: 'You will probably not go to prison for your attack on the professor, but they will imprison you for a long time for knowing and believing that what I'm doing is right.'

Samira spoke with a quiet scorn: 'Like the sister of Ameen Yusef…?'

Sa'eed shook his head and lowered his gaze, another admission of her capacity to shock him. For a few seconds he was stricken with the thought that Samira was somehow implicated. He knew Ameen well, and his sister, Azza. He had lived and worked and fought and prayed with Ameen in Pakistan and Afghanistan. Ameen had been arrested only days before his intended martyrdom and carnage in Manchester's Trafford centre. His sister was arrested later, on the charge of knowing about his intention and not betraying him. She was convicted and sentenced to ten years. Mobs had screamed at her as she stepped from the police van each day of the court hearings.

For years, commentators and editorials had been asking: 'WHY DO THE TERRORISTS HATE US?' Then they began asking what was for Sa'eed, an equally stupid question: 'HOW CAN THEIR YOUNG, BEAUTIFUL AND EDUCATED SISTERS AND WIVES EMBROIL THEMSELVES IN SUCH EVIL?'

Sa'eed looked at Samira and could see only her purity. Azza's loyalty and her fate had clearly inspired her.

Commentators didn't ask such questions anymore. So many sisters and wives had recently been convicted for supporting and helping terrorists. The commentators had no answers. They didn't understand.

Sa'eed walked over to Samira again, took her hands, and gently brought her to her feet. He lowered his head towards her and lightly hugged both of her cheeks. They stared into each other's eyes. He turned to leave. She couldn't resist challenging him:

'Why did you pretend it was our parents you were concerned about? My actions only shamed them. Your *martyrdom* could destroy them.'

He thought for a moment. It was more than a mere question.

'I couldn't very well have told you the real reason without being certain of your loyalty. Forgive me for not trusting you sooner... not trusting anybody. Allah will strengthen our parents. They will learn that it is not enough to *sit at home and receive no hurt*. We must all fight, *with all our goods and all our persons.*'

She smiled. That was the Qur'anic reference, Sūrah 4, verse 95, that she too would use, to justify whatever help she might offer him. Imprisonment was a small price to pay for the privilege.

Chapter 43

O'Neill visited Lawrence Grove at four o'clock knowing that Martin would be at home and his parents at work. It had been one of those freezing cold, brilliantly bright winter days, with a pale blue cloudless sky. In about an hour's time the sun would complete its most south-westerly path of the year; it's blinding yellow brightness would mellow to a deep crimson and it would slowly sink behind the ancient Observatory on Bidston Hill, the most prominent landmark on the other side of the Mersey. He had calculated that one hour was all he needed.

'Hi Martin,' said an upbeat O'Neill, all smiles, when Martin opened the door. Martin said nothing. He looked more tense than usual. He nodded in an exaggerated way as though he couldn't speak. But he eventually did speak and he managed to say what he needed to say:

'Me mum says not to let anybody in the house when she's out.'

He took a deep breath then and his lips trembled.

It was only a week since O'Neill had called. Too long. Martin's mother had worked on him. His mood had changed dramatically. O'Neill stared at him and saw his mother clad in her black satin shift running towards him from the doorway; he saw her naked flesh enveloping him. He literally tried to shake these images out of his head as he wondered what he might say next.

Martin just stood there trying to keep still, securing himself with one hand gripping the frame of the door and the other leaning on the window sill on the inside.

'Where is your mother?'

'Work.'

'So nobody's allowed into the house until she gets back?'

'No.'

'What do you think about that Martin?'

'Me mum said it.'

'Yes I know, but what do you think about it?'

'Don't know.'

'So you're not going to let anyone in?'

'That's what my mum says.'

'Are you not going to let *me* in?'

'Mum says a can't let anybody in.'

'Didn't you know I'd be calling at this time?'

'No.'

'But didn't I tell you the last time I saw you?'

'Don't remember. It's what me mum says.'

'What does Michael say about all this?'

'Nothing.'

'Do you know why I came today?'

He shook his head.

'I wanted to ask you about the discus.'

Martin's whole body moved awkwardly in various directions despite his tightening grip on the frame of the door.

'You can throw the discus, can't you?'

Martin nodded and then smiled.

'Well... can't I talk to you about it?'

He struggled with this temptation, clearly weighing up the risks. Then he nodded.

O'Neill asked: 'Can I see the discus?'

'It's upstairs.'

'Well, can't you fetch it? I don't have to go into the house; I can look at it here.'

Again Martin struggled. Then he levered himself away from the door, turned and ran up the stairs. O'Neill stood there, a multitude of thoughts racing through his mind and a sense of foreboding. He looked along the hallway, bright, thick-carpeted, newly decorated, ornamented... he saw them again, locked together... the place suddenly looked and felt like a tomb.

Martin came down the stairs faster than he went up, perhaps animated by the feel of the discus in his hand. His smiles suggested that he had forgotten the order he had been given.

O'Neill held his hand out: 'Can I hold it?'

Martin handed it to him. O'Neill took it with both hands. The surfaces of both sides were wooden, smoothed and polished, and joined together by a metal rim.

So this was it, O'Neill thought, the *flying saucer*; the same *object* Mrs Greer nudged out of his sight; the sport not worth mentioning in his school! He repeatedly turned the discus round in his hands, gazing at it with the curiosity of a child acquiring a coveted toy and not certain how to make it work.

'It's heavy,' O'Neill said.

'It's not a real one.'

'Is it not? It looks real enough to me.'

'I made it.'

O'Neill looked up at him. '*You* made it! Where? How?'

'At school. There's a piece of metal inside. I did the wood pieces on the lathe and glued them over the metal. Mr Harper helped me with the rim. It's soldered there... See? It's near enough the right weight, two kilos.'

O'Neill was visibly affected by what he'd just heard: the sheer quantity of words, spontaneous yet precise, articulated without difficulty.

'When did you start throwing the discus, Martin?'

''Bout five years ago.'

'Are you good at it?'

'All right.'

'How good are you?'

Martin didn't answer.

'Where are you at school... I mean, are you amongst the top five discus throwers?'

'First,' he said emphatically and then smiled embarrassingly at the look of amazement on O'Neill's face.

'Look Martin, I know nothing about discus throwing. Could you show me?'

Martin jolted his head back as if feigning surprise. 'Where...? Here?' His voice was full of incredulity.

'No. In the park; it's not far from here, is it?'

Minutes later, they were walking to the park together talking about discus throwing. O'Neill still carried the discus. Despite his mother, Martin had acquired an encyclopaedic knowledge of the sport. He talked confidently about the great champions and Olympic gold, about world records and infamous cheats. The discus, he told O'Neill, is the only track and field event that's never set a world record during the Olympic Games.

'The only discus throwing I've ever seen,' said O'Neill, 'was that famous slow-motion clip they show every time there's an Olympics... It's an old film and the thrower's naked. Don't remember what the film was called.'

'*Arena of the Gods*', said Martin; '1936 Berlin Olympics.'

O'Neill was silenced.

They made their way to the centre of the park. Martin carefully scrutinised all the surrounding area. 'I'll throw it that way,' he said, pointing north.

O'Neill handed him the discus and stood back engrossed.

'Holding it is the hardest part,' said Martin. 'You don't grip it. You just let it rest... there, in them finger joints. Everybody grips it at first.'

He stood still for a moment, his back to O'Neill, his arms seemingly dangling at his side, and the discus resting securely as he had shown.

'You should warm up before you throw,' he said. He was *not* warming up merely for O'Neill's convenience. 'You have to swing it a couple of times. You've got to get it well behind the shoulder; gives it more distance and strength.'

His two massive legs stood apart like giant pillars secured as he completed the preliminary swings. O'Neill could feel ripples of air as the arm came gliding past him. Martin moved into the turn, his left leg going first and the discus trailing at the furthest point behind. On he came, facing O'Neill for a split second. O'Neill's mesmerised stare locked onto Martin's eyes. The speed increased dramatically. He completed the one and a half turns and his right arm shot into the air, releasing the discus with a thunderous roar. It quivered and soared high, silhouetted against the cloudless blue sky, scattering a lone raven in its path. Then it descended more rapidly, thudding into the cold green earth just over the brow of a hill, out of sight.

O'Neill was visibly shaken. 'There's a lot more to it than I thought,' he said.

Martin ran to the spot, returned and asked: 'Would you like to have a go?'

'Oh… okay.' It was the last thing he wanted to do. He took the discus and it felt colder and heavier, more alien than before.

'Let yourself loosen up,' said Martin. 'It's in them joints there you want it to rest. It's hard first time. Raise your arm backward… ah, you're gripping.'

'You bet I'm gripping… it's bloody well falling!'

Martin chuckled. 'If you turn your wrist a bit like that… at the end of each swing, it won't fall.'

'It's still falling… I have to grip!'

'No. You're too stiff. You've got to think you're going to hold it… let your arm relax.'

But O'Neill remained stiff and began to sweat. 'No good Martin; you show me.' O'Neill tried to appear curious and interested by examining the discus in his hand, and repeatedly flexing the muscles of his fingers. There was something about Martin's liberation that perturbed him and he didn't know what it was.

A few seconds passed and O'Neill realised Martin had not responded. He raised his head to see why. Martin stood motionless, looking away from him, staring in the direction of the entrance to the park. His mother was standing there. She wore her old shabby coat and held a shopping bag in one hand.

Why doesn't she move or shout or wave or just walk away, O'Neill thought. It was more threatening, he then reckoned, just standing there making them both wonder how long she had been around. But why was she here? She wasn't due home for another half hour at least. Did she sense that O'Neill might try something like this when she wasn't about?

She turned and walked out of the park. 'I bet your mother's proud of that,' O'Neill said.

Martin shook his head and said nothing.

He would suffer for this, O'Neill thought. 'I'll tell your mum it was my fault, Martin; okay?'

But how reassuring was that, he suddenly asked himself.

'Has Michael ever seen you throw the discus?'

He shook his head again.

'Look Martin, I've been talking to a guy up at the university, Peter Chapman; he's head coach for field and athletics. Do you think we could go up and see him for a chat sometime next week?'

The muscles twitched around Martin's eyes and his mouth. A multitude of thoughts raced through his brain. He stammered out a 'ye...... .s.' It seemed to say something more: YES, OH BOY!

Chapter 44

O'Neill drove into the misty wet grounds. The mist had cleared a little but not from around his feet. He walked slowly up the balustrade steps to the huge oak-panelled front door, its brass and paint still gleaming in the mist. He gave the door a mighty knock then turned his back on it to gaze at Mr Perie's pride and joy, to inhale the fragrance-drenched air. The grass was cut, the trees pruned, the leylandii hedging trimmed. Purple, white and crimson rhododendrons bloomed. The maze of lavender was virtually complete. Row upon row of rose bushes were beginning to bud. He was so proud of his roses and his dahlias; always eager to talk about his roses: 'you just sprinkle a mixture of tobacco and naphtha around the bushes,' he told visiting admirers; 'and there's your result.'

Elderly stooping Mr and Mrs Perie answered the door, together as always. A pretty picture: smiles, greetings; no smile returned; no words. They pretended not to notice for a while, but they became frightened of him. He walked into their spacious parlour dominated by the Steinway baby grand in the bay of their window. He looked round at them, following him like sheep to the slaughter. He sneered. He lifted the heavy brass companion set from the fireside. All its pieces fell noiselessly, leaving him gripping the powerful base and stem. He turned round on them and they stared at him aghast. They were so old and feeble and helpless. They could only raise high pitched muffled cries as he rained down the blows upon them. They both lay at his feet, their skulls smashed open and warm black blood gushing out of them.

But that was not the purpose of his visit. He heard those sickening incomprehensible sounds coming from the other room. He walked slowly towards it and opened the door. He saw the look of terror on the face of their deformed son. Their son was a hunchback, a dwarf, an unspeakable repulsive nauseating deformity with two different eyes, an ugly curved spine and a crooked mouth that could utter nothing but the squeaks and grunts of a wild animal. This was their beloved Tony upon whom his loving decrepit parents spent every hour of every day, wiping the slobbering mouth every minute, keeping him ever so clean as if cleanliness alone was dignity. This was the *thing* whose crooked smile and unfocussed gaze had tormented O'Neill for years, because he had to visit him regularly and he had to look at him and speak to him and try to smile at him; worst of all he had to witness the tender loving care of Tony's decrepit parents. What lunacy possessed them to conceive this monstrosity in the twilight of their years?

O'Neill was upon him in seconds and the contorted face screamed. His outstretched fingers went round its sweating throat and the horrible feel of its deformed body drove him into a frenzy. His nails drew blood as they pierced through the thin pale skin at the back of its neck. Deformed arthritic sticks for arms seemed to crack as they beat down helplessly on O'Neill's vice like grip. He gazed down into the two bulging unequal eyes, the gasping jaundiced tongue drying rapidly in a gaping mouth. O'Neill smiled. He laughed. He watched the ugly useless crucified, crucifying life ebb away in his hands. He looked above him in triumph. No movement, no sound. He gazed down and yelled in terror as the crooked lips in a lifeless body smiled death at him.

He tightened his grip again but the ugly crooked smile grew larger. He heard a terrible sound, a mocking sound, a screaming laughter from the crooked mouth, and he saw a triumphal stare in the bulging eyes. He flung the horrible thing away from him. He rushed out of the room, through the house and into the garden. He opened the garden shed. It was the pitchfork he wanted, the same pitchfork he always wanted to wrench from the hands of the loving father, to ram it through the loving father and his deformed son. He ran back to the room again. It was still there in all its helplessness and its ugliness. He rushed at it. He thrust the fork with all his might. But he went with the fork because it pierced only the air that he breathed. The *thing* was still there. He began to tremble before it. He was about the lunge himself forward again but he heard the shuffling footsteps that he knew so well.

He looked around him in disbelief and saw the figure coming though the door wearing the unmistakeable filthy flat cap, the drunken, stinking, staggering frame of Murphy, Patrick Murphy, who staggered to the main office every day, the drained whiskey bottle stuck to the pocket of his vile smelling jacket. Here he was, throwing himself into another of the Peries' luxurious arm chairs. He looked up at O'Neill through his blood shot watery eyes. It was the drops on the tip of his purple nose which disgusted O'Neill. Yet Murphy always insisted on seeing him, the 'Irish one' and O'Neill always refused to see him, telling the disgusted reception staff to shoot him. He laughed cynically at other social workers who *did* see Murphy, pretending to be interested in whatever nonsense he spoke, pretending to care, trying to humour him, speaking softly and gently to him, never chastising him. He knew they thought of Murphy precisely as he thought of him: a drunken vagabond, a half-wit, a stench-laden, lice-crawling, liver-rotten parasite. They would tell Murphy to call again, and whenever they got him through the door, they came rushing back and gestured the clothes-pegs coming off their noses in a great sigh of relief.

O'Neill rushed at him and snatched the stinking whiskey bottle from his pocket. This was what he had always wanted to do, smash the bottle over the skull of Murphy and ram the jagged ends into his bloodshot eyes. He held the neck of the bottle and raised it as high as he could and swung it down as forcefully as he could onto Murphy's head. But there was nothing there. He tried again but there was nothing there. But there he *was* there looking up at O'Neill, his charred purple lips breaking into a smile, his putrid mouth opening and revealing the yellowing black buckled teeth. O'Neill threw the bottle at him and it went through him. Murphy removed his filthy flat cap, went down on one knee and mockingly bowed to O'Neill, offering up the ravaged skin of his bald head to another blow. But O'Neill now felt paralysed and began to sweat and tremble. Murphy looked up at his helplessness and burst into a fiendish laughter. Behind O'Neill the deformity continued laughing at him. Their laughter blended and intensified.

O'Neill felt a consuming madness that he could not stem. He stepped away from both of them but couldn't take his terrorised eyes off them. From behind came another familiar sound. He swung round to face the infamous hag Sheila McCrory. She was encircled by her seven beautiful, bawling bastards, and her eighth child, the new born, trying to suckle off her shrivelled milkless tits.

NO! NO! NO! This is madness! But this is real! Hear them! See them! Feel them! Touch them! The same Sheila McCrory, the sailor's whore, the hag, the last choice for the bloated bellied sailor boys of a Friday night, who had fucked her a thousand times and more, giving her those beautiful little bawling bastards with their arses bare and their angelic faces pasted with a gluey snotter.

Yes, look again Sean. Sheila McCrory, the ugliest whore in the city, the biggest joke in the office. Morgan said her legs should be tied. Emma tried to get her sterilised. Murray wanted her locked up. If only she could be kept on one of the boats and transported to the other side of the globe. If only she would surrender those foundling bastards to our foster homes, our residential homes, spotlessly clean, good wholesome food and loving care. But look at her. She would never surrender them, not one of them. She would remain what she was: the festering thorn in their pampered flesh. So they would still have to see McCrory and perform their acts of compassion, endless patience and toler- ance, and social work love. And they would return to the office scratching and picking at themselves, boasting that their pleated prim dresses and designer suits would be burnt that night because they had been to McCrory's and her snottering bastards had been crawling all over them and their stomachs had swelled and heaved and churned when McCrory asked them to sit down on her couch and they would not sit where drunken bloated sailor boys had belched and farted and fucked her over the years, leaving the solidified pools of prickly semen. Here she was then, Sheila McCrory and her litter rocking to and fro in Mrs Pirie's rocking chair.

O'Neill lifted the pitchfork. This is what I must do, he thought. Then he smiled and laughed, ignoring the fiendish laughter of

Murphy and the deformity behind him. He charged and drove the pitchfork through McCrory and her children, each and every one of them. Through them it went, unscathing them. A streak of terror went through his own rattling bones. Salty sweat trickled from his brow into his eyes, burning, burning, burning. He reached out a quaking hand. It is a ghost, he thought: 'I'm surrounded by ghosts.' He stepped nearer them. But ghosts were from the dead and these bastards and their whoring mother were all alive. They were alive because his quaking fingers touched the cold withered bloodless skin of Sheila McCrory's bony cheeks. A lascivious smile spread across her lips.

He wrenched the suckling infant out of her skeletal arms away from her shrivelled milkless tits. He swung it by the legs above him, round and round, released it with a deafening gratifying roar, and watched it hurling to the furthest corner of the room, its tiny skull squashed, pulpified, in a glorious deadening thudding sound that made him thrust his arms in the air in triumph.

But when he turned to look at the infantless hag, there she was laughing at him, suckling that same infant in her skeletal arms and each one of her brood raising their lice ridden heads towards him, pointing at him, sneering at him, howling abuse at him, laughing like their whoring mother was laughing at him.

A child cried. He swung round to the last remaining corner of the room and saw a child dressed in white, a young child with beautiful dark piercing eyes staring though him, with crystal tears running down her smooth cheeks, with her hands outstretched towards him in supplication: 'Sean... Sean... Sean,' she cried.

'NO!' He raised the pitchfork again and rushed at the child. There was a merciless scream as the four rods of steel plunged into the breadth of its tender frame, and when he withdrew, the blood gushed from the wounds, staining, darkening, drowning the white she wore. But the child still managed to look up at him. He stared petrified into her beautiful anguished face and she raised both of her hands out to him again. She came slowly towards him. He lunged the pitchfork again and again, but she continued coming to him.

The pitchfork fell from his hands. He grabbed his hair and closed his eyes and he tried to tear the searing madness out of his head. But when he opened his eyes and looked above, he screamed. A one-eyed bird with plundered plumage and mangled wings flew round the room screeching mercilessly. Then it flew straight at him and it went through him and under him and above him. The flapping of its mangled wings and its satanic screeching got louder and louder.

He felt himself disintegrating. He wanted to die. To die quickly. He looked down and the child was at his feet gazing up at him. Her tears still fell and her blood still flowed. 'Sean... why do you do this to me?' she asked. He stood paralysed watching her tiny hands reaching up to him. He dreaded her hands touching him. But the child mysteriously rose up to him and her tiny hands encircled and embraced him. She rested her moist cheeks on his soaking neck.

O'Neill roared a terrible deafening helpless roar, collapsing into oblivion just when he opened his eyes and screamed in the dead hour of night.

Chapter 45

January, 2008. The temperature is below zero, but it is a dry night with a moonlit sky. Ringo Starr is singing on the roof of St. George's Hall, restored to its former glory for the princely sum of 23 million pounds. '*Liverpool I left you,*' he sings, '*but I never let you down.*' Ringo and dozens of other celebrities are all playing their part in the launch of the European City of Culture year, cheered on by a rapturous audience of 60,000 in the streets below, and watched by an estimated 400 million worldwide. The compère gushes on and on about Liverpool, its cultural uniqueness, its undying spirit, its unparalleled contributions to humanity, to politics, humour, civil rights, multi-culturism, trade unionism, sports, and the abolition of slavery. He works himself up into such a frenzy of Liverpudlian self-adulation, that he very nearly falls off the dais.

City of Culture was the last thing on O'Neill's troubled mind as he tried to negotiate his way across the city. He swore at every road block, every diversion, knowing that he was not going to get there in time. How could he have not known what it was going to be like when press and radio had talked about little else all week and gigantic bill boards and massive screens strategically placed at junctions and shopping malls had given the precise time, day, minute and seconds to go, before Liverpool's big year began. Everyday his colleagues in the office had been warning each other about the gridlock on the night. But he hadn't heard any of that. He may as well not have been there at all.

Eventually he made it to Lawrence Grove. The houses seemed darker than usual. The city centre party could just about be heard and the skyline was still being lit up by noiseless fireworks. He stood at the gates of number fifty-five, his unsteady fingers on the cold wet latch. It would be his last visit to this home. He could see Mrs Greer coming at him on that very first visit, making him step aside almost losing his balance;

causing him to reach out and wince with the pain as the thorn of the rose bush pierced his finger. He unconsciously put his hand in his pocket for the hanky just as he had done then but there was no hanky. He shook his head, annoyed that he should so lose himself in a memory of the distant past when he needed all his wits about him to cope with the present. This was not going to be easy, but he was not going to turn back now.

Mrs Greer, in her long apron and her hair bundled in elastic bands was cold and upright as she led O'Neill along the hallway. She never spoke to him. When they reached the living room she left him to fetch Martin who was upstairs. Mr Greer sat in his usual position with the television blaring. He nodded, got up and switched the television off.

Mrs Greer returned, Martin trailing behind her. She too sat in her usual place, making bodily contact with her husband. Martin sat on a high wooden chair nearest the door; he could not have been any further away from them. He looked isolated and exposed and it accentuated the gawkiness often attributed to him. O'Neill sat on an arm chair near the fireplace.

'Is that where you usually sit Martin?' he asked.

Martin couldn't reply, just an awkward nod.

'This is my favourite seat,' said O'Neill, getting up and moving to the side of the television where a pouffe was lodged between it and the wall. He set his car keys next to the television, enabling him to lift the pouffe with both hands. He didn't want to offend Mrs Greer by trailing it along her carpet. He looked at her: 'You don't mind?' he asked disarmingly.

She shook her head, but there was a distrustful look in her eyes.

O'Neill brought the pouffe nearer to them and sat down. 'That's better. How about you bringing your chair closer, Martin? Then we can all see each other without straining our necks.'

Martin did as suggested. He did not particularly want to be nearer to his parents, but this was a bit of a novelty and O'Neill appeared to be in charge.

'Now… thanks for letting me in, Mrs Greer,' O'Neill said, looking at her and half smiling. 'That's more than what Martin did; he wouldn't let me in when I called last week.'

The words sounded like a complaint, but that same disarming tone and his half smile convinced even Martin that he wasn't being entirely serious. The unsmiling Mrs Greer sounded defensive when she said: 'He's not to let anyone in when I'm out.'

'What if he wants to bring a friend in or a girlfriend?'

'He hasn't got any friends. He hasn't got any girlfriends.'

O'Neill's brow furrowed and his eyes narrowed in a deliberate exaggerated perplexity. It was turning out just as he had predicted and prepared for. For a few seconds, he looked at the ceiling above. 'That's just reminded of something else you said about your son, Mrs Greer. You once said to me *he has no feelings either!* Do you remember saying that?'

She hesitated for a moment, long enough to convince her son that she was in difficulty. Then she lied: 'I never said that.'

'Okay… maybe I picked you up wrong,' said O'Neill. 'But let's go back to what you *did* say. He turned to Martin: 'Is that right Martin… you don't have any friends, girlfriends?'

Martin had listened studiously, looking alternatively at his mother and O'Neill. It was tolerable, even enjoyable hearing his mother being challenged like that, but only so long as no one addressed him. He reddened and fidgeted nervously. He couldn't reply.

'No friends, Martin?' O'Neill persisted, his soft ironical tone making it clear what he thought of Mrs Greer's opinion. He could see that their *unity* was having a paralysing effect on Martin. He still couldn't reply.

'Don't you have friends at school? Didn't you have a friend at Hollybank? What was his name?'

Martin knew the name. He stared at O'Neill and struggled to say the name. He looked at his mother's cold contemptuous eyes and he struggled to make a sound, but he couldn't.

'What was the name, Martin?' O'Neill repeated.

'D… Damian.'

'Damian!' That was it. Damian Atkins, wasn't it?'

Martin nodded and sighed. His jaw contorted; his tongue buried itself in his lower cheek. He was visibly embarrassed again, but it was the embarrassment of success.

O'Neill said nothing. He wanted the significance of that tiny resistance to be felt by both of them. Then he said: 'Do you think your mum's unreasonable Martin, not letting you bring your friends in?'

'No I'm not!' she interrupted, before Martin could even think about replying. Mr Greer tried but failed to conceal the slightest nudge he made with his elbow into his wife's side.

'Why don't you let him answer for himself?' O'Neill asked, addressing the question to both of them. He felt in control, applying and increasing the pressure almost imperceptibly.

'Because he can't,' she replied instantly.

'That's right,' said Mr Greer.

'Have you ever given him the chance? Have you ever encouraged him to speak up for himself?'

'It doesn't make a hapennie's worth o difference, whether you encourage him or not,' replied Mr Greer.

'You don't know him,' said Mrs Greer. 'He's never been able to speak up for himself.'

'You can't get a word out of him,' her husband added.

'You may as well talk to the wall,' said Mrs Greer. 'He doesn't know what people are saying to him. It was the same when Mrs Lynch came; she couldn't get a word out of him either.'

'He can't remember anything,' said Mr Greer. 'I bet he can't even remember what day it was when you saw him last.' He turned to Martin: 'What day was it Mr O'Neill called?'

Martin's countenance dramatically changed. He couldn't stand the mocking stares of both of them. He was in visible turmoil; unable to think or speak, his head sinking, his tongue constantly wetting his dry lips. He sat helpless on his pedestal, his sad sparkless eyes not knowing where sanctuary lay.

O'Neill was intrigued by the changing dynamic. But he still felt in control. He could not resist *playing* with them again, surreptitiously exposing them, then he would turn on them.

'See!' Mr Greer said, emphatically; 'didn't I tell you?'

O'Neill stared at Mr Greer, realising he'd watched a bizarre transformation: the anxious frightened accomplice had become the principal psychological attack dog.

'I disagree,' O'Neill said loudly and jovially. 'Don't you disagree, Martin?' He swung round to him in an exaggerated way. 'You're not going to take that lying down Martin, are you? You tell them.'

Martin raised his burning head. For a few seconds he was able to focus on O'Neill. Then he tried to speak but he couldn't utter a sound.

Mrs Greer laughed. 'He doesn't understand a word you're saying.'

'Why not?' said O'Neill, looking perplexed. 'Because I asked him did he disagree. I'll ask him again. Martin, they're saying you can't speak for yourself; you can't remember anything... I'm asking you do you disagree?'

Martin managed to move his head a little and to look at O'Neill, but the words would not come.

'Do you disagree?' O'Neill repeated.

Martin willed himself to reply, his head beginning to sway in frustration. A solitary defiant word eventually burst from his lips: 'YES!'

'You disagree?'

'YES! YES!

The defiance took its toll. His cheeks swelled and his lips quivered. But he managed not to cry.

O'Neill toyed with the notion of extracting an apology from them; but they were visibly unmoved by Martin's suffering and his success. He decided not to risk it. But he couldn't help gesturing to them with his open palms and with an 'I-told-you-so' expression on his face, before he moved onto what he thought was safer ground for Martin.

'How did the coaching go Martin?' he asked.

Martin's eyes brightened. A smile of embarrassment and pride spread across his face. 'Fab,' he said, and then glanced cautiously at his mother.

'Well,' said O'Neill; 'can't you tell us something about it?'

Martin replied immediately: 'Mr Chapman's gonna get me professional coaching. He said a should go on a course.' He glanced at his mother, searchingly, as though he was wondering whether or not she might laugh at him again.

'That's great Martin. Don't you think that's great *mum*?'

Mrs Greer stiffened and said nothing. O'Neill wasn't sure which had annoyed her most: the mention of her son's talent or him addressing her as *mum*.

'I'm surprised neither of you told me that Martin was a champion discus thrower, best in the school?' His tone remained jovial and innocent. 'You never know where this might lead Mrs Greer. In two thousand and twelve your son could be winning medals in the London Olympics.'

There was no response other than a hint of tension creeping over them.

O'Neill turned to Martin again: 'Where's this course going to be held?'

'Manchester.' The novelty of mentioning the place and the images it evoked brought a huge grin to Martin's face.

Mrs Greer burst out laughing. 'Manchester? He couldn't make his way to the bus stop!'

Mr Greer attempted to stop his smirk spreading.

Martin's smile quickly faded; the redness deepened.

O'Neill was annoyed with himself, caught out by the speed with which their dynamic had resumed, and unwittingly setting Martin up in the process. He attempted to look incredulous before saying: 'He made his own way from Hollybank!'

'It took him long enough,' said Mr Greer, suppressing his impulse to laugh as loud as his wife.

'Eight hours,' said Mrs Greer.

'He made it,' said O'Neill. Then he realised that that sounded as if Martin had *just* made it; as if O'Neill himself felt that it was touch and go; that Martin could just as easily have not made it.

'And he wasn't right for a week after it,' Mrs Greer said.

'What were you telling me he was eating all the next day?' asked Mr Greer. A smirk spread over his face again. 'Oh I remember: cauliflower sandwiches!'

His wife and he simultaneously burst into laughter.

Martin's crimson face lowered further, out of sight. He swayed and fidgeted on his pedestal, the deepening humiliation fuelling their laughter.

O'Neill felt himself losing control. He could see and feel Martin's pain and yet he remained preoccupied, fascinated by the chemistry of his persecutors: their facial and verbal cues, the mutual anticipation of their thoughts, the rhythm and the incisiveness of their insults.

O'Neill's hand moved to the inside pocket of his denim jacket. He reassured himself that the Child Protection Order signed by a Justice of the Peace only two hours before was still there. But he could not use it yet. If he confronted them now at the height of their mirth they might not take him seriously; they might laugh at him. He would wait. He would regain the initiative, quieten them, silence them, hint at the fact that he knows what they are doing. He looked over at Martin's bowed head and suddenly repeated to himself over and over again: 'knows what they are doing...' He saw himself lying flat on his back on the bedroom floor trying to muffle his panting breath with his white handkerchief. He saw himself tiptoeing across the landing and his trembling fingers opening the door of Martin's room... *Knows what they're doing... knows what they're doing....* The words kept reverberating painfully in his head.

A sticky sweat was emerging on his brow and his neck. He could feel beads of sweat trickling downwards. He wondered did they notice. He could tolerate them laughing as long as they didn't see him sweating. He casually wiped some drops away with his fingertips.

'We bought him one of those MP3 players you were on about,' said Mrs Greer. She had ceased laughing but her tone was ironic. Her mouth tightened, suppressing the laughter that was sure to come.

'Oh yes,' said Mr Greer on cue. 'He's very good with his MP3 player.'

O'Neill's discomfort intensified as the confidence inexplicably ebbed away from him. 'Is he?' he asked, hearing the pathetic helplessness of his own voice.

'Oh he *is*,' said Mrs Greer.

O'Neill turned to Martin, grateful for the opportunity of turning away from their relentlessness. 'When did you get it Martin?'

'*I* got it for him at the weekend,' Mrs Greer announced before Martin could even attempt to reply.

'Have you downloaded some music onto it?' O'Neill asked.

Martin looked at him painfully. O'Neill wasn't sure whether or not he understood.

'Show Mr O'Neill your MP3 player,' said Mr Greer.

Martin looked up at his mother, his eyes begging her not to do this to him.

'Go on,' she said, driven even more by his supplicating looks.

Martin got off his pedestal, the clawing fear of annihilation not strong enough to resist the powerful sway she held over him. He walked over to the computer desk and opened a drawer. He lifted a brand new box, opened it and timidly removed the contents, the orange and black player in its velvet pouch, the installation CD, multi language instructions, connectors and ear-phones. Everything looked pristine, unused. He returned to his pedestal holding the player and the ear-phones.

'Let Mr O'Neill hear it,' said Mr Greer.

O'Neill realised there probably wasn't anything to hear. He was near certain that the program enabling the player to function hadn't even been installed.

His angry helplessness intensified. He could feel sweat gathering on his eye-brows, and sweat soaking the collar of his shirt. He was a mere instrument now of Martin's torture, no more able than Martin to prevent himself being swept along by their ever-increasing, unstoppable, malevolent waves. Their faces presaged the final humiliation. He clenched his fists, willing himself to confront them, to roar at them: *What kind of people are you? You will never do anything like this again… Do you know what this is… This is a child protection order… Look! Signed by a JP. Your son's being removed tonight and he'll never come back… and you can rot in jail… and… and…* But no words would come from his open mouth and his parched tongue.

Martin stood holding the player in one hand and the ear-phones in the other. He fumbled with both.

'Put the ear-phones on each ear,' said Mr Greer mockingly miming his instruction with both hands.

'Now play it,' said his mother as he secured the ear-phones.

He pressed the joystick and looked at the blank screen. Nothing happened. He pressed the record button, the volume control, the play and pause switch, but nothing happened. He eventually found the power control and slid it into position but failed to hold it there. It slipped back again. Nothing happened. He stared vacantly at the screen.

'Does it need batteries?' Mr Greer said.

Martin unexpectedly raised his burning head and stared at them. It was enough to unleash their loud mocking uncontrollable laughter.

O'Neill sprang to his feet and looked down on them. They ignored him. He took a deep breath and clenched his fists again. He tried to speak to them but only strange incoherent sounds came from his parched lips. It made them laugh even louder, the sight of him standing shapelessly and grotesquely before them like a clown, a silent miming clown performing weirdly. Mrs Greer stretched her finger towards him. Her laughter was so incessant she couldn't keep her finger steady. He began to tremble violently, thinking she was congratulating him on looking even more abject than her abject son.

She leant over the edge of the settee and pulled a hanky from her tattered straw shopping bag. She stretched herself towards him again, waving it only inches from his terrified face. Then she threw it at him.

'You left it behind you… under the bed,' she yelled at him, 'and you're filthy footprints as well… the night you watched me make love to him. You can't take him away from me now.'

'Stop it! Stop it! Stop it!' cried O'Neill.

But she couldn't stop. She taunted him again pointing at the handkerchief. 'I cleaned it for you… nice and white… see!'

Mr Greer had recoiled from his wife. His laughter had decreased, trailing off into infrequent bursts, then silence. He looked with increasing horror at the handkerchief and then O'Neill. He realised. He remembered the mysterious noises as he tried to fall asleep that night: the creaking sounds, someone's feet on the floor, the unnerving sense of a presence all around him, and that final clicking sound coming from the back door…

as O'Neill left! O'Neill, actually seeing his wife make violent love to her son!

Martin watched the three of them. Tears of anger swelled in his eyes and trickled down his burning cheeks. The player and the earphones slipped from his limp fingers. His mother saw them falling to the floor. She stopped laughing.

'You stupid fool!' she yelled.

Martin gazed down on the player. He raised his right foot as though he intended crushing it with his heel. Then he looked up and stared at his mother. He slowly lowered his foot well away from the player. He turned to O'Neill. O'Neill suddenly rushed past him unable to bear the reflection of betrayal in Martin's sad dark beautiful eyes.

Chapter 46

O'Neill ran from the house in Lawrence Grove. He had one hand in his pocket seeking out his keys. He reached the car and leaned on its roof with the other hand. He could not find his keys. He searched with both hands, every pocket, and still couldn't find his keys. Then he remembered: he'd left them next to the television. He looked up at the sky and cursed. He looked back to the house. He could not return. He ran away from the car, down the street and onto the main road. He kept looking over his shoulder to see if there was a bus in sight. He reached the first bus stop and stood there watching every car whiz past in the forlorn hope that he would see someone he knew. The strange faces came and went and there was still no bus in sight. He ran on down the main road.

He reached the next stop. There were a few people there but he did not wish to join them. He hurried on. As he got nearer to another stop he could hear the distinct sound of a city bus not far behind him quickly gaining on him. He sprinted as fast as he could. The green single-decker bus passed him, slowed and then stopped a hundred yards in front of him. Half a dozen passengers got on; the doors closed but the bus didn't move. He was still fifty yards away and still the bus didn't move. The bastard is going to move as soon as I get to the stop, he thought. He reached the doors of the bus ready to scream abuse as the bus moved. But it didn't move. The doors opened and the driver smiled at him and said: 'Oye mate! In a hurry?'

'Yea thanks,' gasped O'Neill, clinging onto the cold chrome frames of the seats as he made his way to the back of the bus. He dropped into a corner seat. He stared at the fluorescent lights above. His heart was still pounding, the painful spasms intensifying. He spread a hand over his left side in an attempt to ease the pain. He could feel the crumpled paper in the inside pocket of his jacket. He took it out and opened it up, and he forgot about his pain. Drops of sweat fell from his brow. They exploded on the paper and drowned whole batches of words. The watery antennae, beautifully symmetrical like stars, spread out and clung onto more distant words. But he could still read:

Sean O'Neill, AN OFFICER OF THE SAID CITY COUNCIL OF LIVERPOOL, (herein called the Applicant) has this day applied under Section 44(1)(a) of the Children Act 1989, to detain and remove Martin McDonald to accommodation provided by or on behalf of the applicant, on the grounds that there is reasonable cause to believe the said child is likely to suffer significant harm if he is not so removed…

He shuddered when he read it. He could still see the pain and despair in Martin's eyes. He stared again at the soggy crumpled Child Protection Order, which he had asked a Justice of the Peace to sign only a few hours before. He had told her what had been happening to Martin and she had signed it immediately. She had wished him well as he set out to remove Martin. She had advised him to get the police to accompany him.

He stretched out his hand to the seat in front. Then he raised his aching head and looked at the faceless passengers. A Bengali baby girl bouncing in her mother's arms turned round and looked at him. No one else moved. The baby's eyes fixed on him. Then she smiled at him. She began gurgling and bouncing more vigorously on her mother's arms, excited by the mutual locking of their eyes. She stretched towards him trying to reach him with one chubby-fingered hand, whilst the other clasped tightly on the cold chrome frame. O'Neill looked away, unable to withstand the intense joy and innocence of her face. He deliberately turned his gaze to the backs of other passengers, but he could still see and feel the baby's efforts to reach him. He lowered his head and stared at the floor; then he gazed unseeingly out of the window. The baby's movements ceased. He looked back at her. She was still staring at him, but perplexed-like, her mouth open and her gorgeous eyes bearing the hint of hurt. O'Neill could not stop the tears swelling in his own eyes.

'Sean… Sean O'Neill,' said the voice as he stepped off the bus at Queen's Square station. He vaguely recognised the voice. He looked round at the thronging masses of peoples in the station, mainly families with small children returning from the great celebratory spectacle in Lime Street and making their way to the buses that would bring them home. The coach Peter Chapman, still in his tracksuit and all smiles, holding the hands of his own two small children, came up to him.

O'Neill was grateful it was night-time.

'Hello Sean; I thought it was you; you didn't ring me.'

'No I didn't... I... eh...'

'Yea I know...' He laughed. 'You've too many other things on your plate! But you've done Martin a favour. Make sure he comes to Manchester. Bags of talent.'

'Has he...? Good.'

'Then we'll get him to Loughborough. I know one of the 3As coaches down there; he specialises in the discus. I'm sure he'd like to see Martin throw.'

The benevolence and the unawareness in Peter's face and voice painfully struck O'Neill.

'He's not as shy as he looks.' Peter continued. 'There's an awful lot of pent-up anger in him. It's a good thing for discus throwing but there's more than usual in that lad. I'd love to see him come on; I think he could make it big. He's got the strength height and power. But it's his anger that sticks out a mile. Anger like that... hi'!

O'Neill ran away from him. He ran down Old Haymarket, and turned into St. John's Lane. He slowed down then, eventually stopping and looking about him. No one seemed to notice him. He felt apart from every single person hurrying past him. He felt as if he was in another world, imprisoned, yet within sight and sound of this bustling world on the move. They were mostly young people, heading for the bars and nightclubs, excitable and gay, joking, laughing, shouting, arguing, embracing, kissing. He stood still for a moment then he ran again frightened by peculiar sensations pressing in on him.

He made his way to the office in the city's Social Services North East division serving the districts of Kensington, Anfield and Everton. It would be the last time he would set foot in the portacabin.

Chapter 47

Their silence continued long after O'Neill had left. Mrs Greer was the first to leave the room. She went to the kitchen and stood over the sink. She removed the clips from her hair and shook her head. She bent her head forward and looked down at her blurred reflection in the shiny spotless steel. She smiled to herself thinking of that hapless fool standing before her struggling for his words... like the suave and dapper Mr Winfield screeching for mercy when she rammed the fork into his neck. He was the officer-in-charge of her sixth children's home. He always invited new admissions to his office. He trapped by stealth and cunning. He raped her and she was only sixteen. He raped her again and again and threatened to kill her if she ever spoke out. She never did but she rammed a kitchen fork into his jugular and stood watching him die, thinking of the father who deserted her and the monster who battered her and the Captain who betrayed her and this dying officer-in-charge who had repeatedly raped her. She hid the fork. They came and arrested her. They interrogated her. She told them nothing. They locked her in a padded cell. She wasn't allowed to end it all... ah Martin! He stood behind her and she saw his reflection in the window pane. Martin would not desert her or betray her or rape her. Martin was incapable of harming her. Who would believe that fool O'Neill now, she thought. She ceased all movement and continued standing with her back to him. She could not see the pained questioning expression on his face.

Martin looked down on her, at her dark flowing hair now stretching almost to the tied bow of her apron strings. She was small in comparison to him and yet, even staring at her from behind he felt the awesome power she wielded over him. He wanted to know why she was so strong and dominant, and why she compulsively rendered him so submissive and weak; why she consistently abused him, humiliated him, and then made violent love to him. He was going to confront her, tell her that she was making his life insufferable and that what she was doing was wrong, was evil, was mad. But as she turned round to face him a kind of paralysis seized him. It was his consciousness of this paralysis that then made him tremble. As she came towards him he shook uncontrollably.

She saw the pain in his eyes and he knew it gratified her.

'What's wrong son?' she said, as she raised her soft hand to his flushed cheek.

But he retreated, frightened and angry.

His resistance took her by surprise. She tried to compose herself. But before she could say or do anything else Martin turned on his heels and charged out.

Visibly distraught she left the kitchen. She returned to the living room hearing Martin's bedroom door closing tightly above. She looked at her husband, despising him as the obstacle to her impulse. She wanted to embrace her son, to console him, to reassure herself that she was still in control of him.

Her husband usually always obliged, always took himself off at times like these. But there he was, stiff and frozen like a corpse, in the same part of the settee, his lifeless posture and the focus of his terrified stare unchanged since she had left him.

She heard the bedroom door open. She listened attentively. She heard Martin crossing to the bathroom. She thought… yes… she could hear him on the landing above. He was coming, descending to her, heavily, noisily, but surely. A slight smile broke on her lips. She sighed as she felt the vibrations of his heavy un-rhythmic pace along the hallway. The door opened and her eyes lit on him. A cold painful shudder went through her. He wore the heavy black anorak jacket she had bought him. His stuffed duffle bag was slung over his shoulder. She could see the outline of the bulging discus at the top of it. He was leaving her, determinedly, yet the look on his face was one of terrible apprehension. He was leaving! He was walking out on his mother at 9.0 o'clock in the evening, a bitterly cold January evening.

'Get that coat off!' she yelled at him.

He ignored her. She leapt to her feet and stood before him.

'What do you think you're doing?'

'A'm going… mum; A'm leaving.' He trembled as he spoke.

'You fool! You're not going anywhere.'

'A'm going to Damian's house mum.'

'To let Damian and his family laugh at you?'

'Mum… please.'

'You heard what I said. Get that off you and get up those stairs.'

'No!'

A voice behind her spoke: 'Lettim go.'

She swung around. The corpse had come to life. He stared at her. 'Lettim go,' he repeated.

'No! I won't let him go. He's my son… *my* son! He's nothing to do with you.'

'Has he not?' Mr Greer paused, ruefully. 'It's all over,' he said, with a quiet despair.

'What…? What are you saying?'

'You know what I'm saying. Can't you see, he's leaving. If he doesn't leave tonight, he'll be taken tomorrow… it's over.'

She swung round to Martin: 'No… no… he's my son… they won't take him… I'm the one who brought him up… I sacrificed my whole life for him…'

'You've sacrificed nothing for him. You've destroyed him. I let you do it. I helped you do it.'

His tone was curiously without remorse. It was a self-pitying tone. He never looked at the victim who stood still towering over both of them. Martin seemed immobilised yet every utterance they made seared through him.

'And you would have still been helping,' she said, 'if I hadn't found the hanky; if we'd never known that fool had been here. You think it's over because O'Neill knows what you are. I don't give a damn. O'Neill will never open his mouth. And if he does, nobody will believe him. Who's going to believe a liar… somebody who breaks into a house to watch…?'

She only just managed to stop. She stared at her husband, and he looked away from her.

'M… um,' Martin stuttered.

She rushed towards him and slapped his face repeatedly with the rigid palm of her tiny hand. He yelled. Mr Greer winced and closed his eyes. When he opened them he saw the coat being dragged off Martin. She pulled him round and removed it completely. He stood there in tears. Suddenly he turned and ran out the door. She heard him scrambling on the stairs and then heard his bedroom door slammed tight.

'See what you've done?' she yelled at Mr Greer.

'You're gonna lose him,' he said, almost inaudibly.

'Am I?'

'You need treatment Marian.'

She burst out laughing, indifferent to the oddity of him addressing her *Marian*. 'Treatment? I need treatment?' Her tone was full of vicious irony. 'And what do you need?'

He didn't reply. He predicted that and his miserable countenance suggested he felt that he deserved it.

She went after Martin. His bedroom door was closed. She put her hand on the door handle and pushed. The door would not open. There was no lock, no key, yet it would not open to her. She pushed on the handle again and pressed her body against the door. Still it remained tightly closed.

'Martin,' she whispered in feigned innocence. There was no answer. 'Martin,' she repeated again and again, less of a whisper, her voice a mixture of command and desperation. But the door remained closed. 'Martin, let me in,' she cried. Then she pleaded with him and wept. She threw herself against the door, weeping uncontrollably. Still it remained closed. She dragged herself away into the chilled pitch-black bedroom opposite. She didn't switch the light on. She threw herself onto a cold unwrinkled quilt and lay in the darkness. She buried herself and her tears within the quilt and like the room itself it felt cold and alien around her. A warm gentle hand touched her. She swung round instantly, her anguish frozen, and her lips, wet with tears, breaking into a startled smile; her arms stretched out: 'Martin... darling...' she sighed. Then she screamed. It was her husband. She recoiled away from him: 'Leave me alone!' she yelled, as she wrapped the quilt around her.

'Marian... for God's sake!' He stood helplessly watching her for a while. He knew he dare not touch her again, that it was futile to say anything to her. He left her, returned to the living room and sat in his usual place. He stared at the silent blank television screen. He closed his eyes and shook his head, in resignation and despair.

'Lettim go!' he kept hearing. It was the first and only gesture of opposition he had ever uttered against her. Not a great act of courage; nothing to write home about. It only served to remind him of what he had always been. She was mad but she had recognised his core of gullibility and cowardice. She had ensnared him ever so systematically, exposed him little by little, step by step, to her inferno and her cruelty within it. She kept testing him along the way, probing his morality and his tolerance. He discovered there was no limit to his tolerance and that he didn't have any morality. When he eventually recognised the nature and extent of her evil, he surrendered to it and immunised himself against the slightest shred of empathy or pity for their victim.

Yes, it was all over now. Martin would be rescued; no thanks to him. The police and other professionals would take over from O'Neill. What kind of person was O'Neill? he suddenly asked himself. What kind of pervert, breaking into their home to watch his mad wife make love to her *darling* son? Everything about O'Neill was bizarre, he thought; but no more bizarre than he was himself. Maybe O'Neill was mad then, just as mad as his wife.

He pondered his own fate: the arrest, the interrogation, being charged, tried, and jailed for a long long time. And the impact on his elderly saintly mother? On his beloved sisters, on his older nieces and nephews, on his workmates... Oh No! How long would it all take, he wondered: six months? a year? maybe two years, and every aspect of his miserable life dissected, pored over, laughed at, condemned, and broadcast to the world. No! It was too much to contemplate. He closed his eyes again and shook his head. When he opened his eyes they lit upon an alien object next to the television. He hadn't noticed it before. He actually had to concentrate for a few seconds before realising what it was: a set of keys. He got up, went over and lifted them. Not his keys; not his wife's; there was a place for everything in this house and keys were never just left next to the television. Were they O'Neill's? Yes they were, he remembered; O'Neill had set them down when he lifted the pouffe. He walked over to the window and pulled the curtain. O'Neill's red Volkswagen was still there. He stared into the darkness of the car's interior momentarily thinking that he could see the outline of O'Neill still sitting there, no doubt licking his wounds and trying to pluck up the courage to come back again. Then he realised he was imagining things; how could O'Neill have got into the car if he didn't have the keys which were in his own hand. Of course O'Neill was not there. He'll be back sometime though, with a spare set of keys. But he wouldn't dare come back into this house, he concluded. He left the keys beside the television.

He stood in the centre of the living room reluctant to sit down again. His hands were in his pockets and his eyes were fixed on the green curly leaves of the carpet patterning. But he saw nothing. He looked around the room. He focussed on his reflection in the heavily adorned mirror above the fireplace. He stepped closer. It was such an ordinary middle aged face, he thought. But he had at least a healthy weather-beaten tan and a good crop of hair for his age. His hair was a sandy colour, matching the ginger-framed spectacles he wore. Their lenses magnified his rather narrow eyes which, when he first looked, displayed nothing more that the weariness and desolation he felt. He stretched nearer to within a couple of inches of the mirror and gazed into the black pupils of his eyes. He had always thought his eyes were brown, but this close it seemed that his pupils were surrounded by a host of moving colours, mainly green. He stared at them quite fascinated. But as he moved closer still he saw something entirely different. The pupils of his eyes looked as if they were rapidly expanding beyond him, metamorphosing into mysterious kaleidoscopic caverns. He felt as if he was being sucked into the caverns. His *ordinary* face was turning into something monstrous, yet his gaze was fixed immovably on the pupils of his green eyes. Sheer panic made him jerk his head away from the mirror. He didn't look back. He went into the hall, put his coat on and went out. He relaxed for a few moments on the garden path and turned his still frightened face to the sky. The wind was getting up. He walked to his car in the driveway. As he opened the car door he paused and thought for a moment. He went back into the house and lifted O'Neill's keys. He closed and locked the door of his own car, got into O'Neill's Volkswagen and drove off.

He drove southwest out of Liverpool, through Runcorn and Northwich, and onto the A530 to Crewe. He turned off this main road, onto a single carriageway, then turned off again onto a minor road. He reached a level crossing and slowed. There was a lay-by on either siding of the crossing reserved for heavier vehicles; he parked there. He got out of the car and was very nearly blown back again by a ferocious gust of wind. He held onto the door and gazed at the railway track. The luminous red and white poles of the half barriers were vertical and they rattled in the swirling wind. The tops of the hedges on either side of the road danced vigorously. He walked up to the track, its steel glistening under the huge yellow lights of the barriers. He looked at his watch and calculated. He returned to the car in the lay-by. He waited anxiously. He was parking illegally. The lay-by was for heavy trucks while their drivers were getting the necessary permission to cross.

The bell startled him. The red warning lights flashed. The half barriers came down. Cars stopped. A queue quickly formed. He turned the ignition key and switched his lights on. Drivers glanced in their mirrors. He looked behind him before moving out of the lay-by. One more car was coming. He knew he still had time. He knew precisely the time between those barriers falling and the train passing. He allowed the car to pass him and his heart beat quickened when he saw the blue light above it and two police officers staring suspiciously at him, parked where he should not have been parked. They passed ever so slowly then stopped. The passenger officer got out. He walked back towards the Volkswagen. Mr Greer thrust the car into gear and shot onto the roadway. The officer halted. He yelled more in terror than command as the Volkswagen came at him. But he need not have feared. Mr Greer swerved beyond the officer and the line of traffic. He shot the car to the first half barrier. He skidded around it, then jammed the brakes, parking neatly across the track. He looked to his right. He knew it was coming from the right. He glanced in his mirror. He could hear the commotion, horns blaring, lights flashing, drivers and passengers yelling. He pressed the lock on his door and all four doors locked. He checked that all the windows were sealed tight.

One of the police officers went pounding towards the car and unwittingly provoked other drivers and passengers to do the same. As he made for the driver's door he glanced along the track to his right. He too knew what was coming from the right. He could see it coming. He pulled and hammered at the door, yelling at the darkened motionless figure of Mr Greer who ignored him. The officer realised and retreated. He shoved and punched back the citizens who had joined him. He glanced back at the oncoming 185, a magnificent sight: one and a half thousand tons of silvery bluish steel rocketing along the track at near enough its maximum speed and O'Neill's little red Volkswagen parked neatly in its way. Neither man nor beast felt a thing. But there was a noise.

Chapter 48

Mary the cleaner was startled. She was just finishing her evening shift when someone who obviously had office keys was entering and making no secret of it. She could hear running footsteps, banging doors, and then breathlessness. The main doors swung open. It was O'Neill. At least she knew O'Neill. She held her hand to her heart and said: 'You gimme a fright Sean.'

'I'm leaving,' he said, gasping for breath.

She was standing at the far end of the room with many filing cabinets and desks and computers separating them. His meaning wasn't clear. Had he popped in to collect something and was leaving immediately? She said nothing but she sensed there was something wrong. He approached her and walked past his own desk, not even giving it a glance. He hadn't taken his eyes off her. He was coming towards her as if he was going to speak to her. When she saw his anguished face and the sweat dripping from him she knew he wasn't going to be talking about the weather.

'Mary…'

'What's wrong Sean?'

'Forgive me Mary.'

'Forgive you! What are you saying? Where have you been?'

'Hell!' He stopped and leant one arm on the desk she had been cleaning. 'I left a fifteen year old in hell tonight.'

The unease spread through her. She didn't know whether or not to interrupt and demand that he cease talking like this at once, or to let him continue in the hope that he might eventually talk sense.

'I wasn't able to remove him,' he said.

'Sean, sit down…'

'I thought I could… that's why I went… to take him away. I got a child protection order to remove him, but I couldn't.'

'Remove who? Who are you talking about?'

'Martin…'

'Martin who?'

'McDonald.'

Martin McDonald. It was a name that had meant nothing to her until recently. She had heard Morgan and others talk about the case late afternoon. O'Neill's name had been bandied about often.

'Where is he now… Martin?'

O'Neill didn't seem to hear her question. He continued, a kind of anguished monologue: 'His mother's destroyed him… she's been sexually abusing him for years… his stepdad knew it… and did nothing about it… they've both been destroying the kid… and I sent him back to them… conning myself that I was only trying to get the evidence… but I wasn't… I was abusing him too… I watched them tormenting him… until I couldn't watch it any longer… and then it was too late… his mother laughed at me… said she'd known all along that I had seen her making love to Martin… Jesus! I ran away from them… I left Martin with them…'

Mary had heard enough. If there was only one blight in this little convenience of a job, it was to hear social workers talk about child sexual abuse. As she went about her daily toil, emptying waste paper bins, polishing desks and cleaning floors, she occasionally overheard them talk about the kids who had been sexually abused; about babies being 'digitally penetrated'; or kids as young as five being buggered or raped. Physical abuse was repugnant to her, but child sexual abuse was inconceivable to her, and when she eventually had to accept that it *was* happening, it made her ill. Worst of all, she sometimes met these kids. Often they were rescued in emergencies and brought to the office as the first port of call, to await social workers finding them a foster home. Indiscreet social workers would tell her what had happened to the kids and even enlist her help in keeping them occupied. She would embrace them and play with them and inwardly cry. But what was Sean O'Neill talking about? *A fifteen year sexually abused for years by his mother?* No! She'd heard enough.

'Come on Sean,' she said. 'Sit down here and have a rest. I'll get you a cuppa tea.' She walked hurriedly towards him. Then

364

she remembered something else he had said. 'Why did you ask me to forgive you Sean?'

He looked at her, his voice quaking and hesitant. 'For hating you.'

She stopped walking towards him.

'You and Morgan...' he said; 'and everybody else in this fucking hole!'

'Why did you hate me Sean?'

He didn't reply.

She stood her ground, watching what seemed like a prolonged agony in his face. But she still waited, an unspoken demand that he must reply.

He tried to. He looked into her eyes that were blue and warm and he could see the pain that he had caused her. He felt his legs weakening rapidly. 'I... I...' He collapsed into her arms, and she held him like a mother and he wept like a child.

'Oh Sean... what have you done to yourself?' she asked helplessly, his sweating feverish head hanging over her shoulder. She thought to herself: this hatred nonsense; it required strength to hate someone and he was nothing more than a wet weeping sack in her arms.

She manoeuvred him in the direction of his own desk and held onto him until he was in his seat. His head dropped onto an old brown file that she'd seen Morgan place there on his way out. She left him and rushed to the kitchen. The kettle was still warm. She rinsed the pot and poured milk into the cup. All the time she wanted to rush back to him, but was unsure of what she might do or say to help him. She tried to make sense of what she'd heard, but it made no sense and she concluded that the poor soul may have gone mad. What was she going to do with him then? She couldn't hear him weeping anymore. She was thankful for that. And he posed no physical threat; she was relieved about that. She wanted to rush out now just to be near him again. She poured the tea and almost threw the pot down. But as she rushed from the kitchen she heard a terrifying roar coming from his desk. The cup fell from her hand and shattered. The scalding tea spread over the tiled floor that she'd polished only an hour before.

Two inexplicable sights came on her as she rushed through the door. Sa'eed sat in a darkened corner far away from O'Neill's desk. How long had he been there? she asked. He was just sitting motionless, staring at O'Neill, oblivious to her presence. And it was obvious that the stricken O'Neill was unconscious of either of them.

She was afraid to go near O'Neill. He was standing staring at the open file on his desk. It had not been open when she left him. His stammering, panicking cry got louder as he raised his head high and closed his eyes. He put his hand to his head and grabbed his hair. Then his hands moved down either side of his face and it seemed as if his finger nails were clawing their way through his bony flesh. He dragged himself away from the desk. For an awful moment she thought he would come to her. But then she realised he didn't even see her. He staggered to the exit door and even when he got to the third and final door, she could still hear his weird terror-stricken cries.

Sa'eed remained motionless.

She ran to the window. O'Neill was gone. She stood trembling for a while, looking at Sa'eed. She looked back at O'Neill's desk and noticed again the open file that had been closed when she left him. She moved closer to it. She remembered the name. Her heart beat heavily as she walked over to it. *'Social workers leave files around… you must never open a file'* they had said to her at the outset. She had never done that, but now she was standing at his desk staring down on the open file. She looked up again one more time at Sa'eed, as if she was aware of him thinking she was doing something wrong. But his expression remained inscrutable and her focus returned to the file. There was an old yellowish photograph of a child, a girl of about seven, pinned on the inside of the file. Mary held her breath as she read the large type-written letters with the strange insignia above them:

CITY OF BELFAST CORPORATION
CHILD CARE DEPARTMENT
CASE OF MARIAN PATRICIA O'NEILL

As she stared at it and pondered its meaning, she heard Sa'eed come slowly up behind her. He gazed over her shoulder at the photograph. 'That's Martin's mother,' he said; 'O'Neill's sister.'

Mary's mouth gaped. She blessed herself and closed her eyes and sighed. 'God take care of him!' she cried.

'He was the only one who didn't know,' said Sa'eed.

Chapter 49

Martin had cried while standing leaning against the door preventing his mother from opening it. He had stopped crying now, mainly because he had heard her dragging herself away from him. He could hear her occasional fits of whining coming from the bedroom opposite. The thought… the certainty, that she would try to reach him again made him feel restless and angry. He moved about the room, sat on his bed, lay flat on his back and got up again. He lifted various items lying about, gripped them tightly and sometimes wanted to obliterate them. Yet he let things fall just as the MP3 player had done. He recalled the events of the night from the moment of high expectancy when O'Neill arrived. He had deluded himself that O'Neill would no longer allow them to humiliate him. He loathed his mother for striking him like that and stripping the coat off his back. She had never done anything like that before and he loathed himself for letting her away with it. But the memory that he dwelt on most was of him standing there towering over both of them listening to Mr Greer *confess* that they had *destroyed him*. Neither of them had even looked at him as they spoke, as if the task of destroying him had been accomplished and Mr Greer was admitting to it and that was that! It was precisely when Mr Greer's confession was sinking in, that moment when a searing clarity was giving rise to an unfathomable hatred of them both, that she struck him and all he could do was stand there and take it, and then run.

Why didn't he run out, he asked himself. Why did he have to run back to his prison cell with his jailor now ready to *take* him should he open the door. He had never looked on it as a prison cell before; she had never stayed there too long, and each time she left, it became his little haven once again. But here he was, convinced of his imprisonment, scrutinising and detesting every choice his jailor had made: the bed, quilt, carpet, curtain, wall-paper, the utter desolation of the cleanliness and the order that she demanded. Apart from his discus still protruding from the top of his duffle bag at the side of his bed, she had chosen and purchased every single thing in this room, including the clothes he wore.

He had the urge to run away from it now. If only she wasn't there. She would stop him, beg him, cling to him, and he then may not be able to run at all. He wiped the tiny beads of sweat from his brow. They reappeared. He went about the room in spurts of movement, conscious of a fire within him and unable to rid his mind of the memories that were fuelling it. He stopped. He stared at the small cabinet at the side of the bed. Suddenly he rushed at it. He lifted it effortlessly with one hand and drew it far behind him. He threw it at the large double glazed window of his bedroom. He threw it with such force that the window frame itself dislodged as the glass shattered.

There could be no mistaking the sound or the room from which it came. Within seconds, Mrs Greer had flung herself from the bed in the opposite room and was rushing across the landing. But she stopped herself. She thought the worst: an empty room and the corpse of her son on the concrete path below. She placed a hand across her mouth and her nails sunk into her cheek. She could feel no pain but she was conscious of the rapid trembling in her lower limbs. She begged for a sound other than the howling wind and the rain wreaking havoc which she could not yet see. 'Martin!' she called out, but she dared not push his bedroom door. 'Martin... please answer me.' She heard only the wind reply and the door teasingly rattle on its hinges.

She dashed along the landing, down the stairs, through the kitchen, and flung open the door onto the back garden. There was no corpse there. She stepped out and looked above. Part of the window frame seemed to hang perilously. She could see the drenched thick curtains being blown in and out gashed on the jagged ends of glass. She hurried back in locking the kitchen door behind her. She ran through the kitchen, up the stairs, and stopped at his bedroom door again. What had he done? she asked. What was he doing? In what part of the room would she find him? She stood there, breathing long and deeply. A certain composure returned to her. There was strength and steel in her eyes. She raised her hand to the door and pushed.

The door opened and the wind immediately slammed it tight again. She knew it was the wind. She held the handle tightly this time and used her shoulder. She forced the door open against the wind. She saw him standing against the opposite wall. Relief surged through her. She looked at the window. The curtains, their ends torn in shreds, came fluttering across the room towards her. Spots of rain came too, hitting the opposite wall. The carpet underneath the window was saturated. The wind howled louder through birch and pine trees in the woodland adjacent to the house.

She stood against the door with the palm of her hands pressed tightly against it. The sight of the room dismayed her. The broken window and the fluttering curtains angered her. Her cheeks were hot flushed, but the sight of her son opposite, only a few feet away from her, seemingly frightened and submissive, reassured her.

She made straight for the window. She drew the curtains and held them firmly. She pulled the divan bed towards her. She placed the headboard against the window, ensuring that the ends of the curtain were held tight against the wall. The howling wind occasionally turned the centre of the curtains into a miniature orange dome and the pelmets screeched in protest. But they held.

She walked towards Martin slowly, unlike the heavy charge of the ugly bearded monster into her bedroom that night more than thirty years ago. She had frolicked about on the bare bedroom floor with her younger brother Sean. Their mother had yelled at them repeatedly and they had quietened for a few minutes, but then started up again. She warned them... and then she shouted at her drunken lover saying that he had no control over them. Marian listened, sensed the danger and got back into bed. But she could not get her brother Sean back into bed and she could not keep him quiet. She remembered the floorboards rumbling as their mother's lover came pounding up the stairs. She made a dive for Sean and threw him back into his bed. She was just about to get back into bed herself but she never made it. He came thundering through the doorway and grabbed her by the hair and beat her senseless.

She was taken from the house on a stretcher and cared for by angels in blue. She never saw her mother or her brother again. When she recovered a strange man with a briefcase came to see her. He brought her to a stinking home and she cried every night. Someone must have heard her cry. They looked a gentle couple, a loving couple. She entered the heaven of their care and she travelled further than she had ever travelled before, thousands of miles it must have been. This must be Daddy, she had thought; Daddy had returned to rescue her. He wore a uniform. She heard other uniformed men call him Captain. Her new found Daddy was a real live Captain. He was big and strong and he spoke with a strange accent that she had never heard before. But his voice was warm and deep, sincere and kind, and she loved him dearly, especially when he lifted her and whirled her round and held onto her ever so firmly, yet gently, smiling, laughing, clasping her hand as they walked back to the door of their beautiful home and he kissed his lovely wife and she held onto both of them.

'Marian, I am not your daddy,' he once said to her.

She didn't understand.

'Your mum and dad were not happy Marian; they separated a long time ago.'

'I don't care!' she cried as she ran and threw herself into his arms and he embraced her and tried to console her.

'But you're with us now darling. We are not going to leave you.'

She remembered the first rows. She had crept down the stairs and listened in the hallway. They were arguing over someone else, the Captain and someone else: 'she... she...' Then she heard the Captain's wife say: '*She* can have you... and the child as well. I hope you told her we've got an orphan, did you? You better tell her now. She can have the orphan! What did the two of you take me for? Did you think I was going to lock myself in these four walls... rearing your orphan while you were fucking your whore? No Allister! You tell your whore and tell Marian too!'

He did not tell her. He gave her an ice cold hug and forced a lifeless, guilt-ridden wave half hidden behind the curtain as the social worker drove her away.

Now she was in her own home and all those pathetic creatures had gone and left her with her beautiful son who trembled before her. She raised a hand to his cheek. 'It's all right darling; mummy won't say a thing.'

'Don't touch me,' he said, stiffening as she came towards him and the walls and the ceiling and the floor closed in on him.

She held back for a few seconds. Then she leaned against his body lightly and turned her head so that she could see no part of his face.

'What's wrong darling?' she asked *herself* as she listened to his heart thumping in her ear.

He didn't answer and she didn't know.

'They've gone darling... they've all gone.'

She could feel him bracing himself more tightly against the wall.

'I don't want you to touch me,' he said, his voice quivering.

'Don't say that darling.' Her hushed voice was full of wounded pride. 'Why are you trembling?' She looked up trying to anticipate his reply.

But there was no reply.

She slowly raised her head. She watched the tears trickling down his cheeks. She threw her arms around him, stood on her tiptoes to reach up to him. She sensed his helplessness now.

'Oh precious... don't cry... my precious baby.' She drew him towards her and smiled. She took him by the hand and led him to the bed. She gently levered him down onto the bed. She removed his shoes and lay down beside him. She put one arm around him and spoke in a whisper: 'Everything's going to be all right darling.'

But she did not comfort him. He raised his knees and clenched his fists as he lay on his side trying to stem the rising tides within him. He felt her hand rise up to his cheek, and he allowed his head to be turned. She slithered along his body, and kissed his parched lips, gently at first, then with a little pressure. He sighed as if in surrender. The tension flowed from his body and tears of anguish ran down the sides of his face. She raised her head and looked at him. He knew what she would say.

'There darling, didn't I tell you?'

She kissed him again, moistening his lips with her tongue and effortlessly slipping it into his mouth, wandering freely, sometimes roughly. She withdrew and kissed his wet eyelids. She raised herself and looked down on him. She thought of all the stupid people who would insist on saying that *he* was ever so like his mother. 'Almost your double,' they would say. She hated him each time they said that.

She unbuttoned his shirt and he trembled again. 'Now pet... it's going to be all right,' she said. She made him rise a little so that she could remove his shirt. She unbuckled his belt and unzipped his fly. She lowered his underpants ever so slowly. She smiled, but he knew it was the smile of scorn.

She placed his penis in her mouth and sucked. She felt it grow longer and she bit into it and attempted to look up at him to see the silent writhing in his face. She then sat on the edge of the bed and undressed herself. She stood up and turned to him. She held her soft mountainous breasts to beckon him. Then she came towards him. She walked to the other side of the bed so that she could go down upon him, over his head, kissing his lips, devouring his mouth, then moving down, sucking his penis and pressing her vagina onto his lips. She could feel his lips on her vagina but she could feel no movement. She pulled his head against her and lay heavier upon him. She still could not feel the tongue which always excited her. She turned and stared at him threateningly. He did what she wanted him to do. She could not see the agony in his face; she could not feel the vomit churning in her stomach; she knew nothing of the destructive urges within him. She turned and sat on him. His penis pierced far into her, so large, so beautiful, so vulnerable, as she wriggled and swayed and gasped and gazed above and saw nothing but felt every joyous power she had ever known.

'Isn't this wonderful darling?' she said, without looking at him.

Martin stared at her, with her long black shining hair gliding behind her swaying head. He stared at the pale white tender throat. How tiny it was. He stared at the huge drooping breasts which he had always suckled for as long as she desired, which had so often smothered him and secured him each time she had humiliated and crushed him. He raised his head and he could see far into the black holes of her nostrils. He stared into them and could only see two permanent mocking eye-holes laughing at him for surrendering to her.

He lunged forward and grabbed her by the throat.

She brought her head forward, startled, angry. Their eyes met.

'Lie down,' he said, virtually lifting her and turning her on her back. He lay on top of her and pierced her and smiled in a way she knew could not be a smile. He had never lain on her before. She had never allowed him to lie on her.

She gazed up into his eyes and saw a strange world that confused her. But she was conscious of the glorious piercing fountain within her, stretching, reaching further than it had ever done before. It brought pain onto her.

'Put you arms around me darling,' she pleaded.

He came down on her and locked her within his arms and kissed her violently. She closed her eyes as the ecstatic pain of her son's strangulating hold intensified. She wanted to cry out but she didn't. She surrendered to him. She gasped: 'Oh precious... my darling pet... fuck me!... fuck me!... fuck me forever!'

He began thrusting as she wanted him to, again and again, in brutal anger. He replenished her and withdrew. She lay in a triumphal ecstasy, her eyes closed, her lips smiling. Seconds later, she screamed in agony as one massive blow from something, from somewhere, buried itself in her abdominal flesh. She opened her eyes and screamed again as another blow fell just an inch below. Her pelvic arch fractured, then it collapsed as the third blow fell. She opened her eyes again, conscious of some terrifying, crucifying obliteration of bone and muscle within her replenished womb. She tried to raise herself, and at the same time groped in the air with a tiny hand in a futile gesture of resistance. But her knuckles shattered in the path of yet another blow. She fell back unsure of whether the worst pain was coming from her disintegrating womb, or from her bloodied and broken hand that so pathetically failed to shield it.

She knew what his weapon was now. He raised the discus high above his head again and rained blow after blow upon her.

She tried to escape by turning on her side. But her legs were trapped around him and her battered womb lay open to him and the sight of her blood fusing with his semen drove him into a frenzy.

There wasn't a mark on her face and in death her beautiful dark searching eyes, remained so.

Chapter 50

Sa'eed quickly caught up on O'Neill. He pulled the car into the kerb fifty meters in front of the figure that looked like a drunken slavering man running wildly to nowhere. He got out of the car and stood in the centre of the narrow pavement to ensure that O'Neill could not pass. O'Neill staggered up to him expecting Sa'eed to move aside. It wasn't until he was nearly upon him that he recognised him. He stopped and looked into Sa'eed's eyes and burst into tears. He went down on his knees, panting breathlessly, exhausted. 'Sa'eed,' he cried; 'help me… what have I done?' Then he fell over and lay on the freezing cold pavement, still stammering out his cries and his wails.

Sa'eed gently turned him over. He took a firm hold and lifted him onto his shoulder. He got him to the car, opened the passenger door and skilfully manoeuvred him in. Residents had watched from the safety of their curtained windows and now that the injured or drunken stranger had been lifted from their pavement, they came out of their front doors to watch Sa'eed drive off.

Sa'eed's mind worked feverishly. He could do what he wanted with O'Neill, but so too could he easily jeopardize his ultimate objective, by a wrong move, or an injudicious utterance. Patience was all that was required for the moment. 'Where do you want to go?' he asked.

'Back to hell!' said O'Neill. His self-pitying cries and his wailing were more subdued now. He sat forward with his head in his hands. His elbows rested on his knees.

'To Martin's home?' asked Sa'eed.

'Martin's hell,' said O'Neill.

Where else, thought Sa'eed; a family reunion! 'Are you sure?' he asked.

'Yes. My car's there… and my car keys.'

'Why's your car there?'

'It doesn't matter.'

They said nothing more on the journey. 'It's not there,' O'Neill said, as they drove into Lawrence Grove; 'my car's not there!'

But he quickly forgot about his car when he saw three police cars and an ambulance outside the door of number fifty-five. 'Jesus Christ!' he yelled. Sa'eed tried to restrain him as he leapt out of the car. They saw Martin being led to one of the police cars in handcuffs. O'Neill yelled out: 'Martin!' but Martin didn't look round. O'Neill rushed towards the driveway cordoned off by fluorescent *scene of crime* ribbons and blocked by a burly constable.

'No further,' the constable said.

'I need to...' O'Neill stuttered.

'Who are you?' asked the constable.

'I... I'm...'

'Family,' Sa'eed said; 'Mrs Greer is his sister.'

O'Neill swung round, stunned that Sa'eed knew.

'Hold on,' the constable said. He went inside the house. Two minutes later, he emerged behind a plain clothed officer who directed O'Neill to one of the police cars. He motioned to Sa'eed to stay where he was.

O'Neill and the plain clothed officer got into the car and were there for some fifteen minutes. Sa'eed could hear O'Neill wailing again and thumping his feet on the floor of the car. He saw him rocking back and forward on the passenger seat. The officer got out then, put his notebook into his inside pocket and went round to the passenger side to assist O'Neill. He called Sa'eed and asked for his help. 'I've told Mr O'Neill that his sister and her husband are dead,' he said to Sa'eed. 'Their son Martin has been arrested. This is a murder enquiry. Mr Greer was killed in a road accident earlier this evening. The circumstances make it look as if it was suicide. Mr O'Neill here is insisting that he wants to see his sister's body. That's not possible. When we're finished examining the body it will be taken to the morgue. We will need Mr O'Neill then to identify the body. Will you take him home now and ensure he's all right. We understand he was here tonight before these events occurred. We will need to interview him when he's in a better state.'

Sa'eed was still reeling from the news and its impact on O'Neill. It took a few seconds for him to realise the request being made by the officer. 'I'll take care of him.' he said.

'Do you know if Mrs Greer had any other relatives?'

Sa'eed shook his head.

'Thank you.' The officer turned to leave.

Sa'eed called after him: 'Where's the car… Mr O'Neill's car? A red Volkswagen. That's what we came for. And the keys. He left the keys in the house.'

The officer turned back: 'Nothing can be removed from the house. The car…' He hesitated, then he said: 'it's been pulverised.'

'Pulverised?' Sa'eed looked at him and waited.

The officer didn't speak for a few seconds then came back towards Sa'eed. 'It was a red Volkswagen that Mr Greer was driving when he had the accident,' he said. 'He was hit by a train travelling at over 160 miles per hour. We're not going to ask anybody to identify Mr Greer.' He turned and walked back into the house again.

Sa'eed looked in at the wailing crumpled heap in the passenger seat of the police car. Conflicting emotions were stirring within him. Not pity. He felt elated and grateful and awed by the guidance of his Saviour. If, he conjectured, O'Neill was devastated in discovering that the prey he had hunted so ruthlessly was his sister, how much more vulnerable and receptive would he be now, in learning of her murder by the son he had tried to rescue? And whose folly other than O'Neill's had caused this catastrophe? He prayed silently in thanks.

For the second time within the hour he reached down to lever O'Neill into a position in which he could support him on his feet, or if need be, to lift him. Another constable came over to assist him. They shouldered O'Neill over to Sa'eed's car. Sa'eed strapped him in, thanked the constable and drove off. He drove to his own flat in Smithdown Lane. He stopped outside the flat, turned the engine off and put the handbrake on. He looked down on O'Neill who sat with his head bowed and his eyes closed and who clearly didn't know and didn't care where he had been driven. There seemed to be no more tears left. Sa'eed listened to his whimpering and watched him trembling. He assumed that O'Neill wished he was dead. He reckoned he would be dead if he was left alone this night. He stretched over, reached for the collar of O'Neill's jacket and wrenched him upwards and towards him. O'Neill's head fell forward helplessly. He obviously didn't give a damn what Sa'eed or anybody else did to him.

'Look at me,' Sa'eed demanded.

O'Neill remained limp, his head still bowed. Sa'eed shook him violently. 'Look at me,' he repeated.

O'Neill raised his head and opened his eyes. He looked into Sa'eed's eyes and barely recognised them. They were fierce, intense and full of hatred.

'They've been laughing at you for weeks,' Sa'eed said. His mouth contorted; his teeth gleamed in the beam of the street light that lit up his face. 'What do you think they'll say about you now?'

It took a few moments for the words to register. O'Neill ceased his self-pitying whimpering. 'Who... who's been laughing?' he asked quietly.

Sa'eed relaxed the grip on his collar. 'Everyone,' he said. 'The whole office. Nobody wanted to tell you. You were the only one who didn't know.'

O'Neill's focus shifted from the pupils of Sa'eed's grey eyes. He stared vacuously over Sa'eed's shoulder at door numbers on the opposite side of the street.

'How long have they known?'

'Since Morgan got those file notes... from your *friend*, Maggie.' There was a note of scorn in his use of the word *friend*. 'She's been sitting on them for months. Morgan told Emma first. Everybody knew within hours.'

Sa'eed released his hold on O'Neill's collar and watched the initial stupefying effects of his words. He could see myriads of thoughts racing through O'Neill's mind: how in the past few days some staff had been looking at him and others studiously avoiding him.

O'Neill suddenly began to shake. Sa'eed grabbed his lapels, steadied him and then wrenched him nearer again. 'What did you expect?' he shouted.

O'Neill shook his head; his lips arched and swelled. He had nothing to say.

'You know what these people are,' said Sa'eed. You know the kind of lives they lead.'

But it was his own life that O'Neill this moment was trying to cope with; a life disintegrating, his head throbbing, his heart swollen and bereft, his mind in anguish unable to block memories that were torturing him, and now at the mercy of the mere youth he mentored. He knew Sa'eed was the life blood. He knew that if Sa'eed had not turned up tonight he would be dead.

'It's only liars and fools and hypocrites can keep the sham going,' said Sa'eed. 'Isn't that what you told me?'

O'Neill nodded limply.

'And you're the biggest *fool* of them all, sleepwalking your way into a disaster that *your friend* Maggie could have told you about months ago.'

O'Neill clutched his hair with both hands and forced a loud anguished sigh from his blubbering lips.

'You never prepared me for their cruelty and their cowardice,' Sa'eed said. 'Don't you think it cowardly and cruel that they didn't tell you?'

There was something of a lifeline for O'Neill in that question; a diversion from the devastation he was feeling, a temporary focus on its cause. He didn't have the physical strength nor the composure to answer, but Sa'eed could see the answer in his eyes; could see that he had touched the rawest nerve; regenerated the hatred in his heart.

'You knew all about these people long before I did. You made me ask myself questions that probably would never have entered my mind. You made me laugh at the ridiculousness of the job itself... at least *you* knew it was ridiculous. You never fooled yourself that you were doing anything other than stalking child abusers and exposing colleagues stupid enough to have something else in mind. It was all great fun for you. But you hated the people around you. I hated them too watching and listening to the way they talked about you. They laughed at you rather than face you and tell the truth. Some of them probably regret you finding out who Marian Greer was; they'd prefer it if you'd never found out; if you could be strung along for years while they laughed. Now they've got something much bigger to *laugh* at. Imagine what they're going to think when they hear what's happened tonight. They'll be laughing at you for years when they talk about that hapless *Irish* fool, the arrogant know-all who spent months working with a mother and didn't realise it was his sister! You've got Maggie Lynch to thank for that.'

'No! No!' O'Neill shook his head, but it was more of an expression of helplessness than resistance. 'Maggie tried... I know now she tried to tell me... she's been trying to tell me for months... I made it impossible for her... I never gave her the chance.'

Sa'eed pondered his options: to relent or to quash O'Neill's puny resistance, this uncharacteristic, guilt-ridden, sentimental loyalty to Maggie.

'The *chance*?' he asked, incredulously. 'What's *chance* got to do with it? If you see someone you know heading for disaster and you can stop them by telling them something they won't want to hear, what do you do?'

O'Neill lowered and shook his head.

'The only reason you wouldn't tell them is because you don't care what happens to them. In fact you might even wish it to happen them, especially when you know everyone else feels the same way.'

O'Neill managed to utter 'no' but it was almost inaudible. He may as well have waved his hands in surrender, if he had the strength. He bowed his head low again.

Sa'eed looked down on him, remembering words that kept re-echoing in his mind: *seek out a fourth member whose hatred... is faith in itself.*

Chapter 51

In the name of Allah, Most Gracious, Most Merciful.

To my beloved and revered Sheikh Omar Abdel Rahmān, great teacher and dearest friend, As-salamu Alaikum!

The end of our mission is near. This is likely to be my farewell letter.

Let me first celebrate the news from Afghanistan: the daily elimination of British forces by our Taliban brothers continues. Over one hundred and fifty now dead. What are British troops dying for in Afghanistan, I hear people ask; when are they coming home? When many more are dispatched home in body bags and draped coffins; that's when the troops will come home.

I need not remind you of your success against the Danes. You may, dear Sheikh Omar, have even heard the bomb in Islamabad! I watched film of their Embassy that is no more, and their corpses scattered everywhere. I could almost smell rotting Danish corpses. Thank you, almighty Allah.

In Holland, politician Geert Wilders has produced a film arguing that our Holy Qur'an is no better that Hitler's Mein Kampf. He seems hell-bent on causing us even greater offence than the Danes. Has he forgotten what happened to his compatriots Pim Fortuyn and Theo van Gogh? We slaughter those who offend Islam.

In New York, the Muslim-hater Pope Benedict prayed at ground zero for the 'redemption' of all jihadi Muslims. It is as our brother and most cherished leader Osama proclaims: 'a new crusade' against Islam.

The Catholics in Britain crow. They are foolish to do so. As even the stupid Danes must now realise, the Pope and his Muslim-hating flock must pay a price. **There is not a population but We shall destroy it before the Day of Judgement or punish it with a dreadful penalty. That is written in the eternal Record.**

In my last letter dear Sheikh Omar, I described the fate of children in this supposedly civilized country. I have since encountered evil that I cannot attempt to describe. I also said that by the time I write to you again, more children will have died horrific deaths. There have been twenty children, mostly babies, murdered since I last wrote to you. The most recent is a baby 17 months old. He was beaten to death, covered in bite marks and bruises. He had eight broken ribs. His back was broken. He had finger nails pulled off. His left ear was hanging from his head. He swallowed a tooth that had been punched out of its socket. His gums and lips were torn.

There is another kind of child murder in this cursed country dear Sheikh Omar, which is unmentionable. Amazingly, it doesn't warrant any condemnation despite being a deliberate, premeditated act. It is occurring more and more as a consequence of divorce, which is the fate of most married couples. Nearly all divorces are fractious and harmful to children, but I am now referring to situations in which the spouses harbour murderous intent towards each other. It happens like this: A husband discovers the affair of his wife, or, his wife discovers the affair of her husband. The resulting sense of betrayal and hatred is such that he or she feels life is not worth living. But they rationalise: why should I kill myself and leave the person who is the cause of it to reap the benefits of their wicked affair **and take my children?** So they plot and plan. Yes, they will take their own lives, but they will take the lives of their children with them. And that's what they do. Before killing themselves they kill their children. During the past year, more than thirty of these murderous parents have poisoned, drowned, strangled or suffocated their children; they have thrown their children over hotel balconies in foreign lands; they have held their children in their arms and leapt in front of high speed trains, and the most common method of all: they have simply ran a knife through their children's hearts. All for revenge.

There are no Muslim parents capable of ending their children's lives merely to seek revenge on the husband or wife who has betrayed them.

Finally, let me tell you of one more case, dear Sheikh Omar. It did not result in death, but it summarises so much of what I see in Abington. It happened in an estate just like Abington. I mentioned before: there are many Abingtons in Britain.

A nine year old girl was kidnapped by her own mother! She was drugged and locked up for three weeks. The mother rang the police to say that she was missing. Tens of thousands of people searched for her. The mother's aim was to claim an award put up by a national newspaper for the child's release. The stupidity of the mother was matched only by her cruelty. There are millions of cruel and stupid parents in Britain. There are millions and millions of children dependent on them.

In my training dear Sheikh Omar, I have been taught that when small children are grossly neglected and cruelly abused in their earliest years they emerge from childhood full of hatred and self-destruction. They either turn in on themselves or they kick out at those all around them.

'Kick out' is a most accurate term. When my beloved brother in Allah, Sharif Mahdi, the husband of my beloved sister Samira, was kicked to death in a Liverpool public park many years ago, it was a rare crime. But since then, a kicking-to- death cult has emerged. Gangs of youths, some only twelve or thirteen years of age, who are the cruelly abused and the betrayed children of earlier years, now roam the streets searching for victims that they can kick to death. There is approximately one person kicked and beaten to death in this country every two weeks. This surpasses the number of such attacks in any other country in the world. Kicking to death, whether you are a participant or a viewer, is rapidly taking over knifing someone to death for popularity and thrills. It is much slower and far bloodier and painful. It necessitates a contribution of ferocity from each gang member. The sight of the victims' blood pouring from their mouths, their eyeballs dislodged from their sockets, their teeth lying scattered on the pavements, and their head and face swelled to an unrecognisable grotesqueness, apparently drives the perpetrators crazy. They just cannot stop kicking until they have no energy left to kick. By this time, their victims are dead, and yet this cruelty does not satiate them completely. Their ultimate prize is filming it, and displaying it on the internet as a trophy.

The origin of this degeneracy and violence lies in the neglect and immorality of parents. But everyone knows that the evil of alcohol consumption accelerates that degeneracy. City centres are now out of bounds for most adults, such is the extent of teenage drunkenness and its accompanying violence and vomit.

As I wrote above, the alternative for those who do not kick out is to turn in on themselves. The principal means by which they do so is to kill themselves. This is substantially less problematic than killing others, but the number of children and teenagers killing themselves in

384

Britain is staggeringly high. Younger and younger children are killing themselves. A child of eight hung himself two weeks ago. Some youths even sign a covenant of death with their friends and indulge in multiple suicides. This country has the highest rates of teenage suicide and teenage mental illness in Europe.

It also has the highest rate of teenage pregnancy. I have calculated that there are at present over 150 teenage (unmarried) pregnancies in Abington (two of which are twelve year old girls). The government is in despair about this problem and the resultant spread of sexually transmitted diseases. Its solutions are typically Godless. Such 'solutions' are administered under a huge bureaucracy called 'Family Planning Services.' Family Planning employs all kinds of professional people. They have as much in common with the teenage girls of Abington as you dear Sheikh Omar, now have in common with the middle classes you deserted.

The number of staff employed in Family Planning has increased a thousand fold. Its tentacles have spread into every county of the kingdom. Everyone admits – even government ministers who fund it – that it is an industry whose power and influence increases directly in proportion to its uselessness. Its schemes and project for reduction of teenage pregnancies never fail to reach new levels of absurdity and dangerousness. Their latest suggestions include abortion on demand, sex education for the under fives, sexual diseases education for 11 year olds; freely available contraceptive pills, the implanting of long-term contraceptive devices in 12 to 16 year olds (without their parents knowing), the establishment of sex clinics in every school, and mass inoculation of every girl over 11 to prevent them developing the cervical cancer commonly caused by sexual activity. You see dear Sheikh Omar, in Britain the authorities, the parents, the schools, and the doctors, have all given up supporting and encouraging children to abstain from sexual intercourse. They believe sexual intercourse is not just expected from eleven years onwards, but inevitable. Which is why the number of teachers convicted for sexual liaisons with pupils rises inexorably.

The final solution for teenage pregnancy is abortion. Here again Britain leads the world in the number of abortions carried out on teenage girls. I have shadowed social workers many times whose response to pregnant teenagers is as sinful as it is harmful. They ask as few questions as possible, and they refer the child to a doctor who they know will book them into an abortion clinic instantly. 'Abortion Rights' is the latest publication freely distributed in Abington. If the girl refuses to consider abortion, the social worker will sin even more by applying subtle pressure and calling upon other professionals to do likewise, believing that if the pregnancy reaches fruition it will be a disaster for both mother and child.

Kill not your children for fear of want. We shall provide sustenance for them as well as you. Verily the killing of them is a great sin.

And what about the mothers of these children? What about women in this country in general? The Qur'an tells us that **Men are the protectors and maintainers of women because Allah has given the one more strength than the other.**

Women's groups and government ministers in this country often condemn Muslim countries for the way they treat women. They go out of their way to vilify our moral and family codes and they provocatively provide funds and opportunities to entice our daughters to leave the parents who seek only to do good to them.

Allah binds us to the responsibility of protecting women from sexual exploitation and enslavement. In Britain billions of pounds are spent promoting pornography that exploits and enslaves women. Government permits it, even encourages and profits from it. The pornographers openly canvass in advertisements and the internet, enriching their coffers still further and degrading the mostly poor and uneducated women they entrap. The vast majority of these women become further enslaved in drug addiction.

It is ironic that Britain lectures us about the abuse of women. Last year 360,000 British women were battered in their homes. They are the ones who were courageous enough to report what was done to them; it is believed that there are at least as many more too scared to do so. I have seen women in Abington with broken noses, blackened eyes, jaws so damaged that they cannot be opened, and pregnancies terminated by the kickings they received. In Britain as a whole, one woman is murdered by the man closest to her, every day. All over the country there are refuges for battered women. The perpetrators, their husbands and boyfriends, usually walk free. This is the country that boasts of its sexual equality.

*I came here on a mission, dear Sheikh Omar, to wage war on the enemies of Islam. But nothing has prepared for me for the moral wasteland in which they live and operate. How do you explain this wasteland? How can they not know that their wickedness in neglecting and abusing their women and children so diabolically will eventually provoke the wrath of Allah? Why do they not sense that **they are hanging over the wide and bottomless pit of fiery hell, hanging by a slender thread, and the flames of divine wrath are flashing all around it, singing it, burning it?***

I said in my last letter that I have changed, but only in the sense that my motivation has not stayed the same. I remain dedicated to Allah and to the mission he has entrusted to me, and in the midst of this cruelty and depravity my determination to fulfil that mission has intensified far more that I ever could have predicted. To attack this physically diseased and morally decrepit country however is no longer the challenge I once thought it was; a much greater challenge lies in awakening its inhabitants out of the faithlessness which is the root cause of all their evil. I pray to mighty Allah that I not only deliver fire, but enlightenment and catharsis too.

Use my letters dear Sheikh Omar, in your teachings. Let my observations and my experiences demonstrate to our brothers and sisters who await the call that we underestimate the extent of Satan's hold. He holds this sad and brutal nation in a vice. Expose its hypocrisy and cruelty as I have described it, and let your students laugh when they hear fools proclaim that this is a country of freedom, justice, tolerance and civilization.

Through the power and Grace of Allah,

Your loving Sa'eed.

PART VI

Chapter 52

Maggie and Bell considered themselves reasonably fit, but the fifty-five steps of Liverpool's Catholic Metropolitan Cathedral still left them breathless. It wasn't the only entrance, but it was always the more appealing and uplifting, both literally and for some, spiritually too. It was a drab and wet Wednesday evening and they were attending the first of two rehearsals. The second would be on Saturday afternoon before the evening's performance which would be attended by Church and Civic dignitaries. The choristers would be led by the Liverpool Philharmonic Orchestra and choir, conducted by the electrifying young Russian Maestro Vladimir Petrovin, for a performance of Verdi's *Requiem*. Merseyside's Theatre of Contemporary Dance would also participate, a recent innovation in choral concerts that some regarded as revolutionary, and others, a gimmick. The dancers, according to the publicity blurb, would *personalise the horrors of the Apocalypse as envisaged by Verdi in the thunderous Dies Irae movement,* prompting a local music critic to scathingly ask 'what did *personalise* mean... how could you *personalise* music's most powerful and best known evocation of terror and confusion?' Stuffier and more traditionalist critics reminded their readers that the *Requiem* was already Verdi's most blasphemous and self indulgent work, so a few Scousers prancing about in the cathedral's aisles wasn't going to make it any more or less so.

Maggie would not have been here had it not been for Bell. Bell had been the constant support after the near abduction of Alice, the deaths of Michael and Marian Greer, and the trial of Martin now detained at *Her Majesty's pleasure,* for life. Maggie had sunk into the deepest despair, incapable of thinking that anyone other than herself was responsible. It wasn't only the magnitude of what happened, the obliteration of a family, that had weighed so heavily on her conscience, but also the consequences on the one family member remaining, Sean

O'Neill. She assumed that O'Neill must have endured some kind of inescapable psychological disintegration. Even when exonerated by her employers and a coroner (how they reasoned, could murder, suicide and the incest which had been occurring over years long before any professional got involved, be attributed to anything other than the family's own depravity?) she still could not alleviate herself of guilt. She took another extended leave period. She missed her own choir's *Requiem* rehearsals for months. She went on a retreat to the famous St. Beuno's Spirituality Centre in North Wales where a saintly monk tried to convince her she had done no wrong; indeed, her *motivation* (which she regarded as a *paralysis*) was understandable, even laudable. Her husband Keith, her doctor, her parish priest and Bell all knew what she was craving for: contact and some kind of reconciliation with O'Neill. They warned her against contact. They speculated on his state of mind and what he might do. That only made her feel worse, intensified the yearning to see him. But nobody could tell her where he was. He had resigned, or more accurately, simply had never returned to his office, not even for his personal effects. He seemed to have disappeared off the face of the earth.

That made her nights even more sleepless, convinced her that he had taken his own life and that it was only a matter of time before she would learn of his putrefying corpse being discovered in some woodland. It would be the final catastrophic act in a drama that evolved, she believed, out of her own moral cowardice.

But that seemed a long time ago now. The great healers in her life, her family and friends, Bell in particular, her job, her Catholicism, and time itself, slowly rescued her. She never forgot O'Neill, but the memory of him faded and the pain that such memory provoked became a little more tolerable, less pervasive. Eventually there was no pain at all, only brief intermittent memory and some regret. She still yearned to know what had happened to him. She still prayed for him every day, lit candles for him in her local church; submitted petitions to the Blessed Virgin Mary. Perhaps she shouldn't have been too surprised then when she almost collided with him in *a church* as she and Bell made their way inside.

Like the amphitheatres of old, the beautiful nave rotunda of the Metropolitan Cathedral has equal sectors of seating divided by aisles, the seating narrowing and the aisles converging onto the central holy sanctuary. Maggie and Bell were walking down one of these aisles towards the altar and to the space behind it allocated to the choirs. They didn't see O'Neill and Sa'eed walking down another aisle. Nor did O'Neill and Sa'eed see them. There was much pre-concert activity in the cathedral, with lots of choristers in all the aisles, some there for the first time gazing around them, passing Maggie and Bell or being overtaken by them. The same was happening in the aisle O'Neill and Sa'eed moved in. The two couples were getting nearer to each other and still didn't realise it. At the end of the aisles all four were at the foot of the magnificent Macedonian-marble altar and only a few metres away from each other. That's when they nearly collided and when Maggie and O'Neill looked at each other for the first time in over six months.

It sent tremors of fear and guilt through her. Yet *he* looked remarkably self-composed, unembarrassed. Despite her attempts to trace him and her daily prayers for his well-being, she realised that at this moment in time he was the last person she wanted to see. She had so desperately wanted to see him on her own terms, in a location of mutual choice. Now she didn't know what to say to him or whether or not he intended saying anything to her. He kept his eyes on her as he got nearer, and she then saw in his eyes a look of terrible intensity that she could not comprehend, but he walked past her and said nothing.

Sa'eed spoke to Maggie and smiled. In the paranoiac state momentarily induced by seeing O'Neill and the deliberate slight of walking past her, she wasn't sure whether or not Sa'eed was feeling sorry for her. He didn't look sorry and he certainly wasn't embarrassed. 'Remember,' he said; 'you and Sean told me I should join a choir and sing the *Requiem*.'

She barely managed a half smile and said 'well done.'

She had an urge to turn away from Sa'eed to see where O'Neill had gone, but she strove instead to regain some composure and engage with him. Lots of thoughts were racing through her mind: the inexplicableness of the encounter; the apparent

393

friendship between Sa'eed and O'Neill. She had first been aware of some kind of relationship when she met both of them at the case conference on Martin. Sa'eed had then been a mere student on placement. He was quite obviously something much more to O'Neill now. She'd been told that O'Neill had spent a day or two living with Sa'eed after the night Martin was arrested. Their relationship had obviously endured. She didn't know of any close relationship that O'Neill had with anyone else. Maybe Sa'eed had been as much a lifeline for O'Neill, she thought, as Bell had been for her. But what was it about Sa'eed she asked, that made him a friend of O'Neill.

Bell had never met O'Neill before but assumed that's who he was when she saw how Maggie had reacted to him. She had tensed, anticipating a confrontation in which she might have played some part, if only to usher Maggie away from it. She was relieved when O'Neill walked on past.

She certainly remembered Sa'eed. Her instant response on seeing him was to look around for Azeer. The suave and overpowering teacher and his ice cold student who sat with them in the Piazza Verdi in Busseto, were indelibly imprinted in Bell's memory, and inseparable too; she had never thought of one without the other. But Azeer was not there and everything about Sa'eed seemed to vindicate what Maggie had told her a long time ago, after meeting him and O'Neill at Hollybank: this was a much more emollient Sa'eed, without that cold friendless stare, able to smile genuinely and willing to take the initiative in engaging them.

'You're not going to be sitting under that drum again, are you?' she asked. They laughed at each other. Maggie managed to smile again.

'I'm singing with the tenors,' he said, 'I'll be right in the middle of them. They'll help to protect my ear-drums, and cover up all my mistakes.'

'Is Sean singing tenor too?' Maggie asked, wishing she could explore far more interesting lines of enquiry about O'Neill.

'He's bass,' said Sa'eed.

Maggie looked around and sure enough, O'Neill had reached the bass section and was choosing where to sit. Her enquiry would have to wait.

She wasn't interested in small chat any more. People around the altar were on the move and the three of them were standing in the way. They parted.

Maggie and Bell were silent as they made their way to the rear of the altar to the sector of seating reserved for the sopranos. Maggie was still visibly affected and Bell could not think of any comforting words to say.

Each of the four voice sectors had a specially constructed tiered platform with a stairway at either side. Together, these platforms half-encircled the altar. The soprano sector, as always, was at least twice as big as the other sectors. 'Let's get into the middle', said Bell, echoing Sa'eed's desire to be amongst as many faces and voices as possible.

'That was O'Neill,' Maggie said, inviting her to comment.

'So I gathered.'

'He didn't attack me. He didn't verbally abuse me.'

Bell didn't respond. She knew there was some irony in Maggie's words. She could appreciate that O'Neill's apparent *restraint* was not exactly a source of reassurance. It was the expression on his face that had baffled them both.

'What was he thinking when he looked at me like that?' asked Maggie.

'I don't know.'

'Did he hate me?'

'No. It wasn't hatred. He *didn't* want to stop obviously, but that wasn't hatred in his eyes.'

Maggie thought for a moment. She hoped Bell was right. 'What then,' she said, 'contempt?'

'Maggie! Give over. Get a seat, sit down and shut up!'

They had got halfway up the staircase of the soprano section. Many of the seats had been taken.

'Get into the middle,' repeated Bell, thinking her friend was too preoccupied to care where they sat.

They moved up another row to just past the central row. In the middle of the central row an Asian woman sat alone. Maggie had noticed her on the way up the staircase and glanced at her a number of times as they moved along the row behind. Pakistani, she presumed, and pregnant apparently; she didn't wear a ring. She was five or six years younger than both of them, exceptionally beautiful, with large soulful eyes, strong cheekbones, no makeup, and lips, silent and closed. A silky white headscarf covered most of her black hair, the type of cover that would loosen often and would need constant repositioning. If this woman needed a head cover, Maggie wondered, why didn't she wear a hibab? Was she Muslim? How could a Muslim woman be sitting in a Catholic cathedral preparing to sing Verdi? But wasn't Sa'eed Muslim? And didn't Azeer say that the *Requiem* was immensely popular in Egypt. He wasn't joking as Maggie had then thought; she had checked that out for herself. Perhaps though, this woman was not Muslim. Maggie suddenly realised it wasn't the woman's religion she was curious about, but her colour. She had never seen a non-white person amongst Liverpool choristers before.

They were sitting in the row behind this woman now, two or three seats to her right. Maggie had the perfect elevated view of the side profile of her face which was serious and proud but not serene. She felt a tinge of guilt in staring at the face intrusively and not being seen doing so. She looked away but often felt compelled to look back. The woman's aloneness and colour made her so conspicuous.

Maggie glanced around at the four groups of choristers inquisitive to see were there any other non-white faces. She saw another amongst the contraltos; an Asian woman, but not Pakistani, nor Indian; further east perhaps, Malaysia? Indonesia? She wasn't sure and was too far away to hazard a guess. Like the Pakistani woman in front of her, this other Asian woman seemed to be on her own. She engaged with no one. She occasionally looked up but never looked around her. Her head was lowered though not low enough for her to be reading the music.

Maggie looked at the Pakistani woman in front of her again, and then back at the woman in the contraltos. There was something similar about these two women apart from their presumed Asian roots. She wondered did they know each other and had they come to the rehearsal together.

She glanced over the four choir sections again. She couldn't see any more non-whites faces other than Sa'eed. She wondered did Sa'eed and the two women consider themselves *black*. She always had difficulty in labelling the earth's two billion people whose skins could be any one of a dozen shades of brown, as *black*.

She sought out O'Neill and found him in the middle of the basses. She wondered what precisely he thought and felt the moment he saw her earlier. She quickly realised that she could wonder and stare at him now as long as she pleased, because there was something in his demeanour and posture that told her he was not going to reciprocate. He wasn't only ignoring her; he seemed also to be exaggerating his determination to ignore her. But that would mean that he was at least thinking about her. Was he loathing her? Considering her beneath contempt? Or had he just made a conscious decision to banish her from his thoughts for ever.

He seemed genuinely engrossed in the cathedral itself, his head repeatedly turning almost full circle, taking in its many chapels and its modernistic sculptures and carvings. Occasionally he looked directly above at the extravagant baldacchino reaching down from the central tower symbolically protecting the sanctuary below. At one point she couldn't determine precisely what it was he was staring at, but his focus seemed to alternate between two darkened narrow recesses opposite each other, some twenty metres high, in the main rotunda body of the cathedral. The recesses were fenced off by metal railings which were flush with the walls on either side. She saw O'Neill looking to the floor of the nave below the railings. There was a door directly beneath each railing, opening she presumed, onto a staircase that led to the recessed balconies. It took her a few moments to work out what these darkened inconspicuous recesses were for. A couple of barely visible, unused stage lights at the back of one of them provided the answer; they must be where camera crews and technicians are unobtrusively located when important religious ceremonies are being filmed. Little wonder she hadn't noticed them before.

The choir sections rapidly filled up. The orchestral players and their choir colleagues also took their seats. A thousand amateur singers may mess up a thousand times, but the two-hundred strong Royal Liverpool Philharmonic choir would not. Their stronger and more disciplined voices would always save the day. They took up a central position nearest to the orchestra and the conductor's podium. Maggie could not help herself noticing and dwelling on the fact that every single member of the Philharmonic choir was white.

The diminutive Vladimir Petrovin in tight blue jeans and a checked shirt walked onto the makeshift stage to be greeted with enthusiastic applause. Neither of the two Asian women applauded and Sa'eed's applause seemed timid to the point of silence.

Petrovin exuded all the confidence and authority that reviewers unanimously remarked upon. He was strikingly handsome, a large open face, a characteristically Russian face with Nurevey-like features, mischievous and mysterious: the pregnant smile, the gleam in the eye, the full and sensual lips that curved at either end. He made some self-deprecating comments about his *English*, and then punctured the rising tension with an irreverent joke about mutual misunderstanding at the *Easy Jet* desk in John Lennon airport. He told them he expected the soloists to be joining them later; 'late as always', he added, with a smile. 'No no!' he corrected himself. 'They insisted on staying away until we'd finished with the opening bars of the *Dies Irae.'*

They all laughed. Petrovin explained the much publicised role that the students of Merseyside's School of Contemporary Dance would play. He mocked the more sensational of the press condemnations and assured them of his own enthusiasm for such an innovation. He *advised* them to enjoy the dancers whom they would see for the first time at the Saturday rehearsal; but on Saturday night, they had to forget about them. They must never take their eyes off him. 'That's right... I don't expect anybody to have to look at the music of *Dies Irae*... you all know it off by heart...' He allowed the murmurs of doubt to circulate in response to that, his widening grin telling them he wasn't serious.' You keep your eyes and your mind on me!'

Petrovin succeeded in holding Maggie's attention only intermittently. Her mind wandered. She glanced over at Sa'eed again and at the two Asian women. None of them appeared to be joining in the fun; none of them smiled or laughed at Petrovin's charm and humour. She was uncomfortably aware of an inquisitiveness about all three of them that was rapidly becoming obsessive. Was that it then: the colour of their skin, a reflection of the limited parameters of her social life, her job and family? She remembered Keith bantering her about the exclusivity of choral societies; middle class, mostly middle age and elderly, and white only. She had resented him saying it only because she believed it was true. She worked with lots of minorities, but she didn't socialize with any of them, and she certainly had never had the chance of singing with them. Like many *Guardian*-reading, left-leaning professionals working in the multicultural melting pot of Liverpool, she had consciously chosen to live in a middle class Edwardian town exclusively white. She never had any difficulty in accepting the universality of racist tendencies, including her own, but was she a racist? Was she not merely looking at them but also offended by them? She had never had to ask questions like that before. She made a conscious effort to stop looking at them, but that only made her think about them more.

Petrovin invited them to 'warm up' with a few exercises; he told them to relax, enjoy themselves, give of their best. He gently mocked and mimicked their initial timidity. He promised them that Saturday would be a wonderful night. They believed him. He was ready now to begin. He stepped off the podium and stooped towards the leader of the orchestra, seemingly to clarify some finer details about the score.

Bell and many other choristers reacted to this brief interval by flicking through the *Requiem's* pages. She sought out passages that had previously given her grief and hummed and recited the words as softly as she could. Maggie was aware of her friend's anxiety but she had preoccupations of her own that she could not contain. She nudged Bell, leaned into her and whispered: 'how many non-white people would you expect to see in a choral concert like this?'

Bell resented the diversion but seemed interested in the query. She closed her score and looked around the four singing sectors.

The Pakistani woman in front was the last person she looked at. Then she said ponderously: 'I was thinking about that earlier on; I've never seen a black person singing choral in Liverpool. Maybe down South it's different. I never went to concerts when I worked there. But you're more likely to see Pete Doherty in *Songs of Praise* than a black face in a Liverpool choir.'

Maggie smiled, thought about this for a moment, and with tongue in cheek, decided to defend this implied aspersion on Liverpool's multi cultural credentials. 'I sang Messiah with three thousand... *down South... in the Albert Hall*,' she stressed, and there wasn't one black person in either the audience or the singers.'

'I know. I was thinking about that too... Isn't that why... what-you-call-her... was having a go at the Albert Hall?'

'Margaret Hodge, Minister for Children! She was having a go at the *Proms*, not the Albert Hall; she said the *Proms* weren't culturally diverse enough.'

'The Proms... Albert Hall... same thing,' said Bell. 'She's onto something. You should have written and told her... since you've told everybody else that story. She might have quoted you.'

Maggie ignored the mildly sarcastic tone. 'We've got three non-whites in a choir of a thousand here tonight,' she said. 'Liverpool's doing well then, isn't it?'

Bell looked at her companion conscious of the rhetoric and irony in the question. 'What are you thinking?' she asked.

'Liverpool's not just doing well... I'd say three non-white singers in a chorus doing Verdi's *Requiem* in Liverpool is beginning to look like a revolution.'

'But the chorus is from all over Merseyside, not just Liverpool, and probably from outside of Merseyside too.'

They turned away from each other. Bell opened her music.

Maggie could not resist looking again at Sa'eed and the two Asian women. Her unease grew and her conscience stirred. She was aware of emotions and perceptions thrusting her towards the prejudicial stereotyping that she loathed, that she dared not mention. She closed her eyes and made a conscious mental effort to resist. When she opened her eyes and looked straight ahead she could nevertheless sense that Bell was looking at her, had maybe been looking at her for some seconds. Then she heard Bell say:

'If there had been a fourth black person sitting where O'Neill's sitting now, I might have been worried.'

Bell's focus returned to the music, but she knew the impact of her words.

A stunned Maggie glanced from Sa'eed to O'Neill, and from the Asian alto to the soprano.

Bell slowly raised her head. She had a mischievous sparkle in her eyes: 'Joking,' she said with a smile.

'Testing, you mean,' said Maggie.

Chapter 53

Keith waited up for Maggie but had then got too engrossed in a documentary to be genuinely interested in how the rehearsals had gone. She told him she was tired, which was a huge understatement; she was physically exhausted, and yet in a kind of emotional turmoil that would ensure she would not sleep. She kissed him, went upstairs, and looked in on the kids.

She went into her office and turned the computer on. She could feel the qualms of the earlier evening re-emerging. On her journey back tonight she had recollected once again Keith's harmless banter about choral societies being all-white. Maybe it wasn't like that any more. But even in thinking about it as she sat waiting for her computer to warm up, she felt uneasy, embarrassed almost, as though what she was about to do was, at best, undignified, maybe paranoid, more probably, racist. After the shock of seeing O'Neill and all the questions it had raised, she had ended up preoccupied, if not obsessed, by the colour of people's skin. She was conscious of the total disconnectedness of these two experiences. There was nothing she could do at this moment to enlighten herself about O'Neill's return, but she could satisfy her curiosity as to whether or not choral societies were *still* exclusively white.

She went online and keyed in 'Amateur Choral Societies in the Northwest.' Up they came: Salford, Oldham, Hoylake, Birkenhead, Formby, St. Helens, Bury, Chester, Congleton... the number seemed endless. She picked one at random, *Hoylake*. She entered the site. *Welcome to Hoylake Choral society*. Below was the group portrait, over a hundred members, all white. She went into another site, *Formby*; it was the same. She then systematically went through the web pages of each one them. All white. Then she returned to *Search* with the intention of looking further afield. She typed in Preston Choral Society, then Blackburn, Burnley, Manchester. She studied the faces. All white.

Maybe the small screen was misleading, she thought; or maybe there *were* non-white members of choral societies who were just not there when the photographs were taken. But she didn't really believe that and she ended up repeating the question she'd asked herself in the Albert Hall: Why are choral societies *still* such bastions of whiteness? Now she felt less embarrassed returning to another question which had dogged her all night: why would three black people, one a Muslim, and the other two apparently known by no one, want to sing Verdi's *Requiem* in Liverpool's Catholic cathedral?

She closed the computer down, went to her bedroom and undressed. When she returned from the bathroom she sat before the mirror to comb her hair. She stared at herself, and memories and feelings about O'Neill came flooding back over her.

Their relationship was nothing short of a catastrophe, a proven catastrophe in the corpses of his sister and the nephew he tried to rescue. He had now returned to Liverpool – was he ever away? – and her guilt laden memories had returned with him. But it was the memory of the return itself that would keep her awake in the night: the near collision at the altar, the enigmatic expression on his face as he silently passed her by. She still didn't know what it meant, if it meant anything at all. That briefest of encounters rekindled the dormant desires to reach out to him again, to try to explain, to apologise, to seek his forgiveness.

She recoiled from such a contact. She knew that whatever had happened, he could be a vindictive person, brutally over-reactive whenever he felt slighted or humiliated by others. Now she believed no one had given him greater cause for revenge than herself. She imagined him telling her to 'fuck off' if she made any approach to him. Or something worse. It could provoke his fury, a hatred that would frighten her, that would simply humiliate and overwhelm her.

But would that be the extent of his revenge, she then asked herself, believing as she had always believed, that it was her inaction that had brought about his woes. If so, it was a humiliation that she could not only withstand but might welcome. It would serve partially as a penance and punishment that periodically she still felt she needed to endure.

She imagined beyond the initial contact and the fury. How might he react to the truth, the real honest-to-God truth that although she more often than not lacked the courage to tell *him* of Marian Greer's identity, she did on one occasion actually pluck up the courage to reveal it to *her boss* Mike. It was not particularly courageous, but it certainly would have led to O'Neill finding out much sooner – if Mike had been around at the time!

That seemed pathetic now, more likely to intensify rather than assuage a desire for revenge. No, she could not say anything like that.

How about telling him, yes… the same God's honest truth, that when she was on the verge of telling him, he had, infuriatingly for her, driven himself up another blind alley, convincing himself in all his arrogance that he knew what was happening in this case, and impervious to a contrasting (correcting) view from mere mortals like herself.

What might his reaction be, she wondered, if she pleaded that the only reason she didn't tell him was because she couldn't bear the thought of the devastation it might have caused him. But she instantly knew there was something reprehensible about such a stance, as though she was uniquely, his keeper, his protector. She was prepared to *play* that protective role because she had learnt not just that Marian Greer was his sister, but also, that Marian had been almost battered to death trying to protect O'Neill from their mother's newest boyfriend. That was why, she then deduced, that in her bedsit all those years ago, he denied Marian's existence. How could she dare to risk reminding him of that, of the moment she asked him how many children were in his family and after the prolonged silence, he lied to her that he was an only child. She believed now that he must have carried an excruciating guilt all his life.

All of these excuses were pathetic, she decided. But even if they weren't, even if just one of them had contained a modicum of decency or comprehensibility, they were all still worthless and pathetic as a consequence of her final act. That took place on the morning after the night before, when he without warning or invitation invaded her family home whilst her children slept.

That was the last straw. He had forced his way in, ignoring her pleas not to, only days after the nightmare in Stapleton Woods. Typically, he had come both to attack her (on the basis of another half-baked speculation about her motives) and also, incredulously, to impress her! He just could not resist telling her of his lunatic break-in and his witnessing the crime! And then he himself in her eyes committed an even greater crime; albeit unwittingly, unintentionally, but no less unforgivable for that: when he opened her living room door to leave and momentarily terrorised her daughter, hunched beneath him, listening, already in tears because he, a stranger, had been shouting at her mother.

That was it. She could take no more. She *wouldn't* take any more. On the following day she stapled all the relevant papers that she had deliberately withheld to protect him and posted them to her secretary. She asked Judy to ensure that they were passed onto Morgan. She did it consciously, but determinedly. She knew that Morgan would read them, but O'Neill most likely would not. He never *wasted time* reading old case file notes, he often liked to tell her. It would not take much reading on Morgan's part... *Belfast location, the children Marian and Sean O'Neill, dates of birth etc.*, for him to realise that man and child was that same Sean O'Neill, and more sensationally, that Marian Greer was his sister. Morgan's gratification and his predictable indiscretions had always weighed heavily in her calculations; another excuse maybe, but still a powerful deterrent to disclosing what she knew. But after that night she didn't care any more. She didn't give a damn what Morgan did. She was finished with O'Neill. If he had ever made contact with her again, or come near her home or family, she would have applied for an injunction against him.

Before tonight's encounter in the cathedral, Maggie believed she had coped with her own guilt through faith. Prayer had enabled her eventually to accept God's forgiveness, but not before an exasperated priest had repeatedly told her what she already knew: that it was sinful to hold onto a sense of guilt when God had cleansed her of whatever sins she assumed had caused it. And it was an even greater sin she knew, to *feel* as she unpredictably and inexplicably felt on occasions, that the near abduction, rape, and murder of her daughter had been both a punishment and a warning.

Since the encounter in the cathedral tonight however, Maggie's perceptions had painfully altered. She began thinking that what had seemed like a slow recovery, her return to work and routine, her reconciliation with God, was based not so much on priestly absolution and Godly forgiveness as on the increasing conviction shared by all those who knew him, that O'Neill must be dead. He must have killed himself. Sad, but convenient.

How inconvenient that he had reappeared. God forgave but she knew that O'Neill would not. Now that he had reappeared she realised that she hadn't really forgiven herself. No matter how much priests and friends would rail at her for self flagellating, she could never forgive herself or forget the moral cowardice that enabled her to watch O'Neill unwittingly enmeshing himself more and more calamitously in his sister's diabolical family creation. She was convinced he would not just think of her as a moral coward, but that he would also hold her morally culpable for the death of a whole family, his family, which he didn't even know existed. Whatever the level or degree of responsibility she carried, it surely warranted greater retribution than being told to 'fuck off.' That would be no retribution. That would be both a relief and an escape for her. It would simply mean what it said: *'Fuck off!* And something like: *You're the pits! An unforgivable cowardly bitch. I never want to lay eyes on you again*! Hurtful, but hardly proportionate to the suffering he had endured, which she believed she had caused.

But no! O'Neill had something else in mind, she now thought. And she increasingly read as much in the recall of their silent encounter before the altar, in particular, that expression on his face. That was, she now believed, a controlled expression masking his desire for revenge, a revenge he had obviously been harbouring since the events of that cold January night.

She hopelessly tried to pray before getting into bed and she soon gave up trying to read. She lay awake hoping that Keith would watch something else besides the documentary. She began trembling and then crying. She regretted coming to bed. She dreaded Keith finding her like this. He didn't need this; he didn't deserve it. She got up often and slipped to the bathroom, determined he did not see her like this. She returned and asked the same questions over and over again. Where had O'Neill been? What had happened to him? Why had he come back? Who had rescued him? Somebody must have rescued him... did Sa'eed really rescue him? She had heard of the recollections of the few who had seen him that last night, Mary the cleaner, the coach Peter Chapman and the detective inspector who had taken him into his car and disclosed what had happened. They had all described someone at best, reduced to a crumbling emotional heap. The inspector went further: he suggested to Bell (who had made enquiries on Maggie's behalf) that O'Neill would remain permanently deranged. 'He'd never recover,' he said.

Sa'eed, who had apparently taken him in for a few days after, merely told anyone who asked that he *was in a bad way,* but he would be okay. But then O'Neill disappeared, 'just walked out' according to Sa'eed. No one knew where to. Nobody saw him. Few really cared. He didn't even turn up for the inquest or the trial. Many expressed sympathy and concern. All were convinced he'd snuffed it. Some thought it no bad thing.

Why had O'Neill come back? The longer she dwelt on it the more incredulous it seemed that he had returned to a city in which fate had been inescapably cruel to him. She had earlier concluded that he must have revenge in his heart, but she was not so neurotic to believe that she was the only target of that revenge. Maybe those working colleagues gratified by his humiliation and his demise were also in his sights; maybe his employers, maybe the city itself. Maybe... but *she* had to be the likeliest target!

Would harming her or killing her satiate him? Even that wasn't proportionate to the obliteration of his family. *His family.* What about *her* family? *Her* children? *Her* husband? *Her* home? Was this his malign purpose? The ultimate revenge? She helplessly imagined him scheming the destruction of Alice,

Rebecca and Keith as well as herself; but then she imagined something worse: him deliberately avoiding killing her, leaving her alive (as he had been left alive) with the corpses of her family. She shuddered at this thought.

These were crazy thoughts. But then she reasoned that his suffering was of a magnitude that made such a purpose conceivable, and, that his hatred of her and his lust for revenge must be potent enough to compel him to carry it out.

She shook her head as if trying to clear it of such *nonsense*. She breathed deeply, closed her eyes and thought positively. O'Neill must have been re-born. He's had extensive therapy of some kind. He's achieved a spiritual renewal. He's fallen in love! Such things can happen. They happen all the time. Personal tragedies converted into opportunity and triumph. How better to celebrate than by joining a thousand strong chorus to sing Verdi's *Requiem* in the Metropolitan cathedral?

That's better, she thought, sighing with relief. How could she think otherwise knowing in her heart of hearts that O'Neill was a survivor? But then she suddenly rose up from the bed and stretched out to her shoulder bag which earlier she'd let casually drop to the floor. She grabbed her copy of the *Requiem. How better to celebrate than by joining...* Sa'eed Jama... to sing Verdi's *Requiem!* What am I saying? she asked herself; what am I thinking? What a fool!

She could see Sa'eed again with eyes of cold steel and Azeer sitting opposite him, both of them emotionless yet pregnant with suppressed emotion and staring into each other's eyes. She was flicking through the *Dies Irae* as the memories came racing back to her. She was reading the same words as Azeer pretentiously called out that night: *Day of wrath and doom impending... Heaven and earth in ashes ending.* She closed her eyes again and prayed. She prayed that she would not lose control again. But the prayers were not as strong as the memories: the whiff of mockery in the air; the sense of being laughed at; the pompous, boring, over-confident Azeer, who actually knew little about Verdi and nothing about *Aida* and everything there was to know about the *Requiem*... like the 9/11 pilots who knew nothing about flying other than flying in a straight line onto their targets.

408

She flicked through the pages beyond the *Dies Irae*. She knew it all by heart. She knew it, but she had sung it meaninglessly for years. She had striven in her spare time in pursuit of diction, expression, breath control, trilling and expanding her range, but she knew she had never really listened to the words she was singing. If by accident she had heard the words, she hadn't given them a second thought. She reached the long final movement *Libera Me*. She knew that too, but she had merely been singing the Latin by rote. She read the translation:

Lord, deliver me out of ever lasting death, Oh Lord, upon that day of terror, when the earth and the heavens shall be moved.

When Thou shalt come and the whole world know the fire of judgement, trembling, terrified and full of despair am I,

Till the trial be at hand, and the wrath, the wrath to come…

Then came a repeat of the *Dies Irae* with more prophesy of disaster. It got worse and worse. Thirty pages of repetitive pleading for mercy and forgiveness followed. She stared at the famous final page in which the solo soprano's barely audible plea for liberation and redemption remains unanswered.

Maggie felt sick. She put a hand to her mouth and bit into her knuckles. She saw Azeer and Sa'eed again staring cryptically through each other. She saw O'Neill walking past her at the altar; the indecipherable look on his face. There was neither forgiveness nor mercy in any of those three faces.

The conclusion was as mind-boggling as it was inescapable. Bell's *joke* was no joke after all. O'Neill must be the fourth man. It had to be a conspiracy. They were going to commit an atrocity! Sa'eed, O'Neill and the two women… they were going to do it in the Metropolitan Cathedral during the *Requiem*. They were going to blow themselves up in their strategically central positions and take four or five hundred tightly crammed singers with them, and she and Bell were only a few feet away from one of them. Now she knew why Azeer and Sa'eed were on the verge of exploding in laughter in Busseto: because this is what they were anticipating; this is what they were rehearsing. It would be the irony of all ironies, when a thousand-strong chorus in a Catholic cathedral would be yelling out about hell fire and damnation and Azeer's four disciples, in the name of Allah, would rain down that hell fire upon them.

Maggie put both hands on her head and wondered was she going mad. No, she wasn't going mad, not as far as Azeer and Sa'eed were concerned. But how could O'Neill have become a disciple of Azeer? How could he have become an Islamist terrorist? She couldn't answer. She couldn't even believe it. But he had returned to harm her, no question about that. He had known for a long time that she intended singing the *Requiem* on this occasion. So this had to be his ultimate revenge. The self-destructive nature of such an action must surely have appealed to him. After what he had come through, – surely after all that, she reasoned, there was no greater appeal to him than to annihilate himself and the innocents around him at precisely the same moment when he would be gazing across the marble altar of Liverpool's Metropolitan Cathedral and watching an accomplice simultaneously annihilate the woman he held responsible.

Chapter 54

'Good evening sir, good evening madam.' Alojzy checked their tickets and then said: 'may I…?'

Search! No, he couldn't bring himself to use that word. It was too direct, too challenging and unnecessary. He gesticulated with a gentle opening of the hands, timidly beckoning to the *Cynthia Rowley* shoulder bag on the lady's arm.

Alojzy detested moments like this. He just could not take such responsibilities seriously. As if anyone, let alone this well-heeled middle class couple, would attempt to conceal a weapon or a bomb on their person as they entered the church! Not just any old church, but Liverpool's Metropolitan Cathedral of Christ the King.

To counter the offence he was certain he caused people like these (who were also regular Sunday mass-goers whom he had recognised) Alojzy sought to ingratiate himself in whatever way he could. One effective way he mistakenly thought, was to enlighten anyone staring at the name on his identity pass. 'It's *Ah-LOI-zi*' he would say with a broad smile, momentarily forgetting his task of searching and vetting; 'it's the Polish equivalent of Aloysius.' Some snooty adults were peeved at this assumption by a young man – *another one of those happy Poles would you believe* – that he knew what they were thinking. Others were bemused.

The lady returned the smile and removed the bag from her shoulder. She unzipped it and held it out for Alojzy. His cheeks reddened. He barely glanced at it and was already nodding his appreciation before anything that had caught his eye had registered. 'Thank you madam,' he said, almost overcome with gratitude; 'you can sit anywhere except the first two rows nearest the altar.'

The couple thanked him and moved off to be quickly replaced by another. There were at least thirty people in the queue and a similar number in the two additional queues, all strategically spaced and directed by the cathedral guides to avoid them overlapping around the chosen entrances. They were the early birds, getting there long before the concert started and choosing the best seats. The circular nave however ensured that no one would be too far away from the performers.

Alojzy was no exception in his negligence of security matters and in his lack of confidence. His colleagues at the head of the other queues were similarly pleasant and ineffectual. But you could hardly criticise them for that. They were not *security* trained. They had never been told what precisely to look out for. They had never been tested in spotting the clothes a would-be bomber might wear: the unusual combination of looseness and tightness evident in a bulky suicide vest, the body parts that looked conspicuously disproportionate, impacting on the naturalness of movements. They had never been encouraged to discretely move closer to people and to look into the pupils of their eyes, to be aware of the slightest nervousness, or a reluctance to make eye contact, or to discern the various kinds of tension in a voice, a tautness in the skin, a tremor in the fingers, a sweaty moistness on the collar. Real terrorists of course were professionals, and may not so easily provide such clues, but seldom in retrospect of an atrocity, had those in close proximity with the perpetrators not observed something of significance which a more vigilant attendant would have felt compelled to report.

Aloyzy and his friends had been living in Liverpool, attending and working voluntarily in the cathedral long enough to know that security had never been an issue before. As well as the handbags and the shopping bags which no Catholic female parishioner could do without, briefcases, rucksacks, duffle bags and school satchels had been floating in and out of the cathedral for more than forty years, and never once had the owners been invited or told to open them, or to remove them and leave them at the desk of the official guides just past the main entrance. Terrorists of any persuasion, simply did not bomb British churches. Never had. Never would. But a gesture to security was being made for this *City of Culture Year* event. Searches were obligatory, by hand too, unfortunately for Aloyzy.

412

Nobody seriously considered the need for metal detectors or scanners.

The choristers had been in the cathedral most of the day, having had a three hour rehearsal earlier in the afternoon. They were dressed in their concert attire. Many of them resented this unusual encumbrance, but the strategically minded organisers couldn't trust a thousand scruff-wearing amateurs to go home at the end of a Saturday afternoon rehearsal, get changed, and get back to the venue on time; and as everyone had to accept, there certainly weren't the facilities for a thousand males and females changing in the cathedral grounds.

For those who had seen enough of the cathedral, they bided their time by sitting outside with the lunch packs and flasks they'd been advised to bring. The weather was kind to them, a clear and sunny September day. No matter how calm or sultry it might have been elsewhere in the city, there was always a bracing breeze felt as one stepped outside of the cathedral. The choristers spread themselves all over the fifty-five steps, as wide as the cathedral itself. The higher steps were more sought after, offering not just the breeze but a vantage point for looking out over the Liverpool skyline dominated by the cathedral's gothic Anglican rival at the far end of Hope Street. The steps were ideal for a break, for congregating and camaraderie, for last minute practice, or for just being alone and watching the world pass by. Near the bottom of the steps on the right was the information centre, book shop, and booking office, all sharing ground floor space with the rather chic Piazza restaurant, popular amongst students and university staff. Now it was packed with hungry choristers and all those too disorganised or uninterested in packing lunches and carrying heavy liquids. Like Bell and Maggie.

As soon as Maggie got the chance she commandeered two of the restaurant's comfortable lounge seats and shoved them tight to the window near the door. She positioned them at an angle in such a way that she and Bell had their backs to those nearest them. It looked blatantly uninviting to any one of their chorister colleagues who might care to join them. If it was privacy Maggie was wanting, perhaps such efforts were uncalled for, as the din made by the gabbling and the feasting rendered it almost impossible to hear what anybody was saying, unless both speaker and listener were very close, staring at and lip reading each other.

Maggie had eaten half of her panini. She gulped some water down. She had wanted to have this conversation many times since Wednesday. In her near hysterical state then, she had lifted her mobile, highlighted Bell's number, but failed more than a dozen times to connect with it. She was now grateful that she had resisted it. She would have blurted out all her thoughts and fears and Bell would have thought she was mad. She would have that conversation now without the hysterics. The 'plot' somehow seemed less plausible on Thursday morning, less plausible in the sense that she felt no compulsion to tell anyone. Then she tossed and turned in her bed for a second night, convinced that an atrocity *would* happen. She had no idea why it gained credence at bedtime but seem incredulous in the morning. She desperately wanted to know what Bell might think.

'You said you were only joking on Wednesday,' she began distinctly low-keyed, 'when you said you'd be more worried if there'd been another black person in place of O'Neill; what did you mean?'

Bell looked half amused, half perplexed, as though she sensed the question had been 'burning' in her friend's mind and that Maggie knew exactly what *the joke* meant. 'It was only a joke, Maggie,' she repeated emphatically; 'O'Neill was the odd one out. We've got three young black people, one in the middle of the tenors, one in the middle of the altos, and one in the middle of the sopranos. If there had been another black person stuck in the middle of the basses in place of O'Neill, then yes... I might have been curious... suspicious... worried. If we'd seen something like that a week after 9/11 we probably would have been running out!'

Her mouth was creasing into a smile as she finished in anticipation of what was coming next.

'Suspicious of what? Worried by what?' asked Maggie, her expression and tone making it plain to Bell that she would have to spell it out.

414

'What *you* yourself would have been suspicious of. Had it been four, four young Asians say, and each of them stuck in the middle of a big group of people, all rubbing shoulders with each other, and packed as tight as sardines…'

'And…'

Bell sighed, sensing that Maggie was not going to let up. For a brief respite rather than rudeness, she reached into her handbag and retrieved mirror and comb. She lightly dabbed and flicked the comb through her hair. She then looked down at her full-arm white blouse and black skirt that all the women choristers were obliged to wear; after five hours of continual sitting and standing, and wandering about aimlessly for most of the remaining time, her clothes were becoming an irritant, just like the drift of the conversation itself. 'And what?' she said, mimicking Maggie with a questioning frown.

'So if O'Neill had not been there and a black person in his place, you would have been thinking of the possibility they were four suicide bombers.'

'But O'Neill *was* there,' said Bell emphatically. Her head was bent over like a mother trying to reason with a recalcitrant child; her eyes were open wide, and her suppressed smile suggested she was thinking that was the end of the matter, and that Maggie should think likewise.

Maggie stared at her long and hard. 'But what if O'Neill *was* the fourth suicide bomber?'

Bell threw her head back and let out an instant hysterical laugh. It was somewhat contrived. Onlookers glanced at her. She straightened up and composed herself. She gazed at Maggie and said nothing for a while.

'I thought,' said Maggie, 'on Wednesday we might have been exaggerating in saying we'd never see a black person in a choral society in the North. When I got home I accessed the sites of all the choral societies in and around Merseyside. Some of them I'd never heard of. They all have full screen photographs of their members. How many black people do you think are amongst them?'

'Tell me.'

'None! Not a single black person to be seen.'

'Maggie! Shut it!'

'No! *You* explain it! Every bloody year we have to listen to our committee moaning about *not enough ethnic representation*. They mean not enough dark skins. Like every other choral committee they stand on their heads and scream from the rafters about how much they want ethnic minorities... black people, to join, and still, black people never join. But so what? If three thousand choristers can sing the Messiah in the Albert Hall without a single black person amongst them, then there's nothing for us up North to explain or feel backward about. But what needs explaining to me is why four black people, one of them we know is a Muslim, suddenly turn up to sing Verdi... Verdi's *Requiem* in... of all places, a Catholic cathedral in Liverpool?'

'*Four black people*?' asked Bell, a note of vindication in her voice.

Maggie looked stricken; caught out.

Bell stretched forward to drive home the point: 'There's only three.'

She waited a few moments and then said: 'Maggie... you're getting obsessed with colour. You're like those neurotics at airports and rail stations who ask for black people to be removed off planes and trains. That's the effect of 9/11 and July seven. You're so obsessed with colour and so hell-bent on associating it with terrorism that you forgot one of the four you're talking about is a white guy; somebody you've known for years.'

Maggie fumed at the suggestion, disgusted at her lack of concentration which had provoked it. Bell continued:

'We have people like that coming into our stations every week, mostly Fridays – get it off their chest before it spoils the weekend. Some of them are cranks, some neurotics, some of them genuinely scared, some perfectly normal serious people. We've got to take them all serious. We've got to listen, ask questions, and record. Then when they've gone and the DO reads out what some of them have said, we think it hilarious. There's always black people involved, nearly always Pakistani in their teens or early twenties. I think every Pakistani young person in Liverpool has been seriously suspected by some white person of being a terrorist. That's the way it is. Human nature.

That's what the government has done. They've turned vigilance into an obsession. Imagining plots that are nowhere except in peoples' heads. Like this one of yours. I don't know how my bosses in Canning Place might react to it... even if O'Neill *was* black!'

'O'Neill's the decoy,' said Maggie firmly, provoked by Bell's withering scepticism.

'Oh my God!' For a few seconds, Bell closed her eyes.

'He's the one,' said Maggie, unafraid to say anything now, 'who stops people like you believing that a plot's being planned. Clever, isn't it? You're suspicious of three black strangers and where they're located and you're looking at the place where you'd expect the fourth black person to be... there's always a fourth person in these plots, isn't there?... but the person you see is white, and, just as you say, I know him; lots of people know him; he's a local social worker, as interested in politics and terrorism as you and me are in sumo wrestling! That's clever, don't you think?'

Bell remained motionless.

'People don't realise that that same guy has probably got far more reason to do this than any mad Islamists. The other three presumably are looking for martyrdom; Sean O'Neill's wanting revenge, to commit mass murder and leave us all with a mighty bang.'

'How did O'Neill become a part of a terrorist plot?' Bell asked, calmly and expressionless.

'I don't know. You may as well ask: how did *they* become part of O'Neill? I don't know, but he's been away long enough to prepare for it.'

'You think O'Neill has become a radicalised Muslim and a suicide bomber within six months?'

It was the one deduction that Maggie could not make. It was the same question that she conveniently put aside 'on Wednesday night. O'Neill, a vengeful mass murderer? Potentially, yes. A suicide bomber? Possibly. But, a Muslim convert, radicalised? She was vaguely aware of headlines in the *Guardian* only a few days before, a leaked MI5 document acknowledging that would-be Islamic terrorists originated in the most diverse of backgrounds, and had trodden vastly different paths on their journey to extremism. Despite that however, Maggie, in her wildest flights of fantasy could not imagine O'Neill being spirited off to some Pakistani Madras to be brainwashed by lunatic Imans in between daylong Koranic prayers and chants. She was not however prepared to admit it.

'It's happened to others.'

'But did it happen to Sean O'Neill?'

'I don't know. Who knows how he was affected? How would *you* be affected if your family was wiped out, and you thought you had played a part in it, and you felt that everybody who knew you had gloated about it? Who would you go to? Who do you think would be able to help?'

'You still think it was *your* fault, don't you?'

Maggie didn't reply.

'You've always thought it was your fault, haven't you?'

'Partly my fault… yes.'

'And this idea of a plot… do you know what, Maggie? It's you! You're still wanting to punish yourself; you're almost wanting it to happen! You're warning me that it's going to happen because you've convinced yourself it needs to happen.'

Maggie stared beyond Bell. She shook her head half heartedly, as if she was opposing and digesting simultaneously what she'd heard.

'So what are you going to do about it?' asked Bell. 'Are you going to report it?'

Maggie didn't respond. Another bothersome question neatly kicked into grass on Thursday morning, despite having told herself repeatedly throughout the sleepless night that she must report it to somebody. All the anguish of prevarication, the doubts and fears which had plagued and paralysed her for months as O'Neill fell helplessly and unwittingly into his sister's inferno, flashed across her mind. The excuse then was her certainty that O'Neill would destroy himself if she told him who Marian Greer was; and maybe destroy her too if he found out she'd known for as long as she did. Her excuse now was that she knew there wasn't a shred of evidence of an impending atrocity, and she didn't want to make a bloody great fool of herself by suggesting to anyone other than Bell that there was.

Bell was no longer looking sceptical or even dispassionate. Her eyes had softened, her voice sympathetic: 'I take it that means no?'

The tensions of the past few days suddenly drained away from Maggie. She felt her face reddening and tears swelling in her eyes. She could not stop the tears from flowing.

Bell reached across and put one of Maggie's hands in her own two hands: 'why are you doing this to yourself Maggie?'

'I know it sounds crazy,' Maggie blurted; 'but I know he's capable of this... Those two women... nobody knows them... where did they come from... it's only in a Catholic church that no questions are asked... no security... have you seen the *security*? Everyone's a child of God, and welcome... even a bunch of suicide bombers. No security needed. They've spoken to nobody, those women... I've watched them... they barely open their mouths... I don't believe they're singing at all... and the one in front, supposed to be pregnant... I keep thinking she's loaded up with bombs... Where are the four of them now? I haven't seen any of them since the rehearsal ended. Have you? I bet they're away somewhere getting fitted out with suicide vests or belts or whatever... I... I... I think I even know... when they're going to...'

Maggie managed to raise her head and look at Bell through red moist eyes. Her expression mirrored her stuttering hesitancy; as though she was saying something that she knew might convince Bell she needed certifying. But before she could finish, Bell stared at her and said: 'I know what you're going to say.'

Maggie was silent.

'The *Dies Irae*,' said Bell; 'near the beginning, when you get your ear drums shattered, second time round.'

Maggie's lower jaw dropped.

'Busseto,' said Bell. 'Azeer and Sa'eed. I haven't forgotten.'

'No... no... but why... how come you.... you don't think it's crazy then?'

'No. But that doesn't mean I think it's going to happen.'

419

'Why were you resisting so hard then?'

'I wasn't resisting what you were saying, just what you were letting it do to you.'

Maggie sensed an ambiguity in the tone; she waited.

'Look Maggie, I understand why you feel the way you do and what you're thinking. Okay, I'll admit, that *joke*… for a moment on Wednesday night, I *did* take it seriously. When I saw Sa'eed and the two women taking up their positions I kept looking around for Azeer. I kept thinking about Busseto and the bass drum. You say you were watching the two women; I was more interested in whether or not they were in contact with the men. I'd noticed them long before you did. Just as you said, they spoke to nobody; and appeared to go out of their way to speak to nobody. It was all very odd. You were right: if they were going to bomb us all to Kingdom Come, O'Neill *was* the decoy. I watched the four of them a bit more discretely than you did. I seldom took my eyes off them while you were staring at them and letting your imagination go crazy. I wanted to see was there any communication at all between the women and the men. If they were bombers who could see each other they were certain to look at each other, even just a glance, some tell-tale expression, not as obvious as the way Sa'eed and Azeer stared at each other that night, but some sort of look all the same. But there was nothing. Four hours of rehearsals and no contact of any kind.

Maggie looked deflated. She felt stung by the earlier implicit suggestion that she had temporarily lost control. She realised Bell's strategy: firstly to agree and comfort, empathise and reassure, in effect calming her, but then lay bare the paranoia which had been driving her. Bell had not finished.

'You're not going to report it because there really isn't anything to report, is there? But thirty minutes from now you'll probably feel the urge again to *do something about it;* because you're going to believe there *is* something to report.'

The insight was impressive; the detail inaccurate: Maggie knew she'd be changing her mind in five, not thirty minutes.

'Something else,' Bell said; 'the way you reacted when I asked you had O'Neill become a radicalised Muslim. He would have had to, wouldn't he… in order to become a suicide bomber? But you didn't answer. You gave some excuse about it happening to others. But the look on your face told me what you were thinking: that it was a crazy idea, crazier than the idea of a plot itself. No matter how badly he was affected by what happened to his family, Sean O'Neill wasn't the type to fall into the clutches of Osama Bin Laden… was he?'

Maggie shook her head, not in disagreement, but more in exasperation at the ridicule of the question. 'Where are they?' she said.

'In the cathedral I would think; I can't see them on the steps out there. Do you want to check?'

Maggie nodded.

They got up and left the restaurant. As they went outside and glanced over the hundreds of choristers spread out over the fifty-five steps, Maggie said: 'I want to look round the back of the cathedral… and the car park too.'

'Okay,' said Bell.

Chapter 55

A pleasant and noisy chaos had descended inside the cathedral one hour before the performance was due to commence. You could tell who the tourists were, particularly those visiting the cathedral for the first time. They didn't want the performance to begin just yet. Many of them stood in or near the centre of the nave rotunda. Some had miniature binoculars sitting perpendicular on their horizontal faces. Their necks stretched and strained as they gazed up at the stunningly coloured central lantern tower, the world's largest stained-glass construction, towering over every other building in the vicinity. It was still able to capture the very last rays of a September sun sinking deeper and deeper behind Welsh hills. The best way to see the central tower, the tourists are told, is during a summer's day when the sun's rays collide with its thousand panes of coloured glass, of different shapes and sizes, different angles, registering every colour imaginable. Inside, the rays are converted by the colours of the panes, and, depending on the time of the day, can spotlight any part of the floor beneath. Even the deepest and darkest recesses of the cathedral can be emblazoned. When bored school kids visit and are able to stand in spotlights of blue, or red, or yellow, or whatever colour they desire, then they feel their visit is worthwhile. Adult tourists also indulge in this game but more discreetly.

There seemed to be a lot of tourists with camcorders and cameras and binoculars. When they had had enough of the tower they circled the cathedral, stopping and filming its many sculptures and crucifixes, some exquisite and some grotesque. Then they would enter one or two of its diverse chapels, each one dedicated to a particular saint or a humanitarian cause. The Amnesty chapel was always a great favourite. And of course there were a fair share of tourists and concert goers apparently more preoccupied with people-watching than with any of the cathedral's architectural and artistic delights. There was after all, rank, beauty, poise, wealth, style and jewellery to gaze at, to zoom in on surreptitiously. There were some very important people attending this concert.

As the cathedral masses swelled the cumulative scents of perfumes filled the air leading gradually to a distinct atmospheric change. It was pleasant for some, detested by others, and noticed by all. The scents were particularly potent where three hundred sopranos literally rubbed shoulders with each other.

The cathedral was nearly three quarters full. Sa'eed, O'Neill and the two Asian women simultaneously left four different clusters of people comprising tourists, concert goers and choristers, many of them related. The organisers had decided that assembling an orderly procession of over a thousand choristers and leading them onto the makeshift balconies was too problematic, so they exhorted them all to make their own way to their seats at least thirty minutes before the performance began. O'Neill and Sa'eed converged and then walked together. They occasionally looked on either side of each other and behind. A casual observer may have thought they were merely looking out for other chorister friends. Many eyes lit on Sa'eed, on his black skin, and his whiter than white shirt, with bow tie and a double breasted dinner jacket untypically buttoned over. His left hand remained in the pocket of the jacket.

They separated. O'Neill walked towards the sector stand for the basses, Sa'eed towards the tenors. Sa'eed looked over the 120 tenor seats. He knew precisely where his seat was, having claimed it for a second time at the afternoon's rehearsal. More than a dozen of the tenors' seats were occupied. There were three tenors sitting in his row. He glanced at each of them as he approached. He looked searchingly into their eyes as he got nearer. He recognised all three of them. They had been at both rehearsals. They stood up to let him pass. One of them looked at him and smiled. 'We got in early before we have to sit on top of each other,' he said.

'I know… me too,' Sa'eed replied, thanking them for making the effort of standing to let him pass. But he moved past them quickly, unwilling to converse anymore with them. He made his way to seat number 8, in the centre of the central row. Others were also making their way to the tenors' sector and as the seats around him were being increasingly filled, he relaxed. He opened the *Requiem* and soon gave the impression of being seriously preoccupied.

The two Asian women did not converge though they ended up walking quite close to each other. The taller pregnant Pakistani woman walked in front towards the soprano sector. The other woman was younger and more petit in every respect. Her smaller face and stature, her narrower brown eyes and less darker skin all suggested an Indonesian origin. A silk shawl draped over her shoulders merging with her long black hair. Both women walked differently and at a different pace. They carried copies of the *Requiem* under one arm. Each had placed their other hand in the single pocket of their black skirts.

When Maggie and Bell re-entered the cathedral, Sa'eed, O'Neill and the two women were clearly visible, each of them seated in the middle of their respective voice sections which were nearly full now.

'Looks like they didn't go outside,' Bell said.

Not so, Maggie thought; there were numerous other ways of exiting the cathedral besides the main entrance. Maggie knew the cathedral well, unlike Bell who had never been inside it before their rehearsal on Wednesday, and she remained convinced that the four had hidden somewhere in the precepts of the building completing the preparation of their deadly cargo. Once again Bell had to take her in hand, steady her, and gently usher her towards the altar and the choir stands behind.

As she approached the altar, Maggie's vision encompassed the whole of the arc formation made by the four choirs. The larger soprano section and the altos were in the centre of the arc, the tenors on the left hand side and the basses on the right. The nearer she got, the more conspicuous was her changing focus from one choir section to the next. She avoided looking directly at Sa'eed, O'Neill and the two Asian women, yet they were the only people she was conscious of. She felt that if she dared look at anyone of them they would have realised how scared she was.

Then she thought to herself: how crazy! She was making it

easier for them! She did not want them to see her looking at them because if they did and saw her fear, they would think that she suspected them. But was that not a good and necessary reason to look at them, to stare at them with the utmost suspicion and fear in her face, so that they might *think* – or, if she stared at them long and hard enough they would *know* – that the game was up; that Maggie Lynch knew what they were about, and that if Maggie Lynch knew, her more assured and more discreet police friend must know, and that the cathedral's security personnel must know, and the anti terrorist police must know, and that all these forces were about to pounce?

But where were all those people?

As she and Bell reached the altar Maggie had one last glance from one end of the chorus arc to the other. Every member of the chorus was above ground level and she and Bell would have to climb many steps to reach their row. Yet as she reached the first step, it felt as though she was falling into a chasm, a bottomless chasm from which she would never return. Not for the first time that day, she was gripped by an urge to turn back and run, but as usual, the grip loosened, gave way to the counter thought that her paranoia was taking over again.

They got to their seats and sat down. Maggie knew she would not and could not run now. She was grounded, trapped. She looked at the Pakistani woman in the row in front of her, the only one of the suspected four who could be looked at without the threatening prospect of a return look. Maggie wondered how the people on either side of this woman felt; the seating was so narrow and the overall space afforded to the choristers so limited that the three bodies could not help but touch over a sizable area, particularly their arms. She wondered did the women on either side feel anything unusual. Did *they* suspect anything too? Surely they suspected something when this woman between them, this Pakistani, this *black* woman, or was she *brown*, or just simply *non-white*, or however she referred to herself, surely those who sat on either side of her thought it odd at least that she had never once spoken to them during two rehearsals, had never looked at them, never smiled… would they not at least be suspicious of that?

The choirs and orchestra were now in place. The principal violist joined them. The host emerged from nowhere, a large, stocky white haired man who nobody knew or recognised. He launched into the predictable *City of culture* spiel about Liverpool's great choral tradition, its love of Verdi and how fitting that his *Requiem* be performed in the cathedral on a night of so special a year. He paid tribute to the chorus who had travelled 'from every part of the Northwest…'

Bell nudged Maggie: 'Hear that… from all over the Northwest! Not just Merseyside.' There was a hint of banter as well as reassurance in her eyes.

The host thanked the Right Reverend Bishop McBride and his staff who had made everyone feel welcome, and all the volunteers of the diocese who had given so much of their free time. He announced *with sadness* that Bishop McBride would not be able to join them; he had been taken ill during this afternoon and had asked for his sincerest apologies and regret to be conveyed. There were murmurs and expressions of approval when the host said he didn't want to go on too long. He finished with a crescendo and gesticulated flourish pronouncing the arrival of Petrovin and the four soloists.

Petrovin wasted no time. The soloists sat down, took deep breaths, and held their heads high. Petrovin reached both hands forward and moved his fingers in a revolving motion. Every single member of the chorus and the choir rose simultaneously. He raised his right hand holding the baton. His eyes were fixated on the cellists. For five seconds, nothing stirred. Then his baton moved and the bows of the cellists moved. Although only Petrovin, the cellists, and those nearest them, could hear the opening notes, everyone knew the *Requiem* had begun; it took a few seconds more for everyone else to *hear* that it had begun.

These ancient rituals of commencement had a remarkable calming effect on Maggie. From the neurosis-inducing self absorption in which she had indulged over three days, here she was transformed, virtually picked out of herself, confronted with the inescapable responsibility of participating in something bigger and better than herself, and led by a mesmerising conductor whose eyes were almost hypnotic in their effect. It was simply impossible in those opening moments to cling onto any thought or memory that was not solely concerned with the performance in hand and the desire to do one's best. Maggie wanted to cry with joy.

Requiem... Requiem... Requiem ae-ter-nam.... Dona, dona eis, Do-mi-ne.

She held her music firmly, fixed her eyes on Petrovin, and increasingly felt that her voice was emanating as much from the depths of a grateful heart as from her expanding lungs. She felt liberated; she felt that that her nightmare was over.

And light... .for ever more... Thy light for ever more...

It had all been in the mind, she thought. She had foolishly afforded it the privilege of something worth thinking about, and the more she had thought about it, the greater its acceleration and expansion into a terrifying reality that took hold of her and that she could not purge.

The soloists rose.

Kyrie e le i son... Christe, Christe e le i son.

The chorus joined them. The tempo quickened, the volume increased. The pages were having to be turned more rapidly. Bell's nervous fingers turned two pages accidentally. She grimaced, lost her place and cursed. Maggie could see out of the side of her eye what had happened. She had difficulty suppressing her smile as she moved her head fractionally and leaned over towards Bell. She raised her voice a little and sang the notes emphatically to help Bell get back on track. She had one more glance at her friend's music. Bell had retrieved the situation; she was on the right page, singing the right notes. For a fleeting second Maggie saw something else. Over the top edge of Bell's music, the right hand side profile of the Pakistani woman in the row in front came into full view. It was a perfect profile. The face was expressionless, the dried lips were hardly moving, and her eyes were focussing on neither the music nor the conductor. She was staring tensely into nothingness and appeared wholly detached from the world. A few moments before, Maggie in her contentment had sworn to herself that she would not look at either of the two women, nor Sa'eed, nor O'Neill. Now she was staring at the Pakistani woman in resurrected fear. Her concentration evaporated. Her voice lost its poise and balance. She made a supreme effort to fix her eyes on Petrovin and to concentrate again, but when she did that she realised that the Pakistani woman remained conspicuous within her sphere of vision. She could feel the focus of her eyes being drawn back to this woman. She could feel herself losing control again. She could not block the Pakistani woman from the periphery of her vision. She deliberately stopped looking at Petrovin. She buried her head in the music and refused to look up. But that was a habit alien to her, trapping her more effectively and serving only to intensify her returning sense of catastrophe.

Christe e-le-i-son… The first movement was over.

The chorus remained standing when all she wanted was to sit or lie down. Now she wanted to run again. She could feel waves of panic spreading over her. But she could not run. Why did she do this to herself? she asked. Why did she have to wait until she discussed it with Bell? Why did she not report what she believed without even mentioning it to Bell? How could she risk what her panic-stricken mind was telling her now and had been telling her on and off since Wednesday: that she was about to be incinerated? She thought of her children and her husband and she wanted to yell out. She had a desperate urge to stretch out a hand and grip Bell like a vice and beg her to hold onto her. And within this chaos of her mind she felt herself drawn again to its origin, an impulse to look at the Pakistani woman; an even greater urge to look over at her co-conspirators, at O'Neill most of all.

She resisted. She was conscious that she had resisted it and was grateful. And she suddenly became hopeful. If only she could hold on for mere seconds. She knew that the repeated thunderous opening bars of the *Dies Irae* would all be over in fifteen seconds. This nonsense then, this paranoia would be over too. She would be free. She would relax and enjoy, surrender her whole self, her mind, body and emotion to her beloved *Requiem*.

Petrovin raised his baton. He looked once at the second percussionist, who had quietly taken up his position beside the extra large bass drum. The percussionist was tall and well built, and yet looked dwarfed by the drum. He held one drum mallet in both hands which he had drawn as far back as possible, ready to strike. Petrovin then motioned to the orchestra.

A terrifyingly authentic scream reverberated around the aisles. Maggie jumped. She literally jumped, and a split second before her own scream was about to be unleashed, she realised she had forgotten: there were other players in this drama. Sixty students of *Merseyside's Theatre of Contemporary Dance* had surrounded the nave and screamed in perfect unison, a solitary piercing scream. Petrovin never flinched. From imagining herself being incinerated, Maggie suddenly felt humiliated. Her little jump had not gone unnoticed. There were half suppressed smiles everywhere. Everyone around her knew she had jumped. Some, including Bell, had felt her jump. The humiliation was worse than merely imagining being blown to smithereens.

Petrovin's baton flashed and the percussionist struck.

The shoeless dancers came surging chaotically yet silently down each aisle encircled in a fiery follow-spot glare. They made it seem as though they were running for their lives, but they were hardly moving. They were covered from head to toe, but the garments they wore were so tight that every curve and bone was accentuated. Naked, they seemed; hopelessly exposed. They were all different people, different in age, size, shape, motion, colour and weight, but they uniformly mimed suffering and terror.

The percussionist struck a second time, a third, a fourth, a fifth. Each strike intensified the mimers' terror, made their mouths gape and arms shoot out and their fingers claw and cling to each other. They all made a futile attempt to run faster, yet their terror, their panic, made certain they were getting nowhere.

Petrovin locked eyes onto tenors and basses. They began, a rising fortissimo, but merely a prelude to the much louder and more effective sound of the sopranos and altos.

Maggie, now literally shaking to the core of her being, joined in. No, she didn't join in; she was engulfed, swept along, no more able to *think* or *act* differently than the spellbound audience could do anything other than listen and watch.

Together with the Philharmonic choir, a thousand voices pronounced God's *Day of Anger,* his wrath, his revenge. It took only seven bars of music and seven seconds of time. The visibly awed audience held its breath as the whirlwind of strings plunged chromatically through two whole octaves into hell's inferno. The percussionist stood ready for the repeat.

Maggie wants to close her tear-filled eyes. She *knows* this must be it. She *knows* they are fast approaching the moment... the memory... that precise second when Azeer and Sa'eed could not stop themselves signalling with the barely disguised triumphal scorning look in their eyes.

The percussionist raises and draws back both arms, ready to strike. Maggie looks at the Pakistani woman, and then she is convinced that she is doomed. The woman isn't singing. She has her eyes closed and is praying.

Maggie's paralysis is frighteningly strange to her. She knows she is about to be incinerated, yet she is paralysed; disempowered by the event, by the sheer power and force of the music and the occasion. She is utterly helpless to do anything other than sing! She cannot even pray. She cannot even say: 'God help me!'

Then she dares to do what she swore she would not do. She looks over to Sa'eed. He prays too, with one hand raised to Allah. In these dying seconds the conspirators have ceased living in this world; they are about to join Allah in heaven; perhaps they believe they have already arrived.

She looks at O'Neill and a shudder runs through her. He *is* looking at her. He is smiling at her. He is raising a hand in the air as though he too is making that last humbling, sacrificial gesture to Allah. She was wrong then; so hopelessly wrong in thinking him incapable of such a conversion. But then she sees he is doing no such thing. He is doing something worse. She realises to her horror that he is sickeningly, gratifyingly, evilly, raising his hand to his mouth and mockingly blowing her a kiss.

The percussionist makes the first of the repeated five strikes and instantly Maggie sees part of O'Neill's head blown off with his hand still in the air, that same hand that gestured the mocking kiss he blew.

The percussionist strikes a second time and the whole of Sa'eed's head is blown off. O'Neill and Sa'eed can no longer be seen.

A third strike. The Indonesian woman in the middle of the altos suffers a similar fate.

A fourth strike, and the head of the *pregnant* Pakistani woman only a few feet away momentarily expands but just as quickly disintegrates.

Maggie collapses.

Chapter 56

In the famous Lutyens crypt beneath Liverpool's Metropolitan Cathedral a strange and tense meeting had just taken place behind locked doors. Bishop Brian McBride and his auxiliary, Father Tony Greenwood sat facing two grim faced men. One of these men they both knew well, Jim Foray, the Chief Constable of Liverpool, a long time friend of the Bishop, a regular Sunday church-goer, and occasional guest at the cathedral's concerts. The other was a smaller, stocky built man, of Middle East origin, who the chief constable had introduced as Detective Chief Superintendent Abu Hassan, head of Merseyside's Counter Terrorism Unit, part of the UK's newly constituted *Office for Security and Counter Terrorism*. Neither of the visitors wore the uniforms of their ranks; they were nevertheless suitably attired in bespoke suits and ties. Both men and their wives and the Bishop and his assistant should all have been sitting in the VIP row of the cathedral nave, listening to the Verdi *Requiem*. Their places had been taken by four male and two female counter terrorist agents, which was only a fraction of the number of counter terrorism staff, plain clothed Special Branch officers, and police marksmen who had been mingling anonymously with the chorus and audience during the past two hours. If there was only one common characteristic shared by the four men now sitting round a table in the bowels of Liverpool's Metropolitan Cathedral, it was the one that had been moulded and entrenched by similar experiences in their contrasting lives: a profound sense of the unpredictable nature of life.

The meeting had lasted nearly an hour now, which had seemed like an eternity for each of them. The ashen-faced Bishop hunched over the table was frail and frightened, and had to excuse himself to pray at one point in response to what his visitors had told him. His auxiliary, Father Greenwood, was of a different metal: young, thin, wiry, with a face so solid and steadfast, with large dark blue eyes sunk beneath thick black eyebrows, with cheekbones so bare, and the hollows so deep, you could have been excused for thinking he periodically starved himself, gloriously though. He reminded one of a sixteenth century Jesuit, certain to embrace suffering and sacrifice of the most extreme kind, perhaps the only experience in life that might allow his closed lips to break into a smile. The ultimate challenge for Bishop McBride was not in seeking Divine intervention but in moderating the responses of his strong-willed auxiliary, who had become increasingly belligerent throughout the meeting, and who had to be physically restrained, then threatened with arrest when told what the two visitors, in the interests of public safety, were requiring. It wasn't actually a request, but a command; the Chief Constable and Hassan had convincingly demonstrated there was no alternative to the actions they proposed.

The table around which the four men sat was littered with photographs, X-ray prints, and copies of a four page article or letter. There was also an open Dell XPS laptop with a large screen. The photographs had obviously been taken without the subjects, Sa'eed, O'Neill, and the two Asian women being aware of it. They had been taken from various angles, heights, and locations inside the cathedral, and some had been enlarged, focussing very close up on the chest and stomach areas. All four individuals were easily recognisable to the elderly Bishop and his assistant as members of the Verdi chorus, with Sa'eed and O'Neill in their black dinner jackets, and the two Asian women in their white blouses and black skirts. At the outset, Father Greenwood recalled seeing them at various points in the day. But he didn't mean O'Neill, whom he couldn't recognise from Adam, and he didn't say that the only reason he recognised the other three was because of their colour; they were the only three non-whites in the thousand strong chorus.

The laptop had been running unedited disjointed film that also focussed on these same four choristers. Foray and Hassan had given a running commentary. Numerous camcorders had obviously been used, filming from different locations and heights, often zooming in on each of the four, on the manner of their walk, on the clearly visible signs of tension in their expressions, on their comparative isolation when they joined their sections, and the oddity that each of them always had one hand hidden from view.

In comparison to the film and the photographs, the X-ray prints were rather indistinct. They highlighted a fusion of objects, clothing and anatomy that required repetitive explanations from Hassan and the Chief Constable. But that was nothing to the challenge the two men had earlier faced in explaining why they were there in the first instance.

*   *   *

Earlier in the week Hassan had received an anonymous letter telling him to be at his Liverpool office the coming Saturday, 5.0pm. 'Typical,' he lamented; '5.0pm; two or three hours before we're due at the concert.' He hadn't had a Saturday night off since he was appointed. His wife had booked the tickets for all four of them, and he had been looking forward to it for weeks, until that is, he heard that *Merseyside's School of Contemporary Dance* would also be performing. He disliked such innovations. He had attended *Carmina Burana* in the City's Anglican Cathedral a couple of years before and felt the whole night was ruined by weirdly garbed dancers fleetingly appearing in every aisle, gesticulating and miming in a way comprehensible only to themselves and their tutors. Nevertheless the music was worth hearing. So too would be the *Requiem*. He could just close his eyes and listen.

The phone would ring, the anonymous note said, and an *important* message would be delivered. *Your computer should be running*, it added. His initial response had been that this was another racist crank, some idiot time wasters, compulsively wanting to make contact, take the piss out of any new face the local news threw up. That was the cost of the publicity which he shunned but which his political masters imposed upon him. He was the first Muslim to achieve Chief Superintendent status which he did without too much fuss. But being appointed Commander of Merseyside's newly created Counter Terrorism Unit had to be an altogether different affair. The London-based Director General of the *Office for Security and Counter Terrorism,*

Sir Nicolas Holmes, was convinced Hassan's appointment would prove a major propaganda coup, helping to gain the trust and cooperation of the many Muslim communities in Liverpool.

Hassan had ordered his two deputies, Chief Superintendent Andy Roberts and Chief Inspector Bill Yeats to join him. Yeats had a notepad and pen in hand, a lifetime's habit unaffected by state-of-the -art technology all around him. As they sat around the phone it was clear that all three men, having had a few days to consider the note, now hoped there was something more than a mere bogus call.

The phone rang at precisely 5.00pm. Hassan activated the speaker. They heard a distinct and calm Ulster voice speaking slowly on a recorded message. They looked at each other, perplexed. Similar thoughts raced through their minds: Provisional IRA malcontents… The *Real* IRA… *Continuity* IRA… they'd all been stirring things in Ulster over the past few months. There was always a ragbag of hardliners in every terrorist group that would fight on or try to resurrect the movement in another form. The voice spoke:

By the time you get this message, you'll have about three hours to prevent a massacre. I and three others are strapped with bombs which we intend setting off this evening during the Verdi Requiem in the Metropolitan Cathedral. During the past half hour, I've sent our photographs to the e-mail address on your website. When you get to the cathedral your men should be able to identify the four of us.

There was a long pause. Hassan realised he was being given time to turn to his computer, key in and access the organisation's mail box. That was the moment when he was almost convinced it was a send up, and that he was about to access a few hard- core pornographic photos, most likely adorned with Islamic features, Muslim women, and hate-filled graffiti. Since the Government's campaign pleading for the public to report anything suspicious, the phones and sites and e-mail boxes had got repeatedly clogged. Three quarters of the workload was spent following up leads that were useless at best; much of the other mail was just vile.

He swivelled the computer screen so that his colleagues could see it. An e-mail with an attachment had arrived. He opened the picture attachment, and stared at four faces, obviously four different nationalities. Below them were two photographed sheets of choral music that he recognised. A bar of the music was circled and the first beat of that bar heavily underlined. The voice continued.

You will be receiving the usual martyrdom nonsense in a video which the four of us have made, in due course. You now have the opportunity to ensure that there will be no martyrs, just the corpses of would-be mass murderers. We are the operatives of an Al Qaeda cell managed by Dr Abdul Azeer az-Zahrany of the Al Jamiah Islamic Academy in Knowsley. Sa'eed Jama, top left, is a Somali and the leader of the cell. Tonight he will be located exactly in the centre of the tenors. Faridah Ibriham, top right, is Pakistani and she will be located exactly in the centre of the sopranos. Endah Wulandari is Indonesian, and she will be located exactly in the centre of the altos. I will take up position in the centre of the basses.

Another pause. Then the voice spoke, much more slowly, more gravely.

We will detonate the bombs on the first beat....

'... Of the thirteenth bar of *Dies Irae,*' Hassan abruptly said, cuing onto the circled note on his computer screen where the bar of music was clearly marked 13.

Of the thirteenth bar of the second movement, Dies Irae, the voice continued. *I've shown you where on the score that is attached.*

The three men stared at the screen.

Don't waste valuable time speculating on whether or not this is a hoax call, or what my motivation is likely to be. Suffice to say that I freely embarked on this mission in the belief that it would serve my purpose. I have had no previous links with Al Qaeda, no knowledge of any of the team other than Sa'eed Jama, and no respect for Islamic terrorism.

I have spent six months preparing for the mission. I've worked alongside the people who ordered it and planned it. They rescued me so that I could contribute. But they didn't tell me that was their main purpose when they rescued me.

Before you come running through the doors of the cathedral, you must know that all four of us are committed to detonating our bombs prematurely should any attempt be made to storm the building or to evacuate it or to shut it down. If we hear and see ambulances and fire engines lining up outside the building we will detonate. If you put a stop to people coming in we will detonate. There are at least a thousand tourists and choristers already inside the cathedral now and many will be killed. We are resting now after the rehearsals of this afternoon. You can easily find us. Your equipment if not your eyesight should be able to verify that we are wearing suicide vests. But we will be amongst the largest groups in different parts of the building. We will remain separate from each other but in sight of each other. Should any of your forces try to approach us or stun us we will detonate. You may succeed in stunning one or two of us, but you will not succeed in stunning all four of us in different crowds in different parts of the cathedral at once. Apart from turning the pages of the music we will be keeping a finger on the detonating buttons at all times. That is, the finger of our right hand, except for Sa'eed Jama, who is left handed. Only when the second movement begins, will your men have the opportunity to take all four of us out simultaneously. The music will be deafening and the dance drama will be a major distraction. The audience and the chorus will initially think your killing us is part of the drama, long enough for you to get our bodies out. There are two small dark balconies in the cathedral. They are normally used by film crews and technicians. They are the ideal location for your marksmen. We will be no more than fifty yards from the barrels of your guns. A single bullet should suffice for each of us, that type of mushroom bullet that will penetrate but not leave the body. Aim for the head. The explosive we are using is ammonal and is piped quite high on our chests. Faridah will appear pregnant. She carries twice as many pipes of ammonal as the rest of us, because there are twice as many sopranos as any of the other three voices. We have calculated that, given the compactness of the four choirs, I and Sa'eed and Endah will kill at least fifty people each, when we detonate. Faridah will kill at least one hundred and fifty. There are likely to be many more casualties.

Another pause followed, at least ten seconds. Then:

If you don't know the music I'm referring to, you still have time to listen to it. The Verdi Requiem. On the first beat of the thirteenth bar of the second movement, Dies Irae. As marked.

No more was said. Hassan and his deputies stared questioningly at each other. Yeats' eyes conveniently skimmed through his notes, accurate and comprehensive enough as a result of the pace and clarity of the voice. Hassan lifted the phone and dialled. He knew that the number, irrespective of the time of day or night, would give him immediate contact with Sir Nicholas Holmes.

'Sir Nicholas… Hassan. Hear this.' He pressed the forward button on his phone.

* * *

In the room of the crypt, Hassan's mobile signalled an incoming call. He was watched intently by the other three men. Bishop McBride had both hands clasped in prayer. Hassan listened without saying a word. Then he placed the mobile on the table. He looked at the Bishop and said:

'Reverend Bishop, I have to inform you that the four terrorists have been eliminated. Their bodies were quickly removed. They were, as the X-rays demonstrated, strapped with high velocity explosives which have now been deactivated. The explosives were encased in piping which also contained separate capsules of a highly inflammatory liquid. My experts inform me that if the bombs had exploded, they would have instantly killed at least four to five hundred people. They would in all likelihood have killed more. The density of the choristers, and their highly flammable clothes and perfumes would have greatly intensified the fire-ball effect, possibly incinerating the whole chorus and orchestra. We do not know why the circuiting between detonator and explosives on one of the terrorists… this one' (he pointed to the photograph of O'Neill) 'was deliberately sabotaged, obviously by the wearer himself. It's not uncommon for a terrorist to renege at the last moment, to run away, or simply not to detonate. But it would not have made any difference. He was sufficiently close enough to one of his accomplices to ensure that the explosion and fire-ball effect would have activated his own bombs.'

Kieran O'Hagan qualified as a social worker in 1974, and specialized in child protection work in inner city areas for over twenty years. He has published eight critically acclaimed books on child abuse and related topics, and scores of articles for national and international journals. He was a Reader at The Queen's University, Belfast, until 2000. A feature of his books is the use of fiction to dramatize the emotions and trauma of much child abuse work. *The Verdi Solution* is his first novel.